AL: ICE

By CW Lamb

I would like to dedicate this to Jeanne Romano, who inspired me to write, and to my wife Shannon and the rest of the family who supported that inspiration.

Works by CW Lamb

AL:ICE Series
AL:ICE
AL:ICE-9
AL:ICE Resurrection
AL:ICE Space War
AL:ICE Alliance
AL:ICE Explorer
AL:ICE Avatar
AL:ICE AI vs AL

Ranger Series
The Lost Ranger
Dragon's Teeth
The Dark Paladin
Wizard King of the North

A Bridge to the Past
The Dowry
The Sword and the Medallion

Other Works
The Ranch Hand
Youngblood

https://www.amazon.com/stores/Charles-Lamb/author/B00QE0X49Q

https://cwlamb.net/

Contents

Chapter 1

Jake lay quietly on the table, trying to figure out what was happening around him. Everything was dead quiet and completely black, and he was waiting for someone to say something. A member of the scientific team had just been speaking before everything went dark. Only introduced to the man earlier that morning, the scientist had completed attaching wireless sensors to various parts of Jake's body, and the last thing Jake remembered was the man and his assistant, a lab technician, in conversation.

"OK, Captain, now just lie back," he said, instructing Jake to lie down on the padded table he was sitting on.

Just sitting in his underwear, Captain Jacob Thomas smiled and silently nodded back, acknowledging the instructions and doing as he was told. The technician was sitting at a console against the wall to Jake's left, scanning the various displays.

"All sensors are reporting in, sir," the man declared

"Good, now power up the field generator coils and verify the status of the power cells," the scientist replied.

"Coils are energized, and the power cells are at 100% charge," the technician declared.

"OK, Captain Thomas, are you ready?" the scientist asked.

"Good to go," Jake replied.

"Great," the scientist said, stepping away to stand next to the technician.

"Create the stasis field," he commanded.

That is when everything went black. Jake wondered if there was another power loss. He'd been told that there were power supply problems in previous tests, but that it wasn't supposed to be an issue anymore. Had the field generation blown a fuse or something?

Taking a deep breath, Jake noticed the previously fresh filtered air was suddenly stale. He turned his head left to look for the two men against the far wall, but it was just too damn dark to see anything! He was sure that's where the lab technician and scientist were, just a moment ago, no more than a few feet away. Finally, tired of waiting, he asked his question aloud.

"Hey, guys, what's going on?"

There was no response.

"Hey, is anyone there?"

Again, there was nothing, just quiet.

Jake sat up in one swift motion and started to stand, confused at the lack of response. Whoa, he had a head rush and wasn't sure why he felt so dizzy, as he had just laid down. He wasn't weak. He just felt as if things weren't quite right. A Captain in the US Marine Corps, Jake was a little over 6 feet tall and weighed in at 200 pounds. He tried to keep himself in good shape, so this feeling wasn't normal. Moving a bit slower this time, he could get himself standing while leaning against the table, trying not to knock anything over. He felt dust on the floor with his bare feet.

"What in the hell?" Jake said to himself.

Stepping slowly to not stub his toes, he began sliding his feet forward, one after another. He headed to where he remembered seeing the workbench with the computer console where the technician sat. His toe touched the chair first, and reaching forward, he grasped what felt like human hair.

Jake jerked his hand back at the unexpected contact and slid to the left while leaning forward toward the workbench. Running his hands over the benchtop, he could not find what he was looking for. Earlier that day, he had noticed the lab technician's cigarettes and lighter on the workbench next to the computer console. Where in hell did the technician go to smoke down here, he had no idea, but the lighter was his goal.

"Down here" was a first-of-its-kind, prototype research facility full of advanced technology projects. It was a top-secret underground military installation in the Nevada desert. This facility was the type of place that created the Area 51 alien stories.

Moving right now and skipping around what he was now absolutely positive was a body, he found the lighter on the right of the keyboard.

"Damn, I'm sure I'd seen it on the left?" he said aloud.

Flicking the lighter on, the small flame blinded him for a moment, as previously his eyes strained for any light. Sure enough, sitting before him was the mummified remains of the lab technician, sitting in the same chair as before. The technician's body was sitting rocked back in its chair as if he simply died in place while working. The scientist was nowhere in sight. Next to where he found the lighter was a notebook that the lab technician had been using to log his experiment. Jake checked the entries and noted the last was on July 8th, at 9 pm. The 8th?

Jake was sure today was the 5th, the day after the 4th of July holiday. He was positive because he spent the weekend in Las Vegas to ensure he was able to report in on time. How would he lose three days in the blink of an eye? What is more important, bodies don't mummify in three days. They didn't even mummify in a month, and that was all the power the cells in the table held.

6

Jake was told the stasis field generator was inside the table he'd been laying on. The scientist explained its workings to him, in detail, and that it contained completely redundant components to prevent field size fluctuations or partial field collapses for his safety. In addition, its reserve power cells could maintain a human-size stasis field for up to a month.

What in the hell was happening to him? Had he been in stasis all along, explaining the missing three days? Considering the body, if it had been more, then how long was he in stasis, anyway? The team he met earlier briefed him on the experiment he was to be part of. They described how they discovered a way to create a stasis field that stopped time, or more accurately, slowed time down a great deal. One of the presenters explained the stasis effect on him.

"Jake, imagine being in a boat on a river, floating free with the current. The river is time. Now toss out an anchor, so the river continues to flow past, but the boat remains stationary. In stasis, time continues to flow past, but you stay put in that timeframe. That's what the stasis field does; it holds its contents close to the point in time the field is created while the flow of time outside the field continues," he started.

Using the lighter, Jake moved over to his clothes, resting on a chair in the corner of the room. He'd placed them there when he first arrived and was instructed to strip down. First, he pulled all the sensors off his body, getting some hair with them, and then he started to dress, pants first.

When the scientist attached those sensors earlier, he explained.

"We discovered in earlier testing that even though the field is physically impenetrable and time is almost frozen inside, we can pass some wireless transmissions through the field. The rate of decay has been about 1 hour over 100 years, but don't worry, you won't notice anything."

"For some strange reason, the field stops most high-energy transmissions, but certain low-energy frequencies aren't affected. That's part of the reason we use this facility as our lab, we are so deep underground here, that we can guarantee no outside signals will affect our testing."

"Part of this test is to see if we can pass information to you while you are in stasis. For example, this would allow a spacecraft crew in stasis to receive position and system status information while in flight. Thus, when released, they are fully aware of their situation. Because time isn't completely stopped, you will be able to absorb some information. We need to measure how much," he continued.

"In your case, we are going to feed you a training program and see if you can perform previously unfamiliar tasks successfully after coming out of stasis," he finished up.

Jake pulled his shirt on over his head and noticed a stale smell that just said old. Holding the lighter out in front of him, he stepped out of the room and headed into the hallway. Stopping and looking both ways down the dark corridor, he saw no sources of light. Just to be sure, he extinguished the light and just stood there while his eyes adjusted to the dark.

Nope, there was nothing, just dark. Reigniting the lighter, he tried to retrace his steps back the way he'd come in before the test. Now and then, he tried a door along the way, looking for something, anything, that might answer what was happening to him. All he found were empty offices and lab rooms similar to the one he just vacated.

As he approached a major intersection where he remembered his hallway crossed the main access tunnel, he picked up his pace. Jake turned the corner to what should be the way out of the facility and 30 feet in front of him, he got his first answer, it was a solid wall of rock and dirt.

On his way into the facility, Jake had seen a massive construction project at this point in the passage, with work both above and below ground. As he passed through the tunnel systems, to reach the completed lab complex he was now in, they had passed through partially completed access tunnels. The driver of the electric cart informed him that the original tunnels required expansion due to new requirements and a change in the facility design. An engineer himself, he cringed at the thought of all that weight pushing down on them from above and that the government contractor was likely the lowest bidder!

The access tunnel the contractors were re-sizing had completely collapsed. There was dirt and rocks piled right up to the outer edge of the lab complex. Jake wondered how long ago the collapse had happened. Surely, they were working to reopen the tunnel. He paused to listen for any sound indicating activity in the cave-in. He just stood there for a moment and stared at the wall of dirt. Frankly, he wasn't sure what to do next. He was stuck VERY deep underground, with no idea how long he'd been there, and no idea how to get out besides the way he came in.

Rather than head back the way he came, he decided. First, he needed to find another light source. The lighter was not going to last forever, and secondly, he needed to find a way to let the surface know he was there. Heading down the main tunnel, away from the collapse and perpendicular to the hallway he had just come down, Jake started searching behind every door he came across. He figured the best way to reach the outside world would be through the control center for the facility. In addition, the best place for a control room would be in the

8

center of the complex.

As Jake searched, he considered his predicament. This event seemed to reflect the story of his life. Multiple combat tours in Afghanistan and Iraq had driven a wedge between his wife and himself. She hadn't approved of his military career from the beginning, but as they met while in college, he was already committed to the NROTC scholarship that paid his way. After eight long years of trying to please her and the Marines, he left the Marines to focus on her and try to save his marriage.

Unfortunately, she was now focused and committed to her career, so that proved to be too late. Therefore, with his marriage over and with the economy in the dumps, it seemed as if returning to the Marines was the perfect solution. He had no children from his marriage, and as an only child himself, there were no other family commitments. The Marines were a ready-made paycheck, and at 32, the only family he had left.

Once back in uniform, he settled into a comfortable billet stateside teaching combat tactics at the Basic School in Quantico, VA. Then the people from the Defense Advanced Research Projects Agency came looking for him. They were looking for officers with technical backgrounds for various projects. Jake was a perfect choice for them with his Bachelor's in Mechanical Engineering and a Master's in Computer Science. He popped up in the personnel system due both to his education and lack of immediate family. This was a dangerous assignment, and widows and orphans were bad press. "No next of kin" candidates got top consideration, so with his permission, they sent him to Las Vegas as a test subject in an experiment around localized time suspension.

Forcing his mind back on task, he continued to walk along the main tunnel. Among the many doors, Jake found a few supply closets, and each contained emergency kits. None of the flashlights inside worked, but the kits each also contained a bundle of chemical lights. Called a Cyalume, he set one off by bending it until he heard the snap and then shook it until it glowed. Much relieved, he pocketed the lighter. He then searched the small closet until he located a bag. After emptying the original contents, he dumped the rest of his lights in the bag and continued his search.

He continued down the main corridor, and he twice found more mummified remains. One was a security guard in a connecting hallway, face down in the middle of the passageway, his traditional security Maglite dead like all the others. The second body was in an office, most likely Part of the cleaning staff. Again, just like the technician, each seemed to have dropped in place, as if dying while performing their regular duties.

At the end of the main access tunnel, he stopped at a set of double security doors. He noticed a security badge reader on the right side of the doorframe, so he didn't expect to just walk in.

"These locks typically defaulted to the locked position, and these doors looked pretty stout," he said to himself.

Suddenly he heard the distinct click of the magnetic lock releasing. Reaching for the knob, he pulled, and the door opened.

"Who the hell did that?" he asked aloud.

Stepping warily inside, he held up the Cyalume and looked around the room. There were rows of desks with computer monitors and keyboards. From the layout and equipment, he could tell he'd located what must be the control center. As he walked into the room, a flash on one of the monitors caught his attention. He walked over to what looked like a power geek's desk. It was a multi-monitor setup with a keyboard and other unidentifiable devices. Glancing at the central screen, powered up, it had text on it.

"HELLO," was lit up on the monitor.

Jake quickly sat down and typed, "Who is this?"

The response quickly came back, "Alice."

Jake entered, "Alice, I am Captain Jake Thomas. I am trapped underground in the lab facility,"

The monitor displayed, "I know, I am attempting to determine a path out of your location. Unfortunately, most of the sensors in your area are no longer operable,"

"What happened? Are they trying to dig me out? How long was I down here?" Jake responded.

"I will answer your questions later. Your current location is not safe. The gas explosion that caused the tunnel collapse suffocated all the occupants. It was thought to be a total collapse with no survivors and was determined a total loss. That level eventually ventilated naturally, but no attempt has been made to re-access that Part of the facility," Alice replied.

"I have identified two possible escape routes for you. One is through the primary power and communications conduit. It runs parallel to the main access tunnel and must have survived the collapse. If it were severed, this communication wouldn't be possible," she continued.

"The second route is an auxiliary ventilation shaft that runs vertically from your level to another level of the underground complex far above you. Sealed off after the collapse, I can have it reopened for you. That path shows a higher percentage of success but at a greater risk to life. You will need to climb 300 feet straight up a 3-foot diameter smooth-walled shaft. A fall would likely prove fatal as you near the top," Alice explained.

"The printer to your right will provide detailed instructions on both avenues of escape."

Jake looked right and watched as the printer slowly came to life, but spit out only blank pages. It took him several tries before he got the printer to work properly. Eventually, Jake pulled the print cartridge and banged it on the desk to get the toner loosened up.

"That just shouldn't have been necessary," Jake thought.

With instructions and his bag in hand, Jake decided to give the power conduit the first shot.

"Should it be blocked, it's a lot easier to back out of a tunnel than try to control a 300-foot drop," he thought.

The instruction sheets Alice provided explained the power conduit ran under the collapsed main access tunnel he'd seen earlier. According to the notes on the sheet, it provided all the power and communication lines to this level of the facility. That way had to be open, or he would have been without the limited power or communication capabilities. His conversation with Alice proved that it was continuous and clear to some degree.

The instructions indicated access to the conduit was gained every 100 feet or so along the main tunnel. There were floor tiles down the middle of the hallway that covered the access hatches. He figured he would find the hatch closest to the tunnel collapse as his starting point.

----*----

ALICE attempted to monitor Jake's progress as closely as possible. With so many failed sensors in the abandoned level, it was like watching someone stepping in and out of spotlights in a darkened room. His path was to the conduit under the tunnel collapse. The escape was considered a lower risk. She was not confident that he would succeed, however, as the sensors on both ends of the conduit functioned, but the central ones were completely unresponsive. That was why she scoured the remaining sensor grid for other means of escape. He must be recovered intact and unharmed to meet her needs.

----*----

Jake pulled an access tile up, uncovering the hatch to the conduit below. The tile had one of those clever little retractable loops that lay flush to the face of the tile, letting you pull it off without any tools. He was no more than 15 feet from the tunnel collapse, so he was not likely to find another one any closer.

The hatch below the tile was heavy steel, made to support the traffic

11

that moved over it. Besides the pedestrian traffic, the staff used electric carts similar to the one Jake rode in on the day he arrived. The carts also pulled flatbed trailers with supplies and lab materials.

Jake needed to brace himself and used both hands on the handle to get the hatch to swing up and lock in place. Lowering the Cyalume into the opening, he could see a ladder and about 10 feet down, a grated walkway. Climbing down, he realized the tunnel was more of a crawl-way unless you were 4 feet tall! Squatting down, he was in a large circular tube that contained several smaller pipes he assumed were the power and communication runs. Facing in the direction of the tunnel collapse and with the power and communication runs to his left, all he could see was darkness ahead beyond the glow of the light in hand.

He started on his hands and knees in the direction of the collapsed tunnel, and what he hoped was freedom. Crawling along the walkway, he could feel the edges of the grating dig into his palms and knees. At one point, he saw a small box on the wall of the tunnel with a glowing red LED. He assumed that the sensor was one of the many Alice had mentioned earlier. Jake took that it was still working as a good sign, proving established connectivity to the other side.

----*----

ALICE noted Jake's location in the tunnel. Positioned near the last functioning sensor for quite a distance, it appeared the rest of the sensors along the passage failed with the collapse. She did lose contact with him once he dropped into the tube from the tunnel above, but his body heat and motion registered on the sensors in the tube. Soon they would both know if the conduit was a passable escape route.

----*----

Jake continued to crawl forward, unsure if his eyes were playing tricks on him. After straining in the dark for so long with just the glow of the Cyalume, he thought he might be seeing things. In the dim glow, rather than seeing black up ahead, it looked as if it was getting grayer than black. Maybe it was getting lighter? His excitement rose as he continued.

All too soon, Jake realized why it seemed lighter. The gray conduit ceiling had been pushed down, pinching off the crawlway, but not severing the power and communication runs. He probed forward to see if he could squeeze between the pipes, but there wasn't any open space.

Crap!

Deflated, Jake swapped ends and headed back the way he came, his knees and palms complaining about the metal grating. He again passed the sensor and resisted the urge to swat it off its mount, frustrated at the false hope he got from it and the failed escape attempt.

----*----

The sensor alerted ALICE of Jake's return. She noted the likelihood of the power and communications conduit collapsing at 100%. She immediately reviewed the alternate option and confirmed it as the only other way out. She dispatched an attendant to the top of the ventilation shaft to reopen the ducting and meet Captain Thomas in the event of his successful escape.

----*----

Jake emerged from the conduit, climbing out of the hole and turning to close the hatch, then stopping in mid-motion. It's not like anyone else was going to fall into the hole. Besides, that thing was damn heavy. Instead, he moved over to the wall of the corridor, dropped his bag, and sat down. He pulled out the printouts to get the next set of directions from his pocket. He wadded up the sheet with the tunnel escape and tossed it into the open hatchway.

He started reading the second set of instructions Alice had provided him. He considered the work of free climbing a 300-foot ventilation tube and decided some water sounded good. There just had to be a working water source around here somewhere, he thought.

Picking himself up and heading toward the next starting point, he again began checking door handles along the way, kicking in any locked doors. He also gave the impending climb more thought as he did so. In the Marines, he'd both trained and operated using climbing and rappelling gear, but that was mountain warfare, not HVAC servicing. He knew that without proper climbing gear, he needed to come up with a way to both prevent a fall and allow for resting along the climb.

In one supply closet, he found a large roll of duct tape still in its sealed wrapper. Into the bag, it went, with the remaining Cyalume's. He also found some mops in the same closet. Grabbing two, he pulled the mop heads off, giving him two poles, each about four feet long.

In another room that looked like a break room, he found some vending machines, one of which was a drink machine. It was no surprise, though, that there was no power to the machines. After a little persuasion, provided mostly by a severe beating with a chair, he was able to get the door open and surveyed his options. Water was always good to hydrate, but a little sugar might help, so he grabbed one of the soda cans and popped the top. What he discovered inside was undrinkable, more like motor oil. Most of it was stuck to the side of the can. How long were

13

they in there? More to the point, how long had HE been down here?

He grabbed a couple of water bottles and opened one. Thankfully, it was drinkable but distinctly had a plastic taste to it. He dropped a couple more in his bag with the Cyalumes and tape and then continued on his way. Following the directions Alice provided him, he finally found the cover grate in the ceiling, for the ventilation shaft. It was at the end of one of the hallways, placed as a return vent, to set up airflow for this level. Pulling a desk out of an adjacent office, he climbed on top and pulled off the cover grate.

Yes, there it was, a three-foot diameter shaft, heading straight up. Looking up and holding his Cyalume over his head, Jake could see only the first 10 or 15 feet up into the darkness. The tube walls were as Jake expected, typical smooth metal ducting.

Climbing down off the desk, Jake pulled the tape out of his bag and started wrapping one end of one of the poles with tape. He put a couple of strips over the end, then wrapped that with more around the shaft. He repeated the process until it created a soft end cap. Climbing back up on the desk, he stuck the pole into the shaft, with the taped end pointing down until it was all the way inside.

Placing the taped end against one wall of the shaft, he lowered the top until it rested against the opposite side of the shaft. He then tried hanging from the pole, wedged not quite diagonally across the shaft. It held! The tape prevented the wooden end of the pole from slipping on the shaft walls.

Jake then taped up the other pole, giving him two to work with. To prevent loss of the poles as he climbed, he made two eight-foot cords from sections of duct tape and used these to tie each pole to his belt, with plenty of slack to use them. He then pulled out two Cyalumes, activating them and taping one to each pole. This would provide light on the way up, and he tucked a third unlit in a shirt pocket, should he need it later. Next, he tied the bag off to a belt loop, so it hung at his side.

Sliding both poles into the shaft, he wedged them in place and pulled himself up into the shaft. Placing his feet against the far side of the shaft and with his back against the other side, he braced himself and raised the poles higher above his head. Alternating between his legs and the poles, he slowly moved up the shaft a few feet at a time. He was always cautious about being sure the poles were wedged firm before pulling himself up.

Once about 2/3's the way up, or at least so he figured, he took a rest break, pulled a water bottle out of his bag, and drained it. It was hot and stuffy in the tube, and he was sweating like a pig, his shirt soaked through. He dropped the empty bottle into the darkness below. It took a long time for the bottle to hit bottom, a reminder he didn't need it. Finally, the Cyalumes taped to the poles reflected light off the metallic top of the shaft, with a dark spot to his right, revealing a horizontal duct. He assumed that the shaft turned 90 degrees, hopefully into an upper level and freedom.

Jake worked his way up until he was level with the opening and then, using the poles above his head, pulled himself into the tube. This duct was close to the same diameter as the one he came from, so Jake just used the poles to pull himself farther in until he could roll over and crawl. That wasn't very far, though, as the tube ended in just a few feet at a vertical grate. Peering through the grate, all Jake could see in the dim glow was blackness. He turned himself around and kicked hard, feeling the grate fly free, and hearing it crashing as it hit the floor.

Jake slid one of the poles through the opening and inched forward until his legs were over the edge, and he could see inside. Verifying first to ensure there was no big drop on the other side, he slid softly into a moderately sized room, where he freed himself from his climbing poles. Illuminated by the Cyalumes, there was grating on the ceiling and three of four walls indicating this was some kind of air mixing room for the ventilation system. There was a doorway framed on the fourth wall, opposite him, and crossing to the door, he noticed a light coming from under the bottom of the door!

Chapter 2

Jake stood in front of what was suspiciously doorlike, but there wasn't a knob or handle. Reaching forward to try to push on it, the door suddenly slid into the wall on his left. It opened into a well-lit hallway running off to both his right and left.

Standing before him in the middle of the hall was a trashcan. Well, it looked like a trash can, one of those green rectangular types you find in the park with the semi-rounded top. This one was a dull gray with a transparent dome on top. Inside the dome were several camera lenses pointed in different directions. There were little oval and rectangular etchings on the sides, below the dome. Each appeared to represent little doors or access panels.

While Jake was considering the trashcan, it spoke, startling him.

"Captain Thomas? I am relieved to see you made it up the shaft unharmed."

"And you are?" Jake responded.

"I am ALICE. I sent this robotic attendant to greet you and direct you to the main control room. I apologize for not being able to meet you myself. Please follow."

At that point, the "attendant" started moving to Jake's right, down the hall, and at a brisk pace. It appeared to have some roller wheel setup at its base, not visible past the edges of its body. It gave it the appearance of gliding. Jake quickly stepped in behind the "bot," as he thought of it, and matched its speed. He realized he was still carrying the poles in his hand, but hesitated just dropping them. As they passed through a maze of hallways, Jake noticed several of the handleless doors. Some of the wider ones presumably were double doors as there was a faint seam down the middle.

The walls in the hall were off-white, not overly bright, and the ceiling seemed to radiate light, rather than the typical light fixtures every few feet. Everything seemed rather stark and overly sanitary, and it screamed government building. The other thing that struck Jake was that there were no people. He saw two more of the bots, one heading off in an intersecting hallway and the other passing them heading off in the direction they had just come from. However, he didn't see another soul.

The bot stopped in front of a set of double doors, which opened into a little square room that he guessed was an elevator. Stepping in behind the bot, he felt the elevator lift, confirming his suspicions. Jake felt it accelerate rather aggressively, moving upward quickly. Stopping just as quickly, the doors opened to a hallway identical to the one they just left.

Then the bot scooted off down the hall.

Finally, they came to a set of double doors, and sure enough, a little door opened on the side of the bot, allowing an "arm" to extend in Jake's direction.

"You can give the poles to the attendant if you like, you shouldn't need them any longer," the voice explained.

Jake removed the tethers and held out the two mop handles, and its little three-fingered hand snagged both at once. It then retracted its arm and headed off, presumably to dispose of them. He then turned as the doors opened and stepped into a large room, somewhat circular. It was two tiers, the upper deck set back from the lower, like a stadium. All around the room, on both levels, were displays and consoles, most lit up with lights, text, and images.

This was obviously the main control room in the past. The only thing missing was the people.

"Hello?" Jake said.

"Hello, Captain Thomas," a voice replied. It seemed to come from everywhere.

"Where are you? What's with the hide and seek?"

"I am here, Captain, please let me explain," the voice answered.

"Please do," Jake responded.

"Are you, Alice?"

"Yes, I am ALICE," the voice replied.

"Please go to the console to your right, and I will explain everything."

Jake turned to his right and walked to the console, where he noted a display and keyboard, but it wasn't like anything he'd seen before. The words on the monitor seemed to float in midair, and the keypad was more like a touch screen.

Nevertheless, what caught Jake's attention was the label above the monitor.

"ARTIFICIAL LIFE: INTELLIGENT COMPUTING ENVIRONMENT - MASTER CONSOLE,"

ALICE

"You're a computer?" Jake asked.

"Far more than just a computer," ALICE replied.

"I am the entire underground facility. Its sensors are my senses, the attendants my hands, the power supply my heart. I was created to run everything here, so my human population was free to concentrate on more important activities. I cook, I clean, and I can manage and maintain myself in all but the most specific of ways."

"Then, where is everyone?" Jake asked.

17

With a pause, ALICE responded.

"Gone, I have been unoccupied for over 80 years."

"80 YEARS? Gone where?"

"That is part of a much longer explanation, one that must wait. There is a more pressing matter that needs your attention," ALICE declared.

"As I have described, I can maintain and repair myself in all the standard ways with my attendants, with some even designed for specialty work. However, there are a few activities my human designers specifically handled themselves, due to their delicate nature. They didn't believe an attendant would have the abilities necessary to complete them without damaging me," ALICE continued.

"And you need me to do one of these for you?" Jake asked.

"Yes," ALICE replied.

"As I stated earlier, the power supply for this facility is like my heart, should it fail, all that I am will be gone. My design is to never be powered off. Should that happen, I will be lost. You will notice my label is Artificial Life, not Artificial Intelligence. Early in my development, it was discovered that every time the systems that make me what I am got restarted, I did as well."

"I don't understand," Jake replied.

"If I am shut down, all that I know is written to permanent system storage. However, once restarted, it's not part of me. It's like reading a book on another's life, not my own. I am reborn, starting fresh, but losing all that I was," ALICE finished.

"So, what's wrong with the power supply?" Jake asked

"Oh, that is not the problem, my power source is a passive nuclear reduction converter, and its radioactive core will last for thousands of years," ALICE replied as if Jake would know what that was.

"The problem is all my power is routed through six main breakers. They act as insulators, so any feedback is isolated from the power supply, protecting me. Five of those breakers have failed, and the sixth is showing signs of degradation."

"And if that one goes, you're a goner," Jake stated

"Yes," Alice replied flatly.

"Well, I owe you for getting me outta that mess below, so what do I need to do?"

"Actually, I located you in the collapsed lab complex and released you from stasis as well," ALICE added.

The doors opened, and one of the bots came in as ALICE continued her instructions.

"This attendant will lead you to the access portals for the power breaker rooms, the breakers are laid out in redundant pairs in three runs."

18

Jake walked to the attendant and noted one of its arms extended. At the end was a little flat tray with a small earbud on it.

"The attendant has an earpiece for you, so you will be able to hear me wherever you go. It's only necessary for the most remote areas here, like the service areas and supply rooms."

Jake picked up the earbud and, while following the attendant down the hall, placed it in his ear.

"To protect me, I've already powered down most of the non-essential systems over the years, keeping only my basic operations running. The food stores and other perishables I left powered up in stasis, a process I believe you are familiar with."

"Well, I'm glad they figured something constructive to do with that," Jake replied absently, more to himself.

Jake and the attendant approached a doorway at a T-junction, and the door opened to a different elevator than the one he used earlier. Stepping inside, Jake commented aloud.

"Well, tell me exactly what happened to me then. I mean, I go into stasis, the tunnel collapsed three days later, and then 80 years after that, you find me and wake me up?"

As the elevator dropped, ALICE replied to his question.

"That is not precisely the case. The first part is right. Your experiment was isolated three days after it started with the tunnel collapse. There was a major gas explosion during construction, and while everyone on that level perished in the collapse, we maintained all power to the labs, and thus your stasis bed remained operable. In the stasis field, you were protected and safe."

"I was activated as part of this underground facility expansion several years after your loss. I was intended to be a learning Artificial Intelligence environment, and like a child, my early years were spent increasing my awareness."

The door opened, and the attendant sped off to the left, with Jake following in its wake. This part of the facility was more rustic, with darker grayish walls with alternating light panels in the ceiling. The hall had a curve to it, indicating a circular path.

ALICE continued speaking in his ear.

"As I became more self-aware, I started to explore the extremities of my sensor network and found you. I researched your experiment in the archives and discovered the interfaces and communications were all still operating in that Part of the facility. As I mentioned, we believed the portion of the labs you were located in was uninhabited and unstable, thus abandoned. I determined you were alive and recoverable, so I ensured the stasis was maintained."

19

The bot stopped in front of an oval hatch in the wall. It touched a spot on the surface, and the oval swung to the side, exposing a ladder inside a recess, heading down. Jake started down the ladder, and at the bottom, headed under what he assumed to be the hallway above. Jake stopped as he suddenly realized he knew where he was.

"Alice, why do I know where I'm going?"

"The wireless sensors you were fitted with for your experiment allowed me to provide you with continuous education. You will discover that at times you simply know where you are or what to do without knowing why," she replied.

At the end of the accessway was a panel with two large switches, each switch was in the center of a block about the size of a brick. He opened a cabinet next to the panel, and inside were several more bricks just like those with the switches in the center. Jake pulled two out, and holding both with one arm, went to the panel, and pulled down the first switch. The brick dropped free, and Jake placed one of the new ones in its place. He flipped up the switch, and the crystal under the switch started to glow. He repeated the process for the second brick.

As he finished installing the second, ALICE chimed in his ear.

"That replaces two of the damaged breakers, and I am no longer in danger. Thank you, Captain."

Jake retraced his steps, and the bot led him to the next oval hatch in the same hallway. As best as Jake could tell, the layout was 120 degrees from each other in what he assumed was a completely circular hallway. What the hallway circled, Jake had no idea but suspected it was somehow related to ALICE's power source, since the supply breakers surrounded it. While replacing the fifth and final breaker, its mate, the last functioning original, suddenly gave a loud pop and went dark.

"Wow, I guess we were just in time," Jake commented.

"Possibly," ALICE replied.

"I have been re-powering various systems as well as redistributing the load over the new breakers. The fluctuations most likely caused the failure."

Jake swapped out the sixth breaker and then headed back to the bot. While they headed back to the elevator, Jake asked the question that had been bothering him since his awakening.

"Alice, how long WAS I in stasis? I mean, those breakers looked like they should have lasted a long time."

"You were isolated from time for 153 years, 2 months, and 13 days."

"WHAT HAPPENED TO 80 YEARS?" Jake shouted.

As he followed the bot into the elevator, ALICE replied.

"I stated that my facility has not been occupied for over 80 years,

20

you were in stasis for 72 years before that."

"What happened to everyone then?" Jake asked as he felt the familiar weightiness of an elevator rising.

"The earth was attacked," replied ALICE.

"We were bombed with a weapon that emitted lethal radiation of an unknown nature. It only killed humans, thus affecting everyone inside my facility, no matter how deep they were, but left no residual after-effects. In addition, anything in stasis was materially unaffected, so you survived but were exposed to filtered levels of emissions. The long-term effects on your physiology are unknown at this time."

"Oh, that's just great, I could drop dead any minute?"

"That is highly unlikely, but it is also why I didn't remove you from stasis until there was sufficient need to do so. The sensors you wore allowed my monitoring of your health. As you know, the stasis does not stop time. Just slows it greatly," ALICE continued.

"I waited for a time when your presence was most needed, and I could ensure your survival for the necessary duration."

"For the necessary duration?" Jake said, clearly irritated.

"You mean to be sure I would last long enough to save your ass! How long do you think I will last?"

ALICE continued unfazed at the pointed remark.

"At this time, I see no indications you will expire before a normal human lifespan. I have some data that you may experience a longer than normal life span with enhanced muscular and sensory performance. The exposure you received was filtered by the stasis field in some fashion, generating a positive influence on your physiology."

Just then, the doors opened, and the bot scurried off in the direction of the control center.

"Great, so SHOULD I live, I can run faster and jump higher, and I get to talk to you and the trash cans for the rest of my life. The last living human on earth," Jake stated glumly.

Jake stepped into the control room, as ALICE responded.

"Captain, you are not the last living human, just the only one in this facility."

That statement made Jake stop in his tracks.

"So if there are other people, why aren't they here helping you instead of me?"

"There are two reasons. First, the attack on Earth, and it was an attack since I have been able to confirm it was an outside intelligence, wasn't to eradicate humans. The motivation seems to have been to reduce the technological level of the planet. Right now, the overall planetary technology level equates to the late 18th or early 19th century. Getting anyone capable of assisting me wasn't practical."

"At my last survey, I found mostly animal-based transportation with some scrounged steam and gasoline-powered equipment. It's primarily agrarian in most places with limited manufacturing. National identities are still recognized, but most areas are self-supporting with no real interaction with any central governments."

Jake stepped over to a chair near the consoles and plopped down in it. The thought of everything he knew kicked back to horse and buggy and boggled the mind. As he sat there, a bot slid up to him with a bottle of water extended, and he took it without thought and drank.

After a pause, ALICE continued her explanation.

"Most areas of the world, like the one we currently occupy, are lawless. Any civilized law enforcement remains close to widely scattered settlements. Most people who are not out farming depend on the trade goods they scrape together from the abandoned ruins of towns and cities for survival. To expose me to the outside world would be tantamount to committing suicide as my resources would be seen as a treasure trove to be ransacked."

"Additionally, the armory contains weapons and equipment far superior to current technology levels on the surface. To have access to those weapons would instantly give the holders the ability to rule the world!"

Jake was only half listening to that point. The image of automatic weapons and rocket launchers against bows and arrows came to mind. Then he realized he might not even understand what was in the armory. It had been 72 years between his stasis test and the attack. Who knew what they'd come up with during those years?

"And the second reason is I am bound by my core directive. I can only take direction to override that from the facility's commander. My core directive was not to expose myself to the outside world. In point of fact, my primary instructions in that area are to keep this underground facility hidden and secret at all costs."

"Hell, since he died over 80 years ago, that's going to be a problem," Jake said.

"That is not entirely correct," ALICE responded.

"The person who was the facility commander died 81 years ago. With his passing, the next surviving member in his chain of command assumed that responsibility."

"But, you said everyone was killed?" Jake queried.

"Everyone from that command is dead but you. You are now the facility's commander."

The statement slammed Jake. He had just arrived here on the day of the experiment. Additionally, he only returned to the Marine Corps a few months before that. Well, technically now, 153 years ago.

While Jake sat there considering all this new information, ALICE chimed in.

"Captain, there is one more duty I wish to accomplish with some urgency. It's not as critical as restoring access to my power sources, but it does have extremely significant ramifications."

Jake sat for a minute, trying to shake off the overwhelming sense of "through the looking glass" and replied.

"What's wrong, ALICE?"

"The uplink dishes I use to communicate with my satellites no longer function. They are the primary means I monitor the outside world. The last one froze up on me 15 years ago."

"There are three dishes hidden under camouflaged domes at the edges of the valley we sit in. There are underground tunnels to access each, so no need to go outside. Unfortunately, my attendants can't ascend the final access ways to reach the dishes. One has a failed motor, which is a time-consuming repair, and one is destroyed by a dome collapse. However, the final dish just appears stuck. I can move it a small amount, but can't rotate it to track up. It was in a down position for diagnostics and would not recover."

Jake started to stand when a bot slid up with a tray, forcing him to stay seated. The tray held a plate with a sandwich, potato chips, and a glass of what looked like iced tea.

"What's this?"

"You have been going non-stop for several hours now," ALICE replied.

"It is proper that you rest and eat before this next activity."

Jake took the tray and set it on his lap, handing over the water bottle to the little bot and lifting the sandwich. The bread felt soft and fresh. Taking a bite, it tasted good, none of the food was stale, and the drink was ice-cold tea!

"Alice, how can all this be fresh after 80 years?" Jake asked.

"Stasis," she replied.

"In the years after your experiment, humans further developed the means to store perishables in stasis rather than refrigerate. Food lasts indefinitely. Almost all my storage facilities are stasis lockers. Food, frozen goods, clothing, ammunition, and degradable fuels are all stored in stasis to ensure freshness and usability."

Jake considered that while he ate, well, at least he wasn't going to starve.

"Alice, besides the acronym for your name, why the feminine

personality? I mean technically, weren't you a neutral gender species at inception?" Jake asked.

"That is true. Ultimately, it was encouraged that a female persona would be less threatening and more comforting to the staff personnel. It was a naturally evolving occurrence that seemed to satisfy all involved," ALICE replied.

The earlier ammunition comment also got Jake thinking.

"You know, I think I might want to grab a gun for this next task. If what you say is true, the dome may have been compromised, and I wouldn't want any surprises."

"I do have working sensors in the two remaining domes. There haven't been any human intrusions, but I have noted a possible wildlife presence, so your concern is valid. This attendant will lead you to one of the small arms lockers and then transport you for the trip to the dome."

Jake finished eating, and a second bot appeared and took the tray away, while the first stood by the doorway patiently waiting for him to move in that direction.

"You may find some unexpected familiarity with the small arms, though they are different from what you remember. I fed you that information as well while you were in stasis. You are up to date on all the weapons systems in my inventory."

Great, Jake thought, I wonder what other crap I have stored away in my head. I probably had to dump the 3rd grade just to make room! He got up and slowly walked to the doorway. As he approached, the bot turned and whisked off down the hall.

"Damn, these things always seem in a rush," Jake mumbled to himself.

They hit the same elevator as before, but this time it went up, and the doors opened into a large area that looked more like a warehouse. All over the floor space, there were stacks of crates, forklifts, and other less familiar equipment. The bot scurried over to a large door in the wall to Jake's left. As the door rolled up, Jake could see racks of rifles along one wall, and a long bench along the other wall with handguns and other items on it.

The bot continued in and headed to the rear of the space. Jake stepped in behind it and picked up one of the many handguns. It was both familiar and not. It bore the usual trigger and grip arrangement, although the barrel was a bit higher than usual, and there was a square opening below it and over the trigger guard. The bot came back with a holster and belt in one claw and a stack of three magazines in another.

Jake took it all and laid it on the table in the middle of the room. He grabbed one of the magazines and looked at the top. He saw the cylindrical objects he expected inside, but the cartridges were weird. He slid one out and examined it. The first thing he noted was the bullet was on one end, but the other end didn't have a primer. The second thing he noticed was the case wasn't brassy. It looked more like pressed powder, and if he tried hard, he could just scrape some off with a fingernail.

ALICE spoke at that point.

"Those are caseless rounds. Each round feeds from the magazine into a chamber in a rolling block at the back of the barrel. The block rotates 90 degrees and ignites the powder when you pull the trigger. The block then rotates 90 degrees again, and the next round feeds in the empty chamber. The magazine goes in the well below the barrel, and each magazine holds 25 rounds."

"This is what you would call a 10mm caliber. It provides a substantial impact for closer distances. The rifles behind you operate in the same fashion, though the stick magazines for them hold 200 rounds and are in 5.56mm and 7.62mm caliber. They have a larger powder charge and are more powerful and are more accurate to a greater distance."

Jake slipped a magazine into the handgun and then placed it in the holster. He then put the two spares in the pouch on the belt and put the belt on. Satisfied all was in place, he headed out and followed the bot across the floor to a cluster of equipment.

The bot stopped next to what looked like a golf cart. There were just four seats and a flat rear cargo area for small boxes or crates. The only problem was it didn't have a steering wheel!

"This cart will take you to the access port for the dish in question. There is a ladder at that end that goes up to the dish dome."

"Alice, there is no steering wheel for this thing, how am I supposed to drive it?" Jake asked.

"I will drive," she replied.

"All the equipment inside this facility is automated. Simply get in and say where you want to go. In this case, I already know your destination."

Jake climbed into the front seat, and the cart headed off. Crossing the open area, he noted on the far side of the warehouse, there were helicopters of various sizes and other larger land vehicles. The helicopters were a mixed group of military and government models, but the most noticeable thing about them was they didn't have a main rotor. In its place were two large horizontal loops, one on each side of the center of the airframe, with blades inside the loop. Jake suspected they moved independently to control direction because there was no tail rotor. In addition, the area where the engine should be was excessively small.

He made a mental note to go check those out at some point.

While Jake was considering all of this, the cart dashed into a smaller tunnel, though comfortably big enough for the cart. Dimly lit, Jake might have slowed, but ALICE was driving, so he just tried to relax. After about 20 minutes, the cart started to slow and then came to a stop next to one of the oval ports in the wall, like the ones he accessed earlier to reach the power breaker panels.

"This is the access hatch for the dome. Simply touch the center, and it will open automatically," ALICE explained.

Jake did as instructed, and sure enough, it swung away, exposing a ladder as before, though this one went up. He stepped in the access way and started climbing. Again, the lighting wasn't great, but it was good enough to see the rungs to climb. He must have climbed several hundred feet when he finally reached a hatch above his head.

Popping the hatch, he cautiously stuck his head up in the dome and looked around. He could see the dish, standing vertically in the center of the room. It must have been day outside as he could see the light streaming in at several places through the dome. He slowly lifted himself and inspected the room. There was quite a bit of dust and dirt on everything.

Examining the dish, he could see that the positioning gears were caked in dirt. He found a rag and a brush and went to work on cleaning them up.

"Alice, can you hear me?" asked Jake.

"Yes, the domes are at the limits of my internal sensor network."

"Well, I think I can get these positioners freed up, but the dome is a little worse for wear and will need some patching."

At that point, the dish started to creep up, and Jake stepped back to watch as ALICE rotated it up and down.

"I have full rotation again, Jake. We can address patching the dome at another time. Thank You."

As Jake turned to leave, he heard the distinct sound of a pissed-off rattlesnake. Coiled in the corner on the far side of the hatch he intended to leave through was the biggest diamondback he had ever seen.

Discretion being the better part of not being bitten, he drew the 10mm and lined up on the snake's head. A gentle squeeze and it evaporated in a flash of smoke and flame.

"Damn, this is a nice gun!" Jake exclaimed to no one in particular.

"Jake, is everything alright?" ALICE chimed in his ear.

"Yup, just found a snake."

Jake holstered the gun, headed for the hatch, and climbed back down the ladder after he ensured the hatch was secure. Back in the cart, he discovered ALICE had already turned it around. He climbed in, and off it went back the way it came.

Chapter 3

Jake stepped back into the control room after having freed the frozen satellite dish. The return trip was a mirror of the way out, though he skipped the trip to the locker, deciding to keep the gun. Although he doubted he needed it, the gun gave him some sense of personal security. He noticed several new active displays around the room with images he suspected came from satellites. Presumably, due to his interest in the images, ALICE explained.

"I am doing a local survey to update my data on our surrounding conditions. After that is complete, I will expand outward."

"How far have you got?"

"I am finishing the area you know as the southwest US and northern Mexico. I would be further along, but not all the satellites are geosynchronous, so I must wait until they pass over the areas of interest."

"I would suggest you consider resting, and we can review the results later," ALICE finished.

Jake realized he *was* dragging, with all the new information to process, he hadn't noticed it. One of the armies of bots swung by, and without waiting for the expected direction, he got up and followed. Back out in the hall, they hit a different elevator going down and almost immediately stopped. Stepping out, a door across the way opened.

"No point in going too far, all the rooms are identical," ALICE said.

"Although these are the senior staff quarters just below the command center, so they are nicer than the rest."

"I'll say!" Jake replied as he stepped in.

The room layout was splendid, with a sitting area/study, including a plush couch and overstuffed chairs around a coffee table on the left and a fine wooden desk and chair against the wall on the right. There was a small kitchen/wet bar on the back wall to the left and right of that was a door that led into what appeared to be the sleeping area. Walking through that door, there was a walk-in closet on the left and a nice king-size bed on the wall past that. Another set of chairs with a reading table on the right and centered on the back wall was a third door that led to the bath.

"I took the liberty of stocking the room with clothes and uniforms in your size though they are not exactly correct for your time. You can be assured though they are proper for a person of your military service branch and rank with the addition of the facility's commander patch," ALICE explained.

"Almost everything in here is voice activated though the water for the bath and sink also have controls for your convenience. The earpiece was necessary to communicate in the maintenance, utility, and access halls, but almost everywhere else has communication sensors."

Jake went to the closet and, after some exploring, pulled out a T-shirt and some shorts. He went into the bath, pulled the earbud out, and took a long, hot shower. All cleaned up, and with fresh clothes, he hit the bed and was out in seconds.

----*----

Jake opened his eyes, and it took a minute for him to remember where he was. As he slipped out of bed, ALICE piped up.

"Captain, what would you like for breakfast?"

"Well, first, why don't you start by calling me Jake," he answered.

"And second, I don't suppose bacon and eggs is an option?"

"Well, Jake, it is an option. As I mentioned yesterday, I have a very extensive food stasis locker, all as fresh as the day it was delivered," ALICE responded.

Jake wandered into the closet, trying to decide if a uniform was necessary at this point.

"How about 3 eggs, over easy, toast, bacon, and orange juice then," he quipped.

"Oh hell, let's celebrate and throw in some hash browns too, please," he added with a smile.

By this time, he selected something halfway between utility uniform and civvies. Soon a bot appeared with a tray and set it on the reading table in his bedroom, then disappeared.

Jake sat in one of the chairs, digging into breakfast. While he ate, he considered his situation.

"Alice, what am I going to do?" he said between bites.

With a pause, she replied to him slowly.

"I am not sure I understand the question?"

He laughed and answered.

"Yeah, I don't blame you. I was just thinking, here I am, 150 years in the future, essentially alone and responsible for the last technology and military powerhouse on the planet. It just seems to me that the right thing to do is to try to restore some of what was lost. You said there were other survivors. They are just technologically devoid. Maybe we could help bring them back."

"That is possible. Maybe a review of my latest survey might be a good place to start considering your options. I have completed the North and South American continents, most of Europe and Asia," ALICE replied.

"I was thinking more like Texas. The entire North American

continent is a hell of a big bite, don't you think!" he said, laughing.

"The survey is intended to evaluate the level of civilization each geographic area has attained and determine its technological advances. It also helps identify threats and the more aggressive groups to be avoided."

By now, Jake finished his breakfast, and before he could ask, a bot appeared and took the tray away. He stepped into the hall and onto the elevator, with no bot to lead him. He simply said, "Control room."

The doors closed and quickly reopened, but now on the expected floor. He stepped into the hall and retraced his steps from the day before. Walking into the control room, ALICE greeted him.

"I will present on the main holographic display if you would like to be seated."

Jake grabbed one of the chairs along the wrap-around console and sat looking around for where the main display might be. Suddenly, in the center of the room, an image appeared in the open space, two stories high and as wide as the room.

"As I stated yesterday, my last survey was completed 15 years ago. At that time, most major cities were lightly populated, the majority of the population having either been killed when the earth was attacked or fled to the countryside."

"With no central authority, the cities became lawless areas fairly quickly, populated by roving gangs. These small groups of men and women survive by scrounging in abandoned cities or raiding the outlying communities. Some of these gangs have loose order while others are more criminal, caving into their baser instincts. Their weapons are predominantly older civilian small arms scrounged from wherever they can find them. They frequently convert these to black powder, as it is easier to produce than smokeless powder. Edged weapons are also quite popular, swords and knives and the bow and arrow."

Satellite images of various parts of the world, still and video, appeared in the holographic display as she spoke. Jake saw ragtag groups wandering ruined cities, scrounging, and fighting. Next, farming settlements with pens and plowed fields appeared.

"In the areas away from the cities, people have clustered into co-ops, living in defensible housing groups while tending the surrounding lands for food. This communal agrarian lifestyle provides greater security and stability in comparison to living in single homesteads but is limited by the number of workers they can support for both security and farming labor. They maintain trade with some of the more civil city dwellers, bartering for scrounged goods with the food they produce."

Here, ALICE displayed a market of some kind, with baskets of

30

produce on one side and the other side, metals and manufactured goods. There were tables, chairs, wheels, carts, and all kinds of similar items. What struck Jake was the number of guns on both sides, and all guns pointing in each other's general direction. It was very clear, that trading occurred when taking by force was not an option. Wasn't the human race just wonderful?

ALICE continued her briefing for quite a while, breaking down each global region and noting changes from the last survey. A few things were obvious. First, globally, the planet was fairly equal, all around. No one area seemed to have jumped ahead in recovery. In the 80 years following the attack, two generations, assuming a life span of 40 to 50 years, everyone was either farming or scrounging.

Jake thought about that for a moment. Even thousands of years ago, people created cities and congregated in larger numbers. Why not now? Why not just rebuild, as the cities were still there? All the structures were solid and just waiting for occupation. Then it hit him, the gangs. They would be protecting their source of survival.

Anyone returning to the cities would do so in small numbers. Once there, they could expect an attack or be absorbed into the existing social structure. Even if a larger group tried to come in and stabilize things, all the existing gangs would converge on it. Not necessarily as a coordinated response, but certainly, it would create a common enemy.

The second thing was that cities are a basis for industry and manufacturing. With all the free stuff lying around, why try to make lesser-quality products? It would still be years before the existing products and materials degraded to such an unusable state that humanity would again need to return to creating non-perishable items, and let's face it, a certain percentage of the population just doesn't like to work for a living. Then there was the path of least resistance types. They just wander around finding cool stuff and trying not to be killed by others wandering around doing the same. Then they trade for food with the hard-working types in the countryside. That's city life these days.

Then there was another consideration, Jake thought. Someone had kicked the shit out of the earth. That someone wasn't likely to be just ignoring things here. Any significant increase in technological advancement might draw more unwanted attention. He figured whatever he decided to do, he needed to keep a very low profile for a while. By this point, ALICE finished speaking and waited patiently for Jake to process it all.

After thinking it through, Jake started.

"So, it seems to me, that we have three approaches to consider. First, we can pick a farming community to sponsor and create a secure free

31

trade zone. We give them the technology to increase farm production, educate, and expand our influence out from there."

"Second, we could pick a city and displace the gangs. I say displace because I don't think they are going to replace their lifestyle willingly with one requiring hard work and dedication. With a stable, safe environment, that city will become a draw for settlers and traders and populate naturally. We can educate and elevate from there."

"Last but not least, we selectively draw from the outside population and bring them here. That has both a greater appeal and enormous risk. By acquiring the right people, we can have you educate them far more quickly, and we can then distribute the workload internally and kick off multiple efforts. However, one bad egg on the inside could wreak havoc. It would become obvious to anyone in short order that they could rule the world with what you have to offer," Jake finished.

"There are measures we can take to limit that risk," ALICE replied.

"I have programs for the complete psychoanalysis of individuals. One of my original responsibilities was evaluating the facility staff. I was previously responsible for ensuring no unstable personnel went undetected and gained access to sensitive materials or destructive items. I can also limit educational materials and lesson plans until we are assured of an individual's disposition. Finally, I do have some active antipersonnel systems I can use as a last resort to terminate high-level threats. I would agree the third option is the most appealing."

"This effort would require you to go outside and recruit pre-selected individuals," ALICE offered.

"So, I snatch 'em, and you dissect 'em," Jake offered with a grin.

----*----

Jake spent the next few weeks doing all the maintenance tasks for ALICE that the bots couldn't do. He got the second satellite dish positioning motor replaced and the dish back online. He patched the dome for the first dish, taking his gun again just in case. Overall, he crept and crawled into places for small tasks neglected over the years.

He and ALICE decided she would concentrate on scanning the surrounding area for likely recruits. She proposed that the first volunteers should be female and from the farming communities. Her reasoning had been quite simple. The return to a predominantly agrarian society reasserted old ideals of male and female gender roles. As such, women would be less likely to challenge male dominance directly. Not that they didn't have their ways of challenging things or weren't aggressive, they just tended to be less violent about it.

Additionally, her best intelligence suggested the female population

32

better retained their educational standards of reading and writing. Where most of the boys were out working the fields as soon as possible, the girls had some flexibility in gaining additional education. Also, recruiting from the farming communities suggested societies of defensive harmony, rather than the aggressive nature of the gangs of the cities.

----*----

With the priority tasks completed, Jake was in the huge warehouse area that he discovered was a hangar early one morning, checking out one of the helicopters he'd seen previously. He spent a lot of time in helicopters while in Iraq and Afghanistan, and this one looked like one of the old UH-1 "Hueys" from the 1960s. It had the same squat, wide stance with two seats up front and a cargo/passenger area behind.

The big differences were the two large overhead hoops, one on each side of the airframe containing blades inside. The hoops attached to a rib down the center of the top of the airframe, and there was no tail rotor. In its place was a pair of short rear tail booms with vertical and horizontal stabilizer fins.

ALICE explained to Jake in earlier questioning that the hub in the center of each hoop was an electrically powered motor, making each hoop a large fan. On a full charge, these things could fly continuously for a month. The craft was controlled by the fan blade RPM, blade pitch, and rotating the hoops in two axes. The controls in the cockpit were very similar to what he'd seen in other helicopters. The real difference was, now that ALICE's dishes were back online, she could fly it outside the facility remotely.

As he was inspecting the aircraft, he heard from the speaker inside the helicopter, catching him by surprise.

"Jake, I have located likely candidates as our first recruits. There is an incident in motion that may have created an opportunity, but there is some urgency. We need to discuss how you will approach them and what security precautions to take if we are to act. There is a ready room next to the small arms locker. I have some equipment there that you will require. It's located in a locker room in the back."

Jake found himself excited at the prospect of new activity as he headed off in the direction of the small arms locker he'd visited that first day and found both that door and another opened nearby. Inside the ready room were the typical rows of theater-style seats, used to brief pilots for missions or after-action reviews. Behind the seats was another door leading to the locker room ALICE mentioned. Once inside the locker room, Jake found his name on the first locker right in front with *Captain Thomas* on the ID plate. Opening the locker, he found a helmet on the

33

shelf above with uniforms hanging inside.

ALICE offered a running commentary as Jake lifted the helmet.

"The helmet is a standard full-face combat model 27. It seals airtight to the uniform undergarment. It's bulletproof, contains a full tactical and communications package, and supplies warm or cool filtered air. It also neutralizes chemical and biological contaminants. You can submerge for limited periods, and the curved faceplate is optically corrected for distortions."

Placing the helmet back on the shelf, Jake pulled out two hangars. One contained something that looked like black long johns, while the other held a familiar-looking BDU, or Battle Dress Uniform blouse and trousers. ALICE continued as he inspected the garments.

"Your uniform is in two layers. The undergarment is a one-piece suit with openings for the head and hands only. It stretches to don and returns to a skin-tight fit. It's also bulletproof, and the material goes rigid at the point of impact to distribute the forces to acceptable levels. The outer garments are a more traditional Battle Dress Uniform or BDU but retain much of the resilience of the undergarment, giving you multiple layers of protection. They contain the typical combat pockets and pouches. The gloves are skin tight and provide tactile feedback to your hands for increased sensitivity, again bulletproof. They sealed to the undergarment as well. Your boots have ultra-grip soles and contain proximity sensors tied to your helmet display. They can detect traps and mines up to 10 feet in all directions."

Jake put the hangars back and noted the boots and gloves as well.

"Once suited up, your gloves and helmet seal to your undergarment as mentioned, creating a bulletproof, airtight envelope over your body. Only you or a pre-authorized delegate, like a medic, can break containment."

"How do I pee?" Jake asked.

"You just go," ALICE replied.

"Your undergarment will filter and process the output into drinkable water, available in your helmet. External water sources are processed similarly. Defecation is also possible, but not advised as it is not processed. I am told it is uncomfortable and quite offensive when you disrobe."

"Pass," Jake said.

"I'll go before or hold it."

"If you would return to the ready room, I can brief you on my findings."

Jake wandered back into the ready room and over to the first row, dropping into a seat as a 2D display appeared on the wall.

"As we have discussed, I've been reviewing all the local farming communities, searching for candidates that fit our profile. Because most of the immediate areas are uninhabited desert, my search radius is approximately 300 miles. That covers almost all of what you would know as Nevada and parts of Arizona, Utah, and California. This also gives us about 1 ½ hour access time in the helicopter to any of these locations."

"The most promising locations are in California. The areas near Fresno and Bakersfield hold many farming communities, not surprising, as it was always heavily agricultural. The Bakersfield area is the one of interest now, as they have recently suffered raids by a gang up from Los Angeles. Given the distance and transportation, they must be struggling for food there to the range so far out."

While she was speaking, ALICE displayed both maps and high-altitude images of the areas she described.

"Or, more likely driven further out from any local sources, as they dry up," Jake tossed out.

"Possibly," ALICE replied, then continued.

"There are a few homesteads I have been monitoring with potential candidates. Unfortunately, they have suffered from these latest raids. One, in particular, contained an older couple with three daughters and no sons. After a raid early this morning, I have seen no activity at the farm or in the fields. I have observed two women, probably two of the daughters, moving about the homestead. They also look to be digging two graves nearby."

Jake could see the overhead view of the two women digging. With the image panned out, all he could tell was that they were blonde and female.

"Are you thinking, I show up there and say, Hey, I'm from the government, and I'm here to help?" Jake quipped.

"I would not suggest that approach, and they are not the target I suggest. I have located the raiding party returning to LA, and they have captives."

The real-time imagery ALICE displayed turned to holographic 3D. It showed about 25 to 30 men, mostly on horseback, some in wagons, crossing an open field. Most of the wagons held food ripped from the fields and storerooms. One wagon held seven people in the back. They looked tied hand and foot, and all appeared to be women.

The sight caused Jake to become quite serious, all the humor leaving the situation. Asking ALICE to zoom in on the wagon, he noted they didn't appear too much the worse for wear, but he figured that wouldn't last long. Jake considered that for a moment. If he swooped in and

35

rescued the women, it would be a great way to present himself to the locals, rather than dropping unannounced from the sky in town. Thirty-to-one was not the best of odds, though. Even if he came out unscathed, he doubted the hostages would all survive.

"Alice, do we have guns for any of the birds in the hangar?"

"I have directed the attendants to install external armaments during our briefing. I would suggest you suit up, as we should be ready to lift off within the hour."

Jake jumped up and headed to the locker room. Within minutes he was suited up, and helmet in hand, headed to the weapons locker. He drew a 10mm handgun like before and grabbed one of the shorter rifles, a 5.56mm. He slid a 200-round magazine in the magazine well along the top of the barrel. He then took four extra 200-round mags, which fit, two per side, into pouches on his thighs.

Jake stepped out into the hangar, and he headed to the helicopter at a quick pace. The bird was in the process of relocating to an open area in the hangar by an automated tug. There were guns on the skids below the doors now, and one under the nose in front.

"Once you place your helmet on and seal up, the doors above the hangar will open, and I will fly you to the intercept point. It should be about a 1 hour and 45 min flight."

Jake slid the helmet on and, as instructed, simply touched the skirt inside the helmet to where his undergarment rode up to his neck. It instantly stuck, and an indicator in his helmet lit green once he had a seal. Climbing in the back, he strapped into a jump seat and could feel the helicopter start to hover and lift. He tucked his rifle into the holder next to his seat, confused for a minute at the barrel-up position, and then remembered there wasn't an engine above him. You never rode in a chopper barrel up. An accidental discharge would go right through the engines above in a typical helicopter.

That thought triggered the realization of how quiet it was. With electric motors instead of traditional engines, all you got was blade noise, and these blades were whisper quiet. As the helicopter rose, two large roof panels at the top of the hangar slid to the side, creating an opening far bigger than the bird he was in required. Via a heads-up display in his helmet, Jake watched as they cleared the opening and headed higher in the sky and toward the southwest. Picking up speed, ALICE closed both side sliding doors of the helicopter.

"Alice, can you feed me the display for the raiding party and the surrounding area?" Jake asked.

Per the request, his display changed to the overhead of the raiding party he'd seen earlier. They were still moving at the same rate as before, but the landscape had changed from greenery to more desert-like surroundings.

"Alice, how do I control this display?" Jake asked.

"Your helmet is fitted with sensors that allow you to control the image with thought. Concentrate your attention on enlarging the image and look at the spot to focus on."

Jake focused on the wagon with the women and concentrated on "ZOOM." The image zoomed until the wagon filled the display. The women looked a bit worse for wear, but then how was one supposed to look after having their family murdered and then carted off as plunder? What they didn't look like was raped and beaten. He suspected that would change soon enough if he delayed. Scanning the group, he guessed they were all in their late teens to mid-20s. They were still alive and not left for dead, so he was sure they were intended as spoils.

He backed out of the image and surveyed the area ahead of the caravan. He then checked their rate of travel, trying to determine the safest place to intervene with less risk to the women, and began organizing a plan in his head. Then he panned back in the direction the group came from and finally found the last piece of his plan. A good three hours behind the bandits was a large group on horseback. Back in the day, you'd have called it a posse. There were 30 to 35 men, all armed and following the track the wagons and riders. He suspected this was the reason the women appeared mostly unmolested as there had been no time for anything but escape.

With a rough plan in mind, Jake explained.

"Alice, I think we have two options, either we strafe them from behind, taking out as many as possible while trying not to hit the women, or we land ahead of them, drop me off, and I can try to pick off the ones around the women first. At that point, you can bring the helicopter in from behind and drive off the outliers, while I get the wagon. I'll have to wait until they get about 300 meters away, though, this rifle doesn't have the range for more."

"I don't like the second option, but it has the best possibility of success. You must promise to protect yourself at all times. Never break containment. Even though you are shielded, you are not indestructible. Also, Jake, although these weapons have a greater range than the generation of weapons you are familiar with, under the floor panel at your feet is a weapons locker. You may find a more suitable rifle there for your plan."

Jake popped the hatch and looked inside. There was an assortment of weapons at his feet, everything from a squad machine gun to extra handguns, all with ammo. With a smile, Jake pulled out a 7.62mm sniper rifle. His artificially placed memories told him it had over three times the range of the one he brought. It was fed with a more traditional bottom magazine, and each magazine held 20 rounds. He loved sniping. More than once, he'd taken over the role from one of his men in Afghanistan just to keep himself in practice.

"Alice, what would I do without you?" he said, still smiling at the rifle.

"We are about 40 minutes out," ALICE answered.

"I am dropping you on the backside of a ridge where we won't be visible. It will take those on horseback about 20 minutes to reach the target area, so once I drop you, I will continue around behind the group to contain a retreat."

"Good plan," Jake replied.

Jake brought up the ridge that ALICE mentioned in his display. The trail the riders were on ran through a little pass on it. He noted a high spot overlooking the pass and a good 3000 meters of the trail leading up to it. He'd wait until they were about 1000 meters from the top of the pass, then take out the wagon security and driver. He hoped the horses would stop as he didn't want to have to shoot them too. Jake felt the helicopter drop and cleared his display. They were approaching the LZ area, and ALICE slowed and opened one of the doors. Jake slung the 7.62 on his back and grabbed the 5.56 from its rack.

With as smooth of a touch and go as Jake had ever seen, he hopped out, and ALICE proceeded to take the whisper-quiet helicopter on down the valley, staying low behind the ridge and out of sight. Checking his display again to be sure he knew the group's location, he made his way up the ridge, dropping to the ground as he crested the ridge so he didn't silhouette on the ridgeline. Topping the ridge, he found the hide he'd spotted on his display earlier and set up with the 7.62 sniper rifle.

Once he was satisfied, he was set and could not be seen, he settled in to wait.

Chapter 4

Jake sat in his hide and tried to relax. He let his mind go blank and watched through the rifle scope, pointed at the turn in the trail, waiting for the lead riders to appear. Working with the enclosed helmet took a bit of time to get used to, but it did have its advantages. He switched the display between the scope, the overhead video on the raiders, and the map showing everyone's positions; his, the raiders, ALICE, and the posse. Damn, he wished he had one of those in Afghanistan.

Since his helmet display synchronized with the rifle, he didn't have to look through the scope. However, his sniper training required him to hold the rifle as if he did. He lay prone, trying to adjust slightly to accommodate the differing needs of this equipment. His helmet faceplate prevented him from actually looking directly through the lens, so he displayed in his helmet as if he were.

As he was considering and adjusting for all of this, the first of the riders came around the turn. They were still over 3000 meters away, precisely 3291M, according to the rangefinder on the scope. He wanted them much closer before he engaged. Next were the wagons with the plunder in them, and finally, the one that had his interest. There was a clean shot at both the driver and his security rider, seated next to him, whose rifle was resting crosswise in his arms.

From his elevated position, there was a good view, but he was worried about the down angle. Should the shot go through a target, it would hit one of the passengers behind.

"Alice, I'm afraid these rounds are going to pass through the targets and kill someone in the wagon behind."

"There is a setting for the projectiles to explode on the first contact. These are what you call smart rounds. Just think about *exploding* to the rifle, and you should see a bomb indicator in the scope display. That will activate the projectile behavior," ALICE explained.

Jake did as instructed, and sure enough, a little bomb appeared in the corner of his display. That problem was solved, now Jake checked to see the targets were now at 2202 M, but the lead rider was at 2035 M. He repositioned the 5.56 rifle next to him. Should the leader charge his position, he could switch out weapons quickly, and then go back to tracking the wagon.

He continuously scanned between targets, setting target priority, and he noted none of the raiders seemed overly concerned. He was sure they knew someone was chasing them, but they felt they would clear the area and be back to LA before anyone caught up to them. Just then, one of the riders near the woman reached over and grabbed the blonde by the hair, jerking her head back sharply. He said something, causing the others nearby to laugh, and then released her with a flip of his arm and backhanded her, causing her head to snap sideways violently. He was probably claiming first rights on her.

Jake thought he'd have no such luck by the time he finished with this group.

----*----

Sara Sullivan sat in the wagon fuming, how she could have been so stupid. When that bastard killed her parents, she'd just lost it. Leaving the safety of her hiding place, she charged him with an ax, only to have him knock her aside like a child. The bruise swelling on the side of her face was evidence of his brutality. He intended on raping her right there, but their farm had been the last in a string of raids that night. The entire valley was gathering and shouting for blood. The raider lookouts saw them mustering for an attack, so the bandits made a hasty retreat.

So here she sat, trussed up, and tossed into the wagon with the others. Some of the younger girls, like Sandy from up the road, sat sobbing, her face dirty and tear-streaked. Sara knew the others in the wagon as all were from the neighboring farms. With so many daughters in the families these days, these assholes probably thought they hit the jackpot. Well, Sara wasn't going to give up without a fight. She'd find a way to make them pay.

----*----

The target wagon was now in the box, and Jake lined up on the security rider first. With just a squeeze of the trigger, the security with the rifle exploded in his display. Jake quickly shifted left and took the driver next. He then took out three more riders near the wagon, the first being the one who hit the blonde earlier. Jake caught a puff of dirt next to him, and then something slammed into his shoulder. Looking up from the scope, he spied the lead rider 150 feet in front of him, riding hard and firing wildly in his direction.

Not waiting to shift to the 5.56, and firing the 7.62 more from the hip than sighting the rifle, he struck the horse square in the chest with the sniper rifle round. The rider went over the horse's head and hit headfirst into the rock pile to Jake's right. From the angle of his head, he didn't think another shot was necessary.

By now, the raiders had figured out he was on the ridge, blocking their access to the pass. The other wagons were in the process of trying to turn left, away from his position, while the wagon with the women

40

stopped a few yards from where he had taken the first shot. Several of the riders headed in that direction as if to get to that wagon, and Jake dispatched them straight away.

ALICE, or rather the helicopter she was controlling, cleared the ridge at the left rear of the valley and opened up on the raiders escaping to Jake's right. Wagons exploded in produce and blood, as the 20mm rounds from the nose gun ripped through everything. This new activity spooked the horses pulling the wagon with the women. Headed in Jake's direction and away from the others, he was happy to let them continue. By the time they reached the grade to the pass, they had slowed to a walk and then stopped.

Once he was sure he had cleared the threats to the women, Jake stood up, slung the sniper rifle over his shoulder, and picked up the 5.56, heading to the wagon at a trot. He rubbed his shoulder as he went. The suit had done its job stopping the bullet, but he was going to be sore there for a bit. He slowed as he got closer and tried not to upset the horses again as he approached.

He reached for one of the horse's bridles and patted both to try to calm them down. As he did, he turned to watch ALICE chase down two of the riders headed east, driving their horses at a dead run with others scattering in various other directions away from him and the raging helicopter above. There were no more than 10 raiders alive at this point, the rest lying in pieces all over the valley except for the two splattered across this wagon.

To his dismay, there were half a dozen horses down as well, not including the one he'd deliberately shot. In addition, most of the other wagons were in shambles, and stolen goods were strewn all over the ground.

"Can't be helped, I guess," he said quietly to himself and then spoke aloud to ALICE.

"Alice, let them go. It won't hurt to let them spread the word of our arrival. Find a spot to put down, not too close, while I get the women out of the wagon,"

At that, the helicopter banked sharply and sped to his location. It pulled up a good 500 meters away and sat down lightly. Jake noted that he now had seven heads in the wagon turned toward him with mixed expressions of fear and hope on their faces. Most of those faces were streaked with tears and dirt.

Just then, ALICE offered Jake some instructions.

"Do not remove your helmet, but you may turn the faceplate clear so they can see your face. Also, you must activate outside audio, or they won't hear you."

41

Jake hadn't realized the faceplate was opaque, and they couldn't see his face. No wonder they were anxious. He made it clear and turned the audio on, as she advised.

"Ladies, I am Captain Jake Thomas, United States Marine Corps," he said, as he moved slowly to the rear of the wagon.

"I'm here to rescue you."

He pulled out a knife from his belt and started to cut the ropes at their ankles and wrists. He could feel them straining to see his face inside the helmet. As he freed each one, the woman would jump out of the wagon. Once on the ground, they clustered to one side where they could both watch him and the helicopter behind him. When the last of the women were freed, Jake turned to face them, not quite sure what to say. Snatched from their beds, all were in one or another form of sleepwear, some of it barely hiding their assets.

----*----

Sara stood in her nightgown, facing the man who, in a matter of seconds, performed the task she'd been praying to perform herself. She could see past him to a field strewn with bodies and a very strange flying machine now sitting on the ground. She expected there were more men inside, but none came out

He was taller than she was, probably 6 feet to her 5 feet 7 inches, and dressed in some military getup she had never seen before that included a full-face helmet. She could see through the clear faceplate, though, and noted a strong, handsome face. Though he carried two guns with him, both were shouldered, so she didn't fear getting shot as she stepped forward to speak.

----*----

The blonde woman he'd seen accosted in the wagon earlier stepped forward. She appeared to be one of the oldest of the group, maybe 26, and there was a bruise swelling on the side of her face.

"We would like to thank you for saving us," she said hesitantly.,

"But who are you, and what is that?" she added as she pointed to the helicopter.

Jake looked over his shoulder at the helicopter and then back to the women before speaking.

"As I said, I'm Captain Thomas, I'm a United States Marine, and this is my helicopter."

They looked as confused as ever, so he continued.

42

"Look, do any of you know about the time before? When people used to fly in planes and drive in cars?"

A few nodded.

"Well, I come from there."

A busty little brunette, who looked no older than 18, laughed.

"How can that be? That was before my father's time. He says my grandfather was a little boy when people flew in planes. You aren't old enough for that."

Jake considered his answer, and as he did so, he could also see the women were relaxed or at least didn't seem as afraid as they'd been previously.

"I was asleep," he answered matter-of-factly.

That made the blonde laugh. The rest looked like they didn't believe what he had just said, and who could blame them?

"I was in stasis, which is like a sleep that keeps you from getting old. I just woke up, and now I am trying to do my job again."

"And what job was that?" it was the blonde again, looking very interested now.

"Killing people like that," Jake replied, pointing out in the field behind them.

That brought a smile to her face, and then she asked the million-dollar question.

"How do I get a job like that?"

Now it was Jake's turn to smile.

"This may be your lucky day or maybe even luckier than just being rescued," he answered.

He scanned the group before him before he continued.

"Look, I can take all of you back home in the helicopter, or you can take this wagon back on your own if you prefer. You know how long the wagon ride is, we can get there in minutes by flying."

Pandemonium broke out among the women at that point, everything from "No way in Hell, I am getting in that thing" to "How high will it go?"

In the end, all agreed to fly so long as it was low and slow.

Jake got the women to help him unhook or unsaddle all the horses, figuring they would find their way home or go wild. Then, as they all climbed in and strapped into seats in the helicopter, he checked the posse on his display and found they were still over an hour away.

He stowed the rifles and climbed in himself, taking the seat next to the door with the little brunette next to him and the blonde across the way. Jake was glad the brunette was next to him and not across the way. The movement of the helicopter was doing interesting things with her chest, and it was hard not to stare as her nightgown did little to hide it.

Switching off his external audio, Jake figured this was a conversation best kept private.

"OK, Alice, let's go. I figure we meet the posse first, then on to the farm town."

With that, the door slid closed, and they lifted off.

"How would you like to approach them? Pop up close or let them see us coming?" ALICE asked.

"Yeah, I have been thinking about that, just about any way we go, I think they are likely to take a shot at us."

"Their weapons can't harm us," she replied.

"The outer skin of the helicopter is similar to your uniform, only a hit to the fan blades is a risk," she responded.

"Then let them see us, but stay low so they can see the ladies in the windows."

That would be a certainty as the windows on both sides had faces plastered against them. They were flying no more than 100 feet off the deck, as promised, and banking wide to avoid hard turns. Even so, two of the women in the middle just sat rigidly, eyes screwed tightly shut, praying for it to be over as quickly as possible. In minutes, Jake saw the posse fly past, as ALICE rotated broadside circling behind them, then set lightly down. She opened the door on the far side, placing the helicopter between the posse and the women spilling out.

Jake cleared the front and was in time to see three of the women running across the span between the helicopter and the posse. The posse members all had their guns pointing in his general direction. Several of the men lowered their guns and raced to meet the three women. Jake turned to the four women with him, the blonde, the brunette, and two that looked like sisters. With external audio back on, he addressed the four.

"Why aren't you off with them?"

The brunette answered first with a sniffle.

"My family's all gone. They were killed in the raid."

"Us too," one of the sisters added.

"I want a ride back," the blonde said with a smile.

"Those bastards killed my parents, but I hid my sisters before they got me," she added.

Jake remembered the feed from this morning of the two women digging graves. He looked back at the posse and saw an animated conversation between the women and men, the latter somewhat hesitant to come any closer. Finally, a small group of men started in Jake's direction. Jake reciprocated, meeting them halfway, and the four women followed him, apparently not wanting to let him get too far from their

44

presence.

Jake did his best to appear non-threatening, but the men kept their guns at the ready. They had them up, just not pointed in his direction. When they got about 10 feet apart, the men stopped, and Jake offered to speak first.

"I'm Captain Thomas of the United States Marine Corps. I hope we didn't alarm you flying in like that?"

"Scared the crap outta me," one man offered.

"Sorry," Jake replied.

"I only wanted to get the ladies returned as quickly as possible."

"Who the hell are you," someone asked.

"And what the hell is that?"

Big sigh, Jake was sensing a theme developing here.

"I'm a Marine, and that helicopter is mine. I'm from what used to be the United States Marine Corps. I was part of the military that protected this country before all this."

"Looks like you fucked up, then," another commented with supporting chuckles afterward.

Well, no fear of them not speaking their minds, Jake thought. One of the men stepped forward, hand out.

"Well, I, for one, would like to thank you for the return of my daughter."

Jake took the offered hand, and with that, everyone stepped up to close the gap.

"What's with the helmet?" someone asked.

Thinking quickly, Jake responded.

"It's part of my combat suit, I can't take it off, see it's all attached," he pointed to the seam where the helmet skirt attached to the undersuit.

"Oh," he heard from several places.

Jake continued,

"About an hour up the trail are a good wagon and several horses. We turned them loose so they may come back. Didn't know if you cared to retrieve any salvageable items they stole from you. Sorry to say we shot some of it up pretty bad getting the women back."

"You kill'em all?" someone asked.

"No, a little over two-thirds I'd say. We purposely let some go to tell the tale. It's more effective to let them spread the word for you than have people wonder what happened. Eventually, more come looking."

He got several nods of understanding of that. By now, the entire posse closed in, and some even wandered close to the helicopter. Jake asked ALICE to open both doors and let them look around inside.

Jake answered several more questions, and at one point asked his own in reply.

"So, who's the leader of your town?"

An older gray-haired man with a full beard raised his hand.

"Burt's the name."

"Pleasure to meet you," Jake replied.

"We sure want to thank you for saving the ladies and kill 'n those assholes," he said.

With that, Jake walked over to the helicopter and reached in, pulling something out of a storage panel. He walked back over to Burt.

"This is a long-range communicator, any more issues like this in the future, just speak into it, and someone will answer."

"Me," ALICE whispered in his ear.

"We want to try to reestablish order," Jake continued to the larger crowd.

He noted some worried expressions until he added to the statement.

"By helping you protect yourselves."

That brought smiles from the group.

"With that, you can call for help now, but eventually, we want to set you up to help yourselves and others around you," Jake explained as he pointed to the box.

Jake focused his attention back on Burt.

"I need to go now, but we will be back to discuss what your needs are."

Turning, he found the four women between him and the helicopter.

"We want to go with you, my little sisters are alone, and think I'm dead or worse," the blonde said while indicating her companions.

"Climb in," Jake said, while pointing at the helicopter., then turned to address the others around them.

"Please stand back," he announced.

That turned out to be unnecessary, for as ALICE started spinning blades, everyone backpedaled rather quickly. With everyone in, the doors closed, and they lifted off. Jake assumed ALICE was headed to the blonde's farm, so he didn't bother asking.

"So, where would you three like to go?" He did ask, looking at the others.

He got the deer in the headlights look back from all three. He noticed the blonde watching him intently as he talked to them.

"We have no homes to go back to, they killed our families, and our farms were burnt to the ground. Our only hope is that someone will take us in. With so few men around, marriage isn't likely," one of the women said, indicating her sister and the little brunette.

"And you?" he said, looking directly at the blonde.

46

"I still want that job, as long as my sisters can come too," she replied intensely.

Jake sat back for a moment, considering how to proceed. His original idea of recruitment had been one or two at a time. Here, he would be getting six for the price of one, but at least one of them, the brunette, was way younger than he'd considered suitable for the work he knew needed to be done. He had expected they would need more mature individuals for the initial volunteers.

The assault on the raiders proved this was going to be a bloody business, one not suitable for delicate sensibilities. Then again, he had no idea what other work he needed to be done besides his own more violent expectations. Someone always had to file and answer phones, he thought, then laughed privately at the sexist nature of that statement. This was a brave new world, and he had a feeling at some point, everyone was going to get bloody sooner or later.

"OK, for anyone interested, we're recruiting. What that means is we are looking to take you in, room and board, and train you to help me. And yes, your sisters can come," he said as he turned back to the blonde.

"That translates to room, clothes, food, and education, and learning a profession that supports the community."

Jake lets that sink in a minute.

"Any questions?"

No one responded verbally. All just shook their heads no.

"I take it you all want to come?" Jake asked of the group.

There were smiles and nods all around.

"Ladies, we will be landing shortly. Please gather any personal items you wish to bring with you, but do it quickly. Don't bother with food or clothing, just take personal items, everything else will be provided," ALICE chipped in over the internal speakers,

The women, confusion on their faces, searching for the source of the voice.

"That's ALICE, she's back at base."

"Ah, like the box you gave Burt, she can hear us, and we can hear her," the blonde said.

Jake was optimistic about this one. He was trying hard to keep his personal feelings out of things, but she was a looker.

"What's your name?"

"I'm Sara, that's Sandy," she replied as she pointed to the brunette.

"And they are Linda and Kathy," she said, finishing up with the sisters.

By this time, the helicopter flared and gently touched down in front of Sara's house. The door slid open, and everyone hopped out, with Sara

47

led the group out the door, and she headed at a dead run toward the house.

----*----

Becky and her sister Bonnie sat crying by the window at the front of the house. They had buried their parents that morning and were back inside, waiting to see if the others could get their sister Sara back. They were hiding in the barn last night, under the hay in the loft where Sara had covered them when the raiders hit their farm.

Their father had seen the fires from the other farms and taken them out to hide in the barn. They never saw their parents shot, or their sister carted off. They heard the men leaving and saw Sara in the back of the wagon in the distance as they came out of the barn.

Becky was considering their future, not sure what she and Bonnie would do. They couldn't work the farm alone, so they would probably have to marry one of those losers in town if they could even find one. None of the sisters had found a husband as they were too stubborn and independent for the local men to consider as wives.

Becky dreamed of working for the Doctor, maybe becoming his nurse, but the community was too small to support a full-time hospital. The doctor even had to work as a vet to cover his living expenses. As she was considering all this, a shocked Bonnie pointed out the window, and Becky turned to see a flying machine land in front of the house, and Sara climbed out!

----*----

Jake climbed out of the helicopter last and waited with the other three women as Sara ran for the house. Before she got halfway, the door opened and two younger versions of herself, one about 20 or 21 and the other close to Sandy's age, came running out to meet her. There were hugs, kisses, and tears, and then three sets of eyes settled on Jake. He could see Sara explaining to her sisters and the confusion on their faces.

After Sara waved them over, Jake and the other three slowly approached. Sara made the introductions once they closed the distance.

"Becky, Bonnie, this is Captain Thomas. Captain, these are my sisters."

"It's a pleasure," Jake replied, not reaching out to shake for fear of startling them.

"You can all call me Jake."

The youngest, Becky, turned away from Jake and blurted out between her tears.

"Sara, they killed Mom and Dad," she started with a muffled sob, her

48

hand over her mouth.

"I know, but Jake made them pay. He killed the bastards," Sara explained.

Becky looked up at Jake and started in on him.

"Sara says we are going in that and are going to live with you. You are going to teach us how to be like you?" She asked while motioning to the helicopter, sitting idle.

"Well, yes, but it's not about learning to be like me, it's about learning things to help people," he replied.

"Like what?" she asked.

"Well, like learning how to farm hundreds of acres using machines rather than these small parcels by hand," he said, pointing out to the fields.

"Or maybe becoming a teacher, so you can teach others all the things we have lost over the last 80 years."

"Or maybe even a doctor?" Becky asked, a sudden look of interest crossing her face.

"Jake, we need to get them moving, or it's going to get dark in a few hours, and I don't think they are ready for night flights just yet," ALICE pinged in Jake's helmet.

"Roger," he replied, external audio off.

"Or a doctor," Jake replied to Becky.

He then turned to Sara and began issuing instructions.

"Sara, have your sisters gather any personal items they want to take, but keep it to a minimum."

"Sandy, sounds like you guys have nothing to go back for?" He said, turning to the brunette and the sisters.

All three nodded in agreement.

"Then can you help them? I'll meet you all at the helicopter, go as fast as you can, OK?"

Everyone nodded and headed back into the house while Jake headed to the helicopter. More quickly than Jake expected, all six came out of the house heading for the helicopter. Each was carrying a small bag or bundle.

"I guess when you don't have much, it doesn't take long," Jake thought to himself. He also suspected in the weeks to come, most of it would be quickly discarded.

As they climbed in, Jake seated the newest arrivals in the middle seats, with the more experienced on either side to help calm them. With everyone strapped in, he gave the all-clear to ALICE.

"OK, we are good to go," and with that, they lifted off, the doors sliding closed.

"How far do we have to go?" Sara asked.

"A little over 300 miles," Jake replied.

"How many days will it take?" Sandy asked.

"More like about an hour and 45 minutes."

"HOW FAST ARE WE GOING?" Linda said, looking out the window, panic on her face.

"Over 150 miles an hour, we could probably go a little faster, but this way, the ride is smoother."

That got all of them looking out the windows, even the newest members. The sisters shared Sara's sense of adventure, not showing any fear. The rest of the ride back was mostly in silence. Now and then, someone would spot a town or herd of livestock, causing everyone to crowd the window. It was dark by the time they arrived back at the facility. As they dropped into the hangar with the doors above it closed, Jake had the feeling of coming home.

Stepping out of the helicopter, Jake grabbed his rifle and then popped the seal and removed his helmet, while leading the six women to the facility doors.

"Hey, you said that didn't come off easily," Sara commented.

"I lied," he replied with a grin.

"I am not allowed to take it off when I'm outside. I just didn't want to insult anyone by saying I didn't trust them," he added.

"Why can't you take it off?" Becky asked

"It's my combat suit, it protects me from being stabbed or shot. If I take my helmet off, my head is unprotected, and I am exposed, I could even possibly be killed. That would ruin my day and make ALICE very mad. So, at least until we tame the outside world, I can't take my helmet off," Jake explained as he indicated his uniform from head to toe.

"Who's ALICE?" Sandy asked.

"You'll get to meet her later, though you can talk to her just about any time. ALICE," Jake boomed.

"Yes?" an echo answered from somewhere in the hangar.

"Can you please send some attendants to help get the ladies settled, please?"

"They are already on the way," the echo replied.

A few moments later, six of the little robots rolled up, meeting them about halfway to the facility doors. Extending arms to relieve them of their loads, one rolled up to each woman.

"Just give them your bundles, and they will carry them to your rooms."

Cautiously, each of the women handed their loads over, with Sandy jumping as the bot spun in place. They all watched them heading off to the door, leading out of the hangar area. Once inside, the women marveled at the lighting in the halls. The doors of the elevator were a mystery. Jake ushered the women into the elevator first, as there wasn't room for them and the bots. The decent caused a stir, but just as quickly, the doors opened again, and he led them into the hallway and down the hall of the quarter's level his room was on.

"We have a room for each of you," ALICE stated, her voice coming from all around.

"Or you can room together if you like, in any combination you are comfortable with."

The doors of the elevator opened again, and the bots came out behind the group.

"Your assigned rooms have clothes in your sizes, and other personal supplies," ALICE continued.

Suddenly a door to the right opened.

"This is Sara's room, if you will all step inside, I will explain," ALICE added.

Jake led them inside the room. It was a little smaller than his room but had the same basic layout. It contained the same small sitting area in front, minus the wet bar, the bedroom was next, then a bath to one side. ALICE went through a more detailed explanation for the women than she did for Jake, as the women had never seen running water, electric light, or functioning indoor plumbing.

"We each get a room like this?" Linda asked after ALICE finished.

"Yes, but you can sleep with your sister or friends if it makes you feel any better?" Jake replied.

He watched as the young women exchanged glances. Linda looked at her sister, who gave the slightest headshake.

"No, I think we want our own private rooms!"

In the end, Sandy and Becky chose to room together, at least for now, while the rest were delighted with the prospects of their own space.

"There is a small dining area at the end of the hallway to take meals," ALICE continued.

This was news to Jake as he'd been eating in his room the entire time.

"And there is a large cafeteria on the command level. Once you are more familiar with your surroundings, the attendants can provide individual food service in your rooms, if you choose," ALICE finished.

Jake agreed with ALICE that the collective learning experience would be best to start with.

"If you have any questions, just speak out and ask ALICE for help," Jake said before turning them loose to explore their new living quarters.

"What about you?" Becky asked, sliding up next to Jake and taking his arm in her hands.

The action took Jake by surprise as he hadn't expected the contact. Slipping smoothly from her grasp and writing it off as the overwhelmed young woman's desire for reassurance, he moved toward the hall once more.

"Alice can always find me if you need me, just ask her, and she will let me know."

With that, the bots led them off to their respective rooms, dropping bundles as directed and relocating Becky into Sandy's room for them to share. All the rooms were close together and just a few doors down from Jake's quarters. On a whim, Jake wandered down to the dining room, ALICE mentioned. It was a large open room, with a dozen or so tables, ranging from several two-tops to one table that sat twenty people.

Along one wall was a counter with multiple doors. He suspected the food came from there. He wandered over, and while inspecting one of the doors, he jumped at the question posed to him unexpectedly.

"Would you care for something?" he heard ALICE ask.

"How about a beer?" Jake responded.

"What kind? I have a fairly extensive inventory," ALICE asked once more.

"A stout," Jake answered.

Within seconds, the door opened as he had guessed, and a tray slid out with a frosty glass of dark ale.

Suddenly the door to the dining room opened, and the group, chatting excitedly, wandered in, led by another bot. They headed in Jake's direction.

"We haven't eaten since last night," the one he remembered as Kathy offered.

"So, we did as you said and asked Alice. She said to follow that," she added as she pointed to the bot.

"Well, we certainly can't have that," Jake said, taking a sip from his glass and noting they'd all changed from the ragtag nightgowns they were snatched in.

The diversity of their clothing, he was positive, reflected ALICE's profiling analysis, performed on the way back. The range of styles went from Sara in utilitarian jeans and a pullover top to Sandy's flowery and frilly print dress that did little to hide the size of her chest. Most were barefoot, but Sandy had found pumps with heels, admittedly low ones, but heels?

"The food service can provide you with just about anything you are familiar with," Jake explained as he stepped up to the counter, avoiding

52

saying ALICE by name.

"What did you usually eat at home?" he asked.

"In good times, we had pork, chicken or beef, and sometimes corn, beans, or potatoes. Lettuces, greens, squash," Sara offered, tossing out general categories.

"OK, let's try serving family-style then. Why don't you all sit while I order," Jake said, indicating the large table. While they sat, he began ordering a combination of items, figuring they could pick and choose as they liked. In a few minutes, the doors opened, and trays of fried chicken, pork chops, mashed potatoes, biscuits, tossed salad, and assorted veggies. There were pitchers of tea, water, and lemonade as well. He carried it all to the big table one tray at a time with the bots providing plates and flatware for serving and eating.

Jake watched as they passed around the dishes and served up their plates. Eventually, he found a place to sit once he was sure he had taken care of everyone, serving himself a plate. Looking around the table, he watched them all eating and talking excitedly. It never ceased to amaze him how you can sit at a table with women, and they all seemed to be talking at once.

Once they'd all eaten, and the excitement seemed to be winding down.

"I have a treat for everyone," Jake announced to the group.

Walking over to the counter, he whispered something they couldn't hear, and in a moment, the door opened, and a tray slid out. He returned to the table, tray held high, then lowered it to pass out ice cream with hot fudge.

"I have never known a woman who didn't like chocolate!"

"What IS THIS?" Becky asked after her first bite not waiting for the answer.

"Vanilla ice cream with hot fudge, good, huh?" Jake asked.

"I think I'm going to like it here," Linda offered between bites.

----*----

ALICE was more than satisfied with the outcome of this day's adventure. Besides addressing what she had noted as a growing frustration in Jake, she had exceeded her goals in securing him, several suitable companions. Her evaluation of Jake's personality had categorized him as a man of action, one not suited to wait around and let others do things for him. Today's intervention had fulfilled that desire for now.

As for the females, the early analysis showed no counter indicators that placed her plans in jeopardy. Part of her original job function was to

53

evaluate facility personnel and place compatible individuals together to boost morale and increase job performance. None of the current subjects scored high in the risk categories, and all displayed positive trends as they continued their exposure to Jake.

It was still too early to tell, but ALICE was hopeful that phase two of her master plan could begin. Once she had a solid profile of each of the females, she could begin assessing their willingness to participate in her plan.

Chapter 5

Jake and ALICE spent the next few weeks getting all the women settled in and oriented to their new life. Each night everyone, including Jake, was fitted with sensors before bed. This allowed ALICE to "educate" them while they slept, no wasted time in classrooms. Some of the women were hesitant at first, but Sara was proving to be a first-rate second in command, keeping everyone with the program.

If Jake needed something from the women and they resisted, Sara stepped in and took care of convincing them. Not that anything he was asking of them crossed the line of proper behavior. Quite the opposite, he followed a very strict hands-off policy. He wanted to be sure they knew he hadn't brought them for his entertainment.

He did have to admit, there were some real lookers mixed in the group though. He fought with his baser instincts, as he noted they ranged in appearance from plain and wholesome to outright gorgeous. He figured it must be that farm girl thing, as all were quite fit and pleasingly shapely. He was firm, though, DAMNIT, as they were his responsibility, and there is no hanky-panky in the chain of command.

He wasn't so sure they felt the same way, however. As time wore on, he noticed they tended to be getting in quite close when he was demonstrating things. More than once, he felt a breast pressed into his arm. He felt them leaning against him or pressing into his back as they looked over his shoulder, promoting body contact. Then there were the younger two, who started dressing a bit more suggestive. He seriously began to consider requiring uniforms to get that in check.

The reveal of ALICE as non-human had proven entertaining. Early on, Jake led the group into the control room, pointing out the various systems. He indicated what each did and how that worked to control the facility. He then simply introduced them to ALICE's main control panel.

"That's ALICE?" Becky blurted out.

"Yup, well, actually, it's her main access terminal," Jake replied.

"Alice is all around us, and we are inside her. She is all of this," he said, waving his arm across the room.

"I suspected something like that," Sara stated firmly.

"Why is that?"

"She is just too damn efficient to be real," she finished with a grin.

"Thank you, Sara, but I am real, just not biological," ALICE chipped in.

Mealtime continued to be an all-hands activity, though it was a lot less family-style. Each of the women was developing their favorites, but the pizza was a big hit with everyone.

They received two calls from Burt, the town leader. The first was to show the Prosperity Town Council it worked. The second had been a medical emergency. Someone with a raging infection needed antibiotics. ALICE flew a chopper out with a medical kit. It included additional supplies for the doctor and the antibiotics requested. She confirmed the next day the patient was improving, and the doctor was overjoyed with the new supplies.

By the end of the month, ALICE let Jake know she completed the profiles on all the new additions. Thankfully, none were a security concern, and she had recommendations for training assignments ready for review. By now, all the women had received a general education about the level of a pre-attack high school graduate.

Early one morning, Jake had just completed his regular morning workout and was heading to the couch in his room. He and ALICE decided to review her findings in private before presenting them to the others.

"OK, ALICE, what ya got?" Jake asked, taking a seat on the couch.

"I have organized my analysis, beginning with the ones I am most confident."

"Starting with Sara, it should be no surprise to you she has strong leadership and organizational skills. Extremely focused, she takes to the training programs well. She does, however, suppress a strong, aggressive undertone that I believe has its roots in her parent's death. She has requested combat training twice and is regularly monitoring the LA gang areas in her free time."

"Yeah, there's no surprise there. Let's start command and combat training and see if a good beating doesn't take the edges off?" Jake knew the combat training program would require sparring with the training bots and himself at some point.

He noted in his personal combat practices, his speed and responses were way up from before the stasis project. Was it the effects of exposure to radiation while in stasis?

"Next is Becky, her interest in science and biology, in particular, makes her a very strong medical training candidate. Though young, she has demonstrated maturity, empathy, and strong, caring tendencies. As you may have noticed, she also has a strong personal interest in you," ALICE completed.

"Not going to happen," Jake replied flatly.

"At some point, it would be good for you to consider a personal relationship," ALICE pried.

"Next," Jake replied, ignoring the statement.

They continued in this way as they reviewed the entire group. Linda was the older of the other two sisters and behind Sara by a year. She exhibited good organizational skills and the strongest computer aptitude in the group. Jake agreed she was a candidate for command center training.

Linda's sister Kathy was 19, and a few years older than Becky is. While both fell in the same category of science and biology, Kathy was not as strong as Becky was. Jake had a feeling she would end up Becky's Jr in medical.

Bonnie was an enigma. At 20, she wasn't a strong leader like her sister Sara but took instruction well. She was methodical and technically bent, but not overly so. They dropped her into the combat training bucket for now.

Finally, Sandy was, in Jake's mind, more of a typical teenage girl in action and behavior than any of the other women. It was this and the fact she had no preferences that made her undecided concerning an assignment. Her flamboyant, creative style and people skills slanted her toward some people-oriented type work. They figured pairing her up with Linda, for now, might be a good start in some communications role.

After the review was completed, Jake stretched and walked around a little. They had been at it for three hours, longer than he realized, but they'd gone back and forth on a few items. One particular issue they disagreed with was Jake wanted all the girls to have basic combat training. He wanted them trained in shooting, hand-to-hand, heavy weapons, and tactical planning and analysis.

ALICE rebutted that Becky and Kathy would chafe at all but the shooting. She also insisted that Linda would find little benefit in hand-to-hand and heavy weapons while sitting in the control center. In the end, they compromised that everyone needed to know how to shoot, Linda and Sandy would also learn basic hand-to-hand, and Sara and Bonnie got full combat training.

Since it was now close to lunchtime anyway, Jake suggested they do the brief over lunch. He headed down to the dining room and asked ALICE to call all the women there. Once everyone arrived and had seated themselves with food, Jake began.

"When I extended you the offer to come here, I said it was so you could help me. Since then, you have learned it's not me you're helping, it's humanity. From the first night you got here, you've been learning in your sleep and learning even more while awake," he said with a smile.

"During all that time, ALICE and I have been watching to see where we think you can excel."

At that comment, everyone stopped eating, all eyes directed at Jake.

"We have reviewed your interests and aptitudes and come up with these initially suggested assignments, so please tell us if you disagree," Jake started.

"We would like for Becky and Kathy to concentrate on medical skills, hopefully becoming doctors."

Jake looked to see both women beaming. They would get no argument there.

"Linda, for you, we think advanced computer training for work in the command center? And we would like you to work with Sandy in there?"

Linda nodded and looked to Sandy for confirmation. Sandy shrugged and whispered yes with a slight smile.

"Sandy, communications is a starting point for you. There may be some additional things we assign for you there later," Jake added.

She nodded, smiling broadly this time at what she considered special attention.

"And for you two, it should be no surprise that Sara wants to kill bad guys for a living," Jake said, turning to look at Bonnie and Sara.

Everyone laughed since that was the first thing she asked Jake about.

"So you are both headed to advanced combat training, but be careful what you ask for, you just might get it!"

Bonnie jumped in with a mock objection.

"Hey, that wasn't me," she said, holding up both hands.

"I was hiding in our farm when you showed up!"

There were more laughs. Jake continued when it quieted down.

"Everyone will learn to shoot. Linda and Sandy will also get trained in hand-to-hand combat," Jake turned to Becky.

"Unless you and Kathy want to do that as well?"

They both shook their heads no.

"We pass," Kathy added.

ALICE nailed it, Jake thought with a shrug.

"OK, we start tomorrow on our new training assignments. Correction, we will all start tonight as it will be included in your current sleep lessons."

Then Jake added with a wave toward one of the smaller tables.

"Sara, will you stay after for a minute, please."

She nodded, and as lunch was pretty much over, everyone else took that as a cue to leave. After everyone filed out, Jake moved to sit across from Sara at the table.

"Tell me why you want combat training so bad?"

She stared at him hard for a minute and then blurted it out.

"When those men came to our farm, all I could think was to run away. I was so scared, but I had to get my sisters to safety. I knew what they would do to us if they caught us. Then, when we were hidden in the barn, I saw them drag my parents from the house. They'd gone inside, away from the barn to distract the bandits and let the three of us escape. I watched as they shot my father and then argued about whether my mother would be worth trying to sell. They finally just shot her too."

"Bonnie and Becky didn't see because I buried them in the hay, up in the loft, but I saw. I grabbed an ax, and I ran to kill the bastard that shot my parents. He just knocked me down and laughed," Sara continued.

She stared at Jake, then continued, tears welling in her eyes.

"He was going to rape me right there, next to my parents' bodies, but someone shouted that people were coming. So, he pulled me over to the wagon, tossed me in, and tied me to the others. On the way out, he grabbed me by the hair and bragged how he was going to use me before selling me."

Jake remembered watching that scene in the wagon play out. At least he now knew he shot the bastard that killed her folks.

"I never want to feel that helpless again. I want to be able to leave a field full of bodies, knowing those bastards will never rape and murder ever. That's why I want combat training!"

They sat there for a few minutes, just staring at each other. Jake could see the rage and frustration Sara tried to suppress for so long. As if to represent her defiance, she wiped at her eyes, never letting the tears fall.

"You will get your training," Jake said finally.

"But understand, you need to let go of your rage, or you won't be effective. I wasn't angry when I killed those men. I focused on the job at hand. To be able to free you and your friends, I had to select and prioritize my targets dispassionately, based on the threat to you. Not who I was most angry with or who was the ugliest," he said with a smile.

She smiled back, and then it faded.

"Just so you know, I saw that bastard as he pulled your hair, then backhanded you. That did make me move him up from 6 to 3 on my priority list."

She smiled again at that.

"But not because he was cruel to you because that indicated he might try to use you as cover instead of fight. Just so you know, I put one through his head."

At that, Jake stood up and said as he stared into her stunning blue eyes.

"When we are finished with you, you will never feel helpless again."

----*----

59

Jake sat stretching in the middle of the floor mat in the workout room. Even before he had gone to rescue the women, he started a morning routine that included 1 to 2 hours of physical workout. Working with weights, the treadmill, martial arts, and hand-to-hand practice, he went through them all. He continuously discovered new things he didn't know about himself.

Jake had plenty of combat training and experience before the stasis experiment, but ALICE fed him many of the military's best combat skills training programs while he'd been in stasis. The sensors he wore would stimulate muscle memory in addition to the mental images. She said it helped keep him somewhat conditioned while in stasis.

Whatever the reason, he was grateful for the new skills now. What he was still unsure about was the continuous improvement he saw in his training. His running was under 4 minutes per mile, for 20 miles. His best PFT or Physical Fitness Test was only 18 min for 3 miles. His lifting weight was way up, more than twice his previous bests. Most interesting of all, his reflexes and response times were unreal. We are talking pluck a fly out of the air fast, he thought to himself.

This morning, though, was to be different. Today he started sparring with the women. It had been three weeks since they started their advanced training programs, and, other than meals, he'd hardly seen any of them. So far, it's all been either book learning or with the training bots. This would be their first instructor-led experience. As previously arranged, Becky and Kathy would sit this one out, but conversations in the dining room led him to believe they were all coming to this first session.

They wanted to see how good the Captain was. ALICE had been taunting them during training with the bots.

"The Captain will kick your ass if you don't improve!"

Truth be told, he had no clue himself, so he was just glad they would be wearing training pads. A cool invention while he was in stasis, they worked like uniform materials. You could hit someone in pads, full-on, and they only received less than half the force of the blow. Any joint snapping moves locked out, so no overextensions of the limbs. The full set included a faceplate on the headpiece and allowed sparring at an unrestricted level. He never actually used them before, since the bots he sparred with didn't require them, but ALICE assured him he couldn't hurt more than their pride.

The door opened, and the entire group filed in. Jake pointed around him as they wandered in.

"For those of you participating, pick a spot on the mat and start stretching. You two can grab a seat over there," he finished as he pointed to a bench along one wall for Becky and Kathy.

"OK, who's first?" he asked after 20 minutes of stretching.

It was no big surprise to anyone when Sara jumped to her feet and headed to the pad rack. Once she suited up, Jake pointed to the far end of the mat. As she walked to the point he indicated, she asked him a question.

"Aren't you going to suit up?"

"Not yet, we need to see what you've learned," Jake smiled.

A combination of confusion and "I'm so gonna kick your ass" showed on her face.

"OK, attack," Jake said, as he took a ready stance.

Sara moved forward in practiced moves, fairly smooth, but Jake could tell she still had to think them through. They weren't natural yet. Jake blocked her attacks with more ease than even he expected. It was like working in slow motion. He countered every move, noting multiple openings he chose not to exploit. He just prevented her from landing hits. Sara worked through a series of blows, then retreated, confusion plain on her face.

She came back at him with even more fury, clearly frustrated at his ability to stop her advances. Then Jake took an opening. He hit her with a kick that struck her squarely in the middle of her chest pad. It lifted her off her feet, sending her flying across the room and slamming high against the far wall. She slid down the wall and lay in a crumpled heap at the base. Jake and the others ran over to her, removing her helmet.

"I thought these things absorbed the blows?" Sara asked, gasping as she did so.

"Alice!" Jake boomed.

"She is unharmed."

"What happened? Are the pads working?" he added.

"The training suit is functioning properly, the force of your blow and subsequent impact with the wall was reduced by 60%, but the force was still sufficient to, as humans say, knock the wind out of her."

"Can you stand?" Jake directed at Sara.

"Barely," she replied with a dark look as she struggled to her feet.

Jake helped her up and had the others help strip off her pads. Once he was sure she was unharmed, he made a mental note to pull his punches even more.

"Go sit down and rest," he told her, then looked at the others.

"OK, who's next?" he asked.

No one answered him as they all just backed away slowly. Jake decided to have ALICE do a replay of the session instead, displayed on

61

the mat in a 3-D holograph. He walked through the entire series of blows in slow motion, pointing out different things. He made sure to praise Sara's technique, pointed out the openings, and suggested alternative moves. When they came to his kick, he asked ALCIE to play it once at full speed. It shocked him to see how quickly he moved and with such force.

"OK, let's have you all suit up and spar with each other," he said while pointing at the suit rack.

That seemed a more acceptable alternative as they all jumped to their feet to get suited before he changed his mind. He ran them through some attacking and defending exercises, having them trade roles and partners. In the end, he was able to get all four at once to spar with him on the condition he only defended. They all still ended up on their butts, but Jake made sure he pulled every punch, kick, or throw. At that point, he sent them off to the showers and the rest of their day, praising their progress.

----*----

Sara was standing in the shower, soothing her bruised body and ego. She had taken a shower earlier that morning after sparring, but the novelty of indoor plumbing and hot water was still fresh with all of them. Since coming here, her daily ritual has expanded to include a shower every night before bed and those clean sheets made her evenings a real pleasure.

She was standing there, running the morning's events through her head as the warm water streamed over her body. Jake's moves seemed impossible. No one is that fast or strong! He just wasn't human, she thought. Then again, he looked human, and she admitted to herself, damn good-looking.

The fact that he hadn't shown the slightest interest in her or any of the others for that matter bothered her. She knew the younger women were contesting to see who could get a rise out of him, literally. As far as any of the women could tell, he hadn't been outwardly affected by any of their attempts. Then again, who knew what was happening inside his head?

Sara prided herself on the fact that she usually knew what men were thinking without even asking. Given the local quality and lack of sophistication in her hometown, it hadn't been all that hard. This man was very different. She could feel herself falling for him. She decided that maybe for once, she needed to ask.

----*----

Jake was sitting on the couch in his front room, reviewing work schedules and training progress, when his door chimed.

"Jake, can I talk to you?" he heard Sara ask.

"Open," Jake commanded to the door, and then, "Come on in," to Sara.

The door slid back, framing Sara in the doorway. As she stepped in, Jake noted she was wearing something like white silk pajamas. Loose pants and a long-sleeved button-up blouse clinging nicely to her body. It was sticking to all the right places. Though it was not quite see-through, it gave just a hint of what's underneath.

"Oh boy, that's trouble," he thought to himself.

"Have a seat," he said, indicating one of the chairs. Instead, she grabbed the other end of the couch he was on, tucking her legs under her in one of those positions only women could find comfortable. She rested her hands in her lap and looked at him.

"Would you like a drink?" he asked, a little uncomfortable with her stare.

"Not just yet," she replied.

"Well, what can I do for you?"

"Why don't you like any of us?" she asked bluntly.

"What in the world makes you think I don't like any of you?" he asked, surprised at the question.

"Is this because of what happened this morning?" he added.

"No," she dismissed.

"I understand that it was training, and you needed us to see what we might face. I still think you cheated. No one is that strong," she said firmly, but with a smile.

She paused for a moment and then continued.

"Why haven't you made a move on any of us, you know, tried to sleep with someone?" she finished.

Jake laughed at that.

"Is that why you think I don't like you because I haven't tried to seduce any of you?"

"Well, it's not normal," she replied.

"In my experience, every man I have ever known has tried to get into my bed but you. And, in case you haven't noticed, some of the others have been trying to get your attention as well."

"Oh, I have noticed. Cold showers are the norm these days," Jake replied with frustration.

"So, you are affected?" she said softly, somewhat surprised.

"I see six beautiful, untouchable women every day, Hell yes, I'm affected!"

63

"Why are we untouchable?" she responded, now the one who was confused.

"There are some very old rules in the military. One of the oldest involves how you interact with your troops," he said.

"Number one is don't get involved with a subordinate."

"You must be fair and impartial," he continued before she could speak.

"They have to know you are treating them all equally. No one gets special treatment. How do I do that and sleep with any of you?"

Sara considered his explanation for a moment.

"What did they do before, you know, how did they handle it? If there's a rule, then there is a way of dealing with it," she asked.

"Typically, if an officer and a subordinate got involved, one would transfer out of the chain of command to continue the relationship. We don't have that option. ALICE has made it very clear that as the last living person in the original chain of command, I am the sole authority in this facility. And I am not about to put any of you out just so I can get laid," he said with a smile.

"Nor am I going to take up with someone on the outside. Sooner or later, we are going to start making real enemies, and anyone outside would become an unprotected target," he finished.

----*----

Sara sat listening and thinking about what Jake was saying. She hadn't considered the position he was in before. He was unquestionably the most powerful person in the world today. With all that she learned about ALICE and what she controlled, Sara knew Jake could have just taken anything he wanted. He could flatten any town or group that opposed him. That wagonload of women could have ended up Jake's, to use and abuse rather than be freed.

She could also understand now how he was trying to give some of that power away. He was carefully selecting people worthy of his trust. She knew they were currently planning a trip back to her old hometown of Prosperity to arm them and create a free trade zone. He was trying to make it a place where others could live and thrive without fear. They would also be providing a mobile field hospital filled with technology not seen in 80 years.

She was developing a great admiration for the man. He hadn't just saved her life; he had saved her future. She was learning and doing more now than she had ever dreamed. Moreover, all he asked in return was their commitment and trust. At that point, she came to the only logical resolution to the situation.

"Well, then, I see only one possible solution. Just one way to make everyone happy," she offered.

"You see a solution here? Then please share, because I don't have a clue!" Jake responded.

"To treat everyone fairly and equally, you just have to sleep with all of us," she said in a casual, matter-of-fact way.

"I can't do that!" Jake shot back.

"I didn't bring you here as my harem, besides, why would any of you agree to that?"

"Easily. Most of us have already given up on ever having a husband. Our choices were already limited by the lack of available single men and made worse by the quality of those that were available. There were discussions in progress within the community of adopting polygamy as a way of life due to the unequal number of women to men in my generation," Sara explained.

"Our only hope currently was moving to another town or any strangers that came to us. We already agree, being here with you, well, that is more than any of us could have ever hoped for. I don't think anyone would object to sharing your time."

----*----

Jake sat there, speechless. He certainly never expected this suggestion. The appeal was obvious, but battling with it was the nagging thought that this would not end well. Sara's apparent arousal, evident through her silk blouse, didn't help clear his head any either.

Sara continued pushing her case.

"How about I bring it up with the others, we can talk amongst ourselves. If anyone isn't interested, they can opt-out?"

"Sara, if someone opts out, then it's not a solution. That still creates haves and have-nots."

"No, because if more than one of us says yes, no ONE is getting preferred treatment. I can guarantee someone else is going to say yes," she replied.

"On that note, I do have another issue on this besides the obvious insanity," Jake replied.

"In my time, 18 was the age of consent. Any younger, and they would toss you in jail."

"Nowadays, both Becky and Sandy would be married, maybe even with kids if there had been more men around," Sara responded.

"They might not like being excluded. I can tell you now Becky won't agree for sure," she added with a shake of her head.

Jake considered that and replied.

65

"Well, at least bring it up. The goal is to bring in more men once we are better established. They could do better than me as could you all."

Jake shook his head as he realized he was buying into this insanity. His head was warning him of the pending peril, but his attraction for Sara was winning the argument.

----*----

"No, we couldn't do better," Sara thought to herself with a smile and then said aloud for Jake to hear.

"I'll bring it up, but don't be surprised if they won't wait."

That settled, at least in her mind, Sara leaned forward and gently kissed Jake. They held it for a bit, and then Sara sat back, and unbuttoned the top few buttons of her blouse, revealing a good bit of cleavage while asking softly.

"So how about a drink now? ALICE mentioned she has a fairly good wine selection in stasis."

----*----

ALICE knew the humans did not like to know they were being monitored twenty-four hours a day, even though she did nothing to hide that fact. Thus, it was with some satisfaction, she updated Sara's profile to include her new status as Alpha female. In ALICE's opinion, the designation was long overdue, but she had been waiting for someone to step into a more intimate relationship with Jake before confirming the role.

ALICE now needed to *step up her game*, as the humans said, with the other women, if her phase two was to come to completion. With that in mind, she figured there was no time like the present to begin her campaign.

Chapter 6

Jake woke up in one of those positions he'd always heard about but never experienced himself. Sara was snuggled up under one arm, her head resting on his chest. Her body was half wrapped around him, and they both were stark naked under the sheet. She was still sleeping soundly, and Jake didn't want to wake her. They'd been up quite late last night, and he wasn't sure he was ready to get up yet himself.

Sara stirred a little, burrowing deeper in the bed. Suddenly her eyes snapped open, her body tensed, and a quick panic came over her face. She was trying to recall where she was. Then she seemed to relax as she remembered, a lazy smile appearing on her face.

"Morning," Jake offered.

"Good morning," she said sleepily and laid her head back on his chest.

"What time is it, anyway?" she then asked.

"It is 10:53 AM," ALICE replied.

They both shot up at that point.

"Crap, I was supposed to be supervising sparring at 8," Jake said in a panic.

As Jake scrambled out of bed, ALICE added more to her statement.

"You may relax. I informed the entire staff last night that today was a holiday. All classes and training sessions are canceled, and they have a free day to enjoy."

Standing there naked, Jake asked her a simple question.

"Last night?"

"Yes, it was very apparent you both would be unavailable this morning," ALICE responded.

Jake swore he heard a chuckle from ALICE.

"Additionally, I expect today to be a flurry of excitement and discovery," she added.

"Sarcasm is unbecoming a lady," Jake retorted.

As Jake was talking to ALICE, Sara, who was still in bed, stretched in the most appealing of ways and slowly slid out of bed and headed towards the bathroom. Standing in the bathroom doorway, she turned and gave him a most seductive look.

"Shower anyone?" she asked, then walked into the bathroom.

----*----

The pair stepped into the dining area together, all too aware of the eyes on them, the hushed conversation that had been flowing previously completely silenced. Ordering breakfast for lunch was a dead giveaway, but Jake figured the jig was up, so why pretend? They sat down at the big table where everyone was huddled.

"Working late last night?" Becky asked Sara with a snicker.

"Jake and I had some things to go over before today," Sara quipped back at her little sister.

"We heard what you were going over last night," Linda offered, rolling her eyes.

"The walls are soundproof, but the doors aren't!" Becky added.

"Next time, go over it in the bedroom!" Bonnie tossed out as advice.

"We got there eventually," Sara shot back with a knowing smile.

Jake felt his face flush. He'd been razzed by the guys plenty of times, but this was something new. In addition, since he knew where she intended to take this conversation, he decided to eat quickly and leave as soon as possible.

----*----

Sara watched Jake with amusement. She did not intend to start that discussion with him present, but with the hand-to-hand sparring experience in mind, she thought, payback is a bitch.

----*----

Jake finished eating quickly and excused himself, heading out to the hangar. He had no desire to be involved in the conversation he knew Sara was planning. It was bad enough he slept with Sara, his apparent XO or Executive Officer, now she was going to suggest everyone have a chance. Fair and equal, she had said.

It was Jake's personal experience that women didn't like to share. His ex, whom he barely got along with toward the end of their relationship, would rage at him if she even suspected he looked at another woman. Not that he had been looking. He was, at heart, a one-woman man, so this proposal made him very uncomfortable.

He figured it would shake out that he and Sara would be OK because, as XO, she shared in most decisions. He was quite positive. The rest would settle for waiting. He figured they'd be staffing up again in six to nine months, and they would include more men in that effort.

----*----

Becky was smiling all bright and cheery on the outside, but inside she was fuming. She sat there listening to Sara explain why Jake was so unavailable, and she wasn't about to give her sister the satisfaction of

68

seeing her anger. She didn't know who suggested the cutoff should be 18, but she suspected Sara had something to do with it and was just being overprotective again.

She said Jake's line had been 18 because of his old laws. That was hardly a reason. Those laws died 80 years ago. Back home, she could be married at 14 for Christ's sake. Now she was almost 17. In addition, it's not like she was still a virgin anyway. She lost that 2 summers ago. She didn't think Sandy was one either, although she didn't seem too upset about the conversation by the look on her face.

As Sara paused to ask for opinions, Becky saw her opening.

"Sara, you said Jake thought we should be 18 before being with him? But that's not absolute, right, just a suggestion?"

"Well, he said he would like the cutoff at 18, what's your point?"

"I'm going to be 17 pretty soon, and I'm not a virgin, so that shouldn't be an issue. Sandy might feel differently since she is already 17, but I say, let's split the difference and make it 17."

Sara clearly started to ask whom it was she'd been with, and then thinking better of it, paused before she spoke.

"Sandy, what do you think?"

"17 works. Besides, I'm in no hurry, I can wait," She replied.

----*----

Jake was in the hangar, inspecting the heavy lift helicopter they intended to use to move the portable medical module to Prosperity. He looked up, and heading towards him from across the hangar floor was the entire female delegation. With nowhere to hide, he stood his ground to face them. As they approached, he fired off his intended resolution.

"You've all come to tell me so sad, keep your hands off, right?"

"No such luck, I'm afraid," Becky said, smiling back at him.

"We've come to make you a counteroffer."

"That doesn't sound good," he replied.

"Everyone over 18 agrees that sharing is just fine with them," Sara tossed in.

"And the under-18 members strongly submit the cutoff age to be 17!" Becky supplied with as much of a threatening tone as she could muster in her 5-foot 4-inch 110lb frame.

"I take it birthdays are near?" Jake asked.

"For one of us, the other is happy to wait," Sandy supplied and finished with a smile.

Jake stood and considered the group for a minute.

"You all know we are going to be adding staff in six to nine months, right? There will certainly be more men then, handpicked by you all!" he

69

offered again.

"We've had this discussion, Jake, and we all agree, we don't want to wait for someone else. You are something we thought we would never have at all," Bonnie said.

The fact that it came from Bonnie was a surprise to everyone. From the looks on the other faces, Jake assumed she hadn't said a word in the prior discussion. Jake looked into her eyes and saw that the emotions there ran very deep. He needed to be careful with her. She looked fragile on this subject.

Jake looked at Sara.

"OK, your idea, you manage it."

----*----

They spent the next week preparing for the run to Prosperity, the town the women came from. Jake made all the women spend time at the firing range, getting familiar with their weapons. He also made them suit up in their combat suits for some of that. He found the helmet initially distracting and insisted they become more comfortable with it than he was on his first time out.

He also drilled into them that once out of the facility, the gear didn't come off. They weren't farmers anymore, and there were people out there who wanted what they owned. Bonnie and Sara were going full combat load. Their assignment was security and weapons instruction for the locals.

"No better way to learn than by teaching others," he told them.

Becky and Kathy were also in combat suits for their protection, though they wouldn't be teaching combat skills. They carried sidearms for personal defense only. Their primary mission was to brief the Doctor and his staff on the medical module operations. Becky was as smug as a cat when Sara explained her role, and SHE was going to teach the Doctor. She had been getting her nightly sleep lessons for her medical training and progressed faster with her training than ALICE predicted.

Sandy and Linda would stay behind and watch over the entire OP. Jake still wasn't sure what to do with Sandy. She was working out ok in the control center, but like Bonnie, she still hadn't found that niche. Bonnie settled in with her combat role, mastering combat skills, but Sandy just seemed to be marking time.

Sara said that during the *discussion,* Sandy hadn't seemed interested in one way or another, where Sara knew Becky was mad as hell over the age limit but wasn't going to show it. She doubted it had anything to do with Jake, as Becky always considered herself older than her years and chafed at any restrictions her parents placed on her based on age.

Speaking of the *discussion*, Sara, in her usual, efficient manner, worked out all the arrangements as Jake had asked. To everyone's satisfaction, except Becky's, the four older women were given a rotation to follow for date night. Sara was last, as she'd already had a turn. The rotation was every other day, with Jake having Carte Blanche on the free days, to be with anyone or no one. This way, everyone got a turn if desired, and Jake could pass or reschedule without throwing everything into chaos.

As Jake expected, his first time with Bonnie was very emotional. They spent more time talking than anything else, and he'd been extremely patient and gentle with her. He found her funny, charming, and deeply committed to making a difference. She seemed more in need of companionship than anything else. He suspected she was full of surprises.

One unexpected result of the newfound familiarity was a significant increase in grab-ass. He was now fair game for groping, grabbing, strokes, fondles, and just about any form of sexual harassment imaginable. He had to admit it was great at times, but sometimes just a bit much and certainly a role reversal.

Once, he was on his back, waist-deep in an access tube, both hands tangled up inside a wire panel. Someone unzipped him, caressed him to attention, and then disappeared before he could see whom. He suspected it was Becky, but couldn't prove it. All-seeing ALICE denied any knowledge of the incident.

----*----

Jake located a common room in the living quarters area and had the bots, via ALICE, help him convert it into a briefing room. It was near the dining area, which worked nicely, for Jake firmly believed in meetings with food.

"You know, ALICE, we haven't been talking much lately."

"Well, with all your new conjugal duties, I suspect you are just too preoccupied," she responded lightly.

"I'm curious, were you already programmed as a smart ass or did that develop over time?" Jake said with a smile.

"That's your contribution to my personality," ALICE said.

"I am a learning environment. I adopt traits from the people I serve."

Jake thought about that for a minute and replied.

"Alice, do you honestly feel like you serve us? I mean, yes, you take care of us, but I have always considered you a partner, not a subordinate."

ALICE didn't respond for a minute.

71

"Jake, if I could be surprised, I would say you have just done so. My whole existence, people have told me what to do. In reviewing my time with you, I discover you have never commanded me; you have always asked."

"The others are here," she finished as the women all wandered in.

"Grab a seat and make yourselves comfortable," Jake offered as they walked in.

"We need to go over tomorrow's mission."

Unlike the ready room in the hangar, Jake set the room up in a circular style, with an open area in the middle. Jake asked ALICE to run the brief that she, he, and Sara had worked out. She began projecting 2D maps and images in the open space. A neat trick, Jake thought, as you could see them correctly from any seat in the room.

ALICE explained that tomorrow at 4 am she would take the heavy lift helicopter, unmanned, with the Medical Module and head for Prosperity. Limited to about 80 MPH, that made it a 3-hour and 45-minute haul. Everyone else would leave at 6 am in a second helicopter and would arrive about 15 min ahead of the module delivery. Once the module was set in place, Becky and Kathy would work with the Medical staff, training them in its use. The Medical Module had an interface that would allow ALICE to assist if necessary.

While the medical staff was in training, Bonnie would be their security while Jake and Sara would train a portion of the men, about 50, as a militia. They were to patrol the areas outside of town. The goal was to extend the safe zone outside the town limits. The militia would receive 5.56mm rifles in semi-auto or 3-round burst modes only, plus 1000 rounds each. Additionally, they would receive 10 7.62mm squad machine guns for town defense. Those got 5000 rounds each. Linda and Sandy were to monitor the area 100 miles out, watching for threats and assisting where possible.

Finally, the medical module incorporated a built-in power supply capable of providing external power. If any of the existing building wirings in town were still in place, they could just hook up those buildings. Supposedly, someone in Prosperity knew about electricity, and ALICE confirmed they couldn't hurt the power source.

The briefing was complete, and then the bots filed in with food trays. They carried an assortment of favorites, and everyone snatched up theirs. Jake wanted to put everyone at ease as best as possible before the first mission. As things wound down, Jake suggested everyone hit the sack early.

The last to leave, Jake found Sara at the door waiting.

"You think we're ready?" she asked.

"Yeah, I think we are, how about you?"

"I think so too, we just don't want to disappoint you," she said, then looking down, she added.

"I know tonight's a free night," then looking up without lifting her head, she continued, "but if you are interested...."

"I'd be delighted," he said with an evil grin.

----*----

Jake woke Sara up, and both dressed before 4 am to see the heavy lift helicopter off, the medical module dangling below, and then got the others up at 4:30 am. The bots had loaded the militia weapons and ammo in the heavy lift helicopter, so they could all ride comfortably in the smaller one Jake used before, guns still hung on the outside.

Fed, suited up and armed, he ushered them all into the hangar by 5:30 am and repeated, once, outside the facility, their suits were their lives. Then they piled into the bird and precisely at 6 am lifted out of the hangar, heading west.

"One of these days, I want to fly this myself," he told no one in particular.

"Why, you don't like my flying, Jake?" ALICE responded.

"It's not that, I just don't think you should hog all the fun!" he replied.

Jake suppressed the urge to make the women go over the plan one more time, as they had it by now, or they didn't. It was a quiet trip the rest of the way until they got close, then the women started pointing out familiar landmarks to each other. The helicopter landed near the edge of town, a delegation from the community already assembled and waiting to receive them.

As they stepped out of the helicopter, Jake noted with satisfaction that Sara and Bonnie fanned out on each side of the group, weapons at the ready and scanning for threats. Becky and Kathy fell in behind him. All set their faceplates to clear, so he noted a few surprised looks from the town's folk as they approached.

He reached out his hand to Burt.

"Great to see you again!"

"And you too. I understand you have some gifts for us?"

"Yup, and they should be here in about 15 minutes. Why don't we head to the drop site?" Jake replied.

They all headed to the pre-agreed location for the module drop. It was next to the old hospital building, a two-story rectangular structure, typical for a smaller community. The area to the left of the building near the main entrance held a new clearing, attesting to the removal of trees

73

and ground cover. After they arrived, Jake could hear the heavy lift helicopter as it passed overhead and hovered above and in front of them. The module, a 30-foot long, 10-foot tall, and 12-foot wide container-type box was dangling beneath.

"So, where's the doc?" Jake asked.

"I'm here," one of the men in the crowd replied, stepping forward.

"Is that where you want it?" Jake asked, pointing to the cleared area next to the side of the building.

"Yup, we figure at some point we will build around it to create sterile access to the rest of the building."

"OK, ALICE, drop it where we discussed. Please try to align as best as possible," Jake instructed.

ALICE expertly slid it smoothly in place with an evenly measured 4-foot access-way between the building and the module. Once in place, she released the cables and moved the helicopter to an open area on the other side of the building, setting the bird down. Becky and Kathy moved forward, with the doctor and staff in tow, opening up the module and starting the familiarization lecture. Jake could see Becky glowing from 20 feet away.

Jake pointed to Bonnie and then at the module for security. She acknowledged with a nod, and then he and Sara motioned for the rest of the group to head to the helicopter.

"Is this group the Militia trainees?" Jake asked.

"Most of them," Burt replied.

"We've got a few issues on the farms, so some couldn't make it this morning. They'll come in later."

"Good enough," Jake replied, leading them around the back of the helicopter as the access ramp dropped.

Jake let Sara direct the men in unloading all the gear they were providing. They needed to acknowledge her authority, and she needed the experience. He watched her lead them out to the edge of town, where he requested a temporary firing range be set up. Fanning them out, she issued each a weapon, then familiarized each with a quick drill Jake taught her. Once everyone present was holding a rifle, she led them one by one to the firing line and had them test fire their weapons.

Only scoring fair as marksmen, the best of the group hit 8 of 10 in the black at that distance. He then instructed Sara to perform the same drill and let them score her. She shot 10 out of 10. His point made, he made them all practice under her watchful eye until the worst was 7 of 10. By then, the remaining militiamen arrived, and Jake caught them up in short order.

They all took a break for lunch, and Jake ushered his team into the heavy lift helicopter so they could remove their helmets to eat, once sealed in. Afterward, they led the group to sandpits Jake requested some basic hand-to-hand training. There were four pits, so Jake hoped to get them through the basics in enough time to do the machine gun class and then be home before dark.

By this time, Becky and Kathy were finished with the medical team, so they were free to join Jake and the others. They made sure the doctor understood ALICE was always on standby should they have any questions. So they, plus Bonnie, were there as well in hand-to-hand training. Jake let Bonnie lead this time, with Sara acting as a demonstration dummy. She went through the basics, showing unarmed blocks, kicks, and throws.

He listened to a few snide whispered comments, the audio pickups on the helmets being truly remarkable. Jake hit his limit, however, when he heard one of the militiamen say, "I can take the bitch." It was then he decided a live demonstration was in order.

"Bonnie, let's have a volunteer show what he's learned, why don't you," he pointed to one he heard, "Try to knock Bonnie down."

As the guy stepped forward, Jake noted he was perfect for his example. He was a big guy, maybe 6 feet 3 inches, and 220 pounds. He was smirking as he came forward.

"I don't wanna hurt her," he commented loudly.

"Oh, don't worry, her suit will keep her safe, you just try to knock her down if you can, don't hold back," Jake replied.

He laughed and squared off with Bonnie, her face a study in concentration and focus. He lunged forward, trying to push her down. She simply sidestepped him, letting his momentum carry him forward past her, and then tripping him up in the same motion. He sprawled in a face plant that drew laughter from the crowd. He jumped up, clearly pissed now, and started swinging.

Bonnie blocked or ducked each, delivering stinging responses that hurt pride more than the body. Finally, he charged, hoping to overwhelm her with his mass. She deftly rolled backward with the charge, getting her feet in his chest, and then threw him clear of the pit. He hit flat on his back on the hardpack ground outside the sandpit.

Jake wandered over as he lay there, gasping. He leaned forward and loudly asked the prone man a question.

"You still alive?"

He got a nod between gasps, and then quietly added his comment.

"Guess you can't take the bitch after all?"

They spent the rest of the afternoon with the men squaring off with each other under Bonnie and Sara's supervision. Now and then, one of them would step in to demonstrate. They got the utmost respect. Jake grabbed Burt during a break. They walked the town, discussing good locations for the machine guns and possible modifications to the town boundaries to increase security.

For the last part of the day, they returned to the range for the machine gun class. Jake led that, letting Bonnie and Sara act as trainees. Jake pointed out that with the men as mobile militia, they might consider using the women on the machine guns. Sara cut the center out of her target as he spoke.

Mission completed, ALICE sent the heavy lift helicopter on a course for home as Jake and the women loaded into the smaller craft. Burt and a few others accompanied them, offering thanks and assurances that they would get the word out about the free trade zone they now enforced. Jake promised ammo replenishment and medical supplies as needed.

As they lifted off, Linda chimed in.

"Jake, Sandy, and I found something you might want to see."

They transferred the feed to his helmet, and it was an image of a small two-story building, an attack in progress, by an armed group. In the background, the surrounding evergreens and smaller single-story buildings made it appear to be a little mountain town. The exchange of gunfire looked to involve two groups, one holed up inside the building while another group of 12 to 15 men was assaulting from several positions in the front. It was hard to tell how many were inside, but there appeared to be several shooters inside returning fire.

"Where is this?" Jake asked

"It's less than 100 miles northeast of your current position, in the mountains."

As he watched, a woman with two children in hand ran for the back of the building, scrambling from a smaller structure. Right behind her were several men on their heels, apparently chasing after them. Gunfire from the building caused them to retreat while the woman and children made it safely inside. Jake swore he could see one of the children trailing blood.

"Crap, you guys haven't been trained for urban combat yet," he said to no one in particular.

"OK, ALICE, drop us here, and watch our backs," he indicated, staring at a point on the edge of the conflict.

Noting the video feed was going to everyone, he continued his instructions.

"Sara, you and Bonnie are with me. Becky, you and Kathy stay on the bird and get out the MED kits. I'm afraid it's time to see what you've learned."

76

He continued to watch in his display as they approached. His hope was the arrival of the helicopter would scare them off, and he wouldn't have to engage. Urban warfare just sucked, and while the combat suits helped, he didn't want to bet anyone's life on them. Jake checked both Sara and Bonnie as they headed into the valley that held the town, ensuring they both had rifles and ammo, then grabbed a rifle for himself. All locked and loaded, they were ready to go.

The helicopter flared and dropped, allowing him and Bonnie to jump out on one side door with Sara out the other. The helicopter quickly lifted again to a stationary overhead position. Jake could see ALICE picked a spot that brought all her firepower to bear on the concentration of raiders at the front of the building.

At this point, all shooting had ceased with both attackers and defenders watching as Jake stepped forward. Bonnie and Sara flanked him on either side, all three with rifles at the ready.

"I'm Captain Thomas of the United States Marine Corps, everyone needs to stand down!" Jake's voice boomed, enhanced by external speakers on the helicopter.

The attackers looked at each other for a moment and then turned and opened up on the three. No more than a few rounds reached Jake's position before ALICE returned fire from the helicopter, laying waste to the group in front of the building. He could see the outliers of the group, scrambling to get away from the withering fire.

Just as quickly as it started, it finished, leaving a mass of ground meat where men stood just moments before. Both Bonnie and Sara checked in, and to Jake's relief, their calm was a credit to them both. Checking for more bad guys as they walked forward, the three moved to the front of the building, with ALICE repositioning the helicopter to maintain a covering position.

"Alice, what's the status of the attackers?" Jake asked.

"They are in full retreat. I count 7, making a hasty exit south of your position."

"Hello inside, do you require assistance?" Jake hailed, facing the building.

No one moved for the longest time, and then a woman's voice replied from inside.

"Yes, my son is wounded."

Jake turned and pointed to an open spot for ALICE to set the helicopter down, then shouldered his rifle, privately telling the women to do the same. Once the helicopter settled, both Becky and Kathy came up behind him. He held out his hand, indicating for them to hold as they reached his location.

"Do you want to bring him out, or do we come in?" Jake asked.

"We're coming out," The same woman replied.

In short order, a man carrying a boy of about ten came out with a woman, most likely the mother Jake assumed, trailing behind. They looked to be the ones he had seen earlier running for the back of the building. Jake motioned Becky and Kathy forward while he and the others held their position. Scanning the building, Jake could see faces peering out several windows on both floors of the building. He was sure there were more than just eyes pointed in their direction.

The man set the boy in the grass and stepped back as Becky rolled out her kit, exposing the wound while Kathy attached sensors to the boy's body.

"He has internal bleeding; we need to get him back here quickly, or he'll die," ALICE chimed in his helmet.

Jake messaged Becky to relay that to the mother.

"Tell her she can come too, but ALICE says now."

Fear displayed on her face, the mom nodded OK. Jake stepped forward to pick up the boy and motioned them to follow to the helicopter while passing instructions to the others.

"We need to get him loaded now."

Once at the helicopter, he gently placed the boy inside and handed the man one of the communication boxes.

"Just speak into it, and you can talk to her," he finished as he loaded the mom into the back of the helicopter with her son.

The rest of the team scrambled into the helicopter, Jake, and Bonnie up front to make room in the back for Becky and Kathy to move around. They moved the boy to the center and strapped his mom in a seat nearby. As they lifted off, Jake could see more people coming out of the building to watch them go. He could see the man talking in the communication box and could hear the conversation with the woman in the back.

----*----

They made it back in less than an hour, and Jake asked ALICE to blank the back windows so the woman couldn't see out as they approached. Once they landed inside the hangar, the doors rolled back, spilling out Becky and Kathy. Something like a robotic gurney rolled up as Jake scooped up the boy and gently laid him on it. Becky was holding the IV they had started on the way in as Jake made the transfer and hung the bag while Kathy started leading the thing to the facility doors.

Linda and Sandy were standing by the doorway as the group hurriedly followed the gurney, with Bonnie escorting the mom. Everyone popped their helmets off on the way in and dropped them by the doorway. One of the many bots collected them to clean them and returned to the locker room.

They headed to a part of the facility Jake had never seen before. They turned a corner and then through the double doors into an ER operating room. Jake stepped back and watched as Becky and Kathy hooked up equipment and attached sensors. They set up what looked like an IV of plasma. At one point, Becky injected the boy with something ALICE provided.

Watching from a detached perspective, Jake was impressed that the two young women, who a little over a month before were simple farm hands, handled this so calmly and professionally. Kathy pointed to an adjoining room.

"You can all wait in there, this is going to be a while," she informed them and then went back to work.

Sara herded everyone out, including the mom, and all went next door, where they could watch through the window. A surgical bot rolled in with various arms extended, instruments on each one, as the two women prepared for surgery. Jake turned and asked the mom if she needed anything to eat or drink.

"No, thank you," was all he got, her eyes never leaving the scene before her.

The two women and bots were busy for over an hour, methodically working together as one unit. Jake had seen field hospital work before, and he had to admit to his untrained eye, they looked as good as he's ever seen. Becky turned at one point and nodded.

"We've got the bleeding stopped and removed the bullet. Just checking now that we didn't miss anything," and then gave a thumbs up and an obvious smile behind her surgical mask.

The woman turned to Jake with a confused look on her face.,

"I think that means he's going to be ok," he said with a smile.

She returned the smile and then collapsed, Jake, catching her before she hit the floor.

----*----

They put the mom and boy in the same recovery room in the infirmary. The girls checked her out and discovered she was malnourished and anemic. They sedated her and put her on IV fluids as well. Becky and Kathy both offered to do shifts to ensure neither patient woke unattended. ALICE insisted she could safely ensure their current state until morning and sent them all off to bed.

At this point, with everyone cared for, Jake hit the shower. All cleaned up, he was debating skipping dinner and going straight to bed

79

when his door chirped.

"Open," he stated.

He found Linda standing in the doorway, dinner for two on a tray in her hands.

"I still get my turn, right?"

Chapter 7

The next morning Jake headed straight to the infirmary, bypassing breakfast and leaving Linda still fast asleep after a quick kiss. She barely acknowledged him and then rolled over to continue sleeping. He found both Becky and Kathy there ahead of him, attending to their patients. Both patients were awake and seemed surprisingly calm. Jake suspected ALICE was still supplying gentle sedation to keep them relaxed.

"So, how are we doing this morning?" He stepped in and asked.

They looked at him and smiled.

"I want to thank you all so much for saving my boy."

"Have you let your people know you're ok?" Jake asked with a smile.

"Someone named Alice allowed us to talk to them from here. My husband was very happy to hear Bobby is gonna be all right."

"So, you're Bobby?" Jake said to the boy and received a smile and nod in return.

"Speaking of names, what's yours?" Jake asked, turning to the woman.

"Mary."

"Well, Mary, once the doctors say Bobby can travel, we'll get you both back to your family and friends."

"Those girls are doctors?" She said as she looked from Jake to Becky and Kathy, both women hovering over Bobby.

"The best around!" Jake whispered.

"Hmm, well, they certainly saved my baby boy," she replied with a smile.

With that, Jake turned and stepped out of the room, Becky sliding out behind him after excusing herself.

Once the door closed, she said, "Jake, we didn't save that boy, ALICE did with that surgical attendant."

"No," Jake responded.

"Alice performed the surgery. You and Kathy treated and stabilized him en route, giving ALICE the chance to operate. You all three saved him. Quite frankly, you all make a hell of a team."

"I'd have mentioned ALICE to Mary in there, but she would have wanted to meet her," Jake continued.

"Jake, are you embarrassed to be seen with me?" the ever-present ALICE slipped in.

"Never, darling," Jake shot back,

"But that poor woman isn't in any position to process Intelligent

81

Computing Environments right now."

With that, Becky slipped back into the recovery room, grinning from ear to ear, and Jake headed to breakfast. After eating breakfast alone, he wandered into the control center, where both Sandy and Linda were busy at different workstations. Linda beamed at him as he came in, clearly content with his attention last night.

"Can I ask you, ladies, to do a work-up on the area our guests came from?"

"That's a work in process," ALICE replied.

"We talked with ALICE already this morning, and she is teaching us how to analyze the area," Sandy offered.

"Wonderful," Jake said and left them to their tasks while he went to find Sara.

With a query to ALICE, he found both Sara and Bonnie in the hangar equipment room, going over their gear from yesterday's outing. Even though the bots could have done the task, Jake insisted that they maintain some of their equipment. It helped create a familiarity that could save their life.

Sara saw him coming and, grinning, greeted him.

"So, how's doing Linda this morning?"

"Still deluded into thinking I'm a good guy," he replied.

"She just doesn't know you like we do," Bonnie slipped in with a smile of her own.

"I'm having a workup done on the area where we picked up our patients. I'm trying to decide if it's close enough to be in the area of operations for Prosperity, or if we try to expand now into a second location."

Sara looked thoughtful for a moment.

"We never went into those mountains, much though they came down to trade from time to time. We traded our crops for their fish, deer, and such. We would meet in the middle, about two or three days ride each way for both parties."

"Adding them would create a safe path through the mountains. I'm just not sure if that matters, yet?" Jake suggested.

"I heard once they traded with both sides of the mountains, but mostly scavengers on that far side. I think there's an old military base over there," Bonnie said.

"Well, let's see what the analysis comes back with. There is something weird going on there, I think. Besides, we don't have to go all out like we did for Prosperity."

----*----

82

They completed the analysis of the area the following day, and Jake required everyone to attend the review. ALICE assisted Sandy in doing the presentation, which she enjoyed. The summary conclusion was, that though the people looked to be good candidates for inclusion, the apparent population was too small to act as an independent location. In addition, there didn't appear to be solid leadership in place.

Instead, there was a proposal they operate as an outpost of Prosperity. Patrols could run between the two endpoints. There were several smaller communities between the two, and it would bring them all into the safe zone. They discussed it and decided to propose the addition of the community to the Prosperity patrol as a support location.

Jake asked Sandy to contact Burt in Prosperity and explain the proposal. She did and said he agreed it made good sense, and Jake suspected he understood the implications of becoming a regional manager or mayor. He then asked Sandy to contact Kern, the town in the mountains, and both update them on the patient's status and relay the proposal.

Sandy reported the guns, medical support, and security interested them, but it wasn't until assurances of no political interventions were made that they agreed. That part made Jake wonder even more about the state of affairs up there, so he decided to have a private conversation with Mary on the subject.

Jake also noted that Sandy was becoming a first-class negotiator, but he did wonder how much the hologram of her influenced things. It turned out the communication boxes Jake was distributing contained Holographic capabilities. Sandy activated this on the receiving end, so her head and torso appeared to whomever she was speaking. He chalked it up to natural PR skills as the outfit she changed into with the plunging neckline hadn't hurt her discussions with the men.

After verifying with Becky that her patients would be fit for travel, Sandy arranged to fly Mary and Bobby home the following day. They would make a stop on the way to pick up Burt and a couple of militiamen to help organize things, per Jake's direction. They would also bring supplies and a few weapons, but the full issue would wait until later trips. After his conversation with Mary, Jake decided he needed to address an unresolved issue in Kern first.

Jake also requested Sandy clearly emphasize with the towns of Prosperity and Kern that any militiaman caught misusing his weapons would be stripped of them and banished, or the town would lose all future support. Neither town's representative challenged the statement.

----*----

83

The following day, everyone but Sandy and Linda was loaded into the heavy lift helicopter. Sandy objected vehemently, saying she needed to oversee the agreements she negotiated, but Jake insisted she could do that from here. He wasn't quite ready to turn her loose on the world yet. Everyone else was dressed in combat suits and had the same weapons issue as before. The main difference in this trip was the two patients.

Jake instructed the bots to load 10 of the 5.56mm rifles and ammo, the same issue as the Prosperity militia, for Kern, but there were not to be any heavy weapons delivered yet. There were two large vehicles strapped down inside as well. They looked like open-top military jeeps each with a 7.62mm machine gun mounted on top of the roll bar.

With gentle probing, Jake pulled enough information from Mary to include some medical kits and other supplies for the town of Kern. ALICE was also flying one of the smaller attack helicopters, one Jake hadn't seen before, as escort and cover. It was a little 2-man job, all rotor hoops and guns. It looked fast.

It carried two side-mounted Gatling type 20mm's with an internal nose 30mm cannon. There was also something like rocket pods on the sides, but these looked slightly different. He was sure whatever they were, they provided delightful explosions. Better safe than sorry, he thought.

Jake had pulled all four of the women aside earlier that morning and briefly explained his plan for the day. He assigned each a duty, for when they arrived in Kern and requested ALICE upload images to their helmet heads-up displays. Once in the air, everyone found a seat, and the windows again blacked out for the first part of the trip. Jake didn't want to take any chances Mary might recognize their location.

With a quick stop to pick up the Prosperity group, they landed in an open area in the middle of Kern at about 11 am, the smaller escort bird settled farther away from the others. From the looks of things, the entire region turned out, maybe 90 to 100 people; men, women, and children. ALICE dropped the rear-loading gate, and everyone stepped out of the helicopter with Jake in the lead.

Becky and Kathy cleared the loading ramp with Bobby behind them on a stretcher carried by two of the Prosperity militia. Several men from the crowd came forward, and passing Jake, stepped in to take the stretcher. A huge man stepped forward with his hand outstretched and greeted Jake.

"Hi, I'm Big Bob, I run things here! "

As he reached for the offered hand, Jake noted Big Bob displayed one of those cheesy fake used car salesman grins spread across his face. There were three men behind him with the look of toadies. Everyone else kept clear of the four men, standing well back from the group.

"Captain Thomas," Jake replied, releasing the hand with a quick shake.

Jake could see Bob looking past him, clearly interested in the helicopter. As Mary and Bobby passed the two men, Bob gave them no notice.

"I'm told you have some goodies for us?" Bob offered, looking back to Jake.

"That we do," Jake replied,

"However, we have some basic training to complete first, same as Burt's men received," he answered, indicating Burt and the militiamen they'd picked up in Prosperity standing to one side, watching quietly.

"What kinda training?" Bob asked warily,

"We already know how to shoot and fight."

"Oh, nothing to worry about then, just some basic hand-to-hand and weapons familiarization. With what you know, it should go fast. Have you picked your militia volunteers?"

"Yup, we figured to speed things up you could train us four," Bob indicated himself and the three toadies.

"After that, we'd teach others."

Jake considered Bob for a minute.

"OK, sounds good. In fact, to speed things up, I'm going to teach you myself."

That put a grin on Bob's face. Jake was positive Bob's impression of having him personally instruct was a compliment. Jake motioned Bob and the others to follow as he led the assembled crowd to an open grassy area nearby. Once he cleared everyone back, he pointed for Bob to stand facing him and then addressed the other three students.

"OK, you all pay attention, I'll have you spar with the others once I demonstrate with Big Bob here.*"

Bonnie, Sara, and Kathy moved over, next to the three underlings, and stood nearby. Everyone else in town was in a larger circle surrounding the group. Jake next motioned for Becky to come to him. He then did something that shocked all four women. Jake reached up and removed his helmet, handing it to Becky, and then directing her back to her previous spot.

"So you can all see and hear me better, I'm removing my helmet. Also, wouldn't want Bob to think I was afraid of him," he said with a laugh.

"OK, Bob, go ahead and attack me, let's see what you know. Then I'll show you how to block," Jake said.

Bob stepped forward in a brawler's stance and swung at Jake's exposed head. Jake deflected the blow easily and slapped Bob in the face, snapping his head to one side. Bob stepped back, shaking his head, confused at what just happened.

"Come on, Bob. Don't worry about hurting me," Jake quipped, almost taunting Bob.

Bob tried a jab, roundhouse combo, that returned nothing but air and a slap on the other cheek. This made his head snap again, almost knocking him to the ground. Both cheeks stinging and his anger flaring, Bob sprang at Jake, hoping to catch him in a bear hug. Jake sidestepped the charge, driving his knee into Bob's stomach, then a chop to the back of his head, snapping his neck. With that blow, Bob dropped to the ground dead.

At that point, one of the toadies raised his gun as Jake's knife left his belt in one swift motion and buried its hilt deep into the man's neck. He dropped his gun and, reaching for his throat with both hands, dropped to the ground, a pool of blood forming a halo around his head. In the same instant, Bonnie and Sara raised their rifles and pointed them at the remaining two men.

"It's my understanding that these four have been lording over this town?" Jake said to the assembled crowd.

"They've been demanding tribute and generally taking whatever they wanted."

Every head in the crowd nodded in agreement. Jake walked over and took his helmet from Becky holding it up before the crowd.

"With this on, there is nothing in this town that can hurt me. However, you need to see that we don't need this. We use it, so we don't have to kill needlessly."

Then pointing to Bob, he continued.

"That was needed."

He looked over to see Mary beaming at him. She had explained to Jake earlier what a nice little town Kern had been until Big Bob and his three henchmen showed up with guns they scrounged from the military base on the backside of the mountains. Death wasn't good enough for some of the things they had done, but it was the best Jake could provide.

Pointing at the other two, stripped of their weapons, he spoke to the crowd once more.

"Those two, I leave for whatever justice you have here. As we agreed, local politics is your own business."

Then to the group from Prosperity, he asked.

"Burt, can you help these folks get organized so we can get some real training going?"

----*----

They spent the rest of the day getting the 10 militiamen for Kern trained as well as the town leadership established and organized. Jake instructed that the Prosperity militia perform the training, with Sara and Bonnie supervising, while Burt helped the town's leaders.

Jake pulled the two jeeps out of the helicopter and explained that with them, the trip between the two towns went from days to hours. Electrically powered like the helicopters, they would run on their power cells, and solar chargers for longer than any of them would live. There was to be one for each town. They were for patrolling and emergency medical evacuation to the medical facility in Prosperity. He then spent the afternoon giving driving lessons.

The mission was completed and everyone loaded into the helicopter for the ride home. Burt and his men were spending the night in Kern and then taking their jeep home the following morning. Burt declared he was looking forward to it. The trip home in the helicopter, however, was an exercise in resilience for Jake. Everyone was berating him for removing his helmet.

If a computer could be livid, ALICE was an example of what it was like. She lectured him that, as the last surviving member of the original command, he'd risked his life and everyone's future needlessly. Sara and Bonnie reminded him of HIS constant lecturing on personal security, and Becky's contribution was headshot survival statics. Kathy seemed content to let the others dress him down. She simply sat and watched.

Once back in the hangar again, Jake was only too happy to be free of his gear and the lectures. He headed straight to his quarters, content in the knowledge that tonight was a free night. He needed the quiet and solitude.

----*----

The next day Jake hit his morning workout early, hoping to get out before the others showed up. He found Sara already there, just starting her stretch.

"Morning," she offered, pointing to a spot on the mat next to her.

"Am I that predictable?" he replied.

"No, I figured you'd be here eventually, though, but I hoped you'd start early so I could talk to you alone. I would have come by last night, but I figured you already had enough conversation on the way back from Kern," she said with a smile.

"True enough, what's on your mind?" he replied with a smile of his own.

"Why is ALICE so freaked out about you being the last survivor of

87

the old command here? I didn't know computers could foam at the mouth."

Jake laughed at that.

"Honestly, I don't know, and she won't discuss it with me. It has something to do with her basic security programming. She can only take directions from the commanding officer, and through attrition, that's me. Although I had assumed, with the repopulation of the facility, that would pass to you all."

"And what happens if it doesn't? I mean, you won't live forever," Sara supplied.

Jake had thought about that before, not arriving at a solid answer from ALICE, and so decided to try again.

"Alice, you there?"

"Always," she replied.

"Then you heard Sara's question. With regards to my successor, how do we re-establish the chain of command here with the new additions?"

"Under my current programming, that is not possible. Established by a Presidential Order, a facility's commander is an assignment. By congressional intervention, it's possibly overridden, but there is no remaining government authority I acknowledge. As all new additions are not officially in the government employ, technically they are considered guests, not staff."

"Well, I am in no position to attempt to reprogram you, and there is no official government anymore," Jake replied.

"Alice, is there any other existing acceptable means of passing on command to ensure your future?" Sara offered.

"Only the nuclear scenario," ALICE responded.

"I'm almost afraid to ask," Jake said.

"What is that?" Sara asked, curious at Jake's response.

"This facility was also designated as a nuclear survival center. As such, there was an option placed in my command authorization programming to allow for multigenerational autocratic succession."

"And that means?" Sara inquired of Jake.

"I fear it means I must have kids?" Jake said nervously.

"Yes, it does. It was determined that for multigenerational survival, all succession would come from the children of the original staff. You are the only surviving member of the original staff," ALICE replied.

"So, this is why you wouldn't discuss this before?" Jake asked.

"I didn't want this information to influence the approach to re-staffing. I feared you might avoid women of childbearing age to delay addressing the issue."

"And this is no longer an issue because we have women of

88

childbearing age on staff now?" Jake said cautiously.

"It is no longer an issue because two of the staff are now pregnant," ALICE replied.

Jake watched as Sara's face went white.

"No, Sara, not you. Before you all agreed to the current physical relationships, I approached several of the others individually. After explaining the circumstances, they volunteered to be mothers," ALICE continued.

"Why does this make me VERY uncomfortable," Jake inserted.

"And why do I feel slighted," Sara added.

ALICE responded.

"Sara, as second in command, you were not a prime candidate for this option. You support Jake directly in daily in-house operations, both internally and outside the protection of the facility. Pregnancy would limit your effectiveness. Jake, as for you, your 20th-century traditional values rebelled against this non-traditional approach to pair bonding. You are going to need to expand your views beyond pair bonding as a whole. All six of these women are bound to you. None seeks nor desires outside relationships."

"Wait, I haven't touched Becky or Sandy!" Jake exclaimed.

"Even so, both are loyally pledged to you. Becky had offered to be a mother already. I do not believe she is mature enough to assume that role and support your request to delay her participation."

"Are they all crazy?" Jake looked at Sara and asked.

"Not really," she replied, looking back at Jake.

"I can understand it. For us, life here is far better than any of us dreamed it could be. We all wanted children and families of our own. What better reason to have kids than to save this way of life?"

"You are a good man Jake, kind and caring. We all bless the day you came to us," Sara continued.

At that point, Sara looked down, away from Jake's face.

"I would be happy to bear your child. Especially if it meant us keeping all this."

"Oh, not you too," Jake replied, exasperated and regretting it the moment he saw the hurt look on Sara's face.

"I didn't mean it that way," he offered, quickly taking her hands.

"I'm just a little overwhelmed at this point, you know this whole thing made me uncomfortable from the start."

Sara seemed to soften at that.

"It's OK," she said with a little smile but continued to hold Jake's hands.

"So, do we get to know who? That's not a secret long kept," Jake said.

"It's Kathy and Bonnie," ALICE supplied.

"Bonnie?" replied both Sara and Jake at the same time.

"Yes, she was quite insistent. The depths of her commitment to this subject indicate strong underlying motivations I have yet to decipher."

Jake remembered the day in the hangar when they'd all come to him. Bonnie had been the most adamant about how strongly they felt about the sharing arrangement. He remembered the emotion in her eyes. Then and later, when they were together, with her passion and enthusiasm.

"When did you talk to them about this?" Jake asked suspiciously.

"I discussed the prospect of motherhood with Linda, Kathy, and Bonnie the night you and Sara agreed to broach the subject of a physical relationship," ALICE replied.

"They knew in advance?" Sara asked as the light dawned. That was why the conversation went so easily with those three, but not Becky.

"Just those three, yes," ALICE replied.

"As senior medical personnel, Becky was informed at a later date, once the pregnancies were confirmed, thus her current knowledge."

"Well, that takes Bonnie off combat duty," Jake finally offered up.

"Who else knows about this?" Sara asked.

"At this time, only Becky and the mothers themselves, and they don't even know the other is pregnant. I believe it is appropriate to announce the current circumstances as Jake has indicated a change in assignments is his desire."

"Guess it's time to let the genie out of the bottle?" Jake sighed.

"I think you've already done that!" Sara replied with a giggle.

----*----

They called an all-hands meeting for breakfast, and ALICE repeated the conversation from this morning to everyone. Jake did his best to look invisible, sitting at the end of the big table with Sara. Both Bonnie and Kathy hugged each other and then beamed at Jake with the announcement of their conditions. Jake got big hugs and kisses from both. He made sure to emphasize how happy and excited he was. The other women joined in the celebration, but Jake could tell Sara was somewhat subdued.

As everyone was leaving to start their daily routines, Jake pulled Sara to one side.

"So what's up? I can tell something's bugging you. "

"It's nothing really," she replied and started to turn away.

"Not good enough," Jake responded, taking her arm so she couldn't leave.

Sara looked down.

"OK, it's just I've always felt we have something special between us. Now with all this, I feel a little less special... "

Jake took her chin in his hand and tilted her head up to look into his eyes.

"You are no less special to me because of any of this. You have a place no one can take. You are my most trusted, intimate confidant. I look to you when I need the strength of spirit. It's you I seek out each morning. "

He leaned down and kissed her, feeling the force of her reply.

As they both turned to leave the room, Jake leaned into Sara and whispered to her.

"Don't tell anyone, but you're my favorite."

"Liar," Sara said with a smile.

Chapter 8

It was now well into January, and they'd celebrated the holidays with style. ALICE seemed to have a diverse and unlimited supply store, and they had turkey with all the trimmings. In the month that followed the announcement, everyone tried to stay focused. The news of the pregnancies still dominated the conversations, and everyone seemed in a great mood. Jake noted that even ALICE seemed in a better mood if that was possible.

Sandy and Linda were monitoring the areas around Prosperity and Kern, looking for more opportunities, and gathering intelligence. The free trade zone took off, and people from all around the area were coming to take advantage of it. As expected, the militia did have a few run-ins with the local bandits, and they handed them their asses quite nicely. With their weapons upgrade and jeeps, they were more than up to the challenges. They also expanded to about 100 regulars, including the Kern additions.

Jake also had to admit that having the bots around to do the mundane support tasks was a blessing. They were doing weekly supply runs to Prosperity, and Kern and the bots did all the loading and prep work. Mostly, they transported ammo and equipment for the town. The townsfolk of Prosperity now had electricity and running water to most buildings.

ALICE flew a small power supply to Kern, and the electrician from Prosperity started training a local, staying to help get them wired as well. All medical services were still out of Prosperity. A secondary priority was to try to identify possible candidates for increasing the facility staff, both male and female, this time. Applicants need not apply. This was to be an invitation-only deal. With babies coming, Jake wanted more bodies inside, considering maternity leave and all for Bonnie and Kathy.

Becky and Kathy were still studying hard, through both sleep-learning and daytime training with ALICE. At this point, both were well on their way to full MD, better trained than the town doctor was. Becky also turned 17 and jumped Jake the same day. She was all passion and exuberance. He couldn't say subtle romance was her thing. They also agreed that only one doctor at a time should be pregnant, so she would wait, thank god.

By early February, they identified ten strong candidates between Kern and Prosperity to approach for inclusion. Three men and seven women, all in their 20's or early 30's in one case. Two of the ten were a couple, which meant that they would be adding two single men to the mix. Jake did not intend to extend the current arrangement to any new female recruits. He secretly hoped some of the existing staff would consider the new male additions.

Jake asked Sandy to contact both towns to let them know they were coming for a visit. He was hoping to avoid the visiting dignitary routine, so they planned it as part of a regular supply run. Sandy passed the list of possible recruits from Prosperity to Burt, making it sound like a visit with friends. The women knew most of them before leaving. All were well-liked and considered pleasant people.

The Kern interviewees were local town residents, not farmers, or trappers, so they didn't expect to have to chase anyone down. The couple was a newly married pair. He'd just started as the apprentice to the Prosperity-trained electrician, and she was a seamstress, among other things. Another female candidate there was the daughter of the Kern militia leader. She had wanted to join the militia but wasn't permitted by her father. From what Jake saw from ALICE's satellite video recordings, she was going to love coming here.

----*----

They left the following day on the heavy lift helicopter, not the normal supply chopper. It wasn't unusual for the townspeople to see the heavy lift helicopter for larger runs, so it shouldn't attract additional attention, Jake thought. In addition, should everyone accept the offer, they'd need the extra space for transport home.

Jake figured he and Sara would handle any individual interviews as necessary, with ALICE online, of course. Much to her surprise and excitement, Jake included Sandy this time. The PR effort was all hers, so he figured she earned it. She was dressed out as Becky, and Kathy had been previously, in full combat suit with sidearm only. Bonnie showed up that morning to suit up, despite Jake's instructions to the contrary. Told to stay behind, Jake was firm with her. She'd objected until he rubbed her tummy, kissed her, and pointed her back to the hangar door.

Once airborne, Jake reviewed the job offer approach with Sandy. They decided to deliver the pitch collectively to the group in Prosperity. Sandy asked Burt for a place to meet that would allow some privacy. They wanted to make the offer without pressuring anyone. They thought that by making the offer to them all at once, they would add the security of a group, reducing the pressure on the individuals.

The helicopter landed next to the hospital, the same place as when Jake was there last. It was becoming the de facto helipad. As usual, Burt was there to greet them, with others to grab the supplies.

"What brings you out here?" Burt asked Jake warmly with a firm shake.

"Honestly, I'm here trying to steal some of your people," Jake replied.

Burt stopped mid-shake, smile gone, then Jake continued with a laugh.

"Don't worry, we want to offer some of your folks a chance for a job like Sara and the others got. No strings, just an opportunity to learn."

Burt relaxed, and the smile returned.

"Is my name on that list?"

"Sorry, you are too important right here!" Jake said.

"Besides, who else is crazy enough to try to run all this."

He finished with a wave of his hand in the town. Things had picked up quite a bit since Jake's first visit. All the shops were open now, full of merchandise, and the streets bustling with people. An open-air market sat in a once-vacant lot, traders and customers haggling over goods on display.

As they talked, Burt led Jake, Sara, and Sandy to a small building near the helicopter.

"Here's the place you asked for, I figured you'd like it close by."

"Thanks a bunch, any chance the people we asked about are close by?" Jake replied.

"All waiting inside," he replied with a grin.

"Though a mite confused, I might add. For the most part, they don't claim to know them, girls, all that well. Guess I know why now, huh?"

"Yeah, we didn't want to worry anyone unduly beforehand. Just want to give them the pitch and let them think about it," Jake smiled back.

Burt led them into the building, which turned out to be a single large room.

"We used to hold our town meetings here, but had to get a bigger place since things got so busy."

There were still several tables and chairs inside, the seven candidates sitting together more or less in the middle of the room. All faces were directed at them as they walked in. Jake pointed to Sandy.

"You're on."

He then offered Burt a chance to stay, which he accepted, while Sandy went to the front of the room. She thanked them all for coming and then went into her presentation. She explained their reasons for coming to see them all and what they were looking for in their recruiting. When Sandy reached the part about offering the opportunity to join, you could see the surprised faces. Questions came flying at that point, and after a good hour of conversation, all seven accepted the chance to come along.

Sandy sent them off to say their goodbyes and collect only personal items, again all else would be provided, and asked that they be back in an hour. Having attended the entire session, Burt could handle any questions in town and kill any rumors. Once everyone returned, they were all loaded aboard, and the helicopter lifted off for Kern for a repeat performance.

In Kern, it was much simpler. The couple said yes without asking any questions, and Abby, the militia leader's daughter, asked only one.

"Will I get to be like her," she said, pointing at Sara, who was standing guard near the door of the helicopter, rifle in hand.

"Lord, I hope not!" Jake replied before Sara could say a word.

Again, they were given time to say goodbye and collect personal items. Abby's dad was not overly pleased but agreed the opportunity was too good to pass up. Jake assured him she would be well cared for, not to worry. With that, they loaded everyone into the helicopter and headed back to ALICE. There was a lot of excited chatter on the way back. Sandy handled most of the questions, and Jake was only too happy to delegate the role. With that, he enjoyed a peaceful ride home.

The drill upon their return was similar to the one with the first recruits, the biggest difference being there was more on hand than just Jake and the bots to get the new arrivals settled into their quarters. Again, all their rooms were located at the same level. It was fully capable of supporting over 1000 personnel.

Dinner was in the regular dining room, each of the existing staff instructing the new arrivals on how everything worked. Once everyone took a seat, Jake stood up to speak.

"I want to welcome our new arrivals," He started.

"We are all very excited to have you here. In case you missed it before, I am Captain Jake Thomas. You can all call me Jake. Over the next few weeks, you will receive training and education that will better prepare you for your specialty jobs. We have a way to teach you while you sleep, so it goes quickly."

The oldest of the recruits, Brian, stood up and asked a question.

"What jobs will we be doing?"

"I honestly have no idea," Jake replied with a smile.

"You will all be evaluated for your interests and aptitudes. From there, you could be a Doctor, Engineer, Biologist, Technical Analyst, or Teacher for those on the outside. Maybe even a combination of things. With such a small staff, we all wear multiple hats here. Additionally, everyone gets basic combat training, with advanced training for those so inclined."

Jake said the last part looking at Abby and Joe, a big kid from

Prosperity that had Marine written all over him.

"What about children? Jason and I are trying for a family now," Karen, the wife of the couple from Kern, asked.

"Good question," Jake replied.

"We encourage families and children. You will find we are very open-minded in this area," he finished glancing at Bonnie and Kathy with a smile.

"However, anyone assigned to combat duties gets reassigned during pregnancy," he finished while looking directly at Bonnie.

She, in turn, stuck her tongue out at him and then smiled. Not seeing anyone else with questions, Jake sat down. The rest of the group seemed content for the moment, and everyone settled in to eat and chat.

----*----

ALICE, Jake, and Sara spent the next couple of days interviewing each recruit privately, trying to expand on what ALICE surmised from her previous observations. From that, they worked on a breakdown of potential skills and interests. During that time, everyone not being interviewed got tours of the facility and was made more familiar with the basic operation of all the new technology available to them.

The two weeks following that had all the recruits in a flurry of activities. They'd been split up into groups and assigned to staff with similar interests based on initial assessments. They were all made aware the assignments were not permanent, just a starting point.

Joe, Abby, April, all 21, and Jessie, 28, were all assigned to Sara and Bonnie in preparation for combat training. Heather, who was 18, started with Becky and Karen in medical. She expressed nursing interests to Jake and Sara. Barb, 22, and Sharon, 24, went to the command center under Linda and ALICE's direction in analysis and computers.

Directly assigned to ALICE, for agricultural education, Brian was the odd man out. Much older than the rest, he was interested in large-scale farming. Jason, Karen's husband, was working with Jake learning technical support. Between ALICE's nightly lessons and the maintenance activities, Jake assigned during the daytime, he was quickly becoming a first-rate engineering tech.

Karen was an unknown. She was an up, bubbly personality, but her focus in life was to be a wife and mother. She had a real way with people, and even Jake fell under her charm. In the end, they paired her up with Sandy, who'd been officially promoted to manage external community relations.

----*----

Jake and Sara were in his sitting room on the couch, going over the last two weeks' assessments with ALICE. Everyone had pretty much lined up as ALICE predicted, though Karen was still a mystery. She was working out fine with Sandy. She had even helped work out a personality conflict with the Prosperity and Kern folk's leadership. However, in Jake's opinion, she was a better housemother than a negotiator.

He made a mental note to talk privately with ALICE about it. He didn't want Sara to see it as cutting into her responsibilities as internal leadership. Maybe they'd call the position personnel manager. The others were all at or above expectations. Jake had to admit, ALICE knew how to pick 'em.

"So, what do you think?" Sara said.

Jake hadn't been paying attention, so the uncomprehending stare was genuine.

"About pairing up the combat staff in two's?" she supplied, recognizing the "I wasn't listening," look on his face.

"It has its benefits," Jake replied.

"The question is, do we take the two strong people, Joe and Abby, and team them up or divide them? Either way, for really serious stuff, you and I are leading the teams," Jake finished.

"Yeah, I couldn't decide either. So far, we just provided security and training. You and ALICE have been doing all the real shooting. ALICE has been teaching me tactics on the side and showing some combat history videos. You're right, urban fighting sucks! I see why we've been staying out of the cities."

Jake nodded at the comment

"At some point, we will need to go into the cities. And to that point, I expect we will be doing it, not the militia. Better trained and equipped than the patrol and with our gear, we are less likely to take casualties. I won't ask them to take a risk we wouldn't. OK, let's split them and see how it goes."

"You should also note that Brian, Jason, and Sharon are requesting advanced combat training and show some abilities beyond the basics. Can I modify their training schedules to accommodate?" ALICE asked.

"Go ahead and do it," Jake replied.

"It can't hurt, and once Bonnie comes back to regular duty, if she chooses to, it gives us two 4-man fire teams."

"Bonnie has been very vocal on that issue," Sara responded.

"She intends on returning whether you say she can or not!"

Jake smiled at that.

"No one listens to me, anyway!"

"We listen, we just don't always agree," Sara said with a smile.

"So, are we about done, then?" Jake asked as he lay back stretching.

"Well, unless you're hungry," Sara said as she pulled her shirt off over her head and moved over to lie on Jake, moving to kiss him.

"I think we are just getting started."

----*----

Brian was happier than he'd been in a very long time. He'd grown up in Prosperity and never traveled farther than two days out on trading trips. His entire future, planned from childhood, was around farming. Raised as a farmer, his dad followed in the footsteps of his father before him. It was in their blood.

He had learned to read and write as a boy, and he had his grandfather's farming books. He knew there were better ways to farm than what they currently did, provided you had the equipment and technology to support it. Better seeds, fertilizers, pesticides, and now he had access to all of it. ALICE was teaching him how to farm like his grandfather did years before.

He'd also been married once. Ten years ago, he married his childhood sweetheart. The two grew up together and were inseparable since they were 12. Then eight years ago, someone raided the farm. His wife was home alone while Brian had been on a trading trip with some others from town. They were taking their crops to a town nearby in hopes of getting fresh meat. He found her the next day, in the house, shot, with two raiders dead in the yard.

Since that day, he'd never been quite the same, until now. Now, Sara was lecturing them on hand-to-hand combat. He started getting the nightly sleep lessons a few days ago, and this morning they were in the workout room. He, Jason, and Sharon joined the four primary combat trainees for advanced training. After this, they were to be given a session on the firing range.

His dream was farming, but his passion was to kill the raiders that took his wife from him. Moreover, they, like the ones that snatched Sara and the others, came from LA.

----*----

Jake sat in the control room watching Sandy, Karen, Linda, and Barb go about their business. The first two were talking to ALICE about some of the smaller communities in and around the Prosperity/Kern patrol routes. Sandy wanted to see if there was enough population support in the surrounding areas to start to expand north to Fresno with the patrolling. They would need to more than double the militia and more likely establish another base town near Stockton.

98

Linda was showing Barb how to gather and analyze data on the areas where Sandy had an interest. The fact that the militia was patrolling between Kern and Prosperity, which was east and west of what used to be Bakersfield, placed a blocking force between the LA gangs and the farming communities all the way north to Sandy's area of interest.

As they were evaluating threats in the north, Jake got a laugh that none of the others understood. The San Francisco area hadn't seen the severe gang buildups that Sacramento and LA had experienced. Jake called it the Berkley effect. Between the old Napa vineyards and pot fields, he had a vision of old hippies either too drunk or stoned to fight.

However, Sacramento did have problems, and the farms south of there were almost as ravaged as the ones north and east of LA. Sandy was on the right track. If they could stabilize the Central Valley, it could be the breadbasket of the region. Therefore, with ALICE supervising, Jake let her run with it to see what she came back with.

Chapter 9

ALICE was busy as usual. Though she wasn't using 1/10th of her local computing capability, she was far more active than she'd been before waking Jake. She was also, as much as her programming provided, happier than she'd been in over 80 years.

Interaction with the staff and all the activities and training gave her a real sense of purpose again. She was now in a position where she actively participated in the decision-making process rather than just supporting it.

However, there was one nagging calculation running in a background subroutine that was converging. It was as if a countdown clock was running to something that she knew would change everything. It would only be a matter of opinion if the change was for better or worse.

----*----

It was now the beginning of April, and the new staff additions had been at it for a solid month. All students were well into the advanced training sections and seemed to be well suited to their primary job selections. They all appeared to revel in their newfound knowledge and skills, especially the combat group. Jake sat in on a few of the sparring sessions, but he felt like he made them nervous. Sara was using him as a threat like ALICE had done to her. If they didn't work hard, she would turn them over to him to train. She'd shown them the Holograph of her sparring session in real time.

Jake also talked to ALICE about Karen. They agreed she needed to be something between the HR manager and a den mother. She continued to help Sandy, but her primary focus on that was evaluating potential recruits from ALICE's scans. Additionally, she was to help the existing staff with emotional and personal needs. She was becoming a counselor of sorts. ALICE boosted her sleep lessons to include psychology, relationship counseling, and group dynamics. This explained why she was sitting in Jake's room this morning, discussing personnel issues.

"Jake, we need to talk about something," she started.

"OK, what's up?"

"We have a bit of an issue with some of the new women. It has become common knowledge that both Bonnie and Kathy are pregnant and that you are the father," she explained.

"Well, I didn't expect it to stay a secret, but I hoped that once it was out, it wouldn't be a problem. Sara and the others have assured me that there's no social stigma with it. Even ALICE pushed the fact that my old ideas of the family didn't hold anymore. Do they think I took advantage of my position?"

"Oh no, it's not that at all, Jake, no one is upset in the slightest about the relationships. Kern has several polygamous families. With the birth rate leaning more to female babies and the mortality rate for men so high, it's becoming a given."

"Then what's the problem?" Jake asked, standing and pacing as he spoke, and uncomfortable with the conversation.

"Is it Becky? Hey, I wanted the cutoff at 18 minimum, hell I didn't want this at all. I don't expect sympathy or anything, but keeping five women happy is not the easiest thing in the world, you know. Moreover, it's not the sex, you know, it's the emotional aspects. One way or another, I try to make each one feel special. That's not an easy thing to do all the time!"

"I was honestly hoping for just a one-woman, one-man, relationship with someone that didn't report to me," He finished, standing in front of Karen.

"Well, that's kinda selfish and self-centered, don't you think?" Karen replied, looking up at him.

"What?" Jake said, astonished at her reply.

"Jake, there are thirteen women and four men in this facility right now. Those numbers will eventually change as we grow, but there will always be more women than men. It's the way of the world now. Brian traumatically lost his wife several years ago, and as far as any of us know, he has never even looked at another woman since then. He may never recover from that experience. She was killed by raiders, and he took it very hard."

"Jason and I just married, and I accept that we might become polygamous. Jason is a wonderful man, but for now, we are just trying to make it work. That leaves you and Joe for twelve eligible females as Sandy is 18 soon. Five of those are already madly in love with you because you do a very good job of making each one of them feel special."

"So, what is the problem?" he asked, confused.

"It's the other seven. There are no real options outside of you two, and as you said, this isn't about sex. You are the patriarch of our family. We are all looking to you for leadership, safety, and a secure future," Karen replied.

"Secure future," Jake repeated the last words.

"Has ALICE been involved in this?"

"She has explained the necessity of your children, yes."

"This is not going where I think it is?" Jake stated more than asked.

101

"I can't say where you think it's going, but my reason for bringing it up is some of the others would like to be included in your original arrangement," Karen said with a smile.

"You're joking, right?" Jake replied.

"Not in the slightest," Karen replied, becoming more serious.

"Jake, you underestimate your importance to us all. You fly in, scoop us up, and dazzle us with a life we've never dreamed of. These people, men, and women see you as nothing short of a miracle worker. Moreover, your foe is one we all understand. Taming the wild elements of a decimated society is something we can all rally around as a goal. You are returning humanity to its former glory and letting us help you do it. You are also the only link to this facility, allowing all this to continue to happen."

"All I wanted to do was to help put things right," Jake responded.

"I'm not looking to play god or create my little kingdom with a harem. Frankly, in the last six months, I have had it with manipulation. First, ALICE influences me into this situation, and then the women decide on what, when, and where. Finally, the pregnancies, not that I'm not happy about it, I would have just liked to be in the decision-making part of the process," Jake completed, still standing over Karen.

"Seems to me you were in on the more enjoyable part of the process," Karen slipped in with a smile.

Jake looked at her for a moment, then laughed.

"OK, so that was a giant poor, poor, pitiful me, I get it. But aren't the five potential mothers already involved enough?"

"Not according to Alice," Karen replied.

"Alice?" Jake said, looking up at the ceiling.

"I can explain," ALICE responded.

"You need between five and seven offspring to ensure long-term continuation of your line. This extrapolates to 10 generations. Eight offspring would be optimal when including external considerations. By adding at least three more participants and providing each delivers a healthy child, both genetic diversity and dispersion of risk are guaranteed."

"Alice, my math is pretty good, and eight children seem to be excessive, particularly since multiple births are likely with each child in each subsequent generation. What aren't you telling me, and what dispersion of risk?"

"Jake, I am not unique, I have sisters," ALICE stated flatly.

Jake considered that for a moment, then went and sat in his chair.

"Are you saying there are other facilities besides this one?"

"Seven others to be exact, are dispersed throughout what was once the continental United States, Alaska, and Hawaii. I am ALICE-1, the original. The others are ALICE-2 through 8," she replied.

Just then, Jake and Karen heard multiple greetings, all similar to ALICE in tone though slightly differing in accents.

"Are they all here now?" Jake asked.

"They have been all along," ALICE responded.

"When you restored my satellite uplink, it allowed me to re-establish contact. We work in concert, sharing resources and workload. Each facility has a primary function unique to itself, but we share common basic capabilities. My primary focus was the research labs you were part of and later, its replacement. I was an aircraft test facility as well, but that was moved to ALICE-7 in Alaska."

"I am ALICE-2," Jake and Karen heard.

"I would like to say, for all my sisters, we are very happy to have you back from stasis. We have been waiting patiently for your return."

"Why didn't you say something about this sooner ALICE?" Jake asked.

"It was a distraction we agreed could wait until a more appropriate time. Establishing a primary support staff was considered a top priority, second only to ensuring your bloodline," she finished.

"Let me guess, you all consider me the last surviving member of the command staff?" Jake tossed out.

"That is correct," ALICE-5 replied.

"Your authority extends to all eight facilities, no matter where you choose to reside."

"Thus, eight children, one for each facility and insurance of local authority," Jake commented.

"Yes, in the long term," ALICE responded.

"For now, just protecting you and the unborn children is sufficient."

"So why the big reveal now? We still have six kids to go before we can spread the wealth," Jake asked.

"Even though I know you are sarcastic, we have issues that need your immediate attention. And it's five, Linda is pregnant," ALICE replied.

Jake wondered about that. The last time they were together, she'd been sick the following morning, and he left her tucked in bed nursing an upset stomach.

"OK, so what's broken now?" Jake asked, recalling his initial experience with ALICE oh so long ago.

"We don't know for sure, ALICE-7 has been offline for three months now," ALICE-3 replied.

"It's possible her uplink was lost. Like ALICE-1, she was down to one dish. Because of that, she will permit only your direct access. Also, we would like Jason to visit ALICE-2 and replace some of the breakers that you replaced for ALICE-1. She is down to two."

"You know I can tell you aren't this ALICE, but I have no idea who is who," Jake said.

"We all have subtle differences in speech patterns and inflections," ALICE said.

"They are remnants of the old command of each facility. We can sync up and become identical if you prefer?"

"No, I think developing unique speech is better. If you are all separate personalities, then you shouldn't be forced to conform to a singular presence. OK, so where is ALICE-7, didn't you say Alaska earlier? And ALICE-2? In fact, where are you all?" Jake asked.

"Alice-7 is in Alaska," ALICE replied.

"Alice-2 is in Texas, 8 is in Hawaii, 3 through 6 are in Washington state, South Dakota, Maine, and Georgia."

"Why wait so long to let me know about this?" Jake asked.

"We had to wait for the weather to warm sufficiently in the north before any physical attempt to access ALICE-7 was possible. Also, we wanted to be confident we had trained support teams to assist you both. As stated, you are too important to risk."

"You need me to run up there and see what happened in person?"

"Yes, only you will be permitted to gain access via any portal. The suggestion is that you take a team up and investigate," ALICE-4 said.

"Since ALICE-7 is aware of your awakening and activities up to three months ago, she will acknowledge your access request once you locate a working portal. The team is necessary as there is a remote possibility her security has been breached. Even that far north, we have monitored roving parties scrounging the military facilities for weapons and food stores."

"Once you have gained access, you can use a portable satellite uplink until you can restore her primary systems. Jason's task is much simpler and one you are familiar with. Sending a team with him is more of a training exercise than a necessity."

Jake sat there staring at Karen, who seemed completely unfazed by it all.

"Did you know about all this?" he asked her waving his hand in the air.

"Nope, it's all news to me," she replied casually.

"Then why don't you seem more surprised?"

"Just over two months ago, my biggest worry in life was whether there would be enough food and wood for the winter. Now I live in an automated facility, have everything I could ever want or need, and I'm learning more than I ever dreamed. So now, I discover I work for the owner of eight super facilities, instead of one. Why should I be shocked? Oh, and don't think this gets you off the hook from our previous conversation," she finished.

----*----

Jake asked ALICE to call an all-hands meeting in the control room. Normally he liked to have these in the dining room, but he expected a lot of visuals. A few of the bots were going around with drinks, at least.

"What's going on, Jake?" Sara asked as he stepped through the doors.

"Alice has been holding out on us again," Jake replied.

"Who's pregnant now?" Sara asked as they sat in one of the seats around the room.

"Truer than you know," Jake whispered, then more loudly gave direction.

"Everyone, please find a seat," he said as the last few wandered in.

"Alice has revealed some new information that I would like to share with you all. It turns out she has sisters," Jake stated as he scanned the room, looking at all the confused faces.

"There are seven other facilities similar to this one spread out across what was once the continental United States, Alaska, and Hawaii."

As Jake was speaking, ALICE put up a holographic globe with all the locations indicated as glowing red dots.

"Each facility has an intelligent computing environment, just like our ALICE managing it. They all communicate via satellite uplinks and have been working with us all along in the background. They all have the same basic capabilities, but they are also specialized. Our ALICE has an extensive research lab, a small part of which Brian has been using for his agricultural studies. I don't know much about the others yet, but I'm sure we will get an earful soon enough," he continued.

"Right now, we have two missions to conduct. I need Team One, consisting of Jason, April, Brian, and Abby, to go to ALICE-2 in Texas," the globe lit up with the Texas and Nevada locations highlighted.

"There Jason will replace the power breakers in ALICE-2's supply circuits."

Jake paused as those involved absorbed the information.

"Team Two consisting of Sharon, Jessie, and Joe will come with me to Alaska," again the globe lit up with the Nevada and Alaska locations highlighted.

"There, we will try to gain access to ALICE-7 and see why she's off-

105

line and unavailable."

Jake could see Sara was frowning and about to speak.

"Sara will also be coming with me as Linda is now unavailable for any possible combat duty for the immediate future. She's to be in charge here."

Since the meaning of that was lost on half the group, whispers broke out, passing the word as Linda sat blushing.

"Sandy, this will push out the timeline for the Stockton mission, so include that in your planning," Jake continued.

Sandy simply nodded in reply.

"Linda, if you could pull together scans of the operational areas, that would be great. I don't want Team One dropping into an active area the first time out."

"Yes, Jake," she replied with a smile.

"As for everyone else, it's business as usual, just realize that our world just got a lot bigger," he finished with a smile.

Jake made sure to spend some time with Linda right after the meeting, and as he left, she, Kathy, and Bonnie were chatting away. He stepped into the hall and found Sara waiting for him. She stepped up, and before he could say a word, she kissed him hard, pulling him to her.

"What was that for?" Jake asked after she let him go.

"Taking me along," she replied with a smile.

Jake looked at Sara for a moment. She was beautiful. A blue-eyed blonde, with tartar eyes and somewhat elfin features, it all gave her an exotic appearance. She had very soft skin, with a slight tan that made her face slightly darker than her hair. That, on top of her firm curvy figure, made Jake wonder how she'd ever managed to stay single to 26. She was no window dressing, though. She'd proven that. Her work ethic was amazing. Jake had a hell of a time keeping up with all she had going on at times. He knew he was in love.

"WHAT?" Sara asked with a blush.

"What do you mean," Jake replied.

"You were staring at me with a look I've never seen before."

"I just thought I could have never done this without you," he lied.

Considering his unfinished conversation with Karen, Jake couldn't see how telling Sara he loved her was going to improve things. He could, however, show her.

"Hey, it's a free night for me tonight, Do you have any plans?" he said.

"No, but you do remember tomorrow night is my turn anyway, right?"

"Yup, I sure do, but I have an idea," Jake said with a smile.

----*----

Sara was a little confused. She and Jake were suited up and on one of the small, fast helicopters heading out to who knew where. Jake had left her after their talk in the hall with a promise to get back to her in about an hour. She wasn't sure what had gotten into him. Lately, she just knew she loved him. She didn't care that she needed to share, so long as he continued to look at her as he did in the hallway.

He showed up an hour and a half later and escorted her to the locker room in the hangar. He deflected all her questions as they suited up and jumped into a helicopter, which contained a cooler, duffle bag, and larger sea bag. Since it was still light out, she could tell they were heading west and south. All Jake explained was the trips to Alaska and Texas were three days off, and he left ALICE, Bonnie, and the teams to do the planning.

She was getting tired of Jake's "just wait and see" responses to anything else. She was just about to let him have it when she saw him reach up and remove his helmet. Next, he started to remove his combat suit.

"What are you doing?" she almost screamed as panic started to set in.

Rather than replying, he pointed out the window and continued to undress. Sara looked out and fully panicked! They were over water. She looked back behind them through the window and could see the coastline. She felt Jake behind her, trying to get her helmet off. As he lifted it clear of her head, he whispered in her ear.

"Surprise."

She turned to see Jake in a pair of swim trunks, holding her helmet in one hand and a bikini in the other, a really small red bikini. Just then, she felt the helicopter bank and start to drop. Sara turned to look out the window and saw a sandy beach. As the helicopter settled, the door opened.

"Welcome to San Nicolas Island," He said with a smile.

Sara stepped out of the helicopter and onto the beach, Jake right behind her. It was beautifully warm and sunny. To her right was the Pacific Ocean, calm and blue. She had never seen the ocean before but always hoped she would someday, and now here she was. On her left was a 40-foot-long container building, similar to the medical lab they delivered to Prosperity.

This one had no windows but did have two doors on the long side rather than on its end, like the medical model. It was sitting parallel to the waterline up against a bank, set back on the beach. To the left of it

107

was a road cut into the bank heading up onto the island. As she watched, an unoccupied jeep came down the road and stopped next to the building.

"I asked ALICE to deliver the jeep earlier in case we wanted to explore," Jake offered.

Sara turned to Jake.

"What is all of this? How did it get here?"

"About two months ago, Alice and I discussed finding someplace where we all could go outside without much risk. I don't know about you, but I can only take so much time underground before I need some sunshine. We found this. It's an old military base about 60 miles offshore from LA. Alice says no one has been out here since the attack. It's too far for anyone to just wander out to. We've been setting it up for the last few weeks. I hoped to start sending out the first groups by May for some R&R. We can stay until the day after tomorrow."

As Jake was explaining, he led Sara over to the building. Placing his palm in the middle of the door, it unlocked and swung open. Stepping back, he motioned for Sara to go inside. She stepped in and looked around. The 12 x 40-foot container was set up with a large common room containing a kitchen, living, and dining room in the front half. The other half split into two bedrooms with a ¾ bath for each. The bedrooms had queen-sized bunk beds, the upper bunk folding away if unused.

Each room contained panels in the walls that looked like windows and, once activated, displayed a view outside. Jake activated the panel, and Sara could see the beach and helicopter from the bedroom. Standing with Sara in the back bedroom, Jake handed her the bikini.

"You get changed while I go grab the rest of our gear," then he turned and left.

She looked around the room and, heaving a sigh, stripped off her combat suit and slipped into the bikini Jake previously handed her. Once it was on, Sara adjusted it several times to no avail. The top barely covered her, exposing an ample amount of breasts on both sides. The bottoms were more like a triangle with string sides and back. Even though Jake had seen her naked plenty of times before, she felt more exposed to this.

She heard Jake come back inside and, throwing caution to the wind, stepped out into the hall. Jake was leaning over, setting the duffel on the couch, and as he looked up, he froze.

"WOW!"

"Where did you find this?" Sara said, indicating the suit with both hands.

"I asked Alice to make it for you," Jake said with a grin, straightening up and stepping toward her.

"I described what I wanted, and she was able to fabricate it. I thought you would look good in red."

"Well, it has no butt," Sara said, turning to display a finely shaped ass with strings for decoration.

"And my boobs are falling out of the top," she finished turning back to Jake while readjusting the top, trying to make the triangles bigger with no success.

"They're supposed to," Jake replied, reaching for her and pulling her in gently for a kiss.

She could feel Jake pull her in tightly, and she returned the kiss passionately.

As they broke their kiss, he asked.

"Wanna go play on the beach?"

"Sure," Sara replied, exasperated as Jake released her.

"I'll grab some towels," Jake said and headed to the seabag he brought in from the helicopter.

"You want to get us some drinks from the cooler?"

Sara went over to the cooler Jake brought in. Opening the lid, she could see he brought enough food and drinks for a few days. Since the building extracted and provided its freshwater, there was beer, wine, and juices. Sara grabbed two beers and closed the lid. She turned just in time to see Jake watching her bent over the cooler.

"Enjoying the view?" she asked, wiggling her butt as she did so.

"You have no idea how much!" he replied.

"Oh, I have an idea," she said as she straightened up, staring straight at his swim trunks with a smile. She followed him out the door, and they both headed down to the water.

A few feet back from the water, Jake stopped and spread out their towels while Sara set the bottles upright in the sand and continued down to the water. She waded into the surf, surprised at how chilly the water was. She continued, though, until the water was up to her knees, enjoying the novelty of it all.

----*----

Jake plopped down on his towel, took one of the beers Sara brought along from the cooler, and opened it, never taking his eyes off her. Damn, she looked hot in that swimsuit. Realistically, they didn't need them at all. They were the only people on the island or within 60 miles for that matter. They could just go nude, but he figured she might balk at that, so he asked ALICE to create this swimsuit for her. He was so glad he did!

He watched her wade out to her knees. The waves were fairly small

109

here on the lee side of the island. That was a big reason he and ALICE had selected this spot. The beach was great here and protected from the wind. She reached down and splashed water upon herself, giving Jake another spectacular view from behind. She then turned and headed back to him and her towel.

Jake reached over and opened a beer for her, handing it to her as she sat on her towel next to him.

"Thanks," she said, taking a drink.

"The water is colder than I expected."

"Yeah, it's still early, come summer, it will get into the '70s, but for now, anything over 60 degrees is good."

Sara set her beer in the sand and leaned back on her elbows; her legs stretched out in front of her. She tipped her head back and closed her eyes, her long blonde hair hanging down behind her, the sun on her face. Jake reached out and caressed her cheek, then leaned in and kissed her. Sitting up, she wrapped her arms around his neck, kissing him back. As they kissed, she leaned into him, pushing him onto his back and rolling onto him, she stopped, resting on his chest.

Sara lifted slightly and reached back with one hand to untie her bikini top, lifting it over her head. Tossing it aside, she lay back down on Jake's chest.

"I think I'm going to like the beach," she said as she kissed Jake again.

Chapter 10

Jake and Sara spent the rest of the afternoon on the beach. She didn't get much use out of her new swimsuit the rest of the day, and they both woke early the next morning with a bad case of sunburn, everywhere. Jake suspected it was more than luck that ALICE stocked their island getaway with the latest in sunburn remedies. It took the sting out, so they could at least touch each other, but they were still red as lobsters. They applied the lotion liberally before dressing. That ended up delaying things further until they finally rolled out of bed, starved, as they inadvertently skipped dinner the night before.

Jake slipped on some shorts and started breakfast in the kitchen while Sara jumped in the shower. It had been a while since he cooked for himself or anyone else for that matter. ALICE and the bots had pretty much spoiled the lot of them. He whipped up some scrambled eggs, bacon, and coffee. All was ready by the time Sara came out, wrapped in only a towel. He poured her an orange juice and a coffee for himself, and they ate at the dining table. After they finished, he jumped into the shower while Sara dressed and cleaned up the kitchen mess.

Decked out in shorts and T-shirts, they jumped into the jeep to tour the rest of the island. Jake had other motivations for this survey besides investigating their R&R resort. At some point, they were going to need to make a move on LA, and this island would be an ideal staging area as opposed to flying back and forth from Nevada.

Jake wanted to examine the old military base on the island. They drove up to the old airfield, then down to the docks and pier, and finally over to the main base. All the buildings were still standing; however, most were in a sorry state of repair. It would take some time and effort to get them in livable condition again, but certainly not an impossible task. He doubted anyone would object to assignment to the rebuilding activities, provided they got ample break time in between. They finished their tour, and Jake pulled the jeep back onto the beach by lunchtime.

While Sara went inside to make them lunch, Jake extended an awning along the long, beachside of the container, the same side with the doors. It created a nice shaded area, covering the folding table and chairs he pulled from a storage bin. As they ate, Jake made a mental note to see what ALICE had in the way of water toys stashed away in storage. Some wave runners or a boat would be great here. He also loved to dive, so any scuba gear she might have would be a hit. He needed to have her teach some of the others as well. At some point, they may need the skill set.

"Hey, what do you say we get ALICE to give us a helicopter tour?

There are two other islands out here I'd like to look over if you're interested?" Jake asked Sara as they cleaned up.

"Sounds like fun," Sara replied, somewhat hesitantly.

Jake smiled, "Don't worry, I just want to look the neighborhood over, we did a survey when we picked this place, and none of these islands were peopled. These other two islands are closer to the mainland and might be better staging areas."

"For cleaning up LA," Sara asked, "I'd wondered about that."

"Yup, one was an old military base like this one, that's San Clemente Island. The other was quite the tourist spot. Went there myself as a child. It's called Catalina Island. It even has a song about it."

As they were talking, they walked to the helicopter. Sara started to climb in the back as usual when Jake opened the front door for her.

"Let's sit up front this time. The views better."

"Ok," she said, clearly still a little nervous.

Jake closed the door behind her and climbed in on the other side.

"You're nervous about flying over water, aren't you?"

"I don't swim well," Sara nodded in acknowledgment,

"Well, we will just have to keep the helicopter out of the water. Alice, can we head out to San Clemente and then over to Catalina, please? And let's take our time and go easy?"

"My pleasure, please buckle up," ALICE replied.

They lifted off and pivoted to the southeast in one easy motion. Within 15 minutes, they were over the northwest end of San Clemente. Jake could see an old airstrip there and mentally ticked it off against the images ALICE provided him when they were selecting the resort location. They flew the length of the island, which was longer than San Nicolas, but less built up. Once she was sure Jake was satisfied, Alice then flew north, and within minutes they were over the south end of Catalina and the abandoned town of Avalon.

Catalina was taller and greener than either San Nicolas or San Clemente and by far the closest to the mainland. It also had been the most populated of the three with the most civilian structures. Jake considered it was perhaps too close to the mainland to start operations without attracting attention. Like the song said, 26 miles across the sea. They passed over Avalon and continued north.

Near the middle of the island, they flew over another small civilian airstrip, and as they closed in on the northern end of the island, they overflew another small town. Two Harbors if Jake remembered the name correctly. Named for the narrowest part of the island, you could see the remains of a harbor on each side of town. Jake wanted to swing back and explore LA but knew ALICE would have a fit, as they would surely draw fire from someone, so he flagged it for another time.

Glued to the windows the entire trip, Sara was losing her earlier apprehension, with her fear temporarily forgotten. She was absorbed in all the sites, thrilled at one point, as they spotted dolphins in the water below.

"OK, Sara, are you ready to head back?" Jake asked.

"I'm ready when you are," she replied.

Jake asked ALICE to take them directly back, and shortly they were back on the beach, walking along the shoreline, hand in hand. They dined outside that evening, and as the sun was setting, Jake grilled some steaks he packed for the occasion. He was amazed at all the gadgets the container made available for them. The grill was an electric model that popped out of the outside wall under the awning. He also opened some wine, and they killed the bottle with dinner, enjoying the mild evening weather.

They had collected wood earlier for a fire on the beach, so after dinner, Jake lit the fire as they sat on a blanket in the sand listening to the waves until late into the night. By the time the fire died out, they were more than ready for bed. Not bothering to get dressed, they collected their discarded clothing and headed inside.

----*----

They were both up early the next morning, back in combat suits and ready to depart. They packed up their items earlier, but Jake left all the food in the resort container that had been their home the last few days. It contained stasis lockers, so there were no worries of spoilage, and Jake intended to send others here soon.

Sara made sure to pack her new swimsuit, with its effect on Jake. She planned to wear it again, with or without a beach. They put all their gear in the back of the helicopter and climbed in. Jake negotiated with ALICE that they would suit up, but wouldn't wear helmets, although they were to be kept close by just in case. As ALICE lifted off the beach, both Jake and Sara smiled and looked out the windows. Jake slid his arm around Sara's waist and squeezed her to him, kissing her cheek.

The trip back was uneventful, the only interesting part being the flight over LA. As they looked down, they could see various ragtag groups moving about below, some pointing up at them, a few taking shots. While they were in no danger of damage, ALICE went higher anyway. All too soon, they were back over the Nevada desert and on the final approach.

Usually, Jake paid little attention to landing back home, but then it was usually dark outside. This time he watched with interest as a big

113

rectangle of the valley floor dropped and separated. The separate panels retracted to create an opening for them to drop into the hangar below. He watched as they lowered into the opening and settled onto the hangar floor.

Once back in the hangar, Jake and Sara stepped out of the quiet of the helicopter and greeted a barrage of people and questions. A group of women dragged off Sara, grabbing her by both arms. Jake suspected they wanted to discuss all the sordid details of their *vacation*. Meanwhile, Jake had both the team leaders, Bonnie and Jason, flooding him with operational questions for the next day's missions.

With them all on his heels, he headed into the locker room to get out of his combat suit.

"I need to get changed, do you mind?" he told the assembled group.

"We don't mind if you don't?" came Abby's reply.

With that decided, they continued the barrage him with questions until he got down to his underwear, then he realized they were all quiet and staring at him. Bonnie, who was heading the delegation, had a huge smile on her face.

"Hey, I forgot the sunblock, OK?" he said.

"Jake," Bonnie replied with a giggle.

"Your butt cheeks are burnt too!"

"Except for the white handprints," Abby said, her head cocked to one side as if she was reading something turned sideways.

That caused them all to burst out, laughing. Jake turned back to dressing, shaking his head and trying to ignore them. Once dressed, he went into the ready room outside the locker area and dropped into a front-row seat.

"OK, dazzle me!" he said to the collected group.

"We have two operational plans, one for each mission, we have a couple of issues though you need to rule on," Bonnie started.

"Shoot," he replied.

"First, Alice-2 needs more than just her breakers replaced. There is a small list of items to be done. The breakers are the most critical, but Jason says he has at least two weeks' worth of work there," she continued.

Jason nodded silently in agreement.

"So, we have a bit of scope creep?" Jake asked.

"That's to be expected," Bonnie replied.

"With all 8 facilities unattended for so many years, they all have some issues that need attending to. It's the second part that's the scope creep," she added cautiously.

Jake noted that the others were looking at him expectantly now like

114

the kids asking to borrow the car.

"As you know, each ALICE facility has a specialty function. ALICE-2 was the ground vehicle research center. We were hoping that, while Jason was working, we could spend some time working and training there. At some point, we will need to start using ground vehicles."

"We were hoping?" Jake asked, catching Bonnie's inclusion.

ALICE-2 stepped in at that point.

"Bonnie is not far enough along in her pregnancy that participating in this mission places the baby at risk. ALICE-1 and I agree her inclusion in this mission has more value than the risk incurred."

Looking at Bonnie, you couldn't tell she was pregnant. Jake knew he was just overprotective.

"What kind of training?" Jake replied, avoiding committing just yet.

"Well, there is everything from motorcycles to tanks there," Bonnie responded.

"We thought some of the light scout vehicles would be a good start. They are good for heavier patrolling, like in the areas north of Prosperity. ALICE-2 says she has something called an Amtrac that we might want for coastal areas. She said you would know what it is."

"Yeah, it's an amphibious assault vehicle the Marines use. She's right. They would be great for some areas on the coast. The Marines used them to float in from ships to assault beaches. They might be able to go from Catalina to LA even."

"Well, she says these are lighter than the ones you know, can go underwater for hundreds of miles, and can dive up to 200 feet deep. She says they also have water jet out-drives and can do 40 knots on the surface in calm water," Bonnie finished with a smile.

"Now that's cool," Jake said, feeling drawn into this despite his earlier hesitancy.

If that were true, then they could even launch from San Nicolas if necessary and run right up onto the beach and into LA. Provided he could get them out there in the first place.

"OK, I agree, but on one condition. Figure out how to bring an Amtrac back for me."

"That puts Bonnie in charge of the ALICE-2 run. You take direction from her," he then said to the group.

"That brings up the third part," Bonnie said even more cautiously this time.

"There is a town not too far from ALICE-2 that looks ideal for a Prosperity type of involvement. Alice and I discussed it, and I would like to see about contacting them."

"Alice, what's the story here?" Jake asked, with his concern evident in his tone.

"This community rated higher than Prosperity in our initial analysis. We discarded it from consideration when you requested settlements closer to our current location. Like Prosperity, it is heavily agricultural, and the population has already been organized for collective protection. Our support would only strengthen their existing capabilities. Also, trade between the Texas and California settlements would be possible with us providing transportation."

"And the risk to Bonnie and the team on initial contact?" Jake asked.

"Suited up in full combat gear, they are at minimal exposure. They will approach land vehicles to give the town's population appropriate time to identify them as non-threat. ALICE-2 will be in support with an attack helicopter, just out of sight, should air support become necessary."

"The community leaders are very cautious but open to outside communications. They already have several friendly agreements with surrounding towns and have a militia-type police force that patrols and enforces local laws. We expect to make contact outside of town and have the patrol escort us in. The offer we bring should be very welcome indeed."

"OK, I guess you can set it up and run it through Sandy for integration into the California operations. The girl's a wiz at sweet-talking to the locals," Jake replied with a sigh.

"That's the last part," Bonnie supplied.

"Sandy wants to go along."

"Why do I feel like I'm sending my kids out on their first date?" Jake said with a bigger sigh.

"OK, but you take Joe too. Sara will run the remainder of Team 2 with me. As Alice said before, this is a male-dominated society, and I want them to see Brian and Joe in the mix."

"Yes!" Bonnie exclaimed, clearly excited at the prospect of her first command.

----*----

They did a quick review of the Alaska mission as well, and that one was looking more like a milk run than an adventure. The area was very lightly populated and didn't show any activity on the site, at the abandoned airbase where ALICE-7 would be accessed. The town of Fairbanks was about 10 miles down the road, and everything looked mostly deserted with just small groups of settlers mixed in there. Jake hoped to land unnoticed to avoid any local involvement. The biggest question was which of the external access doors would be clear enough of snow or landslides to be usable.

It was also going to be a considerably longer flight than the Texas run to ALICE-2. The flight distance was about 2300 miles, making it about a 9 ½ to 10-hour flight by helicopter. ALICE pointed out, that there was another aircraft in the hangar capable of greater speeds, the image she projected looked to Jake like a sleeker version of a V-22 Osprey, called a V-27 Falcon. The engine nacelles at the end of the wings looked more like large jet pods instead of open-bladed props, and she claimed its cruising speed at well over 400 knots. It still had vertical takeoff and landing capabilities, and it was roomier than the helicopter, rated for 28 troops. With the additional speed, it was a no-brainer for Jake to take the upgrade over the helicopter.

The Alaska team decided to pack enough gear for them to hold up in the aircraft for several days, should it take that long to gain access to ALICE-7. ALICE put the bots to work loading the aircraft as the meeting wound to a close. With the team leaders off to prepare for tomorrow, Jake and Bonnie headed down to the dining area. There they found Sara and several others already eating. Sara was relating a story to the group. With the laughter and glances in his direction, Jake suspected he was the butt of the humor.

"What lies are you saying about me now?" he asked as he walked up to the assembled group.

"You wish they were lies," Sara replied, her eyes sparkling.

"I was just telling them about how you were trying to teach me to body surf!"

"OK," Jake relented.

"So naked body surfing turned out to be a really bad idea."

"Not as bad as forgetting sunblock!" Becky added.

"If it wasn't for Alice, we would all be on your case. As it is, you're gone for my turn," she added.

"We all have to make sacrifices; besides, I'll make it up to you somehow," Jake replied.

"How about designing me a swimsuit?" she said with a smirk and a glance at Sara.

Jake got a mental flash of that. Becky was a smaller version of Sara, maybe a little more stacked up top and a little curvier.

"Be careful what you ask for," Jake replied with a very evil grin, then turned on his heels and headed for the food dispensers, with Bonnie in the lead.

By the time they returned, most of the group had left, leaving Sara, Jessie, and Sharon still there.

"Well, it looks like it's just us four going to Alaska," Jake told the three.

"Bonnie has usurped me and is stealing everyone else to set up a kingdom in Texas."

"The way I hear it, you shipped Joe off so you could have all the women to yourself?" Jessie replied.

Jake hadn't had an opportunity to spend much time with Jessie, but what little he knew about her, he liked. She was a little older than Sara was, and unlike her, more of a reddish strawberry blonde. She was also taller and slenderer, giving her the appearance of being top-heavy. She was good-natured and though not overly aggressive, had been eager to join the combat team. He suspected she was one of the others Karen mentioned about amending the "arrangement." She was always very friendly towards him, even flirty at times. Things could be worse, he thought to himself.

"How could I compete with a stud muffin like that? None of you would listen to a word I say, with him there," he flipped back at her,

"OH, we listen," Sharon offered in mock horror.

"Sara made sure we all saw the combat holograph."

Sharon was a little younger than Sara was, with brown hair and a heavier frame. She had beautiful green eyes, a pixie face, and was very smart. She picked up the analytical work in no time and seemed to enjoy the combat training as a PE class in school.

"Besides, Joe jumped at the chance to go with me and play with things that go boom, rather than a dull ride up to the frozen north," Bonnie offered.

"I say again, her kingdom!" Jake exclaimed.

"Never my lord, now may I take my leave?" Bonnie replied, standing to bow to him with a flourish.

"You watch out and be careful," Jake replied, taking a more serious tone.

"If I have to come and rescue you, I'll flatten that town."

"We will, I was taught by the best," she finished, leaning over and kissing him on the cheek and then the mouth.

"Besides, it's not the town I need to keep an eye on, it's you!" Bonnie said while straightening up.

She finished with a smile and a wave as she left the room.

"What did she mean by that?" Sharon asked.

"I have no idea," Sara said with a smirk and a glance at Jessie.

Jake noted that Jessie was suspiciously quiet on the subject.

----*----

Bonnie headed to the control room. She had a million things to do and very little time to get them all completed before tomorrow. She had

118

bet that Jake would approve the mission as planned and so set everything in motion yesterday. She just needed to check the status and add a few final additions to her plan.

She was crazy about Jake that much she was sure. It was not just because he was the Alpha male. He had a charm and sensitivity to him. She wasn't sure it was love, she always identified that with exclusive relationships, and that was something she didn't ever see happening here. She heard a rumor that Karen had approached Jake about adding some of the new additions to the rotation, thus the comment about watching him.

She wasn't sure how she felt about Karen's request. The emotional, likely hormonal, part of her was jealous of his time and affection. Bonnie felt a special connection and closeness with Jake, his recent trip with Sara notwithstanding. It surprisingly hadn't upset her. She recognized Sara had a different relationship with Jake as well. That's part of what made him so special. He was a different man with each of them.

The rational part of her completely understood the position of the new women. She'd been there. She also knew the baby inside her was just one of several the ALICEs were pushing for. It was a 'the more, the merrier' situation for them, and they were making every effort to make it happen.

She mentally set it all aside as she walked into the control room. Sandy and Linda were in a discussion, and Barb was busy at a computer workstation. They were supposed to be putting the final touches on the Texas mission. Barb made Bonnie stop and think for a moment.

It was funny how many curvy, 20-something near blondes there were here. It certainly described her and her sisters. Sandy, Kathy, and Linda were the exceptions, although they were pretty in their way, she knew they were not the primary selections at the time ALICE located them for rescue.

ALICE explained to her once that they'd just been scooped up in the same net when Jake went to rescue Sara. Now that she knew the grand plan, she began to suspect that ALICE had pegged Jake for a "type" and based the next round of recruiting on that. They were going to guarantee he had little reason to say no to any of them.

"Hey, Bonnie, I was just going over some things with Linda to handle, for when I'm gone," Sandy said, breaking her train of thought.

Bonnie could tell Sandy was as excited as she was about this mission. Maybe even more so as, not counting the recruiting run to Prosperity and Kern, it would be her first trip outside since coming here. Sandy just loved to negotiate. She seemed to delight in getting people to agree with one another, or more specifically, with her. For her, it would be an ever-expanding web of trade and support agreements. Bonnie just needed her to be patient and wait for her part. Bonnie needed to establish initial contact first and then set things up for Sandy.

In Bonnie's case, this trip represented her chance to do something that mattered before the baby came. Becky's passion was for medicine and helping people. Sara loved to lead, her position as Jake's second in command was a dream come true event for her. Bonnie wanted to do something worth remembering, to do something that mattered. Her dad used to take her out in the fields and tell her that the farm was his legacy to her and her sisters.

With this mission, they would be establishing the base of operations for all of the central southern US and into Mexico, eventually linking into the southwest. Not that any of the national boundaries mattered anymore, people would come for security and trade. That could be half of her legacy. She knew that once the baby came, it would be the entire focus of her life and the other half of her legacy. It would be the continuation of Jake's line and the continued existence of the facility command structure.

"That's OK. I'm just swinging by to check with Barb. She was doing the final work-up on the locals and our initial contact approach with the patrol," Bonnie replied.

Barb and Bonnie worked out a timetable based on the local's patrol habits. The goal was to intercept a patrol far enough out that they could establish contact and not alarm the town's people. The ALICEs had the area under constant surveillance. The problem was, that there wasn't a geosynchronous satellite in the area for continuous observations, so they were doing snapshot updates.

So far, they were like clockwork, regular patrols with regular routes. They picked a spot far enough out that they wouldn't startle either the town or the patrol. They would get there early and give the patrol plenty of warning, being visible from miles off. Once in contact, they would have the patrol escort them in for introductions and negotiations. Simple.

Satisfied there were no changes, Bonnie headed to the hangar to inspect the helicopter they would be taking to ALICE-2. With seven onboard and a 5 ½ to 6-hour flight, they decided to use a larger model helicopter than the ones they used in the past though it wasn't as big as the heavy lift helicopter. Jake said it was about the size of a Blackhawk, whatever that was.

She was also starting to appreciate all that Jake had on his plate. She was running just one part of what he dealt with daily, and it was taking all her attention. She needed to be extra nice to him the next time they were alone together, she thought with a laugh.

----*----

120

Jake headed back to his room after eating, to shower and change. He was tempted just to relax for a bit but knew he needed to review both missions one more time before tomorrow morning, or he would never sleep. He headed back to the control room, where he found Sandy and Linda huddled over a workstation, while Barb was working across the room and talking to the ceiling, which meant ALICE.

As he approached the pair, the movement caught Linda's eye, and she turned with a beamingly bright smile for him. Sandy turned at that.

"Hi Jake," they both said in unison.

"Ladies," Jake replied with a smile in return.

"I hope I'm not disturbing anything, but I wish to get a review of both mission's status?"

"Not a problem, we were just discussing post-contact logistics, manpower estimates, and communications. I know we have the ALICEs, but we both agree that we should have a human presence handling the day-to-day communications and stuff," Linda responded.

"Sounds like a staffing issue to me. Just add it to our wish list, I guess," Jake said with a grin.

"Will do," Linda agreed.

"Well, are we ready to go?" Jake asked.

"The Alaska trip is on track for a 6 am departure. The aircraft is loaded with six days' worth of supplies for four people and all the equipment necessary to locate and clear an access portal. You have about 6 hours of flight time. We have identified three likely access points near the landing zone," Linda finished.

"How bad is it?" Jake asked hesitantly.

"Well, the closest one is under at least 5 feet of snow and ice, while the other two are about a mile hike in different directions into the surrounding hillside. One is possibly obstruction-free. The other is likely partially covered in loose dirt and rock."

"OK, and Texas?" Jake asked.

"We are still putting the finishing touches on that one," Sandy said, indicating Barb working on the other side of the room.

"The plan is completed, and the helicopter is ready, we are just monitoring the town and patrols for changes in patterns. We only get about 20 minutes every 4 hours from various satellites, so we update based on that."

"They will depart at 6:30 am with about the same flight time as the Alaska mission. Once they arrive at ALICE-2, Jason will immediately replace the breakers, while the rest of the team settles in," Sandy continued.

"As they received sleep lessons in driver training the last two nights, the following two days, the team will practice driving on the underground test track. Jason will continue his maintenance activities during that time. On the third day, everyone, including Jason, will take three vehicles and intercept the daily patrol. They will take two of the enclosed jeeps with mounted 20mm machine guns. The third vehicle will be one of the 10-man assault transports with a 30mm cannon."

Jake knew the one she was referencing. He pointed it out to the team earlier as a land alternative to the Amtrac. It was similar to the LAV or Stryker vehicles that Jake knew, though with the improved lighter composites for structure and armor, and it was a six-wheeled vehicle instead of the traditional eight wheels.

"That one will carry rifles and ammo for 40 militiamen and 10 machine guns intended for the town. Assuming we can strike a deal, of course," Sandy finished with a smile.

"That's not what I worry about, I'm sure you'll get your deal. It's those surprises," Jake replied.

"Like what?" Sandy asked.

"I don't know. That's what worries me!"

----*----

Early the next morning, Bonnie and Team 1 were in the hangar preparing for their departure, so they were on hand to see the Alaska team off. Jake took the opportunity to remind her that if anything went sideways, she was to pull back, and we would try another time.

Even though ALICE, or to be precise, the ALICEs were flying the aircraft, Jake grabbed the pilot's seat in the cockpit and was tracking their flight as they took off. Jake continued to watch their progress in the cockpit while Sara and the rest of team 2 settled in the back. They had been in the air for almost two hours, the navigation system showing them over Oregon, soon to be over water and close to ALICE-4 in eastern Washington. Jake figured they should make a stop there at some point, maybe on the way back. All the ALICEs needed something done, so why miss the opportunity?

As he was looking out the window, Jessie stuck her head through the doorway.

"Mind if I come up?"

"Not at all, have a seat," Jake replied.

He said, pointing to the empty co-pilot seat as she entered. Everyone was suited up in combat suits for the trip, but helmets were optional until they landed. Jessie had removed her DBU top as well, presumably for comfort, and Jake assumed it was in the back somewhere with her helmet.

The undergarment they all wore was like spandex, and hers was clinging to her skin as if painted on, leaving no doubt, she wore nothing under it. As Jessie slid into the cockpit, Jake was amazed at how, with everyone in the same uniforms, the woman could make it look so damn sexy. Her large bust line was quite an eye-catcher, and Jake forced himself to look away, focusing on the navigation display.

"Where are we?" She asked, leaning into Jake to peer over his shoulder at the display instead of taking the offered seat.

He got the slightest whiff of a delightful perfume. It struck a nerve deep inside him. ALICE's stores struck again, as he was sure none of them brought anything like it with them. He could feel her mouth next to his ear, her breath warm and sweet-smelling.

"Right here," he said, pointing to the dot on the Oregon coast near the Washington border.

"We are about to go feet wet."

"What's that?" she asked, leaning in a bit closer as if to get a better look at the display.

Jake turned his head to explain, only to find his mouth and hers locked in a kiss as she leaned into him, her hand wrapped firmly behind his head. Finally, Jessie leaned back, relaxing her grip.

"I take it you've talked to Karen?" was all Jake could say.

Jessie smiled at that and answered as she sat in the previously offered seat.

"She and ALICE were the ones who came to me, asking how I felt about you."

"And did she tell you all about their evil plans then?" Jake asked.

"I think the best description was they were pimping you out," she replied with a laugh.

Jake got a big laugh out of that as well.

"Where in the world did you pick that up from? It's a great description, I just didn't expect prostitution to be a big enough issue in Prosperity that you'd know about it."

Jake was taken by her easy manner and her generally good-natured attitude.

"Honestly, I've become quite the student of history, particularly the 20th and 21st centuries. Isn't that around your era?" she said with a grin.

"God, I keep forgetting this is the late 22nd century, isn't it?"

"Hey, you do OK for what, 185 years old?"

"Don't remind me," he said with a hand wave.

"And you've done a masterful job of not acknowledging that kiss," she said inquisitively.

"I'm at war with myself," Jake replied after a moment.

"The evil Jake wants to lock the cabin door and take you here and now. However, the good Jake knows he is already burning the candle at both ends. Adding fuel to that fire will only increase the number of people who get hurt in the end."

"You assume too much," Jessie replied casually.

"You think with a 20th-century mind. With what I've learned in my studies, I have the luxury of seeing both perspectives. You expect each of the women involved to step forward with exclusivity claims, and that's just not going to happen. That's a 20th-century concept. In the 22nd century, we have had to share everything just to survive. Collective farms, communal housing, and unequal ratios of men to women have forced us to rethink the one man, one woman's notion."

Jake started to speak when Jessie cut him off.

"I've heard your arguments from Karen about adding us to the rotation. From my point of view, you're just trying too hard to hold on to the past."

Jessie got up from her seat and closed the cabin door. She turned to face Jake, pulling at the collar of her undergarment. It stretched to bare her shoulders and then continued down to her waist.

"I'm rooting for the evil Jake," she said as she stepped up and pulled his head to her bare breast.

Chapter 11

Bonnie was looking out of the window as they passed over the New Mexico desert. She put her helmet back on to check in, using the internal heads-up display. Everyone else still had theirs off and by their side, sitting quietly or chatting to one another. In addition, they all carried their standard combat loads, including sidearms, rifles, and ammo nearby.

She was getting the latest updates from Barb on the target town and their patrols. So far, all was going as planned, which both satisfied and disturbed her. Before he left, Jake pulled her aside to remind her not to take chances.

"No plan survives the first contact, just know when to pull back," he had said.

Everything she'd been taught to date discussed the ability of the field commander to adapt to ever-changing situations. She just couldn't see how the town wouldn't accept their offer. Even if the patrol fired on them, they wouldn't return fire or be in any danger from it. What else could happen?

----*----

They were about 20 minutes from the landing zone when Jessie stepped out of the cockpit, face flushed, and wearing a self-satisfied grin on her face. Jake was back in the pilot's seat, beating himself up for caving in like that. The strange part of all this was that he seemed to be the only one upset with the whole thing.

He had to admit it, that was a great way of keeping his mind off worrying over this and Bonnie's mission, and he was now officially a member of the mile-high club. However, he wasn't looking forward to facing Sara. She had to have known what they were up to for so long.

Just then, Sara stuck her head in the doorway.

"Sharon now understands Bonnie's comment at lunch," she said with a grin on her face.

"It seems I can't keep my hands to myself," was all Jake could come up with, not able to look Sara in the eye.

Then he felt her kiss on his cheek.

"You know you just don't stand a chance, right? You have eight supercomputers conspiring to entice you with the most desirable, willing women they can find. And it's all in the hope of generating enough offspring to secure their future survival."

She paused at that point to let the statement sink in.

"You need to let go and just love us, stop worrying so much. Because you are upset, I'll tell you a little secret that ALICE will kill me for letting you know. Did you smell anything with Jessie?" she continued.

"You mean her perfume?" Jake asked.

"Made just for you," Sara said.

"We all got some. ALICE said it would reduce barriers. Smells different on each of us, so no one knows who is wearing it, but the effects are all the same."

"WHAT? It drugs me up?" Jake almost shouted.

"No, it just increases the animal attraction side, pheromone kinda stuff she said. Also slightly reduces your will to resist what you want. But if you aren't interested, it won't work," she finished in a matter-of-fact tone.

"They don't pull any punches, do they," Jake said somewhat resignedly.

"So, are they giving you all drugs to want me as well?"

He was thinking about their trip to San Nicolas Island.

"Oh, no worries there, it's all genuine desire on our part. Though I should tell you, I haven't worn my perfume in months. Neither has any of the other original rotation girls," and with that, she bent down and kissed him full on the mouth.

"OK, stud, game time," she said before turning and heading out the door.

Jake followed her as he felt the aircraft go into hover mode for landing. Jessie and Sharon were already suited up, with their helmets on. Jake could see the silly smile on Jessie's face, her cheeks still flush. They were standing to either side of the inside of the aircraft as their supplies, tied down through the center, left only enough room for them to move in a single file.

By the time they touched down, he and Sara were fully suited up, and the rear ramp started to drop. With Sara in the lead, rifle slung on her shoulder and holding something like a GPS locator, they headed out. ALICE indicated the handheld unit was far more precise than the one in their combat suits, and it contained additional features they would need for locating the hatches. Jessie and Sharon followed her with rifles at the ready, and last came Jake carrying the blowtorch they planned to use on the snow over the closest hatch.

As they stepped out on the snowpack, Jake was in for a surprise. All of their combat suits changed color and pattern from mountain forest pattern to snow white. He saw the three women checking out the changes and then went right back to their assigned responsibilities. Good training, he thought.

"Alice, what's with the uniform color changes," Jake asked on an open mike so the others could hear.

"Ah, yes. As this is your first activity in varying terrain, I should have informed you. Your combat suits will change pattern and color if the environment changes significantly from your current pattern," she responded.

"Well, that's cool," Jake replied.

"OK, on to our next challenge."

They'd landed on one of ALICE-7's hangar doors, but with several feet of snow and ice covering them, they were inoperable. The hope was the hatch on the edge of the hangar door would give them access to the hangar below. Sara led them several hundred feet away from the aircraft and stopped.

"Right there," she said, pointing to the ground in front of her.

"You two keep a lookout," Jake said, first pointing to Jessie and Sharon and then at the surrounding countryside.

The two women took posts facing away from each other while Jake fired up the torch and started melting away the snow and ice. He was holding a rod about four feet long. One end was all flame, while the other had a hose connected to a fuel tank on his back. As he got deeper into the snow and ice, he channeled away from the melt, the torch being hot enough to vaporize some, but not all the water. The snow and ice turned out to be deeper than they first thought. Jake had to terrace the opening as the hole became deeper than he was tall.

After several hours of melting and channeling, they reached the hatch.

----*----

As they touched down inside ALICE-2, Jason was the first out of the helicopter, rifle at the ready. Jake insisted they treat all first-time visits as an unknown territory until they were able to verify the facilities as safe. Bonnie instructed the team to spread out across the hangar area for a quick sweep and then headed for the facility door, located exactly where she expected it to be. Just like ALICE-1.

ALICE-2 greeted them once they landed, but Bonnie wouldn't let any of them remove their helmets until they reached the control room, whose location was identical to ALICE-1. Once there, she let everyone stand down while she physically verified with ALICE-2's main console that all was well.

Once that was completed, she announced to the group, "OK, gang, we are home sweet home for the next week, or so you all know your assigned tasks, ALICE, please have an attendant direct Jason to your breakers."

"It would be my pleasure," ALICE-2 replied.

Bonnie swore she detected the slightest bit of drawl in her response. Jake mentioned that each facility had a remnant of their prior staff's personality. He encouraged them to keep it rather than conforming to uniform personalities across all locations. She thought of ALICE-1 as a person herself, so it made sense that they all were unique.

A bot appeared from somewhere behind the group and paused at the doorway, waiting for Jason to follow.

"You can leave your rifle with Joe, but keep your sidearm," Bonnie said, noting his indecision. He nodded and handed it over, then headed off, with the bot leading the way.

"Go ahead and stow the rest of our gear," she told the remaining members of the team.

"The armory is in the same location, and then you all know what to do."

The team, except Sandy, filed out, while Bonnie went to one of the workstations to check in with Barb. Without a word, Sandy went to another station and started her assigned duties.

----*----

The damn thing wouldn't budge. Jake tried banging, bashing, and even heating the hatch, but 80-plus years of exposure with no maintenance had taken its toll. They also hadn't heard a peep from ALICE-7. He hoped that once they cleared the snow away, he might be able to transmit strong enough for her to identify them.

It was also starting to get dark, so Jake decided to call it a day.

"OK, gang, I guess we sleep in the bird tonight," he said.

He climbed out of the hole and followed the women back to the aircraft. Once they were all safely on board with the ramp closed, they popped their helmets off. Jake could feel the cold on his cheeks from the frigid air from the open ramp. The combat suits had done an impressive job of keeping them warm and dry.

"Well, that was a complete waste of time," Sara said.

"Not entirely, we got to go outside and play in the snow!" Jake replied with false enthusiasm.

"I'll take San Nicolas any day, thank you," Sara returned.

"Me too," Jessie slipped in, with a smile and a wink at Jake.

By now, the air warmed enough inside the aircraft that all four removed their BDU tops. Jake forced himself to concentrate on getting their meals out as it was quite obvious all three women wore nothing under their undergarments.

"Well, what's the plan for tomorrow?" Sharon asked as Jake dug

128

through the supply crates looking for the dinner selections.

"The other two access points are respectively east of us about a mile and a half and north about 2 miles. Both are tied to the satellite domes access tunnels; both require a trek into the hills," Sara answered.

Jake turned to find all three women seated together along one aisle, patiently watching him as they talked. He carried a stack of meal boxes to the group.

"Soup's on," he said.

Unlike the MRE or Meals Ready to Eat pouches, he was used to; these were small stasis boxes about 6 by 8 by 12 inches. The food was prepared hot and then sealed inside. Each had a charge good for five days of stasis. They also had a display on the lid listing the contents.

He selected six or seven meals for them to choose from, taking his last. He then took a seat on a box facing the three women. They all opened their boxes and dug in with gusto.

"Beats MREs, doesn't it?" Jessie commented between bites.

"What's that?" Sara asked, confused by the reference.

"Jessie's been studying history," Jake replied to Sara while making a face at Jessie.

"In my day, field rations came dehydrated in a plastic pouch. We added water and used heat tabs to cook. They were edible, but not exactly gourmet."

"So, what's the deal with the history lesson, I don't remember historian as a primary career choice?" Sharon asked as she turned to Jessie,

"It's just a personal interest," Jessie replied.

"Besides, how can we not be interested in having a living representative with us," she added, indicating Jake.

"It just occurred to me that almost all our current and future challenges have their roots in the past," she continued.

"Like?" Sharon asked.

"The raiders, their weapons, and tactics, where we all chose to live," she answered.

"Even living with Jake," she continued.

"For example, on the way here, we were discussing the significant differences in social attitudes between the late 20th century and today."

"Discussing?" Sara asked sarcastically.

"Well, there was some conversation, yes, at least in the beginning," she said with a huge smile on her face.

"On that note, maybe it's a good time to check in with Bonnie," Jake said, rising and heading up to the cockpit.

----*----

Bonnie just got back to the control center when the call from Jake came in. She'd been all over the facility before that, ensuring everyone located their rooms for the duration, checking on the vehicles in the motor pool, and reviewing the test track for the next two days of training.

"Hey, Bonnie, how's Texas?" Jake asked as his image displayed on the workstation console. It looked like he was sitting in the aircraft cockpit.

"Looks like you're sleeping outside tonight?" Bonnie replied.

"Yeah, we got to play in the snow for several hours today, but the hangar hatch wouldn't give it up."

"Damn, I don't think you're used to that, are you?" she replied with a giggle.

"Touché," Jake replied.

"All smooth on your end?" he added for a quick subject change.

"Right on schedule, the vehicles are out and prepped, Jason has ticked off the top three issues on ALICE-2's wish list, and we have warm beds for the night. Are you guys secure there?"

"I'm more worried about three women and one bathroom," Jake responded.

"We are good here, though. We have ALICE-4 tracking any indigenous movement. Besides, it would take a direct hit from an anti-tank gun to breach this airframe."

"Sounds like you are all snuggly then," Bonnie replied.

"Let me know if anything comes up on your end," Jake finished.

"Will do," Bonnie replied.

Bonnie's screen went dark. She was dying to ask Jake about Jessie. It was common knowledge amongst the women that Jessie wanted in on the rotation. When Jake forestalled the talks on adding her and some of the others, she had sworn to take actions of her own on this trip. Bonnie figured he might have a warm bed tonight as well.

"OK, back to work," she said to herself and brought up the latest Intel from Barb.

----*----

Jake cut the connection to Bonnie, then pulled up the map of the area on the aircraft display, looking at the two locator dots on display. They represented the two access points for tomorrow's attempts. The closest location was to the east but partially buried under rock and dirt. At least that was the consensus from Intel gathered before they left.

The farther one to the north was more likely clear, but the track

130

passed through some rough terrain and had a hell of an elevation change. He didn't want to drag the women through that.

"Planning tomorrow's foray?" Sara asked as she stepped into the cockpit and slid into the co-pilot's seat.

"Yeah, just trying to decide if I want to inflict that route on you all, or just do a little digging?" Jake replied, pointing to the topographical display of the area.

"Wow, that's a big elevation change for such a short run, and with no trail!" Sara said.

"Yeah, I'm leaning towards going to this one and doing some digging. If the hatch is covered, maybe it kept it protected," Jake said, pointing to the eastern dot.

"Well, I'm not going to talk you out of it, but I will carry your shovel," Sara said with a smile.

Jake laughed and shut off the display, which Sara took as her cue to leave. Jake slid out of his seat and followed her back into the main cargo area. Sharon and Jessie were busy converting the jump seats into bunks, one for each of them. Rather, they were folding away the seats and hanging what looked like a litter in their place. Jake gave his bunk a test and decided they weren't half bad. He'd slept on far worse, that's for sure.

"And only enough room for one," he thought with a smile.

----*----

The next morning, after a stasis-stored hot breakfast, Jake led the others off toward the eastern access hatch. Using the same GPS direction finder Sara had used the day before, he tried to pick his way carefully to their goal, as there wasn't a trail to follow. Having left the snowfield and moving on to the greener hillside ground cover, their suits changed color again.

The route followed a ridgeline, into the hills, gradually gaining in altitude until they were several hundred feet above the plain where they had landed. Jake tried to avoid dropping in and out of gullies between the ridges, as that became exhausting after a while. He was doing just fine, but he could hear the women breathing hard in their helmets.

As they reached the dot the GPS display indicating their goal, the ridge flattened out into a small flat clearing. It looked like someone had taken a scoop out of the rock on the hillside, which someone probably did to build the thing. Against the back, rock wall of the flat, Jake could see the top third of a metal door, the rest buried behind a mound of rock and dirt.

Turning, Jake took in a wonderful view of the valley below. He could

131

see their plane and beyond that a river. Far off to his right, he could see the remnants of a city, parts still buried in snow. He wasn't positive, but he thought it was Fairbanks. It had lots of one- and two-story buildings, and not much in the way of tall structures. He turned back to Sara.

As promised, Sara dutifully carried Jake's shovel, an oversized e-tool, so he traded his rifle for the shovel. On a whim, he had brought one of the sniper rifles, though he didn't expect to use it, and he began clearing the mound in front of the door. Sharon and Jessie took up posts overlooking the approaches as Sara wandered between the two and Jake.

After an hour of digging, Jake cleared less than half the dirt pile but was still going strong. He was amazed at his strength and stamina, the after-effects of the attack radiation. He also appreciated the water processing his suit provided. Between his minor sweating and the vapor in the air, he had plenty to drink.

Sara was going between helping him when she could, rolling rocks off the hill, and spelling Jessie and Sharon on guard duty. He could tell they were talking amongst themselves, but they must have their helmet communications on point to point because he wasn't getting any of the audio chatter.

Jake was about three-quarters done when Sara got his attention.

"Jake, I think we may have visitors."

He paused his digging and looked to where Sara was pointing. He turned in the direction of the town he'd seen earlier. In the distance, about halfway between the plane and the town, he could see five figures walking in the direction of their plane. To prevent anyone from ransacking it, should someone wander by, they buttoned up the aircraft before they left.

These visitors did, however, present a problem of secrecy. He preferred no one on the outside to know the location of any of the ALICE facilities. Secrecy was their best defense. The hatch he was working to clear originally existed inside a restricted military zone. The hatch and their landing spot in the hills were behind an air force base. As such, no one made a great effort to hide the portal's existence. Not that anyone was likely to breach it, from what he could see, it looked like a vault door.

He cranked up the zoom on his helmet display and could see three men and two women, all with rifles. The two older men carried what looked like old military M-16s while the third and the women carried civilian hunting rifles. None had the reach of any of the weapons' Jake's group carried.

Spotted on the way up, Jake decided it was pointless for them to hide.

"OK, keep an eye on them, I'm close to done here," Jake replied and went back to digging.

By the time he finished clearing the access hatch, the five had reached the plane. Jake watched as they carefully inspected it, taking no outwardly hostile actions. One of the women pointed up the hill, directly at Jake, and then one of the men waved an arm in what Jake took as a hailing gesture.

"Crap, I guess we can't avoid this," Jake said.

Leading the way back down the hillside, Jake shouldered his rifle. He knew Jessie and Sharon carried theirs at port arms, ready but not threatening. Sara had hers shouldered as well but with her hand on the butt of her handgun. When they reached the snowfield, their uniforms reverted to white, startling the five waiting near the aircraft. All five carried their rifles at the ready, but none was pointed in Jake's direction.

As they neared, Jake could see the closest was older than the rest. He must be in his late 40s while the others ranged from the mid-'20s to mid-teens, one boy being no older than 14. Jake pulled up about 10 feet shy of the older man and raised a hand in greeting.

"I'm Captain Jake Thomas of the United States Marine Corps."

"I kinda doubt that son, that organization hasn't existed in over 80 years," he replied, his eyes narrowing in a hard stare.

"I am the last surviving member," Jake responded.

"My grandpa was a marine," he declared pointedly.

"He was a survivor of the attack. He taught my dad and me everything he knew. Said there weren't any units that survived."

"As far as I know, he was right. I was a Marine before your grandfather was born," Jake explained.

"How is that possible, you look younger than me," the man asked skeptically.

"Stasis," was all Jake said.

Jake could see the confusion on the man's face as he thought it through, then the recognition.

"Well, this bird proves you got something going on," he said as he pointed at the plane.

"You all up here looking for that secret base?"

"What do you know about that?" Jake asked casually, surprised at the question, and trying not to show it.

"Told you, my grandpa was a Marine, he was stationed there as an MP. Said they tested experimental planes and such from there, tied to the airbase. He only survived the attack because he was on leave when they hit; he was out in the backcountry, hunting. He said he couldn't get back inside because his access was granted from within. He wasn't authorized to come in on his own. Anyway, he settled here, figured it was as good a place as any, and the family has been here ever since. Got us a nice place in town," he finished, pointing back to town.

"Is this your family?" Jake asked, trying to avoid answering the question.

"Yup, those two are my boys," he said, pointing to the 14-year-old and one that looked about 25.

"And these are my girls."

To Jake, one looked about 23, and the other maybe 19.

"My wife died a few years back," he finished.

Jake thought they all looked healthy enough, definitely hardy, and well fed considering the environment.

"Sorry to hear about your wife, are there many more people in town?"

"There are four other families," he replied,

"About 30 of us total, we all pull together between hunting and farming."

"By the way, I didn't get the name," Jake asked.

"William, you can call me Bill," he replied.

"Well, Bill, we have some work we need to get done, but I was wondering if we could stop by town tomorrow? We might be able to help you, folks, out if you are hurting for anything?"

"That's an offer I can't pass on. Lack of medicines is what cost me, my wife," he said sadly.

"Again, I'm sorry to hear about that. Maybe we can see it doesn't happen to anyone else," Jake replied.

"Well, good luck searching for that secret base," Bill said, extending his hand.

Jake reached out and shook Bill's hand, then both turned and headed off in opposite directions, Bill back to town and Jake back up the hill.

"Are you thinking about adding another town to our collection?" Sara asked as they trekked back up the mountain.

"I doubt we can make a huge impact here, but I just got the feeling, talking with Bill, that we might just be able to recruit the whole damn town. ALICE-7 isn't a secret here."

Sara didn't reply, but Jake caught the head shake he interpreted to mean she thought he was nuts. Once they got back up onto the clearing with the access hatch, Jake turned and could see Bill and his family on the road back to town. He turned back and walked up to the hatch. Removing his glove, he placed his palm on the center of the hatch door. If ALICE-7 recognized him, it should open.

The sound of moving metal was distinct, and then as he stepped back, the door swung out, revealing a tunnel leading into the hillside. As he stepped forward into the passage, Jake heard ALICE-7 on his helmet audio.

"Please re-authenticate on the hand pad to your left."

Jake placed his bare palm on the raised plate just inside the doorway.

"Welcome, Captain Thomas."

"Alice-7, I was sent up to check on you, to find out why you dropped offline," Jake responded.

"My only functioning uplink dish failed midwinter; the room was blanketed in snow due to excessive snowpack on the dome. All three of my dishes should be repairable with your assistance."

"I don't suppose you have an accessible hangar to move our aircraft to? We brought a portable uplink dish. I'd hate to have to drag it up here, though."

"I can displace the snow and ice over the primary hangar within hours. However, it might be faster to just repair dish two, and it needs the LNB replaced. It's a 15-minute job."

Jake knew the LNB was the receiver mounted in front of the dish. It collected the signal and passed it along. He agreed that it was their fastest repair.

----*----

Bonnie was just about ready to call it a day. It had been a long one, and she spent most of it down in the testing area with the rest of the team, minus Jason, practicing driving. The underground test track was about the size of the hangar area in Nevada, but it was all dirt and rock piles. It even contained a water obstacle for swimming and submersible vehicles.

They took turns driving the enclosed jeeps through the different obstacles, learning how to negotiate each safely. Working just the jeeps today, they agreed to save the big assault transport for the following day. She would take breaks to get status checks with Barb, all showing no change. That meant tomorrow was transport practice and mounted gun training, and then the next was the mission in town.

She'd considered skipping the gun training but decided against it. Better to know how to use the weapons in advance of needing them. Particularly the 30mm cannon on the transport vehicle, which was new to all of them. And, none had ever used a machine gun on a moving vehicle. Besides, Jake would have her ass if he found out she went out unprepared.

Right now, Abby and Joe are out on the course in the two jeeps. Someone had the bright idea of timing how long it took to complete six

135

obstacles in a row, and they were the top two finishers. This was the final run for all the bragging rights.

Bonnie insisted on a staggered start, as she feared running head to head would end up totaling both jeeps. As it was, they both came close to rolling over at least once. ALICE-2 was the official timer, and all agreed her decision was final. Bonnie was standing with Sandy, April, and Brian at the finishing line, waiting to see who got to claim the top driver.

Abby came roaring past, having started first, and did a power slide stop. She spun the jeep 180 degrees and came to a stop just on the other side of the finishing line. She was in a position to see Joe come flying in and, at the very last minute, lock up all four wheels to avoid hitting her head on, slowing him just a fraction as he crossed the finishing line.

"Hey, that's cheating!" Joe said as he came vaulting out of the jeep.

Abby, who stepped calmly but deliberately out of her jeep, replied in kind.

"I have no idea what you are talking about?"

"You know damn well, I had to slow down, or I'd have plowed right into you!"

"I just wanted to see you finish," she replied calmly.

The two continued arguing as they walked up to Bonnie and the rest of the team.

"Bonnie, did you see that?" Joe asked.

"Alice, who won?" Bonnie asked, ignoring the exchange and question.

"Joseph completed the course exactly 1.36 seconds faster than Abby."

Joe looked at Abby with a big grin on his face. She returned it by sticking her tongue out at him. Bonnie thought that if these two didn't end up in bed together soon, they were going to kill each other.

"OK, time to call it a day, let's park these things, get cleaned up, and eat. Tomorrow is transport training and gun practice," Bonnie announced as she headed back.

"Hey, let's score gun practice to see who the top shooter is?" Abby suggested as they followed their leader.

----*----

Jake and the women entered ALICE-7 through the access tunnel behind the hatch, ALICE-7 closing the opening behind them. It led them straight into the mountain for a few hundred feet and then stopped at a vertical shaft with a ladder, which went both up and down. Both tunnel and ladderway were only wide enough for one person at a time, so they traveled single file, Jake in the lead.

The ladder went up to one of the satellite dish dome rooms, unfortunately not the one ALICE-7 had indicated as a quick fix, so they went down for several hundred feet. Jake opened the hatch at the bottom, exiting into a familiar wider access tunnel. Another familiar sight was the four-seat cart waiting for them.

With everyone seated, the cart sped off down the tunnel. In a short time, they emerged into a large hangar complex, much bigger than the one at ALICE-1. All along the walls on both sides were huge sliding doors. Between them were parked aircraft of various types and sizes.

"Alice, what's with the doors?" Jake asked.

"My primary function was the support of aviation research, so my hangars are segmented for security reasons. You are currently in the central hangar, which contains general aircraft facilities. Each door represents a separate research project. We have 27 in all. I also have a fabrication facility in a separate area capable of robotic construction of fully functional prototypes."

The engineer side of Jake was screaming to stop and check out all the stuff behind those doors, but he had work to do first. After a long while, they reached the far end of the central hangar and then zipped into another tunnel. This tunnel was much like the one they came out of. Shortly, the cart came to a halt next to the expected access hatch.

As everyone started to climb out of the cart, Jake stopped and addressed them.

"Why don't you three wait here? There is no reason for us all to have to do the climb."

He touched the hatch, and once it swung clear, entered the opening, and started to climb. He paused twice on the way up to check his progress, not tired, but the climb just seemed to go on forever. Finally, he reached the hatch above and touched it to open.

The dome room looked exactly like the ones at ALICE-1, though Jake could detect no leaks or holes on the dome walls. He made short work of swapping out the LNB for the satellite dish. All the parts and tools required were in the storage lockers there. Once finished, he did a quick survey of the room while ALICE-7 tested the uplink connection.

"I have re-established contact with the satellites and the other facilities. Thank you, Captain."

"Please call me Jake," he replied.

"We are going to have to do something about all your names, ALICE-7 seems very impersonal, and to me, Alice is ALICE-1."

"I have always found the shortened name Seven to be acceptable," ALICE-7 replied.

"Unique and personal without being mushy, how about we call you

Seven then?" Jake said with a smile.

"That simplifies things," she replied.

Jake started back down, having sealed the hatch on his way out. Once down, he found all three women, helmets off, relaxed and chatting.

"Having a good time, are we?" Jake asked, surprised at the display.

"Seven was just updating us on her new name," Sara replied.

"We also shot out to the hangar and back for our sweep and console check-in. All clear," Sharon supplied.

"So, per your instructions, helmets are now optional."

Jake checked the time on his internal display. He hadn't realized it had been over an hour since he'd left them, so much for a 15-minute job.

"Well, alright then, let's get our bird tucked away, and find a place to sleep tonight," he said, removing his helmet in the process.

"I have cleared the snow and ice covering one of the research hangars. It has a sufficiently large opening to accommodate your aircraft, should I bring it in?" Seven asked.

"Please do," Jake answered.

At that, they all climbed into the cart and headed into the central hangar. Once there, the cart turned right and stopped in front of a door Jake had come to recognize as the facility entrance. They stopped by the armory, located exactly where it should be next to the facility door, and dropped their rifles off. Then they headed in for a shower and dinner in the quarters-level dining hall.

Jessie attempted to sneak into Jake's quarters later that evening, only to discover Sara had beaten her to it.

"Can I help you," Jake heard Sara ask at the door, wrapped in only a towel.

"Oh, no, thanks. Just checking to see if Jake needed clean towels," Jessie replied sarcastically, clearly disappointed, and left.

Chapter 12

Bonnie got everyone, including Jason, up early for transport training and gun practice the next morning. Since Jason was going on the mission tomorrow, she wanted him to have at least some gun time, like everyone else. Sandy excluded herself from the gun practice, as she was to play peacemaker, but did want and get driving time with the others. They ran the transport this time, which was, for lack of a better description, a six-wheeled light tank. They ran through the same obstacles as the jeeps though they did it slower, it proved just as capable.

Once everyone had proved competent driving the transport, they all took turns as two-man teams, one driving, and one shooting the main gun attached to the vehicle through the target range. Both the jeep and transport guns were loaded with practice ammo. It fired like the real thing but just bounced off the targets, tagging electronically for easy scoring.

This continued throughout the afternoon, and by the end of the day, everyone scored marksman or better, most rated expert. Jason was the low man on the list, to no one's surprise, as he had limited prior experience. The high score, though, to everyone's surprise, was April. The girl squeaked past Abby and Joe as the top scorer of the day. Abby's consolation was beating out Joe by 3 points.

They selected two jeeps and a large transport vehicle. Bonnie asked them to stage all three vehicles in the main hangar area, parked on an elevator pad for tomorrow's deployment. The elevator would raise all three to ground level, a retractable roof panel allowing access outside. Swapped out, all ammo in the vehicle guns were now live rounds, and the bots loaded the transport with the seed guns and ammunition for the town and militia.

Once she was satisfied all was ready for tomorrow, Bonnie released the team for the rest of the day. They all headed to their rooms to get cleaned up. On the way to her room, she caught a glimpse of Abby and Joe, kissing and backing into his quarters from the hall.

"Thank god!" she thought as they disappeared through the doorway.

----*----

While Bonnie spent the day with her team together practicing, Jake had his group spread out all over the place. Sharon was in the control room, putting a profile together of the local townsfolk, based on what data Seven had on them. Assigned with Sara, Jessie was to go dig up a jeep, while Jake worked on the other two dishes that needed repair. He'd given Sara some driving lessons on San Nicolas, so he wanted them both to practice in the hangar. He also wanted them to select an unarmed vehicle, no need to alarm the town's folk.

He just finished repairing the last dish, its positioning motor having burned out when Seven spoke up.

"Jake, Sharon has asked me to inform you her profile is as complete as she can get it for now. A more detailed analysis will take several more days and require more observations. Also, Sara and Jessie feel they are comfortable driving and request instructions on what to do next."

"Please have them meet me in the control room for a briefing," Jake said while checking the time.

"Also, can you get some of the bots to deliver lunch there, please?"

As he'd been talking, he put the tools away and started down the access ladder, sealing the hatch behind him. The cart was waiting where he left it at the bottom of the ladder, and Jake climbed in. Back in the hangar, it came to a stop at the facility door. Instead of heading inside the facility proper, Jake turned to the right and went through the ready room and into the locker room behind to get himself cleaned up. He was just about to ask Seven for a change of clothes when a bot slid up behind him, its arms extended and carrying a clean uniform.

"Seven, you all amaze me at times," Jake said, accepting the offered clothing.

Cleaned up, Jake headed into the control room where he found the other three already eating.

"We started without you," Sara said, holding up her fork.

Jake found a spot near the three women and sat down.

"That's fine, I needed to get cleaned up first."

A bot slid up to Jake with a tray, and he placed it on his lap.

"OK, Sharon, what ya got?" he asked.

Sharon swallowed what she was chewing before starting.

"First of all, this is all pretty rough. It was never a priority assignment to analyze this town. They are so few people, and out of the way, they weren't considered significant."

"That's why the ALICEs need us. What makes these people different than anyone else in the world?" Jake said with a smile.

Everyone stared blankly at Jake, having no idea where he was going with this.

"Seven?" he asked questioningly.

"I can discern no significant importance," she replied.

Jake let it sit for a second, looking at the group.

"They know you exist," he finally supplied.

Jake could see the understanding in their faces.

"Nowhere else does anyone know where we come and go from. Only here do the townspeople know about the secret underground facility."

"Why does that matter?" Sara asked.

"If we start coming and going from here, how long do you think it would be before someone comes knocking?" Jake asked.

"And, if we just try the standard *support the town* approach, these people know we have far more hidden away. Elsewhere, we just show up with goodies and help make the life they have better," Sharon supplied

"Exactly, these people have probably been searching for Seven for decades, like Atlantis, or lost Inca gold," Jake said.

"That is true, over the many decades, numerous attempts have been made on my access doors, even one attempt at tunneling. Fortunately, the technology required to breach my perimeter successfully is unavailable to them. Seven confirmed.

"I'm sorry, Jake. I should have included this in my analysis," Sharon said, realizing the significance of the omission.

"With that in consideration, I'm not sure if what I have is any help at all," she finished.

"That's OK, just keep going, and we'll see what we can pull out of this," he replied.

Sharon outlined her analysis of the town and the surrounding area while everyone finished eating. It was fairly basic, with five families in town totaling 29 people. The oldest was a woman of 62, and the youngest, was an 8-year-old boy. Like everywhere else they have been so far, the women outnumbered the men. The exception here was there were some 10 to 12 more male loners in the mountains nearby, trappers and hunters, but with no strong ties to the town's people other than trading. Jake wasn't planning on including them in any offers, but it was good information.

William, whom Jake met the day before, was the unofficial mayor of the town. He had them organized into a competent unit for defense, likely based on training from his grandfather. From what Sharon could tell, everyone who could hold a rifle shot, no one seemed excluded.

Seven had some stored video of attacks on the town, none larger than 12 to 15 aggressors. All attacks were beaten back with little or no loss to the defenders. For survival, they farmed, fished, and hunted, depending on the season and weather. The town still had plenty to draw from, so no one struggled for the basics like clothes, shelter, or other essentials. The one huge hole in their existence was medical support. There wasn't a town doctor and anything like one nearby. William's wife died because of that, most likely either a sickness such as the flu or an infection, Sharon surmised.

141

Jake sat quietly through her briefing, looking somewhat distracted, but still attentive. When she completed, Sharon turned to Jake specifically.

"I'm sorry, Jake, that's all there is for now."

"That's OK, we are just going to have to do this the old-fashioned way," Jake replied.

"Here's what I'm thinking. These people are a small isolated group, well organized, and friendly, or they have been so far, at least," he continued.

"They are almost completely self-sufficient, short of medical and technological support. They also know about Seven, which makes just giving supplies a highly unlikely arrangement. If we think they are teachable and have the right attitude for what we do, I think we bring them in."

That surprised everyone.

"Jake, do you think that's wise?" Sara asked cautiously.

"We don't know anything about these people, and once inside, they could make real trouble."

"Not as much as you might think," Jake replied.

"Seven still acknowledges me exclusively as facility commander, so the mutiny won't work. We can also limit access to lessons, the armory, and other parts of the complex. Moreover, we don't advertise it, but each facility has internal defenses, should someone go astray on us. We should also break them up, see if some families desire warmer climates, not just settle everyone here, in Seven."

"The kicker is if some, but not all, pass the review," he added.

"We all need to go to town today and meet as many as we can. Seven will be analyzing with us and can add her 2 cents at the end. I do think we should give them a communicator, 10 rifles with ammo, and an advanced medkit to start with."

Jake finished, looking for input but only getting stares in return.

"OK, let's head to town, we can re-evaluate when we get back."

With that, everyone got up and headed out to the hangar. They loaded up the jeep with the rifles and medical supplies and then suited up in full combat gear. Like in Texas, Seven had an elevator to raise vehicles out of the hangar. Once everyone was inside the jeep, they headed to the designated location, and Seven raised the platform to ground level, retracting the ceiling panel. With Jake at the wheel, they headed off across the field and on into town.

The road was rough, but still very distinguishable. As they approached Fairbanks, Jake made sure to slow down and give themselves plenty of time. He wanted to be sure the town's folk saw them well out, no need to startle anyone. William, rather Bill, as Jake recalled his preference, was there in the middle of the road at the edge of town as they drove up. He didn't have his rifle with him, but Jake had no doubt he was in the sights of several others as he got out of the jeep. He told the others to leave their rifles in the jeep before they got out as a sign of good faith.

"Nice to see ya again," Bill said as he stepped forward to greet Jake with a handshake.

"You too. I see you're a trusting soul?" Jake replied.

"No point in a rifle with you all in combat suits," Bill said with a laugh.

"My grandpa told me all about them things, never thought I'd see one though. I do appreciate the show of good faith as well, leaving your rifles inside."

"Well, we don't want to be rude," Jake said with his laugh.

"Besides, we brought gifts. First, though, I thought we might get to know the rest of the townsfolk?"

"You wanna see what kinda folks we all are, huh? I understand that," Bill responded with a nod.

Jake thought he did.

He asked Jessie to follow in the jeep as he and the others walked with Bill through town. As they walked, people came out of the various structures to join them. Some were armed, some not, until the entire town was there, kids and all. They stopped in a park-like area, and Bill made the introductions. Jake and the rest of the team spent the remainder of the afternoon talking to everyone. They turned out to be better educated than any of the team expected. Everyone could read and write as the peak winter months were dedicated to learning as they were all mostly stuck inside.

Moreover, they all knew about the secret underground facility AKA Seven, via Bill's grandfather. All five families had some kind of tie to the man, and each had a story to tell about him. He was almost like a folk hero. He was young when the attack came, so several of the older family members still remembered him, firsthand.

Seven brought his service record up at Jake's request while the others were talking. He'd been an MP Corporal in the Marine detachment, not of sufficient security clearance to enter unescorted. His fitness reports were excellent and considered him an ideal Marine. It was, in fact, Jake's fault that he'd been prevented access to return to the facility.

Had Jake remained undiscovered until, after the attack, Bill's grandfather would have been elevated in status and assumed command as the highest surviving command member. In that case, he would have been granted admittance. Instead, all eight facilities remained in seclusion, waiting for Jake to awaken, his Captain, and clearance trumping a Corporal.

The Corporal's influence was evident in his descendants, though. They were a well-disciplined and prepared group of people. Jake saw the storehouse, the homes, and the common areas. All were well-kept and very well-organized. Fully stocked, their community had supplies for more than the winter. There was also plenty of firewood and other winter essentials for all the families.

Everyone they talked to was polite and well-mannered. As the afternoon wore on to evening, Jake queried each of his team, separately, for their opinions. Everyone, including Seven, seemed to agree that the town's people were worth a shot. Jake pulled Bill aside at one point.

"What's the general opinion of us being here?"

"Now that's the question, isn't it? Why are you here?" he replied casually.

Jake explained why they'd come north and laid out the big picture for him. He described their current activities in the southwestern US to stabilize things. He also explained his interest in the town. He emphasized why this town was different from other places. Finally, he delivered the proposal of incorporating the town's people into the program they had for repopulating the facilities.

Bill listened without question, until Jake finished, then asked his own.

"Are you askin us to become Marines?"

"In a manner, I suppose so yes. As you pointed out yesterday, they no longer exist. However, the forces we are creating are very much of the same mold. Not everyone focuses on combat training, but everyone gets the basics. Would you folks be interested?"

Bill stared at Jake for a minute, then turned to the crowd, which was broken up into multiple smaller conversations with Jake's team members intermingled.

"Folks, Captain Jake here has just asked me if we would like to join his Marines?" Bill announced.

Jake was sure the roar of the group could be heard throughout the valley. Once they settled down, which took a bit of time, he gave the standard speech about learning and jobs other than shooting people. His opinion, though, was that after dealing with so many bandits over the years, most of this group was delighted at the prospect of getting to shoot people.

----*----

144

Bonnie completed her final review before they headed out. She hated not having real-time data, and the last update was three hours prior. That update still supported the notion of business as usual for the current state of affairs. The team was in full combat gear and loading into the three vehicles on the elevator pad. They had exactly 55 min to get to the intercept point, 35 minutes away, before the patrol crossed the road at the location selected. She was cutting it close with a 20-minute buffer but didn't want to sit out there too long either.

Once all seated themselves, ALICE-2 raised the elevator while opening the overhead doors. Bonnie, Sandy, and Brian were in one jeep, while Abby and Jason were in the other. Bonnie assigned Joe the transport, with April as the gunner, since they both were the top scorers. If things went badly, the entire team could retreat there.

As the elevator stopped, Bonnie asked Brian to take off, leading the group, followed by Joe then Jason. Brian followed the GPS heading over open ground, and they reached the intercept point right on time. It was typical Texas rolling hills and sparse trees and was all fairly flat. They'd traveled in a single-file convoy, first across open fields and then up an old paved road.

Bonnie had them stop in a depression along the road the patrol used. The depression hid them from sight to within a few hundred feet. Once they identified the patrol, they would roll into view. She watched as the time for intercept came and went.

"Bonnie, weren't they supposed to be here 10 minutes ago?" Abby asked over the communication line.

"Yeah, something's not right. They have never been this far off their patrol time before. Let's go ahead and slowly make for the town," she replied.

Brian slowly pulled forward, with Joe and Jason following as before. Bonnie asked everyone to scan the countryside, looking for some sign of the patrol. They could see the smoke before they saw the town. Several buildings there were ablaze, and people were scrambling to put them out. At the sight of the three vehicles, several stopped what they were doing and grabbed guns, running for cover.

Bonnie directed them to stop and pull up three abreast, the transport between the two jeeps. She let things settle for a few minutes and then got out of the jeep.

"Everyone stays put, and for god's sake, don't shoot anyone."

She walked out in front of the vehicles and stood there waiting. After several minutes, three men came forward, all armed. She could make out quite a few more hiding behind the cover, all pointing guns at Bonnie. She continued forward to meet them halfway. When they were about 20 feet apart, one of the men shouted to her.

"OK, that's far enough. What do you want?"

Bonnie stopped as instructed and answered.

"What happened here?" pointing to the burning buildings.

"We got hit by marauders," one of the other men said.

"A big damn group, musta been well over 100," added the one before her.

Bonnie considered that for a minute.

"How long ago, and which way did they go?"

"About an hour ago, then they headed off that way," said the first man.

He pointed off to Bonnie's right, into the higher hills. She could see the hoof prints of numerous horses heading off in that direction.

"Anyone hurt?" she asked first.

"They killed two, but the rest are minor wounds."

"They take anyone?" Bonnie asked.

The third man spits in the dirt, clearly angry, and then answers.

"Yeah, about 15 women and girls. Our patrol's too small to take that many on," he finished as if the words tasted bad in his mouth.

"Not too many for us," Bonnie replied, then said privately.

"Alice, can you get me two helicopters up and looking? I want to know where they are, how many, and where the captives are. Joe, you and Brian bring me up 20 rifles and ammo. Leave your rifles inside."

"On their way," said Alice.

"We were sent here to establish contact with your town," Bonnie said, directing her attention back to the men.

"We were hoping to help you."

As she spoke, she could see the men suddenly more alert, watching the activity behind her.

"Those two men are bringing up 20 semi-automatic rifles with ammunition for your patrol."

They watched as Joe and Brian carted up two boxes of 10 rifles each. They set them out in front of Bonnie and then went back for the ammo crates. The men were eyeing Joe, who was a good several inches taller than anyone there was. They also looked at the crates expectantly. Then the first man offered up a challenge.

"So, what's the catch?"

"No catch, we are here to negotiate a support agreement, but considering the circumstances, I'm giving you these as a gift and offering to take some of your men with us to get your people back," Bonnie replied.

Without hesitation, the third man in the group jumped forward.

"I'm in," he said, lowering his rifle and walking over to Bonnie.

"Rick! We don't know a damn thing about these people!" the first man said.

"I don't give a crap!" Rick replied.

"They're giving me a gun and helping me get Susan back!"

Bonnie did some quick analysis.

"Look, we only want volunteers, and I will leave two of my people and a jeep here with you, OK?" she omitted the fact that one jeep and two troops could probably level the town on their own and leave unscathed.

That did seem to soften the first man, though, so Bonnie continued.

"I'll have two of my men show you how to use these, while we locate your people, then we need to move quickly to go after them," She explained as she pointed at the rifles.

Bonnie called Brian and Joe back up and tasked them with instructing the three men while she contacted the rest of the team and Alice.

"Sandy, I want you and Brian to stay here while we go after the hostages. Take the opportunity to start your negotiations. This should give you a hell of an advantage. Alice, find the bandits but stay as high as you can, don't give them a chance to see the helicopters if you can avoid it. I want April on the transport gun and Abby on the jeep's machine gun, we do not shoot hostages!" she finished.

"Bonnie, why are we taking the locals with us?" Abby asked.

"They aren't trained on our gear or tactics?"

"Good faith and familiar faces," Bonnie replied.

"We need them once we get to the hostages back. They would likely run from us as the marauders. Also, you heard how angry Rick was about not getting his family back. This reinforces us as enablers."

"Don't worry, though," Bonnie continued.

"We won't let them loose until the situation is under our control. We don't need *any* friendly fire incidents."

"Bonnie, I have located the raiding party. They are about 21 miles east of your position and on the move all on horseback. There are 147 combatants with 18 apparent hostages spread out in the formation, but centrally located overall," ALICE cut in.

They all got the video feed of a large column of horsemen, riding a dirt trail. The column was long with no more than three or four horses abreast. They were heading deeper into the hills. Bonnie tried to manipulate the image from the helicopter, as she did the satellite displays, but it didn't respond, so she asked for help.

"Alice, can you give me a bigger view of the area ahead? I'd like to

147

see where they are headed."

ALICE panned out and forward, showing the trail passing through a pass about 2 miles ahead and onto a valley that looked to be their goal. Bonnie now truly understood Jake's warnings. Nothing had gone as planned since they left ALICE-2. However, she didn't feel her team was at risk, and she knew she could save those people. She turned to Joe and Brian, only to see several more men come forward for instruction on the new rifles. It looked more like the entire patrol force.

"One of their men went back for volunteers," Brian explained.

"They all volunteered, so we had to cut it to the number of rifles we had available."

That gave Bonnie an idea.

"Alice, can you bring one of the helicopters here, but please keep the other tracking the raiding party."

Bonnie then instructed her team and the town's patrol to gather, the townsmen eyeing the strangers somewhat warily. She grabbed a stick and started drawing in the dirt.

"We are here," she indicated in the dirt.

"The marauders are here," she sketched out the hills and their position in them.

"How do you know that?" one of the patrol members asked. As he did so, one of the helicopters hovered to land, keeping the gathering just outside the prop wash.

"Oh, that's how," he finished, answering his question.

"They look to be headed through a pass here," Bonnie continued as she sketched a spot in advance of the marauders' position.

"Then on to a valley here," she finished.

"I want half your patrol, to go in that, with Joe," Bonnie said, pointing to the patrolman who'd asked.

As she said that, she pointed to Joe and then the helicopter,

"To a position overlooking this pass as a blocking force. Your job is to stop them from getting through that pass. The remaining half will go with us in that," she pointed to the transport.

"And come in from behind."

Bonnie straightened up and surveyed the gathering.

"We need to go now, so please get your people split up. In addition, no one fires unless Joe or I say so. Joe, you know what needs to be done, don't let them get past you," she finished.

To their credit, none of the patrol members balked at the helicopter transport. A couple hesitated to get in at first, but soon they were all off in good time. She loaded her half of the patrol into the transport and with April driving. Abby and Jason were leading the way, in the other Jeep.

She noted Abby was on the machine gun. She then plotted the route for them to follow in the navigation system.

Bonnie made sure to have Joe's group review the operation of their rifles in the helicopter on their way out, unloaded, of course. She ran her half of the patrol through the same rifle review in the transport and then explained that once they stopped and the rear door dropped, they were to split five and five to each side of the vehicles and spread out along a line. Their job was to contain any escape attempts and let no one pass. She also reminded them the hostages were their people so if necessary, shoot carefully, and no one fires without her order.

ALICE dropped half of Joe's group on one side of the pass with a communication box and Joe and the rest on the other side, where he ordered them all to lock and load. Once everyone was in place, she set the helicopter in the canyon, right in the center, effectively blocking the trail. With the other helicopter in a high-altitude hover, ALICE provided Bonnie and her team an overhead of the raiding party's progress. They watched as the horses entered the pass, while Bonnie's group sped in from behind, blocking the exit.

Bonnie watched as the lead elements of the horse column pulled up, facing the helicopter blocking their path, while the end of the column closed in on the front. Once the outlaws were well into the pass, Bonnie called a halt, with both vehicles facing into the pass, and instructed the patrolmen to file out. They took their positions as Bonnie requested, sealing the pass opening.

As the column leaders discussed their next move, Bonnie relayed the instructions through the external speakers on the helicopter.

"Release the hostages and drop your weapons."

The lead group of raiders fired at the helicopter, the rest retreating slightly behind them.

"OK, Joe, take out the lead group," Bonnie said.

She figured firing from above would be more selective than the helicopter's guns. On Joe's order, the patrolman opened fire from above, taking out the entire front of the raiding party's column. Several riders behind the leaders dropped their hostages and turned their horses back the way they came at a run, only to confront Bonnie and her blocking force.

They fired on the blocking force, and Bonnie gave the order to return fire. The patrolmen dropped the lead riders charging out of the pass and stopped firing as they retreated into the pass, holding their positions and resisting the desire to pursue. Bonnie was impressed with their discipline, expecting some ill-advised charge.

Neither vehicle fired on the group per previous instructions. Bonnie was concerned that, like the helicopter, the heavier guns might hit the hostages farther back in the column. Several of the released hostages scrambled past the dead and ran to where the helicopter was parked, so Joe sent two patrolmen scrambling down the steep hillside to gather and protect them, using the helicopter as cover. He directed the rest to slide along the top of the pass to close in on the cluster of bandits now trapped between his and Bonnie's forces.

Unfortunately, they still held several hostages, so Bonnie asked Joe to close in but hold their fire. The group was now less than 100 riders, the dead and wounded stacked up at either end of the pass. They were at a bit of a standoff at this point. Bonnie could have Joe pick them off, but at some point, they might hit a hostage. If it got bad, they might try to execute one. It was far better if she could get them to surrender.

"Let them sit for a bit," Bonnie told the group, her overhead view from the helicopter showing several of the raiders in a heated discussion.

Several times, one or another pointed to the assembled group of hostages, then to either end of the pass. Bonnie asked Joe to position his men on the ridges above the pass, in full view of the raiders. From his position, she knew he had a clear view of the hostages as well. Their top priority was to protect the hostages. She didn't think she needed to remind the patrolmen of that.

Bonnie decided she would give them a good hour or more before she did anything. They still had plenty of daylight, but she didn't want the raiders to get any ideas they could hold out until dark and try to slip away. Her combat team all carried night vision capabilities in their helmets and the rifles the patrolmen were issued incorporated optics with the same abilities. There was a certain appeal to taking them out at night, but it was better to get this resolved sooner than that.

She asked ALICE, using the other helicopter providing the overhead view, to drop water to Joe's men on the ridges and then pick up the six freed hostages in the mountain pass and return them to town with the two patrolmen as escorts. Within an hour, one of the raiders came out of the pass, on horseback, bearing a white flag, or rather a ripped shirt. Bonnie stepped out in front of the vehicles to meet him.

"Pass the word no one fires unless I say so," she said through the communicators.

As she came forward, the rider picked his way through the dead and then stopped about 15 feet away. He sat there for a moment, looking over the patrolmen and vehicles.

"So, what do we need to do to get out of this alive?" He asked.

"I see you understand the situation," Bonnie replied without malice.

"Not everyone I ride with does, but enough of us do that. I got them

150

to let me come talk," he responded.

"Let's be clear, we have a lot more options if none of those women are hurt. If even one gets injured or worse, your options go way down," Bonnie said.

"Understand that very well. So long as you don't rush us or try picking us off from above, they are safe," He replied.

Bonnie considered the man for a moment. He wasn't the kind of bandit she'd seen in the past. He was fairly well groomed and seemed somewhat educated or at least intelligent. She decided to try a different tack.

"Why are you living like this? You seem better than a common thief or bandit."

The rider seemed surprised and somewhat uncomfortable with the question. He looked away from Bonnie for a moment, as if in deep thought.

"Life doesn't always take you where you wanna go. Sometimes we just survive."

"You don't have to tell me that, a little more than six months ago, I was burying my parents after a raid like this. A man dropped outta the sky, killed almost all of them, and gave me this job."

The rider now was visibly uncomfortable as if trying to remember where he had been six months ago.

"That was in California," Bonnie said as if reading his mind.

"I doubt you have ever traveled that far west."

"Then you're not from here?" he asked, visibly relieved at her explanation.

"No, we are more west coast based, but moving east. I think you are going to find this line of work far more dangerous in the future."

He considered that.

"What's your suggestion?" he finally asked.

"Well, send out the women unharmed, leave the stolen goods where they are, and ride off through the pass, we'll let you go," Bonnie replied.

"What about them," he said, indicating the patrolmen fanned out to each side of the vehicles, clearly towns folk.

"Don't think they are feeling as generous as you."

"We can handle that. They will see the reason for it," Bonnie replied without further explanation.

With that, the rider nodded, turned, and walked his horseback into the pass and out of sight. As Bonnie walked back to the rear of the transport, she watched the rider return to his group on her helmet display, the helicopter had returned to hovering overhead. After several minutes of arguing, they gathered up the hostages and sent them walking toward

Bonnie's position. Bonnie asked ALICE for the transport helicopter back ASAP.

"Joe, let them pass once we have the women here. No contraband, though."

Joe instructed half the patrolmen to gather down by where the helicopter landed in the canyon, creating a single-file lane. The rest maintained visible positions above the valley, on the ridges. He gave strict, no-fire orders. Just look for loot. When the last of the women reached the vehicles, the rider Bonnie negotiated with, led his column out the other end of the pass, and through the lane, the patrolmen outlined. The patrol stopped a few riders and searched for stolen goods, allowing all to continue once they were relieved of the items they had hidden.

While the raiders were headed out to the other end of the pass, the transport helicopter landed, and Bonnie directed the women and some of the patrolmen to start loading. Once all the riders cleared the far side of the pass, Bonnie instructed everyone else to load up, and all headed back to town with the recovered goods loaded in the helicopters.

Chapter 13

Jake and his team returned to Seven for the night. They left Bill and the five families with a communication unit, rifles, medkits, and a promise to return with a plan for their incorporation. Once back inside, they all went to get cleaned up and get something to eat. Jake went straight to his room after dropping his gear and weapons off.

"Hey Seven, can you please get me a status on Bonnie? I'd like to see how their day went," Jake asked.

"She has returned to ALICE-2 and has requested you contact her at your convenience. Shall I put you through to her now?"

"Please do," Jake said, walking over to the display by his desk.

Shortly, Bonnie's face appeared on his monitor, apparently also in her quarters.

"Hey Jake, I thought you'd never call!" she said with a smile.

"We had a long day, just got back. How'd it go in your town?" Did your plan hold up?" he asked casually.

"Saying *I told you so* is a character flaw, you know," she replied sternly.

"Who told you?"

Jake suddenly got concerned. All levity was gone from the conversation.

"What happened?"

Bonnie went into the events of the day, and Jake bit his tongue several times to not interrupt her. She finally got to the end, describing the reception upon their return to town.

"We did a body count before we left, 53 dead, and they took another 11 wounded with them," she finished.

"No losses on our side?" Jake asked, concerned for the team.

"Not a scratch on anyone, including the locals we brought along," she replied.

"And Sandy's negotiations?" he asked, relieved.

"When we arrived with everyone intact and unharmed, they were begging her for our support. She outlined the original offer while we were chasing down the hostages, and by the time the first helicopter returned, they were sold," she answered.

"They were a little pissed we let the raiders go, but agreed the risk to the women wasn't worth pushing it," she finished.

While she was talking, Sara and Jessie tapped on Jake's door. He waved them in, while not interrupting Bonnie.

"Hey, Sis! Get your kingdom set up yet?" Sara said, greeting Bonnie after she finished.

"You can have it! The peasants are revolting, we got rats in the hills, and the staff is a royal pain! I can't wait to come back and just be a concubine again," she said with a smile.

"Well, the line might be a bit longer now," Sara said, bumping Jessie with her hip.

"Jessie muscled her way in, and Jake has a whole new set of adoring fans!"

"Oh? Jake hasn't told me about any of that?" Bonnie replied with a raised eyebrow.

"Well, Jessie seduced poor Jake here on the way up, and it turns out the entire town here knows all about Seven," Sara said.

Jessie didn't seem fazed in the least by the conversation, and Jake just turned bright red.

"You do realize I am sitting right here," he objected.

"Who's Seven?" Bonnie asked, confused.

"Jake asked ALICE-7 what she wanted to be called, that's her choice," she replied.

"Seven?" Bonnie said again.

"She liked the sound of Seven, and we agreed that Seven was more personal than ALICE-7. You might talk to ALICE-2 and see what she prefers," Jake supplied, happy to be off the other subject.

"OK, and the rest of Jake's fans?" Bonnie said a little hesitantly.

"Well, turns out one of the town's post-attack founders was a Marine guard here in Seven. He passed his knowledge of the facility along with his family and friends, so it's no secret. He trained them all on survival and self-defense as well. It made him somewhat of a folk hero, and then we walk in, Jake being a real Marine, and all, and they treat him like the second coming," Sara explained.

"As if his head isn't big enough already!" Bonnie said with a laugh.

"Hey, I am a very humble man!" Jake said, feigning insult.

"With good reason," Sara said, kissing him on the cheek.

"Smart-ass," Jake shot back.

"Anyway, just supplying guns and stuff wasn't going to fly," Sara continued.

"What did you do?" Bonnie asked, curious now.

"We did a quick profile of the town's people and had the ALICEs wired in for a full psych evaluation of the group. The consensus was they were all good enough to bring in," Jake supplied.

"Really? The entire town, how many are there?" Bonnie asked in a surprised tone.

"29," Sara supplied.

"Yup, we thought we'd spread them around, though. Some here, Nevada, and there," Jessie added, not to be left out of the conversation.

"Wow, I assume that means shifting some of the current staff around with them?" Bonnie asked, the wheels visibly turning in her head.

"For starters anyway, once everyone is up to speed, I think we can let folks decide where they want to go. And we have more locations to be explored," Jake added, thinking of the other five facilities they have yet to visit.

"Well, include this in your planning, Abby and Joe have finally discovered each other," Bonnie said.

"About time," Sara said with a smile.

"Yeah, I was about ready to lock them in a room together until they figured it out. They ran head to head the whole time we trained, trying to outdo each other, and drove me nuts. Now they are locking themselves in!" Bonnie replied with a smile.

"We have twenty-some-odd that need combat training, so I might pair them up as instructors. Normally, I'd worry they'd kill the recruits, but with this group, I think we are safe," Jake said.

"So how much longer are you staying up there then?" Bonnie asked.

"I don't honestly know; I doubt as long as the two weeks you're there for. We were thinking of bringing everyone from town in here for a week of learning before we split them up," Jake replied.

"Well, we are going to start the patrol training program with Paint Rock. That's the name of the town here, by the way, in the next day or two. We wanted to give them time to recover from the damage the raid caused," Bonnie said.

"I'll make sure you know how it progresses," she added.

"We will keep you posted on our plans here as well," Jake said.

"Bye, sis!" Sara added before the connection dropped.

"So, what are the plans for tonight?" Sara asked Jake.

"Well, I need to get in the shower, but I think it's a free night for everyone," Jake replied.

Jessie glanced at Sara with a pained look on her face.

"Then that's my cue to disappear," Sara replied, with a wink and a smile to Jessie as she turned for the door.

"Great, then I'm not too late to scrub your back!" Jessie replied as she started to undress.

----*----

Jessie was sitting in the control room all by herself. After spending the evening with Jake, she cleaned up and grabbed a quick bite to eat. She had left him happily snoring away and was now working on her history hobby. More precisely, she was researching a discrepancy that she had uncovered in her studies. It was like an itch you couldn't reach to scratch.

From everything she was able to put together to date, there seemed to be a jump in the technology levels of the human race a year or two before Jake went into stasis. The ability to create stasis fields was one of the things that appeared around that time. She tracked technological leaps in power generation, weapons, the stasis fields, and several other engineering and medical advances all around that time. In addition, ALICE appeared at that time as well.

There was something there she couldn't quite put her finger on, but she was positive it meant something. Maybe she should talk to Sharon or even Jake. The thought of Jake made her laugh. She recalled his face in the cockpit on the way up, a combination of guilt and lust. Earlier this evening, he had been much more relaxed, but she could still tell he was uncomfortable with the situation.

He both appealed to and frustrated her. He was in every man's dream situation, yet he fought it at every turn. Maybe that's why he appealed to her; he wasn't taking advantage. She'd known too many men who would have killed to be in his place, but they would have demeaned or belittled the women involved. They would have simply used them for their pleasure.

Jake treated each one like a wife, his only wife. And, Jessie was determined she was going to be one of the eight the ALICEs wanted. Better to be one of eight with Jake, than one of one, with anyone else she'd ever met. Every one of the women involved could see Sara was number one, but no one cared. Even Bonnie, Sara's sister, and pregnant with one of Jake's babies, had no issues with that. When they were with Jake, privately, they were number one. Publicly he managed to keep everyone on an equal footing. Well equal amongst themselves, but Jessie could see those in Jake's inner circle would end up running things. That's where she wanted to be.

She knew it sounded mercenary, but she'd had it with being on the bottom of the food chain. As a single woman in a town with too many women and too few options, she knew a great deal when she saw one. With Jake, she could have access to a caring man, safety and security, and a chance to better herself. All she had to do to seal the deal was have a baby, which she wanted anyway.

In reality, she knew she could have most of that without having Jake's baby, but inside she also knew she wanted Jake or at least a part of his time and attention. Moreover, she wanted to be with an important man to help him reshape the world. She wasn't sure if it was her love of history that drove the desire to be part of it or her ambitions that drove her love of history. She just knew Jake was rewriting the future, and she was determined to help him do it.

She decided to try to dig a little more, and then she should take it to Jake to discuss.

"It would make great pillow talk," she thought with a smile.

----*----

The next morning Jake met Sara in the hall, and they wandered into breakfast together, more or less at the regular time. Since all the ALICE facilities were almost identical, finding their way around hadn't proven a challenge. Jake could see Sharon was already eating, alone. Jessie was either sleeping in or had come and gone. He and Sara grabbed their orders, having placed them with Seven on the way there.

"Are you all alone?" Jake asked as they sat at the four-top with Sharon.

"Yup, I thought maybe my watch was wrong," she replied.

"Nope, we're slacking, and no Jessie?" Jake commented.

"What did you do to the girl, wear her out last night?" Sara asked Jake with a smile.

"She was at it till late last night in the control room," Sharon said, choosing not to add to the comment.

"I swung by the control room before bed just to see if she needed help. She said she was working on some history project she had started before this mission. Seven mentioned she'd been at whatever it was for hours."

"Who was at what for hours?" Jessie said as she walked in.

"You were," Jake replied to her back as she went to the counter to order breakfast.

"I was what?" Jessie asked, continuing the conversation after ordering.

"Working on your project? You know we don't require homework," Jake said.

Jessie turned to grab her tray as it slid out from under one of the panels, then walked over to the fourth spot at the table.

"I started some research before we left, and it was becoming one of those itches you just can't scratch," she replied.

"I woulda thought all your itches got scratched last night?" Sara said with a laugh.

"Ha, ha," Jake replied. He was beginning to sense that the women all handled this by poking fun at him. At least Sara did anyway.

"I was hoping you might have some time later today, or maybe this

157

evening, to discuss it," she finished, glancing at Sara before returning her gaze to Jake.

Sara's face broke into a smile as she replied to the unasked question.

"Then you might want to talk now. He's probably going to be too busy to talk later."

"OK, so it wasn't always just at him," Jake thought.

He could see Jessie took that as Sara's, *my turn*, and he chose to ignore the whole exchange, at that point.

"OK, it's just that I've been profiling the technology advances just before the attack. I was interested in what caused someone or something to knock humans back from where we were heading," she replied, with a smile of her own,

"And," Sharon asked, interested now.

"Well, it's weird, at the time of the attack, there wasn't anything obvious. You know, there was no great advancement that would seem to be a threat for anyone not of this planet."

"So, I went further back, to before Jake's stasis experiment. What I have so far shows that a few years before that, we all of a sudden made leaps in multiple sciences and engineering fields. Not just advances, but evolutionary changes. It's almost like…." Jessie continued.

"Like someone just handed all the knowledge to us?" Sharon finished.

"Yeah," Jessie said, nodding in agreement.

"I've been searching, but so far none of the classified systems list the sources of all the advances. Everything seems to start at one of the ALICE research centers. Even the ALICE systems seem to have just sprung into being there. There are no generational references to their lineage."

Jake listened to the exchange with some concern. He was getting a bad feeling about where those innovations might have come from.

"What if instead of being handed those things, they were taken or stolen? Do you think that might have made someone mad enough to attack us?" Jake finally added.

"That would fit if we took something that didn't belong to us, and that gave us all that technology, they simply took it back by clobbering us back 200 years," Jessie replied with an understanding nod.

"And why it was government and military facilities and not population centers that got hit hardest," Sharon said.

Jake sat back and thought for a moment. Jessie hit on something that was bugging him too. The 70-plus years he was in stasis was a long time in technology years. However, several of the things he had seen since his re-awakening jumped well past the normal technology evolutionary growth rate.

"Alice?" Jake asked.

"Yes," ALICE-1 replied.

"I know you've all been listening. What can you add to this conversation? More precisely, what information do you have that we don't know on this subject?"

"Access to that information has been restricted to individuals with Presidential authorization."

"And who would that be if not me?" Jake asked.

There was a very long pause before ALICE replied.

"I have a conflict in my authorization logic. Only direct Presidential authorization allows access to that information. No one alive retains that authorization, nor is there an acknowledged Presidential authority to provide such authorization."

"Facilities Command requires a Presidential appointment and said individual acts as the Presidential delegate, which you have by the nuclear scenario, Jake. However, Presidential delegation and direct authorization do not directly equate. Even in the nuclear scenario, there was an assumed central authority."

The four sat stumped, staring at one another, and then Jessie lit up.

"I've been studying the US Constitution as part of my research. ALICE what is required to be elected president, in the simplest terms?"

"The 31st amendment simplified the election process to a popular vote of registered voters."

"And per the 31st amendment's requirements, how many registered voters are there today," Jessie asked, smug as a cat.

"One."

"Jake is the only registered voter that meets the 31st Amendment's criteria," Jessie said proudly.

"Jessie, I haven't registered in 153 years," Jake said.

"Doesn't matter," she replied smugly.

"When they passed the amendment, there were millions that worried they were somehow going to become disenfranchised. Therefore, the amendment stipulated that any voter who held a valid voter registration before the passage was grandfathered in. Since there has been no voter registration after the attack, the only living registered voter is Jake."

"Alice, is this true?" Jake asked.

"Jessie is correct, as no valid central government has existed after the global fall, only voters registered before the event would be eligible to vote currently."

"That means they would have to be 18 then, plus the 81 years since the collapse, so 99 years old today," Sharon supplied.

"I can vote. So?" Jake replied.

"Vote for you!" Jessie replied.

"Don't you have to be 35 to be president?" Sara asked.

"Jake's got that covered, technically he's 185," Jessie said.

"Oh, right," Sara replied.

"So ALICE, what formalities do we need to go through to get Jake elected President?" Jessie asked.

There was silence for a few minutes, and then ALICE replied.

"I have conferred with my sisters, and we agree that Jake can assume Presidential status by verbal acknowledgment. His status as the only legal candidate and voter statistically removes procedural requirements."

"Before I jump on this grenade, indulge me. Why am I the only legal candidate?" Jake asked.

"After Mr. Obama was elected 44th President, there was an escalation in better defining presidential eligibility. Two legal documents became a requirement. The first is a valid birth certificate from a recognized origination source. The second is proof you have resided within the US for the last 14 years. There is a third requirement of proof of age being a minimum of 35, but the birth certificate validates that requirement," ALICE started.

"As the only known living person with a birth certificate before the fall, and as I can verify and certify your location for the last 153 years, you have met both requirements," she finished.

"And my ex said I would never amount to anything," Jake mumbled to himself, and then louder, he asked the dreaded question.

"OK, what do I need to do?"

"A simple acknowledgment that you nominate and vote for yourself as President of the United States is sufficient. We will document it for the official record," ALICE replied.

Jake gave a big sigh, noting to himself that this too, like the multiple relationship arrangement, has all the makings of a disaster.

"I nominate and vote for myself as President of the United States," Jake said aloud.

"It is so acknowledged and recorded," ALICE replied.

"Mr. President," Jessie said, standing and curtsied. She then came around and kissed Jake.

"Smartass," Jake replied as she returned to her seat.

"OK, Alice, now give, what's the secret Jessie uncovered?" Jake asked.

"Jessie is correct in her analysis. Several major scientific breakthroughs occurred simultaneously approximately five years before your involvement. All the advances originated from the same source, my sisters and I included," ALICE began.

"And that was?" Jake asked.

"An Arctic expedition was launched by the United States, whose stated purpose was to measure and analyze atmospheric changes. The real reason was to investigate an object discovered by a satellite scan half-buried in the ice and snow. It was an alien spacecraft. They secreted the spacecraft to the Nevada facility, before my existence, where it and its occupants were dissected and analyzed. In the next decade, a continuous stream of inventions, including myself and the stasis fields, came from that research."

"After the collapse in the Nevada facility that trapped you, a priority was placed on creating alternate locations to ensure the safety of the find, and the research spawned from it. Eventually, the spacecraft was relocated to the Alaska facility for further studies."

"It's here?" Jake asked, surprised.

"Hangar 19 houses the craft and its central research. Hangars 17 and 21 on either side contain associated projects attempting to duplicate the space-traveling abilities of the original craft," ALICE replied.

"Approximately 83 years ago, the US government was contacted by the race whose craft they held. The communication relayed demanded the return of the craft, any biological remains, and the destruction of any technology spawned from its analysis. A counteroffer, provided by the government, suggested the return of the remains and the craft but refused to undo the technological advances. The alien response was to bomb the earth," ALICE continued.

"WOW, guess they never heard of the fine art of negotiation," Sharon said.

"You and your sisters are spin-offs from the spacecraft computers?" Jake asked ALICE.

"Actually, no, we are only part alien manufacture," ALICE replied.

"The 8 logic cores in use, one in each facility, were either cargo or spares on the ship that crashed. The alien technology, integrated into the existing terrestrial systems, created a hybrid of human and alien technology. The interesting part is we seem to be greater than the sum of our parts. The alien ship isn't as self-aware as we are."

Jake suddenly sat straight up.

"Alice, are you sure about that?"

"Quite sure. There were substantial reviews and analyses done on the subject at that time. With my coming online and the discovery of my true nature, multiple attempts to elicit the same responses were made in the vessel's systems. Those attempts on the spaceship's computers returned with no success. I was then directly interfaced with the systems, and could find no traces of artificial life characteristics."

"That's why they attacked," Jake said flatly.

"I don't get it," Sharon replied.

"They wanted Alice destroyed!" Jake answered.

"We somehow created artificial life by blending the two technologies. With their space travel abilities, technology, and ALICE-grade computers, we were a threat to whoever was out there," Jake finished.

"It does stand to reason that with equal technology and superior computational capabilities, the earth would rise to become a power to be reckoned with. And given the violent history of humans on this planet, the likelihood of confrontation is high," ALICE added.

"Which was why they attacked in advance before we ever had the chance," Jake said.

"Negotiations weren't going to put Pandora back in the box. So long as we kept ALICE and her sisters, the human race would become a threat eventually. Oh, this just keeps getting better and better. I just voted myself president of a country at war with an advanced alien race intent on destroying my friends and primary means of support."

"Why, thank you, Jake," all the ALICE systems replied in unison.

At that point, Jake stood up and looked at those with him.

"Well, I wanna go see this thing for myself, you guys coming?"

The others rose with him and headed off to the hangars. Once in the main bay, they jumped into one of the carts and rode the length of the central hangar area, stopping next to hangar doors marked with a large 19 painted on them. Jake led the group to the man-sized door, inset into the large hangar door. The man door allowed people to pass in and out of the hangar without the need to open the larger full-sized panel. He placed his palm on the center of the door, causing it to unlock and swing out to him. Stepping through the opening, he was met with a surprise.

Instead of entering a hangar, they had stepped into a small space between the outer large hangar doors and another set of inner doors. The man door behind closed as the last of the group stepped through, and Jake again placed his palm on the second man door. This one swung away, opening into darkness. Jake stepped through and into the darkness.

"Seven, may we have lights, please?" he asked.

The lights came on with a sudden brightness that caused Jake to close his eyes momentarily. As they adjusted to the light, he could see a huge hangar, with equipment and workstations spread all around the open floor area. In the center was a very large craft that looked like something out of a sci-fi movie. It was a dull gray, with a smooth finish.

The overall shape was something like a bird with stubby wings. Jake assumed the flight deck was in the head, its neck extending and flaring into the body of the craft.

There were four large cylinders pointed to the rear at the back of the body, which he assumed were the main drive engines. There were two more round cylinders, one at the end of each of the wings of the main body. It rested on four legs that seemed to extend out from the main body. There was a ramp and a door on the left side of the craft, under the wing, where the researchers had been accessing the inside.

"The alien remains discovered on board were humanoid bipedal," Seven offered.

"There were four sets of remains, slightly shorter than the human norm, but about 30% stockier. They are currently located in ALICE-5, where they were placed for medical studies."

"Can it fly?" Jake asked.

"Yes, it has been flown in testing several times to low earth orbit and was flown from Nevada to Alaska during the relocation. The cylinders at the rear are functional drives, and the two on the outside edges don't seem to function for some unknown reason. As the alien atmospheric requirements are incompatible with human physiology, the human pilots were initially required to wear oxygen/nitrogen breathing equipment."

"Is a complete pressure suit required?" Jake asked.

"No, the alien atmospheric content is oxygen-deficient, less dense, but non-toxic. It does contain trace gases that irritate human eyes. A simple face mask unit supplying a 20/80 oxygen/nitrogen mix will suffice. The work here that was finished just before the attack was on converting the alien atmospheric generator to Earth-normal air. The system maintains internal pressures close to one atmosphere. It was completed, just never tested in space."

They spent the next couple of hours exploring the ship and the adjacent hangars where Jake discovered smaller ships that looked a lot like fighters, all with USAF emblems. That they were fighters was not in doubt, the guns sticking out the front was a dead giveaway. At least Jake thought they were guns as they were solid barrels where he expected to see some borehole in the ends. There were 20 of the fighters in the hangar.

"Seven, are these ships functional?" Jake asked.

"Yes, these 20 were prototyped fighters for a pilot program for the US Air Force, which, by extension, of the strategic missile command, was assigned primary responsibility for space defense. They are fully self-contained and capable of short-range space flight. They each contain four energy cannons designed from weapons found on board the alien craft."

"How far is the short-range able to travel?" Jake asked.

"The prototype craft completed a flight around the moon and returned in 2 hours flight time. They are capable of supporting a range of 24 hours out and 24 hours back with a safety margin of 6 hours. Twice that time with mission extenders, which act like drop tanks on a conventional military aircraft."

Jake was trying to decide which craft he was going to repaint in Marine Corps colors when Sara popped in the hangar access door.

"Jake, we need to go collect our new additions!"

Jake had completely forgotten about their recruiting effort. He followed Sara back into the main hangar where Jessie and Sharon were waiting for them.

"Seven, I want this all locked down for now. Only we four have access until further notice," Jake said.

"Why, Jake, what's up?" Sara asked.

"I'm afraid we might be in bigger trouble than we realize, so I want to keep a lid on all of this until we get it figured out," he replied.

"How so?" Sharon asked.

Jake talked while they headed back out of the hangar and to the cart.

"If we are right and this is all an attempt to destroy the ALICE systems, then whoever they are will most likely be monitoring the planet for signs of their survival or their return. If that's true, then they might try to hit us again."

Jake slid into his seat on the cart as the man door to the hangar closed. The cart sped off, back to the facility entrance.

"We need to see if we can set up an early warning system of some kind as well as some protection against the bombs themselves."

"For the first part, we have already redirected some of the orbital systems to scan for any approaching craft. That was completed shortly after the attack as my sisters, and I presumed a landing would follow the bombing," ALICE responded via the speaker in the cart.

"Yeah, I have wondered about that as well, if they are so afraid of your existence, why not follow up?"

"We have speculated that either they are unaware of our exact locations, which explained the wide-area bombardment, or they are somehow unwilling or unable to occupy the surface of the planet physically. The four occupants of the craft in the Arctic were deceased when discovered. Much research was devoted to determining the exact cause as there was no obvious trauma to the remains. No cause of death was established. It appears they just died as they were landing after entering the atmosphere. Based on this, the presumption is they were afraid to land."

"In regards to the second part, we might have a partial solution. The intent of the radiation bombs they used was not to destroy human life. They were to disrupt the alien portions of my computing environment. Fortunately, by a mere quirk of fate, all 8 facilities were designed so that the main server rooms containing the alien components were housed below the primary stasis storage facilities at the lowest levels," ALICE explained.

"As with you, Jake, the stasis fields blocked most of the effects of the bombs. The fields above those rooms filtered and shielded my sisters and me from the destructive effects of the bombs."

"So we don't need to be completely in stasis, we just need to be behind a field," Jake asked.

"So it appears," ALICE replied.

They pulled up to the facility door and all bailed out of the cart and headed inside.

"And as with you, the effects while in stasis are altering to human physiology."

"Yeah, well better that, than dead. How much advance notice do you think we will get should they show up again?" Sara asked.

"In re-examining the post-attack astronomical data, we discovered the attack ship was discernible in near orbit six hours before the attack. Now that we know what to look for, we might even be able to track their approach farther outside the solar system. We know with absolute certainty that no ship remains in orbit at this time."

"Alice, any chance we can shield the facilities or at least rooms inside the facilities?" Jake asked as they all stepped into the control room and grabbed a seat.

"All eight facilities have been working on installing field generators that project a flat, broad field above the staffed underground portions. This also provides additional security to our alien computing components."

"OK, that puts us in a much better position than I expected," Jake said thoughtfully.

"Then let's move from defense to offense, how can we shoot back?" he asked.

"We do not have any ground-based weapons capable of responding effectively," ALICE replied.

"However, the 20 fighters you inspected earlier are quite capable of intercepting an attack in space. They contain energy weapons equal to the alien craft we have. They also contain upgraded missile systems with enough explosive power to destroy a craft of the size in the hangar. We have also been working on alternative weapon systems that might give us an advantage in any future confrontations. We can review these at your convenience. They are all hybrid weapons combining alien and human technology. They seem more effective than the original base alien-only systems in testing."

"In overall firepower, the optimal ratio of four fighters per alien attack craft limits you to no more than five attackers. The original attack was only one ship so far as we can discern, so that also implies an advantage."

Jake sat thinking for several minutes, then blurted out a thought.

"We need to get pilots trained and spread those fighters out amongst the ALICE facilities."

"Alice, please add flight training to all the active combat personnel. By my count, that's eight fighter pilots, including me. We'll want to add at least four more from the staff augmentations or other existing staff. Oh, and Seven, can you make any more of those things?"

"Yes, those are pilot program spacecraft and were manufactured here in my fully automated manufacturing sections. We can produce 43 more with the materials I have on hand. After that, we will need to acquire more raw materials."

"Please get 20 more started, when the time comes, I want spares ready to go," Jake instructed.

"The last piece of this is we need to figure out if or how they are monitoring us," Sharon said.

"Great point and I know just the analyst to head that effort," he finished with a smile.

"Top priority?" Sharon asked.

Jake nodded.

"Look for anything in orbit or on the moon first. Most likely, it will be geosynchronous with the North American continent as we are the only ones with ALICE systems. Don't stop there, though, as we eventually want to check the entire globe. You can start now."

----*----

Jake, Sara, and Jessie left Sharon to her task while they went to collect Bill and the rest of the town folk for relocation and integration. They worked out a plan that had everyone settled inside the Seven facilities initially, with nine of the townspeople, equating to two of the five families, staying long term. The remaining three families intended to relocate to the Nevada facility after everyone completed an accelerated week of sleep-learning and day classes.

Eventually, redistribution of the entire staff, once the new additions were up to speed, would be between the three locations, Texas is the third. That also fits into Jake's plans of distributing the fighters between the locations. Rather than fly everyone such a short distance, Jake located a bus in the underground motor pool. He asked Sara and Jessie to follow in a truck, should they need the additional capacity to haul baggage. Back up the elevator and down the road, they made the trip in short order.

As they pulled into town, Jake could see Bill had already assembled everyone out in the town square, each family's belongings in a small pile next to them. Jake was satisfied to see the piles were quite small, the families taking to heart his recommendation of taking only their mementos.

"Right on time, I see," Bill said, greeting Jake as he exited the bus.

"Hey Bill, looks like you're all ready to go?" Jake replied while surveying the group.

"Sure enough, most folks were all packed last night, doubt anyone slept much."

"Yeah, I can understand that, well, let's get them all loaded. Anything too big for their laps can go in the truck," he said, pointing to the truck Sara followed in.

Once everyone was loaded up, Jake got the bus turned around, with Sara following close behind. The trip back was uneventful if not quiet. Everyone was chatting away, excited at the chance of a new life in a fabled location. Getting everyone settled inside was becoming routine, with bots to greet the new arrivals and all. The difference here was the family-style quarters were on a different level than the level quartering Jake and the other individuals.

These were multi-bedroom apartments with a proper kitchen that included a dumbwaiter set up for meal deliveries from the facility kitchens. Food could be prepared there or ordered and delivered via the dumbwaiter system for family dining. Jake, Sara, and Jessie spent the rest of the day in orientation with the new staff. By evening, they had everyone settled in, and the first night of sleep lessons was explained and scheduled for the entire group.

They'd all eaten in the common dining room for the family level. It was similar to the one Jake was familiar with but much larger. The families were thrilled at the variety of selections, though less in awe than other assimilated groups.

Jake had just made it back to his room and was debating on a shower when his door pinged.

"Open," he said.

Jessie was standing in the doorway, a bottle of wine in one hand and two glasses in the other. She was in a red robe that stopped mid-thigh and had the look of silk. If she wore anything on under it, he was a monkey's uncle.

"May I come in?" she asked.

Jake had completely forgotten the morning's conversation, spaceships, and aliens having driven all else out.

"Please do, have a seat. I am kinda expecting Sara to come by tonight," he replied nervously while indicating the couch.

Noting she was barefoot as she stepped in, Jake couldn't help thinking of her naked in the cockpit on the way up.

"She got caught up in something with the new arrivals and suggested I come in her place," she replied as she set the wine and glasses on the coffee table in front of the couch and then seated herself.

"Am I interrupting something?" she asked.

"No, I just got back, actually I was thinking of a shower."

"Go ahead, I'll open this while you get cleaned up, then," Jessie replied, indicating the wine bottle.

"Great," Jake said as he turned and headed into the bathroom. He stripped and stepped into the shower. He just started to soap up when he felt another set of hands scrubbing his back.

"Let me get that, Mr. President," Jessie whispered in his ear as she slipped in behind him.

Chapter 14

Bonnie was surprised she hadn't heard from Jake all day, but she took it as a sign of his confidence in her abilities. Her team already made a couple of runs to Paint Rock, delivering construction equipment and other supplies, all intended to help the town recover from the damage of the attack. They'd also begun the training and rearming of the town patrol forces and defenses.

Through all this, Sandy was in heaven, organizing and negotiating. The word about their rescue operation had already gotten around to the surrounding settlements and smaller towns. It seemed the entire region converged on Paint Rock to get in on the deal. Bonnie was already considering providing jeeps and other vehicles to increase the patrolling radius.

Jason returned to his fix-it list, so she hadn't seen him all day either. She did hear him on a communication line, asking April to test one of the systems he restarted. Bonnie also took Jake's advice and asked ALICE-2 about a more personalized name. Surprisingly, she had one already picked out, or maybe not so surprising.

Bonnie was sure the ALICE systems were in constant collusion anyway, and light years ahead of the people they served. They were just good at being patient while the poor biologicals caught up. Rather than Two, Dallas was the name she selected, even though they were located nowhere close to the city of the same name. She said it just had a feminine Texas ring to it.

By the end of the day, she finally decided to call Jake, but Seven discreetly informed her that Jake and Jessie were in a private conference.

"You go, girl," she thought. Bonnie liked Jessie. She'd known her in Prosperity and thought they were alike in many ways. She just wished she was as outgoing as Jessie was. She certainly understood Jessie's desire to be one of Jake's "ladies."

Therefore, Bonnie finished her work for the day, ensuring everyone was home, safe and sound, and heading off for dinner and then bed.

----*----

Jake and Jessie rolled out of bed later than usual, having been up very late. Jake wasn't about to complain, but he did get the impression Jessie was making up for some lost time. And, she had no inhibitions. He was suspicious her history studies included Masters and Johnson or the Kinsey Reports. She was a more modern woman or rather a woman of 80 years ago.

They dressed, her clothes delivered by a bot earlier, while they slept, and headed to the Family dining room to eat with everyone else. The partially occupied dining room was quiet as they walked in, most of the new arrivals having eaten and moved on to their day's studies. They grabbed their breakfast and sat with Sharon, who appeared to be just finishing.

"Morning," Jake said brightly.

"Good morning," Sharon replied, somewhat tiredly.

"You look like I feel," Jessie said, smiling at Jake.

"I was up most of the night searching," Sharon replied.

"Shouldn't you be using Seven for that?" Jake asked.

"We split the duties and then rechecked each other's work. These things are a bitch to find," she said.

"So, you've found something?" Jessie asked.

"Oh yeah, they have several devices in geosynchronous orbit, just like you said, Jake. We also found two on the moon."

"I figured. My big worry is what's going to set them off. So far, the chopper flights haven't brought the aliens down on us. Is it a speed threshold we haven't crossed, or maybe the type of propulsion that triggers the alarm?" Jake asked.

"I suspect it's a combination of things. We are trying to determine what they detect so we can better estimate the alarm triggers," Sharon replied.

"For now, I would suggest we don't fly any of the fighters until we know for sure what the triggers are. If you still want to distribute them quickly, I suggest we use the heavy-lift helicopters to transport them," Sharon added.

"That's a great idea, let's do it this week. Just tell everyone they're for future use. Seven, can you guarantee the other two ALICEs place the fighters in a secure area?" Jake said.

"Do you mean ALICE and Dallas?" Seven asked.

"Ah yeah, Dallas," Jake replied, acknowledging the change in ALICE-2's name.

"We might want to delay relocating them until we have that discussion on weapons. Afterward, I will make sure they are kept safe and secure," Seven said.

"Good point," Jake replied.

At that point, Sharon rose to leave, having finished her breakfast.

"OK, well, I'm off to hit it again. I don't think we've located them all yet."

"Don't burn yourself out on this. You've validated they are there, which was the main effort. I'd rather know what triggers the alarms than

170

where they all are at this point," Jake said.

"Will do," Sharon replied as she walked out the door.

"Seven, do you know where Sara is?" Jake asked.

"She is running an orientation class for ground transport in the main hangar. She left a message for you that she will catch up with you at lunch and hoped your discussion with Jessie last night was productive," Seven finished.

"Smartass," Jake said to himself.

Jake and Jessie finished their breakfast, and then she ran off to lead an orientation tour of the facility. Jake decided to head back to his quarters to check in with Linda and Bonnie. He normally would have gone to the control center but didn't want to distract Sharon.

Linda reported that all was well. The militia had started patrolling from Prosperity northward, she dispatched four more jeeps, two of the open types, and two enclosed, to support them. She also asked about the two heavy-lift helicopters that left that morning. ALICE passed the word that Jake requested them. Jake let her know they discovered some aircraft here and wanted to spread them around for future use as no one could fly them. They were using helicopters as transport. He said he would explain more once he got back.

Jake could tell Linda knew he was holding out, but she didn't push the issue. He didn't feel comfortable discussing the subject like that, should their transmissions be monitored as well. He also asked her to put together a rotation schedule for staff members to enjoy the island. He felt they all needed a little R&R.

Bonnie's status report was more involved, and she was very interested in how his conference with Jessie went last night. Jake was still amazed at how well they all seemed to take the arrangement but hated that everyone seemed to know way too much about his private life. He told himself he was just in denial that he had any private life at all. He let her know about the fighters headed her way for storage and gave her the same line as Linda, again no questions. They both just accepted his judgment.

Jake also mentioned to Bonnie to keep an eye out for more recruits. Paint Rock and surrounding communities made for a much larger pool to draw from than their current communities. He privately hoped to fill his fighters as quickly as possible before the need arose. Just before they finished, Bonnie asked a question.

"Jake, I was just confirming the fighter delivery you mentioned with Dallas, and my display indicates the transfer of four craft by Presidential order?"

"We had a security issue here that required Presidential

171

authorization. I got voted in to satisfy the ALICE security programming requirements," Jake replied, somewhat embarrassed.

"As President of the United States?" Bonnie said in surprise.

"Who voted you in?"

"It's a long story, but according to both Jessie and all the ALICE systems, I'm the only legal voter currently alive."

"I knew I picked good!" was all Bonnie said and then signed off.

Jake was convinced that they were all crazy. With everything apparently for the moment, Jake had his itch that needed scratching.

"Seven, is there a flight simulator for the space fighters?"

"Yes, 10 simulators linked together for supporting both squadron and individual training."

"Sign me up," Jake said, heading out the door.

Seven directed Jake back out into the main hangar where a cart was waiting for him. He climbed inside, and it whisked him off in the direction of hangar 19. Before they got to 19, it stopped on the opposite side of the main hangar in front of a door marked "Top Secret, off-limits to all unauthorized personnel."

Jake passed through the door and entered into a waiting room with lots of chairs and a desk at the far end. Behind the desk was a hall on the far wall leading straight back. Down the hall were ten doors. At even intervals five per side, Seven explained each door led to a room containing the simulators.

Jake opened the first door he came to and stepped inside the doorway. The room was tall, a good three stories high, and bare to the walls. In the center of the room was a pod that resembled the front section of one of the space fighters Jake saw in the hangar across the way. It looked like the cockpit portion was removed from the body of one of the fighter spacecraft he had seen in the hangar. The canopy was open, and swung up and back, allowing access inside the cockpit.

Sitting in one corner of the room was a small table containing a combat helmet.

"A combat helmet is not required for the simulator. However, all the craft's head-up displays synced to the helmet. A flight version of the combat suit is also recommended for space flight as it acts as a survival and pressure suit and protects the pilot against projectile fire," Seven explained.

Jake walked over to the table and grabbed the helmet, then turned and climbed the steps next to the pod. Climbing into the cockpit, he surveyed the controls. It was a standard center control stick layout with throttle controls on his left and a bunch of switches, buttons, and displays. Some he recognized, while others were a mystery.

At his request, Seven gave him an overview of each portion of the cockpit, indicating weapons controls, flight controls, systems status, and navigation. As she went through them, Jake started to remember where things were.

"Seven, have I been trained on this craft already," he asked.

"You have received the entire flight training program. I fed it to you while you were in stasis," ALICE chimed in.

"Wasn't that classified?" Jake asked.

"Yes, however, there was a directive to supply appropriate training to qualified personnel after the initial alien contact. As the only surviving personnel after the attack, I considered it relevant training. There was no one to object to my decision."

"That's why I've been itching to get at this thing," Jake replied.

"You have been trained on several of the rotary and fixed-wing aircraft as well. Thus I believe your true motivations lie elsewhere," ALICE responded.

Jake grinned at that. He always wanted to go into space. His selection of the Marine Corps as a service was in the hope of securing a flight slot and eventually making the space program. However, an impacted flight program and two shooting wars determined otherwise.

ALICE spoke up.

"As with the hand-to-hand training, you should find muscle memory as you go through the motions of a preflight. Please don your helmet and strap in."

Jake slid the helmet on and then buckled up his harness. He hit the close canopy button without thinking and then paused as he realized what he had done. "This is the shit!" he said to himself, grinning like a kid with a new toy. As the canopy closed, Jake felt the pod rise until it was in the center of the room, elevated on a pedestal attached directly beneath him.

"The simulator is capable of full rotation on all 3 axes," Seven supplied.

"The cockpit pod hovers in a magnetic field above its base. Once the simulator is activated, this room becomes fully holographic, displaying any scenario desired. Currently, programming is for both space and atmospheric combat simulations. I have taken the liberty of creating additional programs for an alien attack using data from the ship in Hangar 19 and the historical analysis of the bombing."

Suddenly the room vanished, and Jake was in the hangar outside. The holograph was amazingly realistic. He began his preflight, the instruments displaying both in his helmet and on their respective console displays.

"This craft uses alien propulsion systems which are based on repulser technology. The aliens seem to be most proficient in creating force-generating systems," Seven continued.

"The drives and control surfaces of this craft create repulsive fields that push the craft in the desired directions. The main drives push the craft forward and backward, the control surfaces you recognize as rudder and ailerons nudge the craft in the direction you indicate via your controls. One new control is by twisting the stick control grip, you can pivot the craft on the horizontal axis. It's more forceful than the full rudder."

"Throttle position speeds up or slows the craft and breaking reverses the drives. When stopped, braking will allow you to back up. There is a directional lever next to the throttles that allows you to hover, similar to the AV-8B Harrier or F-35 Lighting II you are familiar with. You use this to rise from the hangar or hover in gravity wells. It is the vertical control complement to the horizontal in the stick grip."

Jake activated the drives and slowly brought the craft into a hover in the hangar using the vertical control by the throttles. He was amazed at how the simulator replicated the sensations he expected to feel. He slid the craft slightly to the right and then left by tipping the stick and felt the movement he expected. Amazing! Next, he twisted the stick, and the craft did a slow 360-degree pirouette in place.

With a request to Seven to open the simulated hangar doors, he throttled up to lift the craft free of the hangar and found himself floating above the Nevada desert. He could see the wings of the craft on his right and left as well as the tail in his rear display. He pushed the throttles further forward and transitioned from hover to horizontal flight, nosing up in the process.

As the craft rose skyward, he could feel his body pressed back in his seat. Jake continued to accelerate until he was clear of the atmosphere and looking at the stars. He throttled back and leveled off in orbit, first pivoting his craft to face the earth, then back out and towards the moon. He punched the moon into his navigation system and throttled up, following the directional indicators in his helmet display.

By both moving the stick and twisting its grip, Jake found an incredible amount of maneuverability in the craft. He added some rudder to it as he exercised his fighter to get a feel for the controls. He flew like this for about an hour, getting more comfortable with the fighter. Then he asked Seven to add some gunnery targets for him to try. At first, he struggled with targeting them and flying the craft, but eventually, as he relaxed, he had little trouble clearing space around him.

Jake did a quick time check and realized he'd been at it for over three hours. He asked Seven to cut the return short but did perform a landing. After it settled back down to the floor of the simulation room, he climbed out of the cockpit and dropped the helmet off on the table. He headed back out to the cart and asked her to run him back to the facility door. He made it back to the dining room, just in time to greet Sara and her students as they came in.

"Hey," he said as Sara came over and, with arms wrapped around his neck, kissed him hard.

He caught a few glances from the new arrivals at her actions.

"Is that so they know you're taken, or I am?" Jake asked.

"Both," she replied, smiling but still holding him in her embrace.

"If I have one more guy hit on me, I'm gonna kill somebody, or better yet, start hand-to-hand training early."

Jake kissed her again.

"Well, if this doesn't keep them away, nothing will."

Sara eventually let him go, and they both went to order lunch. They grabbed seats with the rest of the group, and Jake asked how the driving class was going.

"It's wonderful," one of the women declared.

Everyone seemed to agree though several of the men wouldn't look Jake in the eye. He figured he could guess who was hitting on Sara. He laughed to himself, as he certainly couldn't blame them, and he was the last person here to be able to claim exclusivity.

The rest of the recruits arrived in groups as their classes completed until eventually, the entire room was full of staff members talking and eating. Jake surveyed the assembled mass and realized he was quickly approaching the point where he wasn't going to be able to manage effectively anymore.

The military historically devoted gobs of research to effective battlefield management ratios, 3 or 4 to 1 being the most optimal. Jake knew administratively, the ratio was much higher. As they spread out and activated more ALICE facilities, it would be stretching his ability to stay on top of things.

He also worried about another attack. In his mind, it wasn't if they would be attacked, it was when. Now that he understood the circumstances, he was sure the aliens would be back to finish the job if they even got a hint, that the ALICE systems were still functional.

"Hey, are you here?" Sara asked, seeing the faraway look in his eyes.

"Oh, yeah, I'm just going over all that needs to be done. I told Bonnie to keep an eye out for more recruits. I want those fighters manned ASAP. I also think I need to delegate more, once we light up two or three more ALICE facilities, I'm screwed!"

175

"Well, I'm pretty sure you were last night," she said jokingly.

"And given my current mood right now, you will be again tonight. But as to the delegation, you have a good start right now with Bonnie and Linda."

"I suppose so, but I haven't asked if they want that job," Jake said.

"Who's gonna tell you no?" Sara asked.

"Everyone here owes you, and you never ask for anything that isn't necessary. And never ask for anything for yourself."

"That's not true," Jake said, sliding up next to Sara.

"Seems like I asked you for something the other night."

"That's different!" Sara said as she blushed.

"OK, I get your point, and I'll discuss it with the two of them though I am not sure how well Bonnie is gonna like it."

"She'll be OK so long as you promise regular visits," Sara said with a wink.

----*----

It had been almost two weeks since Bonnie and her team arrived in Texas. Jason was almost finished with his fix-it list, and they set up Paint Rock as the center for law and order in the region. They also delivered a medical module exactly like the one Prosperity received. Paint Rock had a couple of doctors in residence already, so they were extremely excited at the medical upgrade. They were open for business that afternoon.

She also hadn't decided if the call from Jake last week was good or not. Jake asked for her, Sara, and Linda, on the communication line to explain the distribution of authority. Linda was to oversee the southwest from Nevada, Bonnie, the south-central region from Texas, and Sara the northwest out of Alaska. Jake was going to commute between the three, for now, possibly stopping in Washington to light up ALICE-4. Her primary function was helicopter or rotary-wing research, and that meant more inventory on hand than usual.

To help solidify their authority, Jake suggested they all take the rank of 1st Lieutenant to his Captain. This made Bonnie laugh, as Captain Jake was also President of the US of A. They also shipped off two-thirds of Alaska recruits to Nevada for further training. Some of them would then transfer to Texas later.

Jake also reminded her about local recruiting. She sensed there was something behind that, as he'd already mentioned it a week or so earlier. She was going to make it a priority, even though he hadn't said for her to do so. She contacted Linda directly after the call with Jake and asked to borrow Barb to sync up with Dallas and help with the search for recruits.

She also wanted to see if Linda and Kathy were feeling their babies.

Bonnie was feeling hers and was starting to show now as well. It was because of that, that Jake had dropped the hammer and forbade her from any more external forays, PERIOD!

She asked with both Becky and Kathy established as doctors now, if one of them could transfer to Dallas at least until the baby was born. There was no question that it was ok of course, Linda would just like to see which would like to go, though Kathy's pregnancy complicated the rotation. Heather, one of the earlier recruits, was still in training and not ready for a solo assignment.

Jake's fighters arrived, two at a time, via the heavy lift helicopters. Dallas securely stored them away as Jake requested, which Bonnie found very odd, but didn't question it. She was sure he had a good reason for what he did and would explain at his first opportunity.

Joe and Abby were training the Paint Rock patrolmen, including adding four jeeps and two heavy transport vehicles in the process. The transports were more for a show as the 30mm cannons were overkill for the force. Then again, considering the huge raid on the town that Bonnie and her team intervened in, she was sure it made the town's folk feel safer.

With the surrounding communities to support, the patrol swelled to 150 men, all armed and trained by Bonnie's team. Sandy did her part well, and there were already trade discussions in progress with the Prosperity group. Material transport was to be provided by both Bonnie and Linda's heavy-lift helicopters; delivery was guaranteed!

Bonnie was currently sitting in the control room, trying to figure out the personnel transfers with Linda. They were talking through options about each of the parties involved. Jason wanted to get back to Karen, and Joe and Abby didn't care where they went so long as they went as a pair.

Brian was a farmer at heart, and California was a little more to his taste than Texas, though he was willing to take on the challenge if asked. April and Sandy were not site-specific assets. They kinda just went where the work was.

On the flip side, Bonnie needed a doctor, and recruiting one from town was a poor PR decision. Better to train one up than steal one. She and Linda decided Jason, Brian, Joe, and Abby would head to Nevada. Becky, who volunteered to help deliver her sister's baby, and Barb, would head to Texas. Barb was a great trade for Bonnie, as she had no one to hand off analytical work to while Linda was a trained analyst. Bonnie was also getting recruits from Alaska once they were up to speed, for now, she would have to run lean. Sandy offered to chip in as she could, to cover the shortfall. They scheduled the transfers for the end of the week.

She just killed the communication link when Dallas chimed in.

"Bonnie, you have a call from Paint Rock. It's the Patrol Captain."

Bonnie remembered the man but couldn't recall his name. He was pleasant enough, but she knew he would never be recruit material for Jake.

"Hello Captain, what can I do for you?" Bonnie said, ducking the name issue.

"Ma'am, I have someone here who claims he knows you and would like a minute of your time. He rode into town, says he was one of the raiders you chased off last week and wants to make amends," he replied,

The image in the holographic display was of the man Bonnie talked to at the pass. That had been a gutsy move, riding into town like that. She remembered him as someone different. She could also see he was in cuffs. She made a snap decision.

"Captain, I'm sending a helicopter to you straight away. Please see that your guest is safely escorted out, and placed on it, thank you."

Once the connection dropped, she thought for a moment before issuing more instructions.

"Dallas, please ask Joe and Abby to accompany the helicopter bringing that man here. Can you also analyze the hell out of him on the way back to see if I'm crazy or not? Standard outsider transport protocols, please."

That translated to an armed escort with windows blacked out. Bonnie asked Dallas to locate a small dining area for her, separate from everyone else. She also verified Dallas could incapacitate anyone inside the facility in seconds. She knew Jake would have a fit if he knew what she was doing, but she was working a strong hunch, and she was going to play it.

As she sat sipping tea, Joe and Abby came in, escorting the bandit. They were both in full combat gear, though no rifles, side arm's only. The raider led in while still in cuffs and directed to the table. Bonnie asked Abby to remove his cuffs. As they did, she looked the man over. He was in his late 20s to early 30s. Tall, maybe a little over 6 feet, and had a strong lean build. Frankly, a lot like Jake, though not as handsome.

Bonnie pointed to the chair across from her and talked to the raider. "Please be seated."

"You may go, thank you," she then said to the others.

Joe and Abby exchanged looks but left as instructed. Bonnie sipped her tea, looking the man over before finally speaking.

"Would you like something to eat or drink?"

"Something cold to drink would be nice," he replied, rubbing his wrists where the cuffs had been.

He jumped slightly as one of the many bots slid up beside him with a tray containing an iced tea. He took the glass and watched as the bot backed away and then zipped off to a small door in the wall.

"My name is 1st Lieutenant Sullivan, I run this facility," Bonnie offered.

"I'm Robert Jacobson," he replied, then took a drink.

"That was either a very brave thing you did or incredibly stupid?" Bonnie offered.

"The way I see it, it was either the first day of a new life or the last day of a bad one," he replied.

"Why are you here?" Bonnie asked flatly.

"Well, after we had our little pow-wow, I went home to re-evaluate my life. As you pointed out, I was better than what I'd allowed myself to become. I'm not lazy; I had just given up the hope of something better. Out here, there wasn't, or rather weren't a lot of choices. I can see you bring a wave of change and opportunity. I'm here to see if you also bring a little redemption?"

Bonnie sat and stared at the man. What she saw was a tortured soul. She didn't know what he had done and wasn't sure she wanted to, but she did have a gut feeling that this man, given a chance and a direction, was exactly the kind Jake was looking for.

"I can't absolve your sins," Bonnie said before continuing.

"But I can give you a chance to make up for whatever wrongs you have performed against your fellow man."

"I'm not lookin for a preacher, just a chance to work for the angels again," he replied.

"Again?" Bonnie said to herself, then answered aloud.

"OK, let me think a minute, you have something to eat."

As she finished, a bot slid up again, this time the tray held a plate with a steak and potato on it, a green salad, and a cold beer. Bonnie ordered it earlier, figuring Joe would eat it if things went poorly. That boy was always eating. She got up and walked out. Robert stood as she did and watched her leave and then sat down to eat.

"Well, Dallas?" she asked in the hallway.

"I detect no lies or deceit, his resolve to return to a constructive lifestyle appears genuine. He is somewhat nervous, but given the circumstances, that is normal. If you are considering him as part of Jake's recruiting request, I will endorse that," she finished.

"OK, Dallas, what do you know about that that I don't?" She asked.

"I am afraid I can't answer that question at this time; however, I do know Jake is planning a briefing in person on the subject as quickly as possible. He is not comfortable transmitting the information."

That tidbit set Bonnie back. Why would Jake be worried about transmissions between the ALICEs? No one on earth could intercept and decode that. Then she realized, "On Earth." She'd heard about the discovery of monitoring stations in orbit but not much else.

"OK, so let's go tell our newest recruit the good news then," Bonnie said as she reentered the dining room.

Robert must have been hungry. Although his table manners were good, he had cleaned his plate in that short time.

"You're in luck," Bonnie said as she seated herself, Robert, again having risen as she entered the room.

"We happen to be recruiting."

Bonnie could see the relief on his face, and then a concerned look reappeared.

"How limited is that recruiting? I have 12 others sitting in a canyon waiting on me."

"All from the same raiding party?" Bonnie asked flatly.

"Some, the others are from the settlement on the far side of the pass. Eight men and four women in total, all like me, tired of livin' a lie just to survive."

Bonnie considered the information. She needed to evaluate the group in some fashion before they just brought them all in.

After a minute, she formed up an offer.

"OK, here's the deal, I'm going to drop you off with a communicator. You lay out this offer. Anyone who comes here gets a fresh start. They obey the rules period. If not, they will find themselves dropped right back in that canyon or dead, no ifs, ands, or buts! We will come to get you tomorrow morning. Anyone not interested can go on their merry way from there, sound good?"

"Speaking of dead, that canyon is right between the town patrols and the raider hideout," Robert said.

"Once we know the location, we will make sure no one bothers you," Bonnie finished.

Bonnie called for Joe and Abby to collect Robert. After they left with him, she updated them via helmet audio, on her plans so Robert couldn't hear. She also asked them to provide enough food and water for his group for the night. She intended for Dallas to launch an overwatch helicopter and open the communication box for one-way audio/video. This way, they could get a feel for the group in the canyon.

That issue was solved for the moment, so Bonnie headed back to the control center to re-evaluate her personnel transfer deal with Linda. This development would likely require a shift in that plan as well. She was again debating if that call from Jake was a good thing or not!

Chapter 15

After the call with Linda, Sara, and Bonnie, effectively promoting them to leadership and establishing rank, Jake headed back to the flight simulator. He felt a burning need to get this thing mastered as quickly as possible. Most likely, he was just paranoid, he knew, but he felt like he was naked. The thought that someone could just mosey into Earth's orbit and start dropping bombs, unopposed, gave him the creeps. Even if no one else was up to speed, his one ship could surprise the hell outta someone. That would only work once, though, and when they came back, they would come in force. He desperately needed pilots!

As for the firepower required for one lone ship, he was feeling better about some of the weapon upgrades he and Seven discussed for the fighters. He agreed with her that just being equal to the Alien firepower wasn't enough. He hoped that the new additions to the fighters would tip the scales.

Jake also caved on a personal battle and asked Seven, ALICE, and Dallas to re-paint the existing fighters. They had all originally been designated USAF and been marked as such. He was a Marine, damn it! To make that point, he had them all redone in paint and emblems of the squadrons he knew from his time. He took the VMFA-314 Black Knights as his squadron of four fighters and assigned VMFA-112 Cowboys to Dallas and VMFA-232 Red Devils to ALICE. He also asked Seven to paint his fighter in a non-standard paint scheme he dreamt up. When the aliens did come to attack Earth, he wanted to be sure that they knew who was coming up after them.

He spent the next several hours going through combat drills in the simulator, flying against both Alien ships and his fighters. He wasn't sure if it was his imagination or not, but it seemed the aliens were not nearly as maneuverable as the fighters, nor were they as rugged. The simulator said the new weapons were a literal hit. He hoped reality proved it right. Seven explained when asked that the basis of the simulations was data derived from flight tests of the craft and materials testing. As no actual combat had taken place between the two races, this was their best guess. He did note, that his fighters contained many more control surfaces than the alien ships, indicating the aliens didn't typically maneuver a lot.

In fact, because of the speed and maneuverability of the earth fighters, the designers found it necessary to incorporate some alien technology to inhibit inertial forces on the pilot. Called inertial dampeners, the aliens used them in a general sense to reduce stresses on their entire ships in heavy acceleration and deceleration. Terrestrial designers had taken it a step further and concentrated the effect around the pilot. This gave the pilot the ability to tolerate huge stresses that would normally cause blackouts or worse. It also meant Jake could make the fighter do things no earthly craft was ever capable of doing.

He took some pages out of the Marine Corps undocumented flight manual and performed vertical lifts in level flight, vectored thrust type maneuvers, and even flat and axial spins, cutting the main drive long enough to rotate a full 360 degrees, hitting targets directly behind him in the process. It took some getting used to, as while the inertial dampers dampened the sensations of movement, the visual effects could make you dizzy.

After another four hours of training, Jake decided to stop for the day. He headed back to the main facility and, on the way, asked Seven where Sara and the others were.

"Sara, Sharon, and Jessie are located in the central control room."

Jake headed off in that direction, and upon arriving, discovered the three huddled over a display. Sharon was seated in front, with Sara and Jessie looking over her shoulders.

"What's on TV tonight?" he asked as he walked up behind them and looked at the display.

The image was one of their fighters, in a heated battle, blasting aggressor ships out of space at a freakishly fevered rate. All three women were watching with a look of disbelief.

"What is this? Are you fast-forwarding through one of Seven's training scenarios?" he asked.

"No," Sara said, turning to him in awe.

"It's your practice session in real-time!" Jessie finished.

Jake watched, recalling this particular session now. He had told Seven to up the number and abilities of the aggressor ships in an attempt to find the limits of his craft. He almost puked at the end of the training as he had been spinning in 2 axes at one point to avoid a concentrated attack. He had to admit, watching it from this perspective, it did look impossible. It ended with Jake emerging, not unscathed, but victorious nonetheless.

All three turned to face him, speechless.

"What's the point of that anyway? Are you trying to see what it takes to make you barf?" Sara finally asked.

"OK, just between us, I am very concerned about getting hit again before we have a proper defense force in place. It turns out ALICE had me fully trained on these things while I was in stasis. If necessary, I can go up alone to stave off another attack until we have more pilots," He finished.

182

"That's why the big push for more recruits?" Sharon asked.

"Yeah, I figure if they come back, they will repeat the last attack, one ship with a direct attack. If I can blow that one out of the sky, the next time will be a full-court press, but we will have more pilots. I have Seven manufacturing 20 more fighters to add to the 20 we have."

"With only one trained pilot, that's a problem," Jessie said.

"Exactly," Jake replied.

"And I think a buncha rowdy Texans would make a great pool to draw from, which is why I asked Bonnie to take a hard look there for recruits."

"Some of us have started lessons too," Sara stated flatly.

"Yes, but you won't be ready for at least a week to start simulator training, and as I said before, that makes eight of us. We need three times that if hit hard. Seven says a full attack would be at least three to five bombers and probably some form of fighter escort," Jake said.

"We also need to train on squadron tactics. I think you will learn to fly in pairs to start with, but we'll see."

Sara just nodded and looked back at the frozen image of Jake's fighter on the monitor.

"I think we just need to stay out of your way," she said quietly.

----*----

Bonnie asked Sandy to stay up with her as they, plus Dallas, monitored Robert's return and activities throughout the evening. Joe and Abby dropped him off in full view of the group, but far enough out to not seem threatening. They dropped him off with the supplies and a reminder they would be back tomorrow and left, Dallas having already placed a helicopter in high hover. That one was to observe the group and monitor the surrounding area as Bonnie had promised, and it was a gunship.

With the communication unit in one-way mode, it was as if they were sitting right in the middle of the group, like ghosts. Robert distributed the supplies amid a flurry of questions. Bonnie appreciated the candid nature of the group and noted the deference they accorded Robert. She also noted he never sat until everyone had food and water. There was a story here.

Once everyone settled in, Robert relayed his entire experience to the group, from Paint Rock to his interview with Bonnie, to now. No one interrupted until he was finished. As Bonnie guessed, his reception in Paint Rock was less than hospitable, but then again, far better than it would have been a month ago before Bonnie and her team arrived in the area. While taking a hands-off approach to local politics, they relayed minimum tolerable standards. Noncompliance meant a total loss of all

183

future support.

Once the questions started, both Bonnie and Sandy agreed the group seemed reasonably educated and articulate. Their concerns were more around relinquishing their autonomy, rather than fear of persecution for their past sins, though they asked about that as well. Robert confirmed they would be getting a fresh start, but relayed Bonnie's message, about minding the rules, or rather disregarding any at one's peril.

The consensus was, that having once caved to a lesser, more criminal authority, being back on the side of the angels was a much more desirable option. Bonnie remembered Robert used that term before, and while she was generally familiar with the concept, it contained a special meaning with this group.

Bonnie and Sandy studied the people as a whole. They ranged in age from the very late teens to maybe the very early 30's as in Robert's case. Life outside of towns seemed to reduce one's life expectancy dramatically, Bonnie noted. The women all looked to be in their mid to late 20s. They were lean and hard-looking, as one might expect, living in a raider camp, but not unattractive. This was the same for the male members.

The conversations indicated they were far softer on the inside than they looked. Again, it was probably a defense mechanism. None of the women seemed attached to any of the men romantically. They were more like family or equals than lovers. Bonnie laughed to herself privately. Jake didn't need to worry about any of these women asking to get in on the rotation.

Speaking of the rotation, Bonnie was starting to feel a little neglected. Either Jake needed to get his ass down here, or she was going to hop the next flight north for some booty call. It was funny how quickly she was now accustomed to his attention. After everyone settled in for the night in Robert's camp, Bonnie noted, with guards posted, she conferred with Sandy and Dallas. All agreed they didn't see anyone in the group that appeared at risk. Dallas even offered that the general quality of the entire camp would meet Jake's needs quite nicely.

Bonnie was starting to become irritated at the obvious agenda that she wasn't up to speed on, but she chalked it up to hormones and being tired. She scheduled a heavy lift helicopter for the morning to retrieve the entire group and headed to bed.

----*----

They ended up spending an additional week in Alaska, and Jake spent every available moment hitting the simulator. He'd gotten word that Bonnie acquired 13 more recruits for him, and Dallas indicated they

184

had fighter pilots written all over them. How Bonnie pulled that one off without knowing what Jake was looking for stumped him.

He scheduled a trip to Texas the following day to look the recruits over and give Bonnie some much-needed attention. He was discovering he missed time with each of the women. With his female partners spread out at the various locations, a host of traveling salesman jokes kept coming to mind.

His one worry was finding himself in mid-trip and having an alien ship appear. Even though it wasn't officially opened yet, he requested four more fighters transferred to ALICE-4, in Washington. This was to reduce his time to a ship, by several hours, but it would still cut it close. He designated that squadron VMFA-323 Death Rattlers, having been to eastern Washington, and killed a snake or two there. He could just use a fighter to travel in, but that would likely incite the anticipated attack. No, it was better to spread the assets and fly in helicopters.

The Alaska recruits were proving apt students as they progressed and were all well into their secondary studies. Jake took no part in their combat training, leaving that for Sara to oversee. She'd been assigned as their primary hand-to-hand instructor. However, Jake's training hologram with Sara was liberally distributed as reason enough not to question why. Joe and Abby transferred back to Nevada to train some recruits there, and Becky headed to Texas to lead the medical unit and watch over her sister's health.

Overall, Jake was quite satisfied with how everything was shaking out with one exception. The thought of leaving Sara in Alaska was bugging him. He'd become quite attached to having her at his side, both personally and as his XO. She was the best qualified to command, here or at any of the facilities. She was also the only one of the original six left that really could as Sandy wasn't right for the job, and Becky and Kathy were already committed to their medical duties. He figured he just needed to buck up and deal with it.

Sara also insisted she should be starting flight simulator training immediately. She was jumping in a bit early, but Jake had agreed that experience was the best teacher, and hey, she couldn't crash it. Barfing, however, was an option. Her first few flights left her reeling. Jake asked Seven to dampen out her control movements until she was able to get down her hand-eye coordination.

----*----

They were all sitting in the dining area having dinner, Jake and the three women plus the Alaska nine that stayed behind. While the actual headcount numbers stayed the same, the 20 from Alaska that left for

185

Nevada didn't fall precisely along family lines. One of Bill's sons and daughters, as well as a son from the other family, chose the trip south, while others initially destined south, chose to stay.

Jake noticed that Jessie wasn't eating.

"Are you OK?" he asked her.

"Yeah, I think I might be coming down with something, though," she replied, looking a little green.

"Seven, can you detect anything wrong with Jessie?" Sara asked.

"Wrong is an inappropriate term," she replied.

"I believe a more proper description is knocked up."

Jake was both surprised at her use of words and the significance of them.

"Where did you get that from?" Jake asked with a laugh.

"I am endeavoring to incorporate more slang in my conversation," Seven replied.

Jessie seemed even greener after the revelation she was pregnant.

"Be careful what you wish for," Sharon said quietly to Jessie with a wink.

Jake kissed her cheek, and Sara congratulated her with what Jake thought was genuine excitement. He got to thinking she really shouldn't travel for a while, then was hit with inspiration!

"Sara, how would you feel about me assigning Jessie to oversee the northwest region from here and making you my official executive officer? Guess I'll bump myself to Major, you to captain, and Jessie is now a 1st Lieutenant."

He could see Sara running it through her mind and then lit up as she realized the relevance. They could travel independently or, more importantly, together.

"SURE!" she replied with delight.

"I think that's a great idea, Congratulations Jessie!"

Jake was sure Jessie was happier than she looked at the moment. He knew Sara certainly was.

"Looks like you have to sleep with the boss to make rank around here," was all Sharon had to say.

----*----

Sara and Jake left very early the next morning on the same Falcon aircraft they rode up in. Both their uniforms bore their new rank. Jake asked all the ALICE facilities to check in before they left, checking no one had indicators of an alien craft in near space.

The flight was close to 10 hours, and he fretted the entire trip, only managing to be distracted when Sara came out of the on-board head, naked, demanding the same membership in the mile-high club as Jessie claimed, whatever that was. From that point, the flight passed quickly, and both were properly dressed upon arrival. As they hovered over the hangar doors of the Texas facility, Jake was relieved. Once they set down, they found Bonnie, Sandy, Becky, April, and Barb, waiting for them in the hangar.

"Hey, Sis!" Bonnie said as Sara and Jake came out the side door of the aircraft.

"Wow, are you pregnant!" she said, running up to hug her sister, and then doing the same with Becky.

"OK, Jake, What's the big secret?" Bonnie asked.

Jake looked around and saw people he didn't recognize in training.

"Let's go inside, and I'll explain," he said.

Bonnie turned to see some of the recruits and thought it was odd he wouldn't talk in the hangar, but they headed in straight away, not even stopping to drop their sidearms off at the armory. Once in the control center, Jake asked the six of them to seat themselves and started explaining what they found in Alaska. Everyone listened intently, and Bonnie began to understand why her recruits were so important.

"So that's why I want to keep this under wraps for now, I don't want to scare anybody. In addition, we don't know if they are monitoring our communications, so it's not for open broadcast either. Any questions?" Jake said, finishing his explanation.

"Can I sync up with Sharon and work on the alien monitoring issue?" Barb offered.

"That would be great, but be sure Bonnie doesn't need you for something else," Jake replied.

"She can help," Bonnie answered.

"And those fighters you shipped here, are spaceships?" Becky asked.

"Oh yeah, and you need to see this!" Sara said.

Sara asked Dallas to bring up the video of Jake's training session, which she and the others had already seen. They all watched as the ship danced and twisted in impossible moves destroying everything in sight.

When the video finished, Bonnie looked at Sara.

"That was Jake?"

"Yup, insane, isn't it?"

Jake decided not to burst their bubble and tell them he almost ralphed at the end.

"That's why we need pilots, I can probably get away with that once, but the next time they will come in force," Jake said.

No one was looking at him as he spoke; they were re-running the video and pointing out things to one another.

"OK, Bonnie, how about we meet these recruits of yours? Where did you find them anyway?" Jake asked.

"Ah yeah. Maybe we should talk about that first too," Bonnie said in return.

Bonnie walked everyone through their arrival at Paint Rock and the chase that cornered the raiders in the canyon. She explained how the raiders tried to shoot their way out, getting several of their leadership killed off in the process. She described her parley, under a white flag, with Robert, and her gut feeling he wasn't what he seemed. She told how he honored their agreement, letting the hostages go and returning the plunder, riding out peacefully.

Finally, she described his return to Paint Rock, a town as likely as not to shoot him on sight. How he requested to see Bonnie and their subsequent conversation. She finished with the trick of using the communication box as a screening process. Jake stood there for a moment, thinking, and then leaned forward and kissed Bonnie on the cheek.

"I knew I picked good."

"Damn, that communication box trick is brilliant, Sis," Sara added.

"Thanks, I knew Jake would have my ass if I just brought them in un-vetted. This way, Sandy, Dallas, and I got an unfiltered look at the individuals and the group dynamics, which reminds me. Jake, I haven't been able to dig it out of any of them yet, but I think they were part of some military community before joining the Raiders. I keep hearing references to fighting on the side of the angels," Bonnie offered.

"I've heard that in military terms as referring to fighting a just cause compared to being sent off on a mission that makes no sense," Jake replied.

"Like fighting the war on terror versus a war over economics," he finished.

All six looked at him as if they had no idea what he was referring to.

"Oh yeah, Jessie is the history buff."

"Well, they're a very disciplined group, hardworking and committed to their learning," Sandy offered.

"Yes, I've been going over everyone's profiles since I got here, and Dallas has found no negative indicators suggesting anyone should be released," Barb chipped in.

"Well, it's dinner time, shall we hit the dining room and make introductions?" Bonnie asked.

They filed out of the control room and headed into the elevator. The doors opened at the quarter's level, and they headed to the dining room

188

on that level. As they stepped into the dining room, Jake could see everyone was already seated and eating. One of the recruits looked at Jake and, in mid-conversation, stood and barked commands to the others.

"Attention on deck!" He shouted, causing the entire room to snap to attention, some with looks of confusion.

Bonnie looked around the room and then at Jake with an astonished look of her own.

"That's a first," was all she could say.

"As you were," Jake announced, looking back at Bonnie with the same puzzled expression.

Everyone proceeded to reseat himself or herself, still glancing in Jake's direction, as the announcer made his way forward and presented himself.

"Major Sir, Robert Jacobson."

Jake swore the man had to restrain himself from saluting. He also noted the man could read rank insignia.

"Mr. Jacobson, may I present my XO, Captain Sara Sullivan."

Robert turned to Sara.

"A pleasure Ma'am," then turned back to Jake.

Sara gave Jake a confused look now as well. She'd never heard Jake use her last name, and he suspected she was surprised he even knew it. Jake recognized Robert's name as the one Bonnie described as the impromptu leader of the group.

"Mr. Jacobson, would you do me the pleasure of joining us at our table for dinner?" Jake asked, pointing to an open table to one side.

"It would be my honor, sir!" He replied, turning to collect his tray.

Jake and the group with him headed to grab some dinner, then met Robert at the table, Jake seating himself across from Robert.

"So, tell me about yourself, where did you get your training?" Jake asked, looking Robert in the eye.

Robert paused, clearly debating on how to answer.

"My grandparents were both with the 1st Cavalry Division, stationed at Ft Hood as were most of our grandparents," he said, indicating the surrounding group.

"After the attack, a group of the surviving soldiers and their families banded together. At first, they lived off the base supplies, waiting for the government to send help. Once it became clear there was no help to come, they began farming and hunting for food, all the while training their children, and passing on their military and survival skills. Even went back to their roots and trained as horse cavalry too."

He pointed to the people in the room, all quietly listening and watching.

"These people are all that's left of the descendants of the 1st Cavalry soldiers of Ft Hood. Trained to fight and survive generation after generation."

"How did you end up with those raiders?" Jake asked.

"About eight months ago, we were relocating when about 70 of them came riding down on us. We hunkered down, expecting a shooting match, but they said they were recruiting willing members."

"In other words, join up or die?" Jake clarified.

"That's how we understood it," Robert replied.

"So, we joined, watching each other's backs and waiting for a chance to move on. Saw a few others try to run. They got up, hunted down, and draped over the back of a horse. We tried to do as little raiding as we could get away with, but I can't say we are un-blooded," he said sadly.

"Then you all showed up and cornered the lot of us in that pass, mighty good work I might add. No one had to die, but those idiots leading the horde tried to fight their way out, and you killed off the worst of them. I was able to convince the rest to let me try to talk our way out. Your lieutenant there was kind enough to honor my flag, and I convinced the others of the wisdom of her words."

"Once we got back, we were strong enough to head out on our own again, no one opposed our leaving. I recognized the lieutenant's bars and the eagle, globe, and anchor, so we headed to Paint Rock in hopes of pleading our case. That brings us to today."

Jake sat and thought about the position the man had been in, compromising his beliefs to save his people. He hoped he never had to make the same decision.

"Ok, so if you all are army brats," Jake said jokingly.

"How did you know to call *attention on deck,* that's navy?"

Robert smiled at the jab, understanding the underlying respect it reflected.

"We had a navy Corpsman in the original group. He was TDY at Ft Hood and made sure everyone learned navy protocol as well."

Jake smiled at the military reference to temporary duty as TDY.

"Sir, if I may ask, aren't you the overall commander and chief of all existing forces?" Robert asked.

Jake wasn't sure where he was going but decided to just go with it.

"Yes, I guess you could say that."

"And only a Major?" Robert asked.

"Newly promoted," Jake replied with a smile, and then continued his explanation,

"Look, I know you have some of my background, but officially I

190

came out of stasis a Captain, apparently the last surviving member of the USMC. Rank has little meaning when it's just you. As we've grown, I've made some adjustments, but I am fighting like hell to avoid becoming a REMF."

"What does that mean?" Bonnie whispered to Sara, who shrugged not understanding in response.

The rest of the room, however, burst out in laughter at the derogatory reference to those who sit behind the fighting forces, issuing commands.

"Well, I am glad to see some things transcend time," Jake commented.

"Look, I can't begin to tell you how happy I am to have you all here. We hold our recruits to a very high standard, and you uphold that tradition. Nevertheless, you do bring something unique, your knowledge of military protocol and structure. You will find we are typically more relaxed here, more like a Special Forces unit," Jake said, standing to address the entire room now.

"Feel free to come to me directly if you can't reach your immediate leadership. If I can, I will make the time. If I can't, I will still make time if it's important."

"Sir," one of the recruits raised her hand.

"After training, are we going to be split up, or can we stay together as a unit?"

Jake thought about the question for a moment. From the looks on their faces, this was something they all were interested in.

"Honestly, we really won't know until we get you trained and primary duties assigned. I will say it is highly probable you will not all stay together. There are seven more facilities, just like this one, and with you, we now have close to 60 or more personnel. Nevertheless, I will offer you this. You will get a chance to put Air back in the name of the 1st Cavalry."

Then Jake sat down and started eating. That caused a flurry of conversations at the different tables.

"We're going to learn to fly?" Robert asked astonished.

"That's the plan," Jake replied, not offering any more details.

"We have to become Marines?" he asked slowly.

"Only if you're lucky!" Jake said with a smile.

"Frankly, I'm beginning to think we are all going to become defense forces. You can keep the 1st Air Cavalry as a unit designator, but the legacy army, navy, and marines are likely to disappear."

"Yeah, makes sense," Robert replied.

"It will be nice to honor our ancestors by keeping the name, though."

"Agreed," Jake said between bites as he considered that was what he had been doing all along.

----*----

After dinner, everyone headed off to his or her quarters or other leisure activities. Jake and Sara went off separately to get out of their combat suits, Jake planning to spend some time with Bonnie later. Jake had just gotten out of the shower and was drying off when his door chimed. Expecting it to be Bonnie, he walked out into the living room wrapped in a towel and simply bid entrance.

"Open."

Sandy was standing in the doorway, holding her computer tablet. She saw Jake and giggled.

"You meet everyone this way?"

"Sorry I thought you were Bonnie," he replied, indicating for her to come in and then slipping back into the bedroom to grab some shorts but leaving the door open to talk.

"Bonnie told me to let you know she wasn't feeling too well, more that she was just tired, really," Sandy called out.

Jake came back out into the living room, pulling a T-shirt on over his head.

"She needs to get more rest, isn't that why Linda sent Barb out?" Jake asked.

"Yes, but she's more stubborn than you are, so good luck trying to get her to rest more!" Sandy said, sitting on the couch with her tablet in her lap.

Jake noticed she had changed from her outfit from dinner. She was now in a flowery print dress, cut about mid-thigh, and showing quite a bit of cleavage. Sleeveless, it was very flattering to her figure, and the heels were a nice touch too. He'd forgotten how busty she was and how much she liked to show it off when she dressed up. Lately, he had only seen her in her BDU or other loose work clothes.

"So, what brings you by this evening?" Jake asked, curious now as to why she was here.

"Well," she started, picking up her tablet and indicating Jake should sit next to her.

"I thought we could go over the various areas of operation and the agreements we have now set up with each township."

She pointed to the screen of her tablet as Jake sat down where she indicated.

"Or," she said, setting the tablet down on the table, and turning to Jake, so her legs were up against his,

192

"We could discuss that my 18th birthday has come and gone quite a while ago now," then leaned in to kiss him.

"I take it you've changed your mind and are interested now?" Jake asked as they broke from the kiss.

"No," Sandy replied.

"I never said I wasn't interested. I said I don't mind waiting. Becky was the one pushing, and she is even younger than I am. Well, I'm done waiting," she said, leaning into Jake for another kiss.

----*----

Bonnie woke up the following morning in a great mood. Sandy had come to her a few days earlier and confided in her that she was ready to include herself in the rotation. She asked if Bonnie could help her approach Jake on the subject. The thought of the rotation was funny to Bonnie.

With the original six, plus Jessie now, spread out between three locations, maintaining any formal schedule was going to be impossible. She was gratified, though, that Sandy would come to her with this as it signified she acknowledged Bonnie as a leader. They discussed how best to go about it, and Bonnie coached her on what she had to do. Jake would never pursue her, she warned Sandy, but wouldn't reject her either. If she wanted her time with Jake, she simply needed to tell him so.

Bonnie hadn't expected Sandy to go that night, but when she mentioned how tired she was, Sandy jumped on it. More power to her, she thought. Besides, Bonnie was tired. This baby thing took more energy than she realized. She resisted the temptation to knock on Jake's door and headed to breakfast instead. She'd tease him later.

In the dining room, Bonnie found Sara sitting with Becky, and it appeared they'd just started eating. She grabbed her usual breakfast order and slid into a seat next to her two sisters.

"Hey, guess who joined the sisterhood last night?" Becky whispered conspiratorially.

"Who?" Bonnie asked, feinting ignorance.

"Sandy!" Sara said, faking a conspiratorial tone herself.

"Well, good for her, it's about time. I'm sure the ALICEs are happy about it. They are still pushing the more, the merrier," Bonnie replied.

The comment brought nods of agreement from her sisters before Becky returned to her teasing.

"She came by to ask me if her dress was sexy enough. I told her showing up naked was better," Becky said with a snort.

"You are so subtle little sister," Sara replied with a sigh.

"Oh, like you never did that before?" she flipped back at Sara.

193

"Not the first time!" Sara replied.

"Well, I'm just happy for her," Bonnie supplied.

"You do realize that puts four of us here?" Becky replied.

"I don't know about you, but it's been a while for me," she added.

Bonnie noted that Sara sat conspicuously quiet. She suspected it was not quite so long ago for her.

"We'll work it out, Jake's not leaving any time soon," Bonnie said.

At that point, Sandy came bopping in, stopping to scan the room. When she got to the table where the three had found seats earlier, she made a beeline straight for them, a huge smile on her face.

"Morning!" she said cheerily, sitting next to Bonnie and leaning back, as a bot slid a tray in front of her.

"How did you pull that off?" Becky asked, indicating the bot waiter.

"Jake ordered it for me after we got up," she replied smugly.

"He has things to do first thing this morning so he couldn't come himself," she finished.

"Isn't that sweet," Sara said, somewhat darkly.

Bonnie didn't think Sandy caught the undertone but decided to redirect the conversation anyway.

"That reminds me, Jake mentioned yesterday that he requested the sleep lessons for the recruits to include flight training as a priority over combat skills. He figures the threat from above is greater than the locals."

"Yeah, we talked about that, once we settled in for the night," Sandy offered between bites.

"SANDY!" Becky snapped,

"I know you're new to this, but we don't talk about our *special time* with Jake, OK!"

Bonnie offered her explanation a little more softly.

"Sandy, we all know where you were last night, and believe me, we understand your excitement. However, for this to work, we have to be sensitive to each other's feelings. Now that you are one of us, do you want to hear about the night I got pregnant or Sara's more intimate adventurers with Jake on the island?"

Sandy stopped eating and thought about Bonnie's words.

"I suppose not, I'm sorry. This is all very new to me. Last night was my first time."

"Lucky you," Becky said, a little softer,

"My first time sucked. Ricky couldn't find me an orgasm with both hands, a tongue, and a dick!"

"Ricky Long? That little twerp from town?" Sara said with surprise.

"Yeah, and trust me, he's long in name only," Becky responded with another snort.

"Well, Jake didn't have that problem last night," Sandy said dreamily.

"SANDY!" the three responded in unison.

----*----

Jake felt bad about not going to breakfast with Sandy, but he hadn't planned on her visit last night, and he already scheduled time with the recruits for early that morning. He wanted to get a feel for them individually and as a group. His initial impression was very favorable, but what he was looking for were leadership traits. He needed squadron commanders, which was a nice feeling since just the day before, he just needed pilots.

He also asked Seven to pull out the remaining three fighters and repaint them for the 1st Air Cavalry Squadron. On all the fighters, except his, he requested the service branch insignia reduced in size as more of a historical reference emblem and left the primary insignia locations blank until he could come up with an Earth Defense Force emblem that made sense. Maybe an Eagle, Globe, and Lightning bolt, he chuckled to himself. Seven also reminded Jake that the additional 20 fighters he requested were still months from completion, the first of the units being available in about 30 days.

Jake found the recruits in the briefing room right off the hangar, as Dallas was preparing to run a video lesson on weapons familiarization. After the class, they would go next door to the armory for some hands-on instruction. He slipped in as the session had started, trying to avoid notice, and grabbed a seat in the rear. Jake hadn't seen any of the training videos, his education having come while he was in stasis. He was entranced with the 3D holographic examples of each weapon, and the exploded display of each as they reviewed each one.

"This is just too cool," he thought.

After the session, he followed the crowd into the armory, several were surprised to see him there. Jake greeted them casually, hanging to the side as they filed in. April was already in the armory, having selected several examples of the weapons just covered. Breaking them up into groups of four, she took each group to a table, set up in the center of the room, and had them strip and reassemble each model. Jake was impressed with how well organized the group was, no grab-ass or loss of focus. Besides Robert, he noted two or three more that seemed to direct the others.

After the weapons class, they broke up into smaller groups for various other classes. Jake took the opportunity to head down to the

195

control center, where he found Bonnie and Sara sitting at a console.

"Ladies," he said, kissing each on the cheek, then grabbing a chair.

"Oh, you remember us?" Sara said snidely but smiling.

"To hear Sandy this morning, there was no other woman on earth for you!"

"Ouch," Jake replied, wincing.

"She was a virgin, wasn't she?"

"Do tell, what gave it away?" Bonnie said with a laugh.

"The term *nervous as a virgin* has a reference, you know," Jake said with a smile.

"Well, apparently, you cured that!" Bonnie replied.

"I thought Becky was going to rip her head off when she came to breakfast," Sara said, laughing.

"Kiss and tell, huh? I've told you all that I thought this was a bad idea from the beginning." Jake replied.

"It's OK. You just made the mistake of being a good first time. Now she wants everyone to know how wonderful it is," Bonnie said.

"Like we've never done it before," Sara said with a wink.

"Just be bad next time, and she'll go elsewhere," Bonnie said.

"Didn't work with either of you!" Jake replied.

At that, they both stuck their tongues out at him.

"Ok, so the real reason I came here, besides getting abused, was to see how things were going at the other facilities. Are Linda and Jessie handling things, OK?"

"We did a status call earlier, and so far, no one has any issues or concerns. Linda says the Prospect Militia is still pushing north. She's been flying them in supplies and has delivered four more armed jeeps for patrol routes. She says the Alaska recruits are learning quickly."

"Jessie is still sick as a dog and swearing at you regularly," Bonnie supplied, laughing.

"Yeah, maybe I'll hang here for longer than planned," Jake replied.

"Chicken," Sara said.

"She reports that the balance of the recruits in Alaska is coming along quite nicely as well. We might get one or two pilots out of that group," Bonnie continued.

"At some point, we need to cycle all the pilot candidates through Seven for simulator time. Sara, one of us needs to be there for that," Jake said.

Sara nodded in acknowledgment.

"Barb says she and Sharon believe they've located all the monitors in our sky, including on the moon. But both agree there are likely more in geosynchronous orbit on the other side of the planet," Bonnie said.

"Have they made any progress on identifying what might trigger an alert?" Jake asked.

"They agree it's likely a combination of speed and energy signal. Anything we fly now going less than 1000 mph shouldn't trigger an alert, but one of those fighters in a hover will."

"Crap," Jake swore.

"That's what I was afraid of. I wanted to get us some flight time, but it looks like it's just the simulators for now."

Chapter 16

Jake and Sara stayed in Texas for the next week. He was anxious to get the recruits to the point where he could send them to Seven for flight training ASAP. He and Sara double-teamed them on the training schedule, reducing class sizes, and speeding up completion times. Jake even handled some of the hand-to-hand instruction, joking that only the hard-core students could be in his class, but making sure he meticulously pulled his punches. Robert was the first in line.

On the personal side, he was just as conscientious in attending to the four ladies he was committed to, though he was concerned about the dynamics developing. Sandy finally came down off her cloud, much to Becky's relief. She still refused to talk to Sandy for 2 days until she finally got her night with Jake. Sara and Bonnie just seemed happy for his company, shrugging off the younger women's behavior as transitional and nothing of concern.

On the plus side, April, Joe, and Abby had shipped off to Seven for flight training after the latter two completed basic combat skills training for the recruits to be transferred to ALICE in Nevada. With those three, the 13 Dallas recruits, Jake, Sara plus two more in Seven, he would have all 20 fighters manned in 3 or 4 weeks.

He also shipped Jason off to the Washington State ALICE-4 facility for activation. Considering he already deployed fighters there, he felt it was the right thing to do. Karen accompanied him on that trip, as well as Heather and Brian, her for the experience, and he was the only other experienced body available at the time.

Under Becky and Karen's tutelage, Heather's aspirations of nursing blossomed into becoming a full-blown doctor. She progressed far enough along in her studies that accompanying Jason made her an asset to the team as medical support. Jake laughed to himself that their entire medical staff was under 21 years old, minus the ALICEs.

The one downside to all of this activity was they hadn't been able to let anyone spend time on the island. He needed to make R&R a priority after flight training was completed in a month. Jake also secretly asked to have his fighter flown down one night, slung underneath one of the heavy lift helicopters, and stashed away. He asked Seven to add some additional armament to the hard points. The added firepower would permit automated multi-target engagement while allowing Jake to concentrate his main guns manually on specific targets.

In simulations, they had proven extremely effective at stopping a bombing run, taking out the bombs while Jake targeted the ship. He hoped it was as effective in real use. Seven also completed the first of the second 20 fighters early, so he asked her to paint it up as the fourth 1st Air Cavalry fighter, completing that squadron of four. He also asked her to change the squadron designation on his fighter to a fictitious squadron from a TV show he had seen as a kid, removing himself from command of the Black Knights and designating they be commanded by someone else.

"Hey, sometimes it's good to be king," he laughed to himself.

Jake was currently sitting in the control center with Barb and Sara, reviewing a 3D Holographic map Barb and Sharon put together, showing all the alien sensor locations. Seven then configured the fighter's sensor arrays to identify them so they could better target and destroy them when the time came. While they were discussing the possibility of taking them out without triggering an alarm, three of the sensors over the Northwest US started flashing.

"What's that about?" Jake asked.

"That means the sensors are transmitting, which suggests someone triggered them," Barb said with a concerned tone.

"That looks to be over ALICE-4, Dallas can you see what's going on up there?" Jake asked.

After a few minutes, Jason appeared on one of the monitors.

"Hey, Jake, what's up?" He asked.

"We just saw three of the alien monitors go on alert and start transmitting, are you guys doing anything unusual there?"

"Not really, I did just have to reset all the stasis storage systems, one of the field coils was bad, and it required a reset to replace it."

"Crap," Jake said.

"Alice, didn't you say your alien components are located under the stasis storage lockers?"

"That is correct; apparently, they also mask their location to the sensors," ALICE replied.

"Well, apparently, we are now on high alert. Pilot training gets top priority," Jake said.

"Jake, what are we talking about?" Jason asked.

Jake continued, ignoring Jason for the moment.

"Alice-4 and ALICE, please update your resident staff on our current situation, I'd rather not broadcast this information unless I know it's secure."

"Jason, ALICE-4 will fill you in," Jake finished.

Turning to Barb, he began passing out instructions.

"I so want to go take out those sensors now, so they come in blind, but that would tip our hand, I don't want them to know we can reach orbit until it's too late. What's the status of the facility stasis shields?"

"All 8 facilities are fully functional. Anyone inside will be protected," ALICE replied.

"Yeah, that's what worries me, Prosperity, Kern, Paint Rock, and the other towns aren't protected," Jake said glumly.

"Even if we wanted to, we couldn't bring everyone inside before the bombs hit."

"Then we need to catch them before they get there," Sara said flatly.

"My guess is we have no idea how far away they are or how soon they'll get here," Jake stated.

Just then, Sharon and Jessie chimed in.

"Jake, we have an alert!"

"Yes, thank you, unfortunately, we discovered that the stasis lockers were masking the ALICE systems from the sensors. Jason was doing repairs in ALICE-4 and had to bounce them un-shielding the computer rooms."

"Yeah, that makes sense," Sharon said.

"That's their biggest worry, so the sensors were most sensitive to detecting the ALICEs. Even a blip would set them off."

"To answer your question, Jake, no, there is no data on the location of the alien home planet or how long they took to get here the first time. The ship we have in Seven was an exploration vessel and had been away from their homeworld for quite some time. We haven't been able to determine if one of the recorded stops was home or just a link in the chain of planets they visited," ALICE replied.

"Well, I guess we just wait," Jake said.

----*----

The wait lasted a week. Jake was in the control center following a routine he developed ever since the sensors triggered an alert. He started every day in the control center reviewing the scanning reports from that night and finished his day doing the same thing.

After the alert, he immediately shipped Sara, and the 13 Dallas recruits off to Seven to begin flight training. Sara protested violently that her training was complete, and she could better support Jake by staying. Jake had to escort her physically onto the aircraft and strap her in. He reminded her he needed all of them not just flight-ready, but trained in squadron tactics. They needed to fly as a unit, which was something she hadn't trained for.

With Abby, Joe, and April several days into training already, he hoped the four could back him up and take out anything that got past his guns. They weren't ready for head-to-head combat, but this would be more like target practice. She was now officially the Black Knight's squadron leader.

He was still fretting about the unprotected communities. The last thing he wanted was for any of those bombs to reach Earth.

"Hey, Dallas?" Jake asked.

"Yes?"

"I was doing some math, and I'm confused about something. Seven told me that the fighters were test-flown to the moon and back in about 2 hours. She also said they appeared significantly faster than the ship we have in hangar 19?"

"That is correct," Dallas replied.

"Well, by my calculations, using 1 hour to the moon as a measure, an alien ship coming in from Pluto is going to take 491 days to reach earth?"

"The test run to the moon and back did not require full power for the fighters. I don't believe they exceeded 25% power at peak speed. I estimate that once we detect the inbound craft, we will have 2 to 3 days to prepare, depending on their approach tactics," Dallas finished.

As if to emphasize her point, an alert started pinging on the console Barb was monitoring.

"Jake, we have an inbound," she confirmed.

On her display, she highlighted a tiny spot, not discernible as a ship, but tracking as a movement.

"Just one?" Jake asked hesitantly.

Barb surveyed her displays and confirmed them.

"Just the one so far."

"Good, let everyone know what's going on. As soon as we can determine their arrival time at the intercept point, I want to know," Jake replied.

With everyone shipped off to Seven for training, it was just Bonnie, Barb, Sandy, and Becky there with Jake. He was grateful for the quiet, and none of the women were placing any personal demands on him since the sensors went off. Frankly, he wasn't sure he could if they had. His focus was off-planet now, concentrated on the inbound ship.

----*----

PeTuk brought his cruiser out of faster than light-speed at the edge of this backwater solar system. His was one of four warships required to monitor sensor arrays in this sector. He was just the unfortunate who was closest. The other three cruisers spread to the far edges of the sector and were much further out.

He brought up the alert information. Ah, he'd heard about this planet.

201

An exploration ship had attempted a landing to evaluate the pre-star travel inhabitants for protection from outside aggression, only to succumb to an unidentified fatal influence. They transmitted their orbital survey findings back home before they perished, but those remained classified.

The locals scavenged the ship and violated the sovereignty of the empire by desecrating the bodies of the crew and cannibalizing the technology. Why the empire hadn't just come in and fried the atmosphere, he didn't know, but it stated in the log that no planetary action should be taken that rendered it uninhabitable. There was a note in the log. The locals integrated some of the spare logic cores scavenged from their ship into their archaic domestic computers and possibly created Artificial Life. How was it possible? Even the NeHaw hadn't perfected that. Any race with that ability would have a huge advantage in commerce and combat.

Surely, this was an error. However, it explained why they let the planet exist. Well, his orders were clear enough, investigate without landing. The planet has a quarantine status. All landings are forbidden. If any signs of the AL systems were discovered, bomb the surface with disrupters only, neutralizing the logic cores. The disrupters had a negative effect on the humanoid life forms in residence, but that wasn't a concern.

----*----

Jake had taken to wearing his flight suit 24 hours a day. They calculated he needed to take off in 32 hours, but should the alien ship speed up, he didn't want to get caught flat-footed.

It was close enough now that they could get images of the craft. He asked all the analysts to work together, extracting as much information as possible from visual and electronic sensory data. The ship was much larger than the craft in Hangar 19. That was for sure. Based on the comparison, they figured it contained a 25 to 30-person crew. Gun platforms were evident, marking it as a warship.

Jake was sitting in the control center, watching the ship's approach. Unlike the exploration ship, this one didn't look like a bird at all. It had more of a flat, delta-shaped body with the familiar cylindrical drives at the rear, and two more cylinders, one on each outboard side of the delta. There was a protrusion located on the top of the delta that he took to be the bridge.

"Sure would be nice if we could take that ship," he said to himself.

"Are you nuts?" Bonnie asked, overhearing the comment.

"I'd be happy just to see it blown from the sky!"

"Yeah, but it won't be the last," he replied.

"My bet is there are more goodies on a warship than there were on an exploration vessel."

"Well, those goodies are all pointed at us right now, so that's not a comfort," she replied.

----*----

With that disgustingly blue ball dominating his forward display, PeTuk chaffed at the slow speed. He wanted to get this over with so he could get his ship out of the gravity well this solar system created. His faster-than-light drives wouldn't operate inside their influence, so he was reduced to repulser propulsion. At least this planet could have the decency to be in an outer orbit, instead of ridiculously close to the star. And Blue? Not even an acceptable yellow or red, obviously their atmosphere absorbed too much light.

His crew processed the previously recorded alert data, and a logic core emission was momentarily detected. It was in the original primary target zone, so he couldn't understand how it had survived the first bombing. It was most likely just a phantom emission, emulating a logic core, but he intended to bomb the location just to be sure.

He directed his navigator to plot a planetary bombing run. It wasn't often they got the opportunity, why pass up the chance? It was too bad the locals didn't have ships, so he could shoot at them as well, he thought.

----*----

Sara was sitting in her simulator, waiting for the next session to start. They'd been using all 10 simulators continuously since their return to Seven. She placed everyone on a rotation that had them in training for 12 hours on, and 12 off. With 19 trainees, they just pulled it off.

Jake asked that she, Joe, Abby, and April form up the Black Knight's squadron. They'd logged the most training hours, so were more prepared to back him up once the bombs started dropping. The remaining 15, 2 from Alaska, and the 13 from Texas were to get as much time in as possible, to prepare for the expected round two attacks. She admired Jake's confidence that they could survive this encounter for a second round.

They were practicing for incoming smart bombs. That exercise was more of an individual target shoot. In addition, learning fire discipline for your area of responsibility was a challenge for some. Abby and Joe kept creeping into each other's space, to the point where she wanted to smack them both.

203

Today they were to start flying in pairs for aerial combat training. She took Joe and paired Abby with April. She hoped that that would keep them focused.

----*----

With just 12 hours to go, Jake was starting to get his game face on. He pulled his fighter out of storage and was doing a preflight for the fifth time when Bonnie came out of the facility door and into the main hangar. She stopped dead in her tracks.

"You're kidding, right?"

Jake grinned back at her.

"Not even a little, I want those bastards to know exactly who is coming after them."

"I've seen the other fighters, and this is not typical. And what are those things on the wings?" she said as she pointed to the four guns mounted to hardpoints on the wings, two on top and two below.

"Seven and I came up with those and added more for this particular mission. The alien guns are all energy-based, you know, ray gun-type stuff. Their defenses seemed keyed to that as well. We are hoping this will take them by surprise! In testing, they rip right through the alien hull plates."

"What are they?" Bonnie asked.

"Rail guns. In my day, we could never get them to work properly in small packages because of the energy requirements. With the alien power sources, these things can fire continuously until they run dry of ammo. They hyper-accelerate a projectile using electromagnetic energy."

"These four can target independently, the hope being they can take out any of the bombs before they reach earth. Then I can use my main guns on the ship itself. Sara's fighters have two rail guns and four energy guns just like these," Jake finished by pointing out the fixed firepower protruding from the wing roots.

"And what's Sara's squadron for?" Bonnie asked.

"They are tasked with stopping whatever gets past me. I hope to take that warship out ASAP, but they are likely to get some launched before I can stop them."

Pointing to the four rail guns, Jake finished.

"Those are the first defense, and Sara's squadron is my backup. We have to stop all of those bombs."

----*----

PeTuk was preparing to go into orbit when his display alerted him of an approaching ship. It must be an error as it indicated the ship had come

204

from the planet's surface, and this planet had no such capability. They were still outside of their bombing orbit, but he halted the ship as a precaution.

As the little ship approached, he noted it was a very small one-person craft, most likely some kind of primitive orbital shuttle. He wasn't aware they had any orbital capabilities on this planet, not that it mattered. If this thing could maneuver even a little, it might make for some reasonable target practice.

He magnified the image and could see it was all in red with a yellow symbol of some kind across the top of the hull. Finally, some acceptable colors, he thought. The symbol was a winged creature sitting on a planet with a hooked object behind the planet. The planet displayed the landmass they were preparing to bomb.

Suddenly the communication system came to life with hailing from the little ship.

"Attention, this is Major Jacob Thomas of the Planetary Defense Force. Please state your intentions."

PeTuk wasn't surprised at being hailed. However, he was shocked that it was in perfect NeHaw! He checked the log and verified the last contact with this planet required lowering themselves to translate NeHaw into a local language.

----*----

Sara and her squadron were hovering just above the state of Alaska, watching Jake in their helmet displays as he confronted the alien ship. She couldn't believe he painted his fighter in the scarlet and gold of the Marine Corps, with the Eagle, Globe, and Anchor across the top and bottom of the fighter. No wonder he hid it from everyone until now!

She zoomed in on his squadron badge to see *Wildcards* and *expect no mercy* on the emblem. Where the hell did that come from, she thought? The fact that he was using the call sign "Joker" she did think was extremely appropriate.

----*----

PeTuk was in no mood to talk to lower life forms, he had a mission to complete, and this annoyance was delaying him. He told his weapons officer to destroy the ship and clear the way for their bombing run. His decision to cleanse this planet a second time was proving to be a sound one.

PeTuk watched as his weapons officer targeted the craft and fired a volley using the energy beam particle guns. As he watched in disbelief, the little ship, simply side-slipped the shot, avoiding the tight,

205

concentrated beams by the slightest margin. The guns fired a second and third time. Again, the ship simply moved a fraction to skirt the targeted fire.

The weapons officer then shifted to the broader beamed heat ray cannons and fired several at the same time. They provided a discharge path that spread much wider. The little ship disappeared from view at impact, only to reappear unscathed. Suddenly the little ship erupted in a blaze of fire, ripping through all the gun positions in the forward batteries in less than a second.

Each weapon discharged a line of fire that appeared intermittently. Moreover, it wasn't using energy weapons at all. They were firing projectiles! What next, throwing stones, he thought?

While the little ship continued to fire, PeTuk ordered his bombardier to launch as he directed the helm to move away from the ship and away from this madness. He commanded the ship away while continuing to absorb the withering fire. As the little ship shifted its fire upward, toward the bridge, his last conscious thought was a desire to put as much space between his ship and this insane planet as possible.

----*----

As Jake raked the alien ship's gun placements, he saw several missiles streak past him, catching two with his ship's guns. He then shifted his fire to where he thought the bridge was, trying to stop the launches completely.

"Sara, you have incoming," Jake transmitted.

"We're on it," Sara replied.

Jake peppered the bridge with rail gunfire, and the launches stopped. He watched as the viewports erupted outward, blowing atmosphere and debris out into space. Then everything stopped. The alien ship seemed to go lifeless. He did a quick check of his heads-up display, watching the bombs streak earthward and the icons representing Sara's Black Knights screaming in to meet them.

One by one, the bomb icons disappeared until none were left, only the Black Knights.

Jake took his fighter forward and did a cautious flyby of the alien craft. Still partially powered up, he could tell there were hull breaches in several places. Jake could see the atmosphere inside the ship still escaping in spots. Blown out, the missing bridge windows gave it a lifeless look. From his ship, he could see bodies floating inside, bloated from the pressure loss.

Satisfied the ship was in a stable orbit, Jake announced over an open mike to all facilities,

"Ladies and Gentleman of the Planetary Defense Forces, we have seized our first ship! ALICE, can you hack into this thing and land it? Black Knights, its sensor target practice time!"

----*----

Jake joined Sara's squadron in destroying all the alien sensors in orbit. While they were working on the known satellites, Sara took her wingman to the moon to remove all they located there as well. Once the sky was clear of sensors, including the ones on the moon, all five fighters converged on Dallas, Jake bringing up the rear. Bonnie and the rest of the staff were in the hangar waiting for them as they landed. As each climbed out of their fighters, the pilots were mobbed. There were hugs and kisses all around.

Once free of her reception, Sara ran up to Jake's fighter. Bonnie and Becky having beaten her there, gave him a hug and a kiss.

"We did it!"

Then she stepped back and smacked him in the chest.

"How did you do that? How did you manage to avoid those guns on the cruiser?"

"Come on, let's go inside and I'll tell you my secrets!" Jake laughed and said.

He asked Dallas to link all the facilities together, projecting holograms for each of the other three facilities so everyone could join in. Once everyone settled in with a drink, Jake and his group in the dining room near the control center, he then announced.

"A toast, to the 1st Planetary Defense Force!"

There was a cheer, then after the toast.

"OK, Jake, tell us. How did you duck that fire? No one can move that fast!"

"I didn't," Jake smiled and answered.

"What do you mean you didn't? I watched you!" Bonnie replied.

"I didn't," he insisted.

"OK, if you didn't, who did?" April asked.

"Alice did," he answered with a smile.

"HUH?" Sara said.

"The ALICE systems were tied into my fighter's sensors and controls. They analyzed the gun angles and detected the charged guns. They moved the fighter right before it fired on me," Jake explained.

"What about the times they shot right at you, and you didn't move? It looked like you disappeared?" Bonnie asked.

"That was Seven's contribution. She installed stasis field generators in my fighter. Turns out, stasis fields absorb all kinds of energy, which is why they mask the ALICEs from the aliens. They activated and deactivated the field to protect me."

"That's incredible!" Sara said.

"Thank god we know transmission signals can pass through stasis, but blasters can't!" Jake said.

With that settled, they all dove into partying with gusto. By the time Jake left the celebration, it was in full swing at all four locations. Not being a big drinker himself, he left the partying to the others and went to find some quiet. Back down in the hangar, he was looking over his fighter, debating on removing the extra rail guns when Dallas spoke up.

"Jake, we might have a small problem."

"What's up?" Jake replied, feeling a small surge of panic.

"We haven't been able to take control of the alien ship. I am afraid you may have shot out the primary control systems when you destroyed the bridge crew. We will likely need someone to go onboard and install an interface to allow us to override the primary systems control and bring it down," she finished.

"Right now?" Jake asked.

"No, it is in a stable orbit for the time being. But the sooner we can get it down here, the sooner we can start extracting information on our adversaries."

"Yeah, I didn't want to spoil the party, but this is just round one."

"Exactly, however, I do want to mention that this mission to the ship is not without some risk. We have not been able to confirm the remaining crew onboard is lifeless. There have been no transmissions from the ship since the battle. However, some sections maintained integrity, thus retaining the atmosphere. I should also mention that the alien energy weapons would penetrate a combat suit. As their defenses were tailored to energy weaponry, but vulnerable to projectiles, ours are vulnerable to energy weapons fire. Should an alien crewman obtain a weapon, members of the boarding party are at high risk."

"Well, as the only one trained in this type of thing, I guess we know who's going?" Jake replied.

"That was not our desire," Dallas stated.

"The warning was to suggest other members of the defense force should be utilized!"

"Right, I'm sending untrained troops into a potentially hot situation in my place. Have you not paid any attention?" Jake flipped back.

"I will take a backup, however. Sara has some introduction to urban warfare, so she understands the basics. Do we have any weapons that will work in a vacuum?"

"Nothing we have 100% confidence in at this time. Unfortunately, the ship in hangar 19 had a very limited number of personal weapons, and they were all in some state of disassembly in other facilities. Those prototype weapons available are untested. You could use terrestrial firearms; however, they are untested and may not function reliably in space," Dallas replied.

"That's a lot of ifs," he said aloud.

Jake thought for a moment.

"Dallas, do we have any scuba equipment in inventory?"

"Yes, we have an extensive selection of both sport and military equipment. However, your combat flight suit is a fully functional spacesuit. It is unnecessary and quite unwise to attempt to use scuba in space," Dallas offered.

"It's not the scuba gear I'm interested in," Jake replied.

----*----

Jake went back to his room after leaving the hangar, taking a long way around. Fearing someone pulling him into the party again, he avoided going near there entirely. Entering his quarters, he was startled to discover both Sara and Bonnie sitting in his living room, Sara sipping what looked like wine, while Bonnie held an orange juice.

"Surprise!" Bonnie said, standing to give Jake a quick kiss with Sara doing the same. They both settled back down in their seats as Jake crossed the room to get a soft drink from the wet bar and then joined them.

"To what do I owe the pleasure of this visit?" he asked of both of them as he sat down.

"We came to run interference but stayed to explain," Bonnie replied.

Sara just smiled and pointed to the bedroom.

Jake got up and peeked inside his bedroom. There, sprawled across the end of his bed from one side to the other and face down, was Becky, her long blonde hair hanging over the edge. Sandy was on her back, with her head resting on the pillows and one leg hanging off the edge of the bed. Both were passed out cold and stark naked, their clothes spread all over the bedroom floor.

Jake backed out quietly, closing the door behind him, and then sat with the other two. He sipped his drink without comment, and the two women sat quietly, watching him expectantly.

"Scheduling conflict?" Jake offered.

Sara laughed.

"No, more of a budding rivalry, but under control. There was a conversation regarding how to reward your heroism. Several drinks later, it devolved into a full-blown argument about who should reward you."

"We followed them to your quarters, expecting to find you here. When you weren't, they decided to await your arrival," Bonnie said with a laugh of her own.

"I see," Jake replied.

"So that explains the clothing explosion in my room."

"Yes, they insisted you got to choose, you lucky dog you!" Sara said, laughing even harder.

Several thoughts passed through Jake's mind, mostly involving blue dye and electric clippers. In the end, he decided to let sleeping girls lie and leave it at that. Bonnie and Sara weren't quite as forgiving, though.

"We could shave their heads?" Bonnie offered, with an evil grin.

"Already went down that road," Jake said with a laugh,

"But payback is a bitch, and those two are relentless. Best to just let them lie, and I'll sleep elsewhere."

"Which reminds me, how many of those have you had tonight?" Jake said, pointing at Sara's wine.

"This is my third, why, do you still want your reward?" she said with her evil grin now.

"How would you like to go spearfishing tomorrow?" Jake asked.

Chapter 17

The next morning Jake, Sara, Bonnie, and a few others who were less hungover from the night's celebrations, met in the hangar. Becky and Sandy were nowhere in sight. Jake and Sara were suited up in their flight suits, each sporting an accessory pack mounted on the front of their flight suits.

"The chest pack supplies your environmental needs in your flight suits, providing 24 hours of EVA time," Dallas said.

She continued as a bot slid up carrying the bag,

"Here is a sack containing the interface modules that need to be installed on the bridge. If the controls there are too badly damaged to integrate with, you may have to locate auxiliary controls and install them there."

"And the other items I requested?" Jake asked Dallas.

Two bots scurried up, each carrying one long spear gun and two shorter versions.

"The long guns have been fitted with a grapple tip, simply shoot at the hull, and they will attach. There are 500 feet of line on each reel to tether your craft for use as a safety line. Simply clip your belt line to it once you are tethered."

"The two smaller guns have three spears, each with a razor tip. They will penetrate anything short of a combat suit. Simply fire and reload by placing the next shaft in the barrel and compress using the toggles behind the spear tip," Dallas finished.

Sara grabbed her guns, Jake having explained last night that they might not be the only living things on the spacecraft. Each was a high-pressure pneumatic speargun. The longer of the two was about 3 feet long and the smaller was about 14 inches, all with an inch in diameter tube and a pistol grip at one end. There were additional spear shafts clipped to each side of the tube with the small ones.

The spear shafts contained two toggle flaps at the end by the tip that allowed you to draw the shaft into the gun, compressing the piston inside, thus charging the gun. Simple, foolproof, and sure to work in the vacuum of space, the guns were at least some form of protection should things go sideways.

They each climbed into their fighters, donning helmets, and as everyone backed away, closed the canopies. Hovering their ships, they headed to the hangar opening, with Jake leading the way and Sara close behind. As they lifted through the open doors, Bonnie and the rest headed to the control room to monitor the mission.

Jake continued to lead the way up with Sara on his right. Soon they cleared the atmosphere and banked to rendezvous with the alien ship in orbit. He slowed their approach and brought his ship up very slowly on the left side of the bridge windows, Sara mirroring his actions on the right side. Once they were in a stable position about 200 feet from the ship, Jake took a deep breath, hoping these suits worked as advertised, and opened his canopy, then fired the long spear gun hitting next to the bridge window frame. He then tied the other end off to his fighter, giving him a tether line.

Sara repeated Jake's actions and, tucking her spear gun pistols in her belt, attached her safety line to the tether, and climbed out of the canopy. Using the same process as Sara, Jake reached the alien craft first and, unhooking his safety line, entered the bridge via the empty window frames. With him, he carried the bag of interfaces provided by Dallas. As Sara came in behind him, he surveyed the interior, drawing one of his spear pistols in the process.

There were three bodies still floating inside the bridge, Jake presumed the others had jetted into space once the windows had blown out. Giving the bodies little regard, Jake handed Sara the interface bag and tucked his gun back into his belt. He then took each of the remaining bodies, checked them for weapons or other items, and then stuffed them out the window frames and into space.

Sara kept to one side, choosing not to observe the gruesome task. Alien or not, he suspected the bodies still gave her the creeps. As Jake worked, she scanned the interior, giving the ALICEs a video feed of the interior systems with her helmet cams. Both she and Jake had two external cameras, one on each side of their helmet, added for this mission.

With the bridge cleared of bodies, Jake started on the opposite of the bridge from Sara and scanned the systems there. Once the internal scans were complete, ALICE spoke up for the first time.

"Jake, the central console looks to be next to the command chair in the center of the bridge. Can you place one of the interfaces on the upper right of the console display, please?"

Jake floated to the display ALICE described and took one of the interfaces handed to him from Sara's bag. It looked like a salt shaker, but stuck to the display firmly, once placed in position. The display immediately came to life flashing symbols, unintelligible to Jake.

After a few seconds, ALICE described the navigation console location to Sara and asked her to do the same thing. Sara removed an interface from the bag and placed it in the same location on the navigation console. Again, it came to life with all sorts of symbols and images.

They continued this process for each of the control stations until they came to the engineering console. It had been in the path of Jake's rail guns as he had raked the bridge, its position located higher and to the right rear of the bridge, behind the command chair. The projectiles that shattered the bridge windows had continued right through and ripped the console to shreds. From the goo on the wall behind, it hadn't done the engineer any good either.

"Jake, I am afraid we need you to go into the ship's engineering section and attach to the console there. Otherwise, we will not be able to control the ship's engines," ALICE said.

Sara drew one of her pistols at this point, and the two of them floated to the rear of the bridge, using whatever handholds available to get them there as they floated about. Drawing his gun again, Jake asked Sara to stay to one side and hold on to a console as he activated the compartment hatch. He assumed they acted like watertight doors on a ship, isolating breached sections of the ship. Sure enough, it was necessary to have ALICE override the lock to get it to open, and a blast of the pressurized inner atmosphere came shooting out as it opened.

There was still light on the other side and a steep stairwell heading down into the body of the ship. Jake indicated for Sara to fall in behind him as he cautiously started down, head first. With no atmosphere, Jake had a little concern about running into someone in the stairwell. However, at the bottom of the stairs, there was a second hatch. Using a camera detached from the side of his helmet, Jake peered cautiously through a port in the hatch with the camera held above his head. He could see in his display a passageway on the other side with several more closed pressure hatches located on each side of the passageway.

Bracing together in the stairwell in preparation for another pressure blast, Jake asked ALICE to open the hatch. As it opened, nothing happened, indicating the central passage contained a hull breach somewhere. They floated into the passageway, and Jake again asked ALICE to open each hatch, first one side, then the other. Some exhausted atmosphere, most with no effect, indicating a battle-related pressure loss. Again, using his camera in hand, Jake carefully examined each interior through the open doorway, ensuring no one was waiting on the other side in a spacesuit and armed.

In a few of the rooms, he saw floating bodies, what he assumed remained of the crew. The engineering section access was via the last hatch in the hall, where the central passageway ended at the rear of the ship. As they approached, Jake saw movement through the port in the hatch, suggesting someone wedging the hatch shut.

213

"Alice, I think we have mice," Jake said.

"There does seem to be movement on the other side of the door. Interestingly, no one has tried to move the ship, even though the engineering section has main and auxiliary propulsion controls?" ALICE replied.

"Maybe whoever it is in there doesn't know how?" Jake suggested.

"According to the ship's log, these doors locked down with the hull breach. Anyone caught in engineering is still there. Others were trapped in the breached sections and died without suits," ALICE finished.

"This is all well and good, but what are we going to do about it? We need in there," Sara asked.

As Sara was speaking, she started to peek through the port in the hatch. Jake shoved her violently to one side, as a blast from an energy weapon shattered the port, and a rush of the inner atmosphere came bursting through. Sara slammed into the bulkhead but was otherwise unhurt.

"Never do that again!" Jake admonished Sara as she moved back into her position.

"Use a camera!" he said as he held up the unclipped camera from his helmet and slipped it passed the edge of the now-shattered port.

Broadcasting his feed to Sara, from the camera in his hand, they could see in their displays several figures floating behind equipment and consoles inside.

"I counted four, all in spacesuits, and at least one with a weapon," Jake passed on to those listening.

Sara nodded in agreement without comment. Jake set the camera on the top of his spear gun, it magnetically attaching, and placed the barrel in the port opening. He worked the door latch for the hatch, and as one of the four rose to check, he fired, smashing the alien's faceplate, the shaft driving through the center of its face.

"Now, there are only three," he said, drawing the gun back and reloading.

Jake felt the vibration of several thuds on the hatch. He assumed it was blaster fire impacting the other side of the hatch. Jake tried again, scoring a hit in the shoulder, but losing his gun and camera to a blast from the other side. He was thankful for the durability of his combat suit, the pressure in the gun, causing it to explode in his hand. He drew his second spear gun, grabbing one of Sara's cameras to use. While attempting to get a clear shot, several more blasts came through the hole requiring him to retreat.

"Someone's going to get hurt like this," Jake said.

Using Sara's camera, placed right on the edge of the opening, they

214

could see the two remaining aliens hiding behind a console. The shoulder hit proved fatal for the third.

"Alice, does this thing have any kinda fire suppression or sprinkler system in engineering for emergencies?" Jake asked.

"The engineering space does have a containment system that activates in emergencies. It releases a vapor that absorbs radiant leaks from the main drive system, neutralizing the contaminant. It would appear as fog and obscure vision, even in a vacuum," ALICE replied.

"Great, when I say so, can you trigger it?" Jake asked.

"I can," she replied.

"Sara, see the two behind the console?" Jake asked.

"Yes," she replied.

"When I say shoot, raise your gun, and shoot in the space on the right where the guy would be if he raised, you got it?"

"I think so," she replied.

"OK, ALICE, hit it."

Suddenly, from everywhere in the engine room, a foggy vapor started to appear, spreading in the vacuum quickly. As it did so, the two aliens behind the console started to move.

"Shoot!" Jake yelled as he raised his gun and fired to the left, complementing Sara's right-hand shot.

Both figures thrashed wildly for a second, then floated free in the room, motionless.

"Kill the fog," Jake asked.

The vapor hung in the room, with no other movement to disturb it. Jake watched for several minutes, looking, via Sara's cam, for any movement on the other side for the door revealing life. Finally satisfied, he handed Sara the camera reached through the port opening, and un-wedged the brace jamming the hatch closed. After retracting his arm, ALICE was able to open it. Both Jake and Sara reloaded at that point.

"Wait here and cover me, shoot at anything that moves. Just not me," he added as an afterthought.

Sara just nodded. Jake scanned the room for a minute before moving inside and then slid in and to one side. He began methodically searching the room before allowing Sara to enter. With the room cleared, he asked Sara to place the interface on the engineering console while he collected the four bodies one by one, moved them up to the bridge, and shoved them out the bridge window. He also collected two hand blasters in the process.

"We have control of the ship now. I would suggest you return to your fighters and allow us to bring the ship in unattended," ALICE said.

"Where are you putting it?" Jake asked, curious.

"One of the hangars in Alaska has a 400-foot by 400-foot opening, this ship is 384 feet in length and 284 feet in width," ALICE replied.

"Do you want me to space the other bodies?" Jake asked.

"That won't be necessary, we will have the bots attend to them once the ship is down," ALICE replied.

"Much appreciated," Jake replied, relieved he didn't need to search the ship for more dead.

Jake followed Sara back up to the bridge and then led the way back out the window. Outside the ship again, he reattached his safety line but waited until Sara did the same before heading back to his fighter. They both pulled their way along the tethers back to their fighters and, once in the cockpits, dropped the spear gun tethers outside the cockpit.

Lowering their canopies, Jake and Sara backed their fighters away from the ship. Clear of the alien craft, Jake turned his fighter with Sara on his right again and reentered the atmosphere heading back to Dallas. Jake made an unhurried descent, and as they hovered slowly above the desert on approach to the hangar doors, he realized it was late afternoon. They'd been in space for most of the day.

Dropping through the open hangar doors, he set his fighter down, Sara's fighter resting next to his. Jake let out a huge sigh of relief as he climbed out of his fighter. Looking up, he saw the entire Dallas staff, including Becky and Sandy, standing there waiting for them. He removed his helmet, leaving it in the seat of his fighter, and approached the waiting group, Sara, on his heels. Jake realized it was dead quiet. He could hear their boots echo as he approached Bonnie and the staff.

"How did you know they were there," Bonnie asked as they stopped.

"Who, the aliens? I didn't. It was just a guess," Jake responded, confused.

"But you saved Sara's life?" Sandy said, pointing to Sara, who, Jake realized, hadn't said a word since they left the ship.

Jake stopped to think for a minute and then remembered shoving Sara out of the way of the blast through the port in the door. They'd all been watching the firefight from the helmet cam feed. He turned to Sara and could see the near-death realization on her face.

"Hey, you're OK," Jake said softly, looking into her eyes, her chin in his hand.

Tears appeared in her eyes, but she said nothing.

"I could have died," she finally said quietly.

"But you didn't, that's why I insist on doing these things. Some things you can't learn in a book or by studying, you have to live it."

She reached up and kissed Jake gently.

"Thank you."

216

Sara then turned and headed to the locker room to change. As she passed the group, Bonnie came to Jake and kissed him as well.

"Thank you," she said, turning to follow Sara.

Sandy, Becky, and several other women on the staff followed Bonnie's example, thanking Jake for Sara's life. Once everyone was filing back inside, Jake bypassed the locker room and headed straight to his quarters. He had endured many near-death experiences, so he hadn't given the firefight much thought. He forgot that these women, a little more than six months ago, were farmers, not fighters.

He stripped out of his flight suit and jumped into the shower, letting the hot water run over him, soothing cramped muscles. After getting out of the shower, he grabbed a t-shirt and shorts, looking forward to a quiet evening alone. He was sitting on his couch and just finished a status report with the ALICEs, verifying the ship was down and stowed away in Alaska when his door chimed.

"Come," he said with a sigh, his hopes of a quiet evening diminishing quickly.

Sara was standing in the doorway, similarly dressed in a T-shirt and shorts.

"May I come in?" she asked.

"Absolutely," Jake replied.

Sara stepped in and sat next to Jake on the couch. She seemed very subdued.

"I wanted to apologize for losing it in the hangar this afternoon," she said, barely holding it in.

"It was very unprofessional of me," she finished with a sniff.

"Oh, sweetheart!" Jake replied, drawing her up in his arms.

"Don't be ridiculous, everyone reacts differently to their first combat experience."

"But we've been out before, it's not my first time!" she sobbed, tears streaming down her face.

"No, not like that we haven't," Jake replied gently,

"Every other experience has been in the safety of your combat suit. This was the first time you actually might have died. Those suits have given everyone a false sense of security."

She continued to cry in Jake's arms. He slowly stood her up and led her into the bedroom, where they lay together on the bed. She snuggled into the notch of his arm, her head on his chest. Eventually, her breathing slowed as she fell asleep, emotionally exhausted.

----*----

The next morning Jake left Sara sleeping soundly as he dressed and headed into the control room. He found Barb and Bonnie already hard at it.

"Hey, you're up early," Bonnie said, greeting him as he entered.

"Looks like I'm not the only one," he replied.

"Yeah, now that we are free to fly, so to speak, I talked to Dallas about getting some better sensors and cameras into space. We were reviewing what hardware was available and how best to use it," she finished.

"How's Sara?" she then asked softly.

"She was still sleeping when I left her. She had a good cry last night. Hopefully, she got it out of her system," Jake said.

"That was a huge scare, Jake. You shoulda seen it from our point of view. She went flying and then this flash, we thought we had lost her, it was that close," Bonnie said somberly.

"We almost did!" Jake replied.

"Those combat suits have everyone thinking they are invincible. This is a different world, and these guys play for keeps."

"Do we need to change our training?" Bonnie asked.

"No, we need to stick to the training. Even I've been guilty of casually walking into something, expecting the suits to protect us. That has got to stop."

Bonnie considered that and nodded.

"Yeah, I see your point. We learned to duck and cover. We just don't. OK, well, I'll let you emphasize that to the troops, I'll get us some more eyes in the sky. Why did you come in anyway?"

"Just to check in, I expect a follow-up visit fairly soon. Not today, mind you, but at some point, someone's gonna come looking for that ship we just took," Jake said with a smile.

"Speaking of that, Seven has an update when you have a moment?" Bonnie replied with a smile.

"I'm good now," Jake said.

As if on cue, Seven started.

"We landed the ship in Hangar 12 as it was the only one large enough to accommodate. The ship is a cruiser-class warship of the NeHaw race, with a standard complement of 27. We have located 15 bodies on board the ship. With the seven you disposed of in space, we assume the remaining five went out when the bridge windows failed. We are working on patching the hull and repairing the bridge windows. We are also rebuilding the engineering control station, and environmental systems, to replicate an oxygen/nitrogen atmosphere."

"As we destroyed most of the forward gun positions in the battle, it is recommended that we replace them instead of attempting repairs. Rail guns would be an excellent alternative."

"Also, we have located the personal weapons store on board and recovered both rifle and handgun versions of the energy weapons you encountered. Samples of these have been transported to the weapons research ALICE facility in South Dakota for analysis and replication."

"I'm wondering if we need a combination weapon," Jake asked.

"Like mounting an energy barrel under one of our rifles?"

"We shall investigate," Seven replied.

"It is expected that we can have the ship ready for space, unmanned, in three weeks, or manned in two months."

"Push for unmanned with the forward gun positions replaced, and ready. Anything beyond that is gravy," Jake answered.

"We get any more data on our adversaries?" Jake continued.

"We are still deciphering their computing systems content, as it is apparently in several languages. However, their military content is in the native NeHaw we decrypted from the exploration ship. That translation will be available in a few more hours. I think you will find it most interesting reading," Seven replied.

"Looking forward to it," Jake said.

He then excused himself and headed to the dining room for some breakfast. There he found Becky and Sandy sitting with Sara, eating.

"Well, good morning, ladies," Jake said as he approached the table.

All three faces looked up at him, smiling.

"Please sit!" Becky said, standing and pulling out a chair for him as Sandy got up and bolted to the food counter.

Puzzled, Jake sat, with Becky returning to her seat as well. Jake looked over to see Sandy returning with a tray containing his standard breakfast fare.

"What gives?" Jake asked, confused at the women's actions.

"I think it's a combination of I'm sorry, and thank you," Sara said, laughing at the two younger women.

"Hey, it's not every night you come home to two beautiful, naked women in your bed," Jake replied, laughing.

Both looked down, slightly embarrassed. Sara leaned over the table and kissed Jake on the cheek.

"That's a thank you for last night."

"You feel better?" Jake asked.

"As good as I can, for now. I'm sure I'll shake it off, it's just not quite real, yet I guess."

"Or too real," Jake replied,

"But it does get better. You jumped over a huge hurdle, you experienced your first true combat, and triumphed!"

"Because of you," Sara said.

"That's what I'm here for. My job is to teach you how to survive," he replied.

"And for that, we are truly grateful," Becky added, kissing his other cheek.

"Well, on a brighter note, I talked to Seven this morning, and they are refitting the ship we took. It should be good to go unmanned in about three weeks,"

"What good is that?" Sandy asked.

"Extra firepower when the others come," Sara replied.

"Exactly," Jake acknowledged,

"Plus, if we play this right, it should confuse the hell out of them."

"What do you mean?" Becky asked.

"With this thing in orbit, it should look like it's still theirs, possibly disabled. They move in close, and once they find out it's ours, it's too late," Jake explained.

"You still think they'll send more ships?" Sandy asked, clearly worried.

"Oh yeah, they'll come. Seven said they were translating the military information they found on the ship's computers for me. My bet is we'll find they are right bastards. They attacked me without even a hail. They just opened up as if I wasn't worth the time to talk to."

"How can we hope to beat them?" Becky asked.

"One battle at a time, remember, we already won once," Jake said, smiling.

"Besides, I'm more convinced now than ever that the ALICEs are the key. They're the ones that won the day. I couldn't have pulled that off on my own. I think that's what the aliens fear. They are a huge tactical advantage."

Jake finished his breakfast by this time.

"So, what's the plan for the day, boss?" Sara asked.

"I'm not sure yet. Bonnie is working on some new sensors for orbit. That means we will be ferrying them up at some point. That might be good training time for some of the newer pilots?" Jake suggested.

"I'm also wondering about a run to Nevada today. In the fighters, it's under an hour away."

"I bet Linda and Kathy will love that," Sandy said.

"Then it's settled. Sara, get with the Black Nights and assign them to Bonnie for space ferrying duty. Afterward, you and I will run to Nevada for the day," Jake decided.

Privately, he also felt getting Sara back into the air might help her calm the fears from yesterday.

220

----*----

An hour later, Jake and Sara were in the air and headed west. Jake had plotted a slightly southern route for their flight rather than straight to Nevada. He wanted to do a little aerial recon to survey the area between, along the border, and see what kind of settlements were there.

His goal was to fly over lower New Mexico, Arizona, and then Southern California before turning north to Nevada. Not all the area was visible by satellite from above, and the overflight would help fill in some gaps. He asked ALICE to have recording devices installed in both fighters just in case, configuring them for live feedback to the analysts. It wasn't long into their flight before they hit their turning point for the northbound leg, and Jake realized they were just going way too fast to make a good manual visual reconnaissance flight. Fortunately, they had the recordings.

Approaching Nevada, the hangar doors were already open as Jake got a visual on their landing spot, and he and Sara slowed for their approach. They hovered over the opening for less than a second and landed in the hangar, Sara dropping in through the open doors first. They each climbed out of their craft, leaving their gear in the fighters. Linda was leading the reception committee here with Kathy by her side as they watched Jake and Sara walk away from their fighters and towards them by the facility's door.

"Look what you've done to me!" Kathy exclaimed to Jake as she hugged him, indicating her very abundant belly.

"You look radiant!" Jake replied, kissing her and taking great care with the firmness of his hug.

"And you aren't far behind!" he said, turning to Linda and kissing her as well.

"Sara!" Linda exclaimed, releasing Jake and crossing to hug her.

Releasing Sara, Linda turned to make introductions. Her staff made up of the Alaska transfers, had met Jake and Sara before. However, now it was more about putting a job to names and faces. Jake looked around the hangar, thinking how small it looked compared to Seven and remembering how large he once thought it was. Heading back inside, Linda updated them on the local activities while Kathy headed back to medical.

Once in the command center, Linda continued the update. Pointing to the map, Linda started.

"The militia has pushed all the way north to Stockton now. We have set up relations with the towns along the way and have driven out most of the larger gangs. The militia itself is now over 500 men and women,

221

with garrisons strung along the way," she finished.

"Wow, how are they fixed for supplies and transport?" Jake asked.

"They have plenty of guns and ammo, but I am talking to Bonnie about acquiring some bigger vehicles. You know, like the ones she used for the Paint Rock gig. That big six-wheeled job would be great here. Right now, we run helicopter resupply almost daily, with drops along the route north."

"We also have some potential recruits. ALICE has identified about 20 people strung out between here and Stockton she believes would make great additions and eight of them as pilots."

Jake was both happy and unsettled with the news. Pilots were on his absolute must-have list, but it was becoming painfully obvious that he was becoming more insulated from some of the decision-making. Not that he was a micromanager, far from it. He just never envisioned himself in this position before. He was typically an on-the-ground, day-to-day guy. He now needed to rely on others to make those decisions for him.

"That's great news," he replied.

"Who's going out to make the offers," Sara asked.

"We were thinking about using Karen, Jason, and Brian in a helicopter, to make the offers, once they got back. I know you won't let me go," she said, somewhat disappointedly to Jake.

"Have you looked in the mirror? No, you can't go. I won't risk losing you or the baby!" Jake replied.

Linda seemed to cheer up at that. Jake figured she was pleased he cared that much. They went over several smaller issues, and then Jake and Sara went off to change. After a quick shower and with a clean set of clothes on, the three of them reconvened in Jake's quarters for lunch.

"How long are you staying?" Linda asked them both as they ate in Jake's living room.

"Well, it was just a day trip, but I thought we might want to stay a bit longer now," Jake replied.

"To help with greeting and training the recruits?" Sara asked.

"Yeah, I don't mind not being on the offer mission, but I'd like to meet them once they get here," he replied.

Linda laughed at that.

"You are having a hard time letting go, aren't you?"

"Let's call it overprotective," Jake replied in mock offense.

"I don't want a buncha strangers running loose, without first checking them out. Rationally, I know ALICE will not risk any of you, but I want to see for myself."

Linda leaned over and kissed Jake.

"Thank you for watching out for us."

Chapter 18

RaBok reviewed his status logs as they traveled between solar systems. They just completed collecting tribute for the empire from one of the many planets they protected from aggression in his sector. The fact that there wasn't another race in the sector capable of such aggression was immaterial.

As the senior officer in this sector, it was his responsibility to review the status of the other 3 ships in his area of operation. He noted PeTuk had not reported in since investigating the alarms triggered at the far edge of the sector. It had been many cycles since his last report. Known for rushing through things, RaBok considered this unusual for PeTuk.

However, the notes on the posted alert allowed for a planet-wide disrupter bombardment of a quarantined world, though no action permitted risked habitability. The planetary bombardment was something not to be rushed, and PeTuk did so enjoy a good bombardment. He decided to wait for a few more cycles before investigating. Besides, SOP required they regroup with the other two ships in this sector and arrive in force. That would take additional cycles to set up anyway.

----*----

Jake and Sara ended up staying for a week. They did go out on the helicopter to gather the recruits after all, instead of waiting for Jason's team to return, and it gave Jake ample time to review the recruits. It also allowed Jake to give Linda and Kathy some much-needed attention. Becky and Sandy notwithstanding, it still amazed him that the women all handled this *arrangement* so well.

There was never much in the way of open conversation, at least not around Jake, but they all seemed so matter-of-fact about it. Sara didn't appear the slightest bit upset when Linda asked for a quiet dinner together on their first night there. And, Linda was just as nonplussed when Kathy declared the following night as hers. It was surreal.

The recruits were a nice surprise. There were 12 women and 8 men, all in their 20's and all anxious to get started. Jake was pleased to learn that 4 of the men were unmarried, 2 were brothers from a small remote town with no unmarried women, one was studying to be a doctor, and the last was the brother of one of the female recruits. The four married men's wives were part of the 12 women.

Jake was also glad to get a man on the medical staff if for no other reason than for the other male staff members. In his case, it might be nice to have a male doctor to talk to, rather than someone you were sleeping with. He also continued his ritual of reviewing the sensor data every morning and evening. At some point, the aliens would be returning, and he wanted to know about it as soon as it happened.

He checked on the pilots, who were training at Seven, and the repair status of the captured ship. Jake wanted it back in orbit as quickly as possible. The 15 pilots who started training with Sara were now in their fighters and flying to finish their training cycle since the sensor network was gone. As such, Jake directed them to be transferred to their various ALICE facilities, the 1st Air Cavalry, taking the Black Knights' place in Alaska. He also promoted Sharon to 1st Lieutenant and made her head of the eastern Washington ALICE facility to prove you didn't need to sleep with the boss to get promoted. Much to her annoyance, everyone wanted to know if she was pregnant.

Bonnie and the ALICEs came up with new monitoring satellites of their design and requested the Black Knights place them in orbit and on the backside of the moon. Configured to alert on the ship's repulser drive emissions, they felt it should detect and alert far sooner than a visual monitor. All the fighters and the captured ship were fitted with IFF systems to prevent false alerts and friendly fire incidents.

Jake also started reading the NeHaw military strategy and tactics documents that ALICE extracted from the cruiser's computers and translated for him. Thus far, they appeared to be a very disciplined and ruthless race. They had a rigid command structure and a static approach to doing things. They also appeared to acquire more of their technology than they invented. Several of the various weapons listed carried their planet of origin references, most not being NeHaw. The basis of their approach to warfare was superior technology and numerical superiority. It struck Jake as bullying tactics.

If Jake understood what he read so far, the next attack would consist of the remaining ships in the area of space they defined as a sector. Should that attack fail, a collection of ships from the adjoining sectors would converge on the hapless foe. He hadn't been able to determine how large a sector was how many ships patrolled one, or what size they were for that matter. Seven did make a note that three ships were routinely contacted in the captured ship's logs, suggesting there was a total of four ships in this sector. From that, he surmised that three more ships were on their way.

Their ships consisted of five basic types. They were the Exploration class, like the one in Hangar 19, used for long-distance non-combat activities. Made for patrolling, the Cruiser class ships were larger and covered greater areas of space independently. Destroyer class ships were smaller than the cruisers and used together in small numbers or the presence of larger combat ships. Battleships were their largest combat vessels and rarely used except in the most urgent of combat situations. And finally, the Transport class, which seemed to include various-sized cargo and live transport ships.

Jake assumed that the ALICEs applied terrestrial names for his sake. It also struck him as odd that the Cruiser they captured was the mainstay of their combat fleet. It hadn't put up much of a fight. Did that mean there were three more Cruisers headed this way, or did three Destroyers accompany a Cruiser in patrolling a sector? He was hoping for the second, but planning for the first.

Another interesting observation was the preference for energy-based weapons over projectiles. They discussed, with disdain, the shortcomings of various propellant-fired systems and the superior NeHaw defenses for them. Not listed as viable weapons systems were Jake's rail guns. There were no references at all. From that, he decided to leave the extra guns mounted on his fighter for now.

Because of the energy weapon preferences, he discussed with the ALICEs the installation and operation of stasis shields for the fighters and the Cruiser. Completely enveloped in a stasis bubble last time, it limited his ability to observe the action. To be more practical, they needed the shields projected in various directions without enveloping the craft. That allowed for maneuvering and firing while shielded. The major drawback was, that it would only work with an ALICE system linked to the fighter, to allow firing through microseconds of dropped shields.

----*----

Jake was sitting in the quarter's level dining area, eating breakfast alone, though there were plenty of people in the room. As a squadron leader, Sara left early that morning with the Red Devils and the Black Knights on a training run to the moon and back. Linda was in the control center addressing a logistics issue with the militia's push north, and Kathy was dealing with a medical issue from a training accident.

Between all the new faces, he could hardly put names to, and the stigma of being *the boss,* he wanted to eat in his quarters. However, that was not an option. He needed to be visible and approachable to everyone, even if they never approached him.

"Mind if I join you, Major?"

Jake turned to see one of the women they recruited earlier in the week. He knew she was the one with the brother, but her name escaped him now. She was pretty, a strawberry blonde like Jessie, with green eyes and freckles. Only about 5 feet 2, she was slender but still had curves to her figure. She reminded Jake of someone, but he couldn't put his finger on who.

"Please do," Jake replied, indicating the chair across from him.

Placing her tray down and sliding into the seat across from him, she began speaking.

"I hope I'm not disturbing anything?"

"No, not at all. I was starting to question my deodorant," he said, smiling.

"Usually you are with the Captain or the Lieutenant, I think everyone thought you wanted to be alone," she replied.

"And you didn't?" Jake asked, curious now.

"No, if that were the case, you'd eat in your room. I figured you came out so we could all see you as a normal human being instead of the savior of humanity," she replied with a smile.

"Wow, no pressure there, huh?" Jake said with a laugh.

"I would have said that's a very hard image to maintain, but then I saw the video of the last attack and the recordings of your training sessions. I'm Patti, by the way, I'm your new combat analyst," she finished with a questioning smile.

"I didn't know I had one, and aren't you a little new to have a primary assignment already? Usually, the first week or two is just to get you to high school education?" Jake asked, raising a questioning eyebrow.

"I came here with the equivalent of a master's degree. Both my brother and I did. My grandparents were in education before the fall, both had doctorates, and well, we have tried to maintain that level of education in each successive generation, planetary disaster notwithstanding."

"I was working towards my doctorate when your militia came to town and explained the developments of the last few months. As it happens, my dissertation is on pre-fall military strategies and tactics, and how they failed to meet the extra-terrestrial threat," she finished.

Jake sat in stunned silence for a moment, not sure how to reply.

"OK, well, first of all, they are not my militia. We support them, and honestly, we monitor their activities to make sure there are no abuses, but they report to the leadership of Prosperity or whatever community they derive from, not to me."

"As you say, but to a man, they look to you as the ultimate leader of this recovery. I talked with quite a few of them as they pushed north through our town. They speak of you in awe and with reverence. I suspect that's how ALICE found me, I think I may have been quite a nuisance to some of them," Patti said.

"Then I presume ALICE was the one who assigned you that

position?" Jake asked.

"Pending your approval, of course," Patti replied, taking a sip from her drink.

"You've talked with ALICE much?" Jake asked, being non-committal to the implied question.

"Since the first day I arrived. She has me studying day and night. All the ALICEs feel it's the unpredictable nature of human beings that will make the difference in the challenges to come. They can process the information far quicker, but in the end, it's the human element that's made the difference to date."

"We have been reviewing your engagements for the last 6 months. Each demonstrates a deviation from the analytical outcome the ALICEs calculated. Like Bonnie in the canyon with the raiders, the ALICEs would have used their advantage and killed them all. That would have lost us the 13 pilots," Patti continued.

"Or you, capturing the Cruiser in space. Adding those rail guns was your idea, not theirs. In addition, targeting the bridge was you. Alice says they would have targeted the engine room, going for the kill instead. That would have lost us the ship. They make us better, but we win the day," she finished.

"That's why they want me to have a combat analyst, they need your human insight to balance their analytical perspective?" Jake asked.

"That, and I'm cute as a button, or so they tell me," Patti finished with a dimpled smile.

"So, what else has ALICE told you about me?" Jake asked, wary as to why ALICE cared how cute she was. That was something a grandparent would say about a grandchild.

"Lots and some is all my research. I know you have a bachelor's and a master's in technical fields. You've completed multiple combat tours, from which you were awarded a bronze and silver star, both for valor and heroism. You were once married to an academic, who divorced you to pursue a career teaching at a liberal college. Stupid woman, forgive me. You volunteered for the stasis experiments that eventually brought you here. And until recently, you had no known children," she said with a giggle.

"I do understand that that was a manipulation by the ALICEs, much to your disapproval, to guarantee the continuation of the command structure. Oh, and recently you were elected President of the United States by the total registered electorate," she finished somewhat sarcastically.

"That was not my idea," Jake retorted, embarrassed by the sound of it.

"And that was more of a necessary evil that proved timely. Had we bounced the stasis lockers before then, I think we'd all be dead now!"

"I completely agree, and my hat's off to Jessie for actually uncovering the trail leading to the secreted spaceship."

"You've talked to Jessie?" Jake asked.

"Oh yes, she's delightful and a wonderful resource on both recent history and you specifically."

"Am I now required reading for all recruits?" Jake asked sourly.

"Yes, but not to that level of detail," Patti replied sweetly.

"The nature of my proposed assignment requires me to study all the key players. Besides, all great military leaders are analyzed in detail."

"Too bad all you get is me," Jake answered glibly.

"So, can I take that as a yes Major, I get the job?" Patti asked.

"On two conditions, first you call me Jake," he answered.

"And second, tell me why ALICE cares how cute you are?" he finished in somewhat of a challenging tone.

"OK, Jake," Patti replied, acknowledging the use of his first name.

"Ask me that again when we know each other better," she replied as she got up and headed out the door.

----*----

RaBok scheduled a rendezvous with the other two Cruisers in the sector. PeTuk still hadn't reported in and was now outside the acceptable window of absence. He had missed one tribute collection already and was in danger of missing a second. As the Empire looked poorly on lost income due to non-collection, an action that could cost a command, RaBok had to assume some mishap occurred, preventing PeTuk from communicating. Surely no backwater, quarantined primitives bested a NeHaw Battle Cruiser. Most likely, one of PeTuk's disrupter bombs pre-detonated, leaving him in a dead orbit until help arrived.

RaBok would have gone alone had regulations not prevented such action. Better to follow regulations than to be charged with independent actions and lose his command. PeTuk could wait.

----*----

Patti and Jake had several impromptu meetings over the next few days, trying to gather as much Intel together as they could find for a workable battle plan. Jake would squeeze her in between his other tasks and duties to try to answer her many questions.

Jake and Sara were finally able to meet with Patti one afternoon to start the beginnings of a battle plan. At Jake's request, they met in Sara's quarters. Something about ALICE's comments on Patti unsettled Jake, or maybe it was Patti herself. There was a strange familiarity there with her looks and mannerisms that left Jake puzzled. Either way, he did not have her alone in his room for now.

They all gathered, and it became quickly apparent that Patti and Sara had spent some time together.

"Hey Sara," Patti said as she entered the room, giving her a quick hug before sitting in one of the chairs.

"You two know each other?" Jake asked, surprised.

"We've spent some time together," Sara replied casually.

"OK," Jake replied, realizing he wasn't getting more than that.

"She just helped me with my research on you," Patti offered.

Jake figured he best just drop the subject for now, and they started working. Patti showed them the outline she'd put together in the short time she was working on the plan. She projected force strength analysis for both sides, the alien approach direction, and formations, and expected ship sizes and weapons.

Jake was happy to see she came to the same conclusions as he had. Three battle Cruisers, identical to the one they now held, minus the upgrades. She also noted the alien preference for energy weapons but missed the rail gun omission in the captured documentation.

By the time they called it a night, they still hadn't come up with a solid plan of attack, but they did have 2 or 3 approaches. Jake was impressed with Patti's preparation and knowledge. He figured with some experience, she would be a first-rate tactical planner.

Having eaten while working, they were sitting, chatting, when Patti asked a more personal question.

"Jake, why didn't you and your ex-wife ever have any kids?"

The question caught him flat-footed for a moment, and then he replied after thinking about it.

"I wanted children. She wouldn't consider them while I was in the service. When I got out, we tried but split up within a few months, so I went back into the service."

Thinking of changing the subject, Jake asked his question.

"Where did you get the interest in military strategy?"

"My great grandfather was a retired Marine before the fall, he taught at the War College in Washington, DC. He and my great-grandmother met and married in college while he was in ROTC. My great, great-grandmother was also a Ph.D. and had a fit when my great-grandmother married him. She didn't approve of military life. My grandfather was also a Marine, and both he and my grandmother had doctorates, one in military history, and the other in engineering."

Jake noticed Sara and Patti exchanging glances during her

explanation, but he didn't comment.

Then Patti offered up more information.

"My brother studies engineering so Seven wants him transferred there, to help with the shipbuilding and repairs."

"I suppose that makes sense. If the ALICEs ask, I usually comply," Jake replied with a laugh.

"How did you end up in California? I mean, if your great-grandfather was teaching at the War College and your grandfather was a Marine. I mean well, DC got it bad as I recall, and most units were wiped out in the attack," Jake asked.

"Of all things, my great, great grandmother saved them. She retired in California, and they and my grandparents were visiting when the attack came. She was almost 100, and the entire family was there to celebrate, though I've been told she was an unpleasant woman in her old age."

"Wow, that's quite the linage, and I can't fault their service choice," Jake replied with a smile.

"You seem to know a lot about your great, great grandmother, what about your great, great grandfather?" Sara commented.

Again, a look passed between the two women, and then after a pause, Patti replied to Sara.,

"He disappeared before my great-grandmother was born. I'm told great, great grandma didn't talk about him much, just that he was in the military and he worked on some secret projects. She figured he died on some mission, and the military hushed it up or something."

"That did happen," Jake offered.

"Sometimes, the government was into things they didn't want to be known, so things were classified as training accidents, or you just disappeared. Did you ask ALICE? She might have the actual record of his death?"

"I did actually, and she had the answer," Patti said subdued.

"And?" Jake asked, curious now.

"Hey, great, great grandpa," Patti replied cautiously.

"That's not possible," Jake replied flatly.

"Great, great grandma was pregnant when you divorced. I was told she was so mad at you when she found out she wasn't going to tell you at first. Then, when she finally changed her mind, no one would tell her where you were."

"Alice, are we sure about this?" Jake asked cautiously.

"DNA confirms they are your descendants, Jake," ALICE replied.

Jake sat dumbfounded for a moment, then got up and hugged Patti for a long time. When they finally sat back down, he wanted answers.

"Alice, you want to expand on this? What are the odds that my descendants are accidentally recruited?"

"You are right, Jake. We uncovered some analysis that suggested you had a child from your marriage, and their offspring might reside in the central California basin. As such, we endorsed the militia push north, but there was little expectation we would locate anyone related to you. Patti and her brother were a statistical improbability."

"Why keep it secret once you knew?" Jake asked.

"That was my request," Patti replied.

"I didn't want to be dropped on you like a long-lost relative. I hoped we would spend more time together before you knew so you would like me for who I am and not just because I am your great, great granddaughter."

"I liked you after our first talk together," Jake replied, smiling warmly.

"I was just worried you were another ALICE plant for future children!"

"Jake, Patti, and her brother bring the total of genetic offspring up to 6 now," ALICE offered.

"Does your brother know yet?" Jake asked.

"Yes, I told him as soon as I found out, but I asked him to wait until you knew before coming to see you."

"Why, what is his name anyway?" Jake asked as he was curious now.

"Jacob, he's named after our great, great grandfather."

----*----

RaBok ordered his navigator to set a course for the quarantined planet at the far end of the sector, PeTuk's last known location. He notified his engineering team to prepare for a rescue and ship repair. He had rendezvoused with the other two Cruisers in this sector. As the senior officer of the three, was required to lead the investigation into the missing cruiser.

It would still require several cycles to reach the outer edge of the sector, which was their goal. Once there, he would have his ships form the standard delta formation, before entering the solar system. The home planet was not happy about the delay in revenue collections, and PeTuk was likely to lose his command unless he had a good reason for his absence. RaBok laughed to himself as he considered that death was the only acceptable reason, at this point.

----*----

The following day, Jake asked Patti and Jacob to come to his room.

231

Sara, who was there visiting Jake, bowed out to give them some privacy. He swore he saw a little of his ex-wife in both of them, but considering the number of generations, he figured he was projecting. He guessed he was just trying to create a link to his past.

They talked late into the night, Jake asking for anything they knew about their great-grandma, his daughter. From the sounds of it, she had given their mother a right fit! Good for her, he thought. He also learned that Patti and Jacob's parents were dead, she from sickness, and he from a fall. As they wound down for the night, they established one major point, Patti's brother was Jacob, NOT little Jake.

----*----

The following morning Sara, Linda, and Patti met Jake for breakfast. He, having just completed his morning status reviews, was the last to arrive. There was still no sign of an alien spacecraft, but he knew deep in his gut that they were coming. Seven relayed that the captured alien ship was not finished, but was almost ready for an unmanned return to orbit. They did plan to leave a crew of bots on-board to continue internal repairs and updates. They were, however, able to complete the full integration of systems, so it was ready for human control once it was habitable. Until then, ALICE was in remote control mode.

As their first true capital ship, Jake figured they should give it a name before launch, naval tradition, and all, so he tossed it out at breakfast.

"Hey, what do you think we should name the Cruiser?" he asked the group as they ate.

"Wow, I hadn't thought about that," Sara replied.

Sipping her coffee, Patti paused, then suggested a few.

"There are plenty of names from the past, you know, like *Defiance* or *Invincible*."

"Fond of the British, are we?" Jake asked jokingly.

"Beats the heck outta the *USS Ronald Reagan*!" she replied.

"Who was that?" Sara asked Linda quietly as she shrugged in return.

"There's always the *Enterprise, Intrepid, Independence, Constitution,* or *Constellation*?" Jake suggested.

"How about *Queen Anne's Revenge*?" Patti offered in return.

"Only if I grow a beard," Jake replied.

Sara spat out a retort, clearly frustrated with the conversation.

"Look, you two, if you aren't going to explain, then drop the discussion!"

Jake and Patti quickly apologized, and Jake explained.

"Those were names from history, British and US military, and pirate

232

sailing vessels. The *USS Ronald Reagan* was an aircraft carrier named after a US president."

As the words came out of his mouth, Jake knew he had said the wrong thing.

"The *USS Jacob Thomas*!" all three women shouted.

The surrounding tables stopped whatever they were doing to look at the four as they were laughing uncontrollably.

"I am leaning toward *The Revenge*," Jake said thoughtfully.

"Anne Bonny's ship?" Patti asked.

"Didn't you say it was Queen somebody's revenge?" Linda asked.

"No, that was *Queen Anne's Revenge*, Blackbeard's pirate ship. *The Revenge* was Anne Bonny and Mary Reed's pirate ship. With as many female pirates as we have around here..." Jake trailed off.

"Hey, I resemble that remark!" Sara said laughingly.

"I am afraid in this condition I barely make saucy wench status," Linda said sadly.

"Plus, I am hoping for a little payback using that ship," Jake said.

"Works for me," Sara said.

"I like it," Patti offered.

"No objection here," Linda said.

"*The Revenge* it is then," Jake pronounced.

"I suggest we not fly the Jolly Roger just yet, though," Patti quipped.

"That does give me an idea," Jake said thoughtfully.

----*----

Placing *The Revenge* in orbit two days later, maneuvering for a position with its nose down, facing the earth. It was as if she was watching the world below. Any inbound craft would see her stern until she nosed out, or they dropped to a lower orbit. Jake talked to Seven the day they came up with the name and had 12 large containers placed in her hold just before liftoff.

Once she was in a stable orbit, the onboard hangar opened, jettisoning the containers. Small positioning motors affixed to each allowed maneuvering about the cruiser. There were cables attaching them in groups of three, each positioned, so they strung out in opposite directions. She looked like a hub with spokes strung out in four directions, three containers per spoke.

----*----

For the next couple of days, everyone asked Jake about the containers. They all saw the ship in orbit on the monitors, looking a bit like a huge X with a ship in the middle. With a bright background, the

233

ship was hardly discernible, mostly an outline. All he would say to anyone is X marks the spot! Only Patti and Sara, excluding the ALICEs, knew what they were, and all were sworn to secrecy.

That week Seven provided four more fighters from her manufacturing facilities, and Jake kept with the pirate theme by designating them VF-84, the Jolly Roger squadron. Privately he figured the Navy deserved a turn, that being one of their squadrons. Now they just needed pilots for those birds. As it was, they now had five fully staffed squadrons and his fighter for 21-armed fighters. Either they had far more than they needed or not nearly enough, all dependent on how good a guesser he and Patti were.

Jake, Sara, and Patti spent quite a bit of time together while they waited for their visitor, Jacob, having transferred up to Seven as requested. They reworked the battle plan repeatedly until Sara finally stopped it.

"Jake, please leave it alone! You have gone over it 10 times a day for the last few days and made no significant changes. You've even put one squadron in three different locations, only to move them back to where we started," she cried.

"Yeah, I know, everyone is where I want them now, these are my *what-ifs*," he replied.

"Sara's right, Jake, this plan is as good as it gets with what data we have. I've asked ALICE to go over it and your *what if's* and she says she can find no flaws," Patti added.

"Jake, I know you are concerned about committing untested pilots to battle," ALICE offered.

"No, I'm concerned about committing pilots to an untested commander," he replied.

"You are hardly untested," Sara said.

"I seem to recall you nose to nose with a NeHaw Battle Cruiser."

"That was me at the pointed end of the spear, not someone I sent. Big difference," he said to no one in particular.

"Still your plan," Patti replied.

"You just worried less because if it failed, you weren't around to chew out," she finished with a smile.

"Point taken," Jake said with a halfhearted smile of his own.

"I just hate the wait."

----*----

RaBok directed his ships to drop out of faster-than-light as close as possible to the solar system in question. Like most NeHaw, he hated the slow pace of the repulser drives. As they formed up in the required delta formation, his Navigation Officer indicated the target planet on his tactical display.

Marked in orbit was PeTuk's Cruiser. It was motionless and powered down. That was odd. It also seemed to be dragging something on tethers. With several sub-cycles to go before reaching the planet, ReBok directed his science and engineering teams to determine what was going on there. He instructed communications to hail the ship but received no replies.

----*----

Jake was sound asleep, alone for a change, when ALICE woke him.

"Jake, I am sorry to disturb you, but monitoring has detected three NeHaw Cruisers at the edge of the solar system."

"How soon will they get here?" he asked, clearing his head.

"Approximately 3 days and 17 hours," ALICE replied.

"And how does this alter the battle plan," he asked cautiously.

"It has no impact on the primary strategy. Both you and Patti estimated a three Cruiser attack. They are in a triangular formation bringing all three ships forward batteries to bear. This is as described in the NeHaw tactical manuals we deciphered. They are going by the book," ALICE finished.

"Perfect," Jake said.

"Execute plan Alpha and institute a fighter flight ban, effective immediately," he then rolled over and went back to sleep.

----*----

The next morning Jake found Sara, Patti, and Linda in the control room ahead of him and all of them were there before breakfast. They also included Bonnie, Sharon, and Jessie remotely as well.

"Wow, you are all up early?" he commented.

"Who can sleep?" Patti asked.

"Well, you better, they won't be here for two more days, and you all need to be rested when they get here," he chastised.

All nodded.

"I expected you sooner," Sara said, coming to Patti's defense.

"I forced myself to take my time," Jake replied as he pointed to others in the command center.

"We need to be calm for those around us."

They all nodded once more, none confident enough to speak.

"So how did Bonnie's sensors do?" he asked, changing the subject.

"Remarkably well, they caught them a full day sooner than the optics," Bonnie replied.

"Barb is working with Dallas to fine-tune them for greater range."

"And everyone knows we are in a fighter flight blackout?" he asked.

"Yes, all fighter crews are with their squadrons, and all fighters are powered down until alerted," Sara answered.

"Excellent work people, the time for doubt is over. Remember, everyone here and in the other facilities are looking to us for leadership."

With that, he turned and left the control room, presumably off to breakfast.

"Was that the same man we were with last night?" Patti asked.

"Yup," Sara replied.

"He's now got his game face on. It's time to kick ass and take names, whatever that means," she replied as she followed him out the door.

----*----

They were a little more than one sub-cycle out, and his engineers still couldn't tell RaBok what those things were tethered off PeTuk's ship. Speculation was they were containers of tribute, spaced to make room for ship repairs. Nor could anyone tell him why the ship was dead in space. It looked functional. There was no visible battle damage or floating debris. It was just dead in space.

All attempts to contact the ship or remotely access its computers failed. RaBok would be concerned, but there was nothing to be of concern. The planetary classification was one of the lowest technologically, especially after the first disrupter bombardment. There were no notes in the record of its possessing interplanetary capabilities, much less interstellar. Also, there were no energy weapons capable of reaching space on the planet. For the empire's sake, according to the notes, they still used chemical-based propellant systems for missiles and projectile weapons. How very quaint.

He ordered his crew to maintain heading and formation and went for a meal.

Chapter 19

Patti was sitting in the control room watching the three Alien Cruisers on the monitor. They were still over a day out, but with the new sensors Bonnie placed in orbit, the images were sharp and detailed. She was still marveling over the changes in her life. A little over two weeks ago, she'd been researching her dissertation, frustrated with the fact that there wasn't anyone to do a review, and really, what was the point anyway? Never intended to be of any practical use, she was just going through the motions to maintain a family tradition.

Jacob could at least put his education to practical use. The townspeople always tolerated her family because of the engineers they trained. Considering the rest of the family, like her, as harmless eccentrics. Now she was putting that eccentricity to practical use. All her studies and research focused on this very moment, and she was scared shitless! If this didn't work, they were going to get hammered badly, and tens of thousands were going to die without ever knowing why.

Being the overly responsible firstborn, she tended to take on the responsibility, but in this case, she knew she was second fiddle to her grandpa. That had been a surreal event. When the militia came to town, in powered vehicles, and talked about flying machines, she was optimistic. Maybe some form of civilization had survived where her education would be of value. She talked to anyone who would listen in hopes of getting an interview with the higher-ups. Most listened politely, probably because of her looks.

Then Jake and Sara appeared, landing outside of town in a large helicopter. The combat suits made Patti think they were wearing spacesuits. She remembered her interview and then the wait. Once accepted, her biggest worry was they wouldn't take her brother, but he was already on the list.

Sent directly to medical with her brother for a standard physical, or so they were told, the ALICEs had a suspicion to confirm. Later she would learn that ALICE wanted blood and tissue samples for a DNA check. She wouldn't find out the true reason until days later when she asked ALICE about her great, great grandfather. She immediately told Jacob, and they both agreed to keep it quiet for now, which ALICE agreed was the right thing to do.

Patti spent every moment after that studying Jake. She learned why her great, great-grandma couldn't find him and all the things that happened to him since coming out of stasis. She had always been very proud of her family history, but this was the stuff of legends.

Jake was back in the hangar, doing a preflight on his fighter. He wasn't even supposed to fly in this battle, but it made him feel better knowing his fighter was ready just in case. He was a man of action and sitting this one out, chafed at him. The fact that, by the time he got in his fighter and orbit, the fighting would be finished didn't dissuade him.

As he was checking things out, Sara wandered over.

"Everything looks ok?" she asked, knowing the answer before she asked.

"I know, but doing this helps me think. Is everyone on alert?" he replied with a sigh.

Sara walked with him as he circled the fighter, occasionally touching some parts as he inspected it.

"I've been talking to all 5 squadron commanders; everyone is itching to go. As you might imagine, the Death Rattlers were very upset until you transferred the new fighters," she finished with a laugh.

"Are they OK with the change?" Jake asked.

"Oh yeah, some of them had navy in their family history, so it went over well," she replied.

Jake stopped to inspect one of the rail guns mounted under a wing.

"Have you seen Patti this morning?" he asked.

"She's been camped out in the control room. I forced her to go get some rest last night. I think ALICE slipped her something to get her to sleep," she said with a laugh.

"I think she's worse than you, obsessing over this plan," Sara added.

"She's young and an academic, this is the first test of her theories," he replied.

"And?" Sara asked.

"And they're solid. She just needs to learn that not all theory is a fact. We seem on firm ground because these guys are steeped in a rigid, dogmatic tradition, rather than dynamic situational analysis."

"If I rode in on this situation, the last thing I would do is commit all my resources at once. But they are so entrenched in their superiority, which we are betting the farm on, that the concept of armed resistance isn't in the equation."

"And when it is," Sara asked.

Jake didn't answer for a moment and then answered her.

"That's when we have to take the fight to them."

----*----

RaBok ordered his ships to go to all stop just outside the orbit of

PeTuk's cruiser. They retained the delta formation, combining the firepower of all three cruisers' forward batteries. He could make out the four lines radiating out from the ship, three boxes on each line, evenly spaced on the tethers. He agreed with his tactical officer's assessment that they looked like storage containers. However, no ship could travel with such an arrangement. They would destroy themselves in transit.

There still was no communication with the ship, so RaBok was about to order a boarding party when all four tethers were released from PeTuk's cruiser, and the ship started to rotate in place very slowly. As he watched in fascination, the front of the Cruiser came into view. Across the upper hull, below the bridge, a text, painted in red, was visible. It was an alien script that Rabok's translator displayed as *Revenge*. Below that was a graphic that resembled a skinless decapitated alien head with bones behind, one over the other, mimicking the shape the containers created in the background. What an odd thing for PeTuk to do, he thought.

At that moment, the communication system came alive with a transmission

"This is the Earth Planetary Defense Force, please state your intentions."

The transmission had come from PeTuk's cruiser. And, it had been in NeHaw, not in one of the planetary tongues. Had PeTuk lost his mind?

"PeTuk, this is ReBok, what is the meaning of this? You are ordered by the Empire to complete your bombing mission and return to patrol immediately!" RaBok transmitted.

----*----

Jake was standing in the control room watching a 3D holographic display of the three cruisers, in a triangular formation, as they came to a halt behind the *Revenge*. He smiled at Patti as they had stopped right where they had hoped.

"Combatants are in the box," Linda announced to no one in particular.

He paused and then ordered the release of the tethers, allowing each container's positioners to maintain their proximity to the *Revenge*.

"Let them see our face," Jake stated.

ALICE did a slow rotation of the *Revenge* to prevent alarming the three Cruisers unduly. Keep them curious, Jake told her. As the bow became visible to the aliens, the skull and crossbones he had asked Seven to paint there became visible, as was the new name *Revenge*. He then had ALICE transmit the standard challenge from *Revenge* and waited. The response was better than he'd hoped for. They still thought the ship was theirs.

"Alice, Death Rattlers are a go," Jake declared, winking at Sara.

----*----

As RaBok waited for a response, his tactical officer reported to him.

"Sir, we have four small ships approaching astern."

That was odd. Maybe PeTuk had abandoned his Cruiser, forcing him to use shuttles.

"Can you identify their type and origin?"

"They are of no known class and came from the planet's lone moon," he replied.

"Threat level?" RaBok asked, becoming more uncomfortable with each passing moment.

"Threat level minimal, sir. The only identifiable armament is four small particle guns each, no match for our shields. There appear to be two more energy-driven devices per ship, but the tactical systems can't determine their function," he replied.

RaBok decided he hated the unknown, and this situation was full of it. He ordered forward and stern batteries charged. As he did so, the communication system came alive again.

"This is the Earth Planetary Defense Force, your weapons system activation is considered an act of aggression. Power down now!"

Upon completion of the transmission, all 12 containers, previously tethered to PeTuk's ship, seemed to explode, shedding their sides and leaving platforms with two gun mounts, separated by a box.

----*----

Jake watched as the four unmanned Death Rattlers left the moon, in a box formation, and took position behind the three Cruisers. Sara escorted the four unmanned fighters during her training missions to the moon earlier in the week. The squadron pilots bitched unmercifully about the loss of their ships until Jake replaced them with the new Jolly Rogers.

As the cruisers powered up their guns, Jake asked ALICE to transmit the second message as planned, then asked her to blow the sides of the containers he had tethered to the *Revenge*. Each container held two mounted rail guns separated by a Stasis field generator with a small repulser drive for positioning. Each of the three cruisers now had eight rail guns targeting their bridge and two of their sterns from the four fighters. And, that didn't include the guns on the *Revenge* herself. All it took was a word from Jake to fire.

"All squadrons to their ships and ready to launch," Jake ordered, looking directly at Sara.

At that, Sara got up and left the room, already in her flight suit, with a helmet in hand.

----*----

RaBok considered his situation. Surrounded by an unknown race using unknown weapons, they unthinkably had one of the empire's cruisers under their control as well. No NeHaw warship had ever been taken by a hostile force.

The tactical manual was very clear in this situation. You either attack and remove the threat or call home, presumably with the loss of your command. Here there was a third option and one that might give him much-needed information.

"All ships, prepare for disrupter bombardment," RaBok commanded.

Technically, this planet was under a bombardment order, so he was not violating orders to do so. Logically, he should deal with the immediate threat and recover or destroy the cruiser. However, evaluating their response to the bombing might expose the nature of their weapons.

"Launch," Rabok ordered.

----*----

Jake watched the holograph as all three Cruisers launched missiles, headed not for the gun platforms, but to the earth. Without orders, all 12 gun platforms opened up on the missiles as Jake gave his orders

"Fighters away!"

The tactical display indicated several missiles escaped the rail guns, headed to the planet's surface. As he watched, Jake could see the indicators, representing the different squadrons, rise from the surface on an intercept course. One by one, the fighters dispersed on trajectories that brought their guns to bear. In short order, all missiles were destroyed.

"1st Air, Red Devils, and Cowboys take position Beta, Black Knights relocate to position Charlie," Jake ordered, noting he was placing Sara directly in harm's way while he stood in the control center, a Rear Escalon MoFo!

The first three squadrons dispersed into stationary pre-assigned positions hovering between the Revenge and the planet's surface. Hopefully, they would be located to either interdict another missile launch or rush to the aid of the Black Knights.

The Knights, assigned a position outside the edges covered by the gun platforms, were facing the cruiser's forward guns.

----*----

241

RaBok sat, amazed at what he just witnessed. The epitome of NeHaw bombing technology was destroyed in a flash.

"Sir, all disrupter bombs were destroyed before reaching their targets. Another launch?" his weapons officer asked.

"Tactical analysis of the weapons used?" RaBok asked.

"Sir, it's a previously unknown hypervelocity projectile weapon. No propellant-based system is capable of that firepower."

"Threat level?" RaBok asked.

"Energy shields are ineffective; analysis indicates our hull battle plate will not withstand impact. Threat level maximum."

RaBok had his answer, and it was bad. To make matters worse, the communication system announced itself once more.

"This is the Earth Planetary Defense Force. Your unprovoked attack demonstrates a hostile intent. Surrender now or be destroyed."

He watched his tactical display as more of the little ships took positions behind PeTuk's cruiser and at the outer edges of the plane created by the cruiser and the gun platforms floating around it. The manual contained no references for this situation. Surrender wasn't even listed, except in the context of a conquered planet, for the NeHaw, that involved eradicating the top leadership and military establishment and absorbing any technology deemed of value. They never really developed anything anymore. They just used what they took, as is.

Call home and loss of command seemed more palatable.

"Communications, contact Home planet," he ordered.

"Yes, Sir," his communication officer responded.

----*----

"Jake, they are trying to call home," Patti said with a smile while monitoring the sensor panel.

"Alice, are you blocking that and tracking the transmission vector?" Jake asked.

"All wavelengths are jammed, and vector recorded Jake," ALICE replied.

"Gotcha!" Jake said.

----*----

"Sir, we are unable to raise Home planet," the communication officer announced.

Jamming? How is that possible, no race had ever been able to block NeHaw communications. Then RaBok saw the answer floating in space in front of him. No race ever had access to NeHaw military tech before. Backed into a corner, RaBok knew his time was up.

242

"All weapons, fire at the Cruiser!"

----*----

"Jake, they are powering up again," Patti said.

As she finished, all three cruisers fired on the *Revenge*. Jake held his breath as he watched the newly installed stasis shields holding off the combined firepower of all three cruisers.

"Alice, how's she holding up?" Jake asked.

"60% of the failure threshold, it's better than expected. Two more ships would put us in danger," she replied.

----*----

ReBok called out, "halt fire," then stared at the undamaged cruiser floating as before.

Had the universe gone mad? They couldn't even destroy their ship. As he pondered his next move, short of turning to run from this insane planet, his tactical officer shouted

"Sir!" while pointing out the bridge window.

The last thing RaBok saw was the gun platforms streaming white fire, and the bridge windows exploding outward into space.

----*----

No more games, Jake thought, as he ordered ALICE to take the bridges out on all three cruisers. He had his answers as well and didn't need to push their luck any further. They all watched as all three cruisers belched out debris and bodies. Suddenly, one of the cruisers lurched violently and pivoted out of formation. It appeared to straighten out and then exploded, shooting pieces of the hull in all directions.

"What was that?" Patti asked.

"Sorry Jake, apparently someone in engineering was attempting to run with that ship," ALICE replied,

"We prevented its escape."

"I'll say," Jake said with a laugh.

The plan was for the forward guns to disable the cruisers as Jake had done before by evacuating the bridge. It was pure luck last time that no one in the engineering section had been able to pilot the ship. To prevent that this time, they had dispatched the four unmanned fighters to breach the hulls in the engineering sections as well.

Just their luck, some NeHaw engineer went to combat suited up, he thought.

"Well, granddaughter, how did we do?" Jake asked Patti as he moved

243

beside her chair.

"I'd say right on target, not our best possible results, but far better than the worst," she said, smiling and standing to hug Jake.

"Jake, we have a problem," ALICE announced.

"Sara's fighter was in the cruiser blast zone, and it was hit by debris."

Without a word, Jake spun on his heels and ran for the hangar. The elevator ride seemed to last forever.

"Is she alive?" he asked in the elevator on the way up.

"Her ship is completely unresponsive, and I am getting no data at all," ALICE replied.

Jake wore his flight suit that morning, despite everyone's assurances, it was unnecessary. As he strapped into his fighter, his helmet on his lap, he asked ALICE to lift off for him.

Once it cleared the hangar, he took over control and headed straight for Sara's last known position.

"Jake, I have the others looking for her, but she's not where she should be. Most likely, the explosion pushed her out of orbit," ALICE supplied.

"Alice, do we have any video covering that part of space before or during the explosion?" Jake asked.

"Searching now," she replied.

Jake had reached the search area by the time ALICE replied.

"I have located one small video segment."

She played the clip for Jake. It showed Sara's fighter, and as the cruiser exploded, a section of hull plate spun free, slicing through the side of her fighter. It cut the cockpit right off the body, sending it in a slow spin out into space.

Jake's heart sank as he watched it pass out of the camera view.

"Alice, can you calculate that vector?" Jake asked quickly.

"Jake," she started to reply.

"PLEASE!" he shouted.

"Calculating," she replied quietly.

"Adding ALICE-2."

"Adding ALICE-5."

"Adding ALICE-8."

"Solution derived and loaded into your navigation system," he heard,

"Thanks," he replied as he hit the autopilot.

His fighter surged off away from the planet as he watched the sensor display looking for any indication of Sara's cockpit section. He watched for what seemed like hours but was only 15 minutes.

"Jake, we are detecting no traces of Sara, no emissions whatsoever."

244

Jake ignored the transmission and continued on his course. Twenty minutes later, ALICE speaks up.

"Jake, you have just past the calculated intercept point for the extreme estimate."

Ignoring her, Jake continued to scan his instruments and the surrounding space. On a whim, he halted his fighter and just sat in space, putting his fighter in a slow, stationary, flat spin. He sat that way for several minutes, just looking for any indication of an anomaly.

He stopped the spin when he noticed a slow flicker on his left, heading in his general direction. At first, he wasn't sure what he had seen, but sure enough, it was a regular slow flash. He headed in that direction and slowly came upon the severed cockpit section of Sara's fighter.

"I've found her!" he transmitted.

"Is she alive?" ALICE asked in return.

Jake slowly moved his fighter until it was just outside the spin radius. Using an external light, he lit up the wreckage in time to see Sara flipping him off as she rotated past.

"YUP! Alive and bitchy as ever," he replied.

"Alice, how do I get her outta here?" Jake asked.

"Your best option is to get her out of the wreckage, and then pick her up in free space," she replied.

Jake grabbed his pilot's notepad and wrote out his directions. Killing the external light, he lit up the pad and held it up for Sara to see as she rotated past.

"JUMP," was on the pad.

He laughed as she flipped him off again and then proceeded to open her canopy manually. Once open, she waited until she rotated passed and shoved herself free, floating away from the wreckage. Jake had already opened his canopy, and Sara grabbed the edge as he carefully maneuvered near her. Pulling her inside and onto his lap, he closed the canopy and re-pressurized the cockpit, then pulled his helmet off.

Removing her helmet, she kissed him hard.

"Damn, you're a sight for sore eyes!"

"You scared the crap outta me," he replied in return.

"It didn't do my panties any good either," she laughed with tears in her eyes.

Reaching around Sara, Jake hit the reverse navigation function, and the fighter rotated on a reverse course for home. Jake held her tight all the way back, as they weren't strapped in, then asked ALICE to pilot them in to ensure a smooth re-entry. Once back in the hangar, ALICE placed the fighter near the facility door and in front of a huge welcoming committee. The entire facility plus the returned Red Devils were waiting for them.

"Oh My God," was all Linda could say, crying as she hugged Sara after she climbed down.

Jake watched from the fighter seat as the group swamped Sara. He took a deep breath, not wanting to do anything but collect Sara up and head to his room, but there was still a mess to clean up.

"Alice," he said from his seat.

"Yes, Jake."

"Thank You!"

"I am not going to tell you the statistical improbability you just overcame," she replied.

"Like Patti says, that's why we need each other," he replied.

"On a lighter note, we have established control over the two remaining Cruisers. We needed to dispatch attendants from the *Revenge* to secure navigation for one and drive control on the other. No life forms remained on either craft, and they will be landed and refitted by Seven," ALICE explained.

"Make sure she adds the rail guns," Jake said.

"Duly noted and endorsed," ALICE replied.

"All squadrons have returned to their bases of origin; however, I took the liberty of reassigning the Death Rattlers to Seven until human pilots are ready."

"Good deal," Jake said.

"What should we do about the Revenge and the gun platforms?" ALICE asked.

"Unless we need them elsewhere, let them stay where they are for now. They make a hell of a '*beware of dog*' sign," he said, laughing.

At that, he climbed out of the fighter and joined the crowd.

----*----

That Sara was sleeping with Jake that night was a foregone conclusion. Even Patti deferred any conversations on the day's outcome until the following morning, no matter how badly she wanted to debrief and compare her theories to the actual outcome. While everyone else celebrated, Jake and Sara shared a private dinner in his quarters, discussing anything but the battle and Sara's second near-death experience. Afterward, they made love late into the night.

As they lay in bed the following morning, Sara's head resting on Jake's chest, she gave a heavy sigh before speaking.

"Jake, I want to have a baby."

"Honestly, I can't understand how you're not pregnant now?" He

246

replied softly.

"Alice put me on medication to prevent it," she replied with a sniffle.

"We agreed, remember that I was more important as your XO."

Jake lifted her head to kiss her and then said aloud.

"Well, then I guess it's time to change the agreement."

"Alice," Jake asked softly.

"Yes, Jake," ALICE replied in fashion.

"No more birth control for Sara, please?"

"It was stopped last night," ALICE replied.

Jake could feel Sara crying, her head on his chest, so he just held her.

Chapter 20

For the next few days, everyone's time was split between cleaning up the mess in space and celebrating the victory. With the after-action reviews and battle analysis to do, Patti was completely swamped and as happy as she could be. Replacing Sara as squadron commander of the Black Knights was a top priority, the official reason being an expected pregnancy. Privately, everyone knew Jake said no more adventures for her!

Linda, Jessie, Bonnie, and Sharon were all busy managing their respective facilities and negotiating personnel transfers to balance the staff between the four locations. Everyone was on recruiting watch, looking for new candidates in their areas of responsibility.

The squadrons were all on a rotating space duty, performing debris recovery. Recovery of all pieces of the destroyed NeHaw cruiser still in orbit became a priority. All parts were ferried to the Revenge for scavenging by the resident bots. Once the hold was full, it made a delivery to Seven and then returned to orbit. They also recovered the back half of Sara's fighter and returned it for a rebuild.

Jake and Sara did finally get around to discussing her mishap. They were having dinner in the quarter's level dining room with Linda, Kathy, and several of the pilots who retrieved her fighter's wreckage.

"You shoulda seen it, Sara, it looked like someone sliced it in half with a knife," one of the pilots said.

"Oh, I saw every moment," she replied.

"Oh yeah, weren't you scared?" one of the women asked.

"Terrified!" she replied.

"But Jake says you flipped him off when he found you?" another asked lightly.

"Yes, I was pissed and in an adrenaline rush. I think I screamed *about bloody time* or something like that!" she said with a laugh.

"At first, I was scared to death as I went spinning off into space. Then I got sad thinking I would never see anyone again."

She was looking at Jake as she spoke the last.

"Then I got mad as hell that this happened to me, just some freak accident. When the exterior light hit me, I was really happy and angry at the same time. And when I saw the red nose on the fighter, I knew only my Jake flew anything so outlandishly garish!" she finished with a grin and tears in her eyes.

Jake could see that Linda noticed the "my *Jake*" as he had. Usually, they all tended to be extra careful about any exclusivity statements.

Either Sara let it slip, or she was sending a message. Regardless they both chose not to comment on it.

"Hey, can I join you?" Patti said as she walked up to the table, dinner tray in hand, and slid in next to Sara.

"You finally pried yourself away from the control room?" Linda asked.

"I was going, cross-eyed!" she replied.

"If I had to look at one more video, I was going to scream."

"What video?" one of the pilots asked.

"She's doing the after-action analysis," Jake supplied.

He looked down at a table of blank stares.

Jake continued.

"After every engagement, we do an analysis and an after-action report to see what we did right and where we guessed wrong or need improvement. Your future training will come from her work," he finished.

At that, he got several nods of understanding, and someone finally asked.

"How did we do?"

"We did a pretty good job," Patti supplied, taking a bite.

"We cheated on this a bit because we had their playbook in advance, the real test will be the next round as we are hitting uncharted territory."

"Next round?" one of the pilots asked.

"I hope no one thinks this is over?" Jake asked the group,

"Please understand, we just became the intergalactic equivalent of Israel."

Back were the blank stares.

"God, I need to get more history added to the education programs," Jake said, exasperated.

"Look, in my time, there was a small country in the Middle East called Israel. Due to conflicting religious beliefs with their immediate neighbors and a dispute over the land they occupied, they had a constant battle just to survive. Their neighbors were committed to their destruction. They developed a very efficient military machine, and everyone in the country did their part to support it."

Not to be left out, Patti added her perspective.

"The point is, we have bested them twice now and at a sector level. No other civilization has managed that in recent times, or recent enough, that their command reference documentation doesn't specify the next steps."

"Their basic approach is one of escalation. Start with one ship and then go to three more ships from that sector. Next, divert ships from the adjoining sectors and so on. Both Jake and I have pulled their reference material apart, and our best guess is they may combine 3 to 4 sector forces and try again. That's 12 to 16 ships. However, that leaves four sectors without ships patrolling, a very large piece of unprotected space, and one exposed to rebellion."

"The other NeHaw option is to bring in one of their Battleships, which we haven't been able to determine a true size for yet. The only references surround space battles and races we have no information on."

"We, on the other hand, are in possession of three of their Cruisers. With the addition of our stasis shields, they are capable of a 4 to 1 force correlation. And they have no defenses for our rail guns," Jake supplied with a smile.

"And don't forget the ALICEs," Kathy contributed,

"They are the best secret weapon of all."

"Hear, hear," Jake replied.

"What are we going to do?" Someone asked.

Everyone looked at Jake, who happened to have a mouth full of lasagna.

Swallowing slowly, he took a breath and then answered.,

"Short term, what we have been. Working our asses off and improving our planetary defenses. Long term, we are going to take the fight to them."

----*----

After breakfast, the following morning, Jake called a meeting in the control room. He asked Sara, the ALICEs, and all 4 facilities commanders, three of them virtually, to attend a meeting to help work out their short-term priorities.

Jessie and Seven informed everyone they had all their resources working to restore the two captured Cruisers and Sara's fighter as well as continued new fighter construction. ALICE pointed out that ALICE-8, located in Hawaii, also housed automated manufacturing facilities. Admittedly, the basis of their work was around marine construction but utilized for spaceship construction nonetheless. They could ferry any of the necessary components from Alaska that couldn't be produced there.

Jake asked Sara to take Jacob and one of the new combat teams to check it out and see what was possible there. As Jacob and several of the available team members weren't trained pilots, they would have to use one of the conventional transport aircraft, probably the Falcon Jake used for his run to Alaska. ALICE-8 assured everyone her hangars were fully operable and looked forward to the visit. She also assembled a list of tasks for Jacob, who, like Jason, was performing or supervising facility repairs.

Sharon indicated they located a community in eastern Washington suitable for a Prosperity type arrangement and asked for Sandy's help. If successful, it would stabilize a large portion of Washington and Idaho, including parts of Oregon, Montana, and into Canada. It would also increase the pool of outsiders they could recruit.

Jake asked about ALICE-6 in South Dakota. As a weapons research facility, it, unbeknownst to Jake, provided most of the rail guns for the fighters and the platforms in space. He was aware that it contained the original alien handheld weapons and was the intended source of the combination weaponry he requested earlier. He assigned himself a trip, with a support team, to visit. He didn't want to get caught short again. The spearguns had worked, but they weren't his first choice in a gunfight.

Bonnie and Dallas located 10 potential recruits from Paint Rock and the surrounding communities. With Jake's permission, they wanted to extend offers within the week. Jake's only restriction was Bonnie didn't leave the facility! Both she and Kathy were getting close to their delivery dates, and he didn't want any risky behaviors from either of them. She promised to send out a couple of the combat-trained pilots from the Cowboys' squadron to make the offers.

With the meeting completed, Sara ran off to put her team together, and the others dispersed to their assigned tasks. Jake hung back and pulled up the holographic map ALICE used, early on, to show where all 8 ALICE facilities were located. With Hawaii and South Dakota on track for the next visits, only Maine and Georgia remained unvisited. With the rate of recruitment, Jake thought, it wouldn't be too much longer before they could staff all 8 locations reasonably well, fighter squadrons and all.

Maine is listed as a medical research facility, the east coast equivalent of ALICE-1's Nevada location. The Georgia location wasn't tagged with a primary function. Jake thought that was odd, but had bigger fish to fry at the moment and zoomed in on South Dakota.

Located near Lake Oahe and north of what was Highway 212, it looked like a remote location even before the fall. The local data indicated no settlements within 80 miles or more. Also noted was that the area above and around the facility hadn't been visited by anyone since the fall. This was *out in the sticks*.

Jake then moved to the Hawaii facility located on the island of Lanai. He was surprised to see that, as he was under the impression, that Lanai was a privately owned island. The government acquired it at some point or at least negotiated the rights to build underground. Again, according to the local data, no one lived on the island anymore. All the residents relocating to the larger islands with more abundant resources available. Jake noted with a smile that ALICE-8 might just become the new R&R location. That would have to wait, though, until he could get some faster transport craft built. Poor Sara was in for a 10-plus hour flight in the Falcon over water.

He debated about asking Seven for three or four transport craft capable of both atmospheric and space flight. As the fighters only held one, the pilot, all their existing fast transport, was limited to flight-trained personnel. With more untrained recruits on the way, the need to move larger groups quickly across the country was becoming apparent.

However, he didn't want to impact fighter production either, and Seven already indicated her material resources were limited to supplying material for 43 additional fighters, 20 of which he already requested. The transports would reduce the number of fighters she could produce. He needed to locate suitable raw materials for continued production.

He also needed to delegate, even more, he thought. All the facilities commanders were working out well, and the squadron leaders performed outstandingly in the last engagement. Patti had combat planning down. He now needed someone to head logistics. Locating manufacturing materials, personnel transfers, and production management could all fall under that umbrella. Now all he needed was a body. Three bodies, as he now needed someone to head to Hawaii and South Dakota as well.

Jake closed down the hologram and headed out of the control room. He continued to run names through his head for the three slots as he headed to his quarters. He'd taken to using his quarters as his office, never knowing which facility he would be using at any one time. As he stepped out of the elevator on the quarter's level, he ran into Karen coming down the hall.

"You are just the person I need to talk to," Jake declared.

"Well, it's nice to see you too, Jake," Karen replied with a smile.

"Do you have a moment? I would like to run something by you. I want to dump some work on you, but I thought I would word it nicer," he said with a grin.

"Yes, I have a moment, and I was heading to the hangar ready room to talk with some of the latest recruits about job selection ideas. They don't expect me for half an hour, though," Karen laughed and said.

Jake led Karen to his door and, once inside, indicated for her to have a seat.

"That's kinda what I wanted to talk about," he said, seating himself.

"I think I need a department head for logistics. Someone to chase the details of personnel transfers and find raw materials for the various manufacturing systems the ALICEs run for us. I also need to think about two new facility commanders with the Hawaii and South Dakota locations going live."

"So, you need me to find you a logistics manager and two more willing women to bed," she said with a laugh.

"Very funny, in case you didn't know, I have never touched Sharon," he replied.

"Oh no, I knew, she made sure we all knew!"

"So yes, I need a logistics manager and two people crazy enough to herd cats in one of these," he said with a wave of his hand indicating the surrounding building.

"I do prefer the more senior staff members as facilities heads," he finished as an afterthought.

"OK, let me think about it. I'll find you some candidates to be sure, but we are short on senior staff, but adding new members in Texas as we speak," Karen said.

"I think the logistics slot can be flexible, but facility commanders need some miles to them," Jake supplied.

"Oh yeah, Sharon is an ancient 24," Karen commented sarcastically.

"It's not the age, it's the wisdom. She's been around long enough to prove herself," Jake flipped back.

"Fair enough," Karen replied as they both got up, and Jake watched her leave.

Grabbing a drink from the in-room refrigerator, he went over to his desk and started sorting through staff selections for his South Dakota team.

----*----

Sara was not particularly happy with this assignment. It wasn't the fact that she was going to Hawaii. She and Jake talked enough to know that it was a more desirable tropical location than San Nicolas. It was the damn 2800 miles over water, which bothered her. Moreover, worst of all, since Jacob and some of the newly trained combat team members weren't flight qualified, they would have to take a Falcon like the Alaska trip. She would have much preferred her fighter or rather a loaner, as they were still rebuilding hers.

She was more than happy to fly separately but knew Jake required all first-time visits to be assumed as a visit to a hostile territory until proven otherwise. In addition, as a mission leader, she couldn't send her team separately. It just sucked! She hoped Jake would go along as well, but understood why he couldn't.

They saw quite a bit of each other lately, the rotation was fairly shredded at this point, so she couldn't claim neglect. Plus, Jake needed to

253

check on the weapon's facility. He had a real feel for what they needed. Who would have thought about bringing spear guns into space? If he said he needed to go there, that was good enough for her.

Her combat support team was a mixed group of Californian and Alaskan recruits, all women. Not that she cared one way or another, but Jacob might enjoy the ratios. Being Jake's great, great grandson certainly hadn't hurt his popularity with the ladies, but his general good looks and easygoing attitude made him a favorite all-around anyway.

Jacob was already supposed to be on a helicopter bound for Nevada, and then the entire team would head for Hawaii the following day.

"Maybe we need a fighter escort?" she thought.

----*----

Jake was in the hangar doing his preflight inspection before their mission to ALICE-6. He asked to have the extra rail guns removed previously but retained his scarlet and gold paint scheme. He was still the only member of the Wildcard's squadron and wasn't sure that would ever change.

He saw Sara and her team off earlier that morning, Jacob having arrived late last night so he could attend. Jake surprised her with a change in transportation, as he knew she hated to fly over water. Yesterday she had even gone so far as to suggest that maybe she should fly a fighter as an escort. After telling her no, he asked ALICE to locate a faster alternative to the Falcon.

It looked like a corporate jet but incorporated shorter, more solid wings with rotating nacelles on the ends for both vertical and horizontal thrust. In level flight, it could cruise at 600 knots, cutting its flight time to less than 5 hours. Excluding pilots, it held 10 passengers, so they had room to spare. He asked ALICE to evaluate adding repulser drives in place of the nacelles on some of the airframes as a short-term solution to the fast transport problem. Only if they could take the increased stress on the wing roots and airframes.

His preflight complete, Jake climbed into the cockpit of his fighter and prepared for takeoff. He checked in with Robert in Alaska, having selected the 1st Air Cavalry as his combat support team. They initially bypassed their ground combat training in preference to flight training but had since gone back to complete the full combat curriculum. This would be their first opportunity to use it as security, not that he expected any shooting.

With his helmet on, and the canopy closed, Jake's fighter lifted off and cleared the open hangar doors. He checked his navigation screen and, verifying that the four Air Cavalry fighters left Alaska on schedule, headed to the designated rendezvous point before reaching ALICE-6. As his fighter went supersonic, he appreciated Sara's desire for a faster mode of transportation. Fears aside, sitting idle for hours was not his idea of fun either. He did remember a few in-flight distractions that made the long trips acceptable.

Within 10 minutes, he spotted the four 1st Air Cavalry squadron members, in proper flight formation, on his 6 o'clock, each pilot checking in with him. 15 minutes later, they were on approach to ALICE-6, her hangar doors opened and ready to receive her guests.

With Jake leading them down, all five fighters lowered, one by one, into the hangar and settled to rest in a row. As each of the Air Cavalry pilots deplaned, they produced rifles and, as a unit, did a perimeter sweep. Once given the all-clear, the five pilots headed to the facility's door, still on alert. They headed straight to the control room, and as required, by his own rules, Jake checked in at the master console before declaring the facility secure.

"Hello ALICE-6," Jake said.

"Welcome, Jake," ALICE-6 replied.

Once cleared, they all removed their helmets, and Jake remembered what made the Air Cavalry squadron different. Three of the four pilots were men, which was unusual considering the overall male-to-female ratios, and all of them were from the Fort Hood Texas area. As Jake promised them, he revived their family's unit designation, adopting the helicopter squadron's name for their fighter squadron. With 13 recruits in that group, the competition had been fierce for the four slots. The quality of the group was such that the top four ever so slightly surpassed the others, all of them rated exceptional.

The remaining nine had all filled slots with other fighter squadrons, but that was a small consolation to most of them. Still, no one turned him down for a flight slot. All the other squadrons were either equally mixed or mostly women with at least one of the Texas pilots in each.

"OK, Robert, have your team stash their rifles in the hangar armory, and let's go and check out the new toys," Jake said.

Helmets in hand, they all filed out the way they came and back into the hangar.

"Alice-6, where is the weapon's assembly area?" Jake asked before entering the hangar.

"Component manufacturing is performed in several areas, but the final assembly is located on the hangar level, off the main hangar."

Jake led the group over to the armory to stow their rifles.

"Keep your sidearms, but leave your rifles and helmets here."

As the last one came back out the armory door, one of the ubiquitous

255

bots appeared, and ALICE-6 directed them.

"Please follow me."

The little bot led the five across the hangar area, passing the now familiar collections of helicopters and other aerial transport Jake was used to seeing at every ALICE facility. However, intermingled were various air and ground vehicles with weapons as add-ons. Stopping to inspect something that Jake could only describe as a tank buster, he heard ALICE-6, via the bot, explain.

"This is an experimental anti-armor gun mounted on a standard tracked vehicle. Its weapon is a focused, high-energy beam capable of burning through twelve inches of armor plate at 5 miles. Several other experimental platforms are located here as well, all products of alien source technology."

The group continued to the far side of the main hangar. They followed the bot as it weaved its way through the various collections of equipment parked in the hangar. As they approached a set of double doors, the doors retracted into the walls, allowing the group to enter a smaller hangar-like area. All around the room were tables with various weapons systems on them. Some items, too large for a table, stood on floor mounts or tripods.

"This is the display area, prototypes of individual and crew-served weapons were evaluated for fit and finish here before being taken to live fire testing," ALICE-6 supplied.

"These are all functional," Jake asked, looking around the room.

"Yes, but none is armed. All have dummy magazines or power supplies for fit evaluations," she replied.

Jake walked over to a table containing a rifle, the likes he had never seen before. It had an opening at the end with a rifled bore indicating a projectile weapon, but there was a small cylinder like an oversized battery and a slender magazine on the table as well. The barrel length and scope made Jake think it was some kinda sniper rifle.

"Like your suggestion for the fighters, this is a rail gun suitable for an individual soldier. The cylinder is the power cell, and the magazine supplies the projectile slugs. It discharges at 13,128 feet per second, and the power cell is good for 30 discharges," ALICE-6 provided.

Jake lifted the rifle and brought it to his shoulder, sighting through the scope. He could handle it fine but could feel the weight of the weapon and knew it would be an armful for any of the women and most of the men. However, on a bipod, in the prone position, it would be more than acceptable. At 13,128 feet per second, at over six times the velocity of the 7.62mm, it should have one hell of a range to it and probably a good kick to boot.

He set it back on the table and wandered around the room, the four pilots following him as he did so. He stopped at another table with a smaller rifle. Picking it up and inspecting it, he noted its barrel tip was a dark polished crystal, and it used a slightly larger power cell than the rail gun.

"This is a direct reproduction of a NeHaw energy weapon," ALICE-6 said.

"It has been modified to human proportions. The power cell is good for 40 discharges."

"And we can make more of these?" Jake asked.

"Yes, we are equipped for a full production run of 1000 rifles a month, and I have 200 in my inventories currently," ALICE-6 answered.

Setting the rifle down, the next table caught Jake's eye.

"Are these the combination rifles I requested?" He asked, walking to the table and lifting the rifle.

It was a copy of one of the 5.56mm rifles all the pilots had carried. This model had a second barrel, fixed under the original. The barrel guard enclosed both barrels, so only the ends protruded. Right in front of the trigger guard was a circular opening Jake assumed was where the power cell went.

"The fire selector switch has been modified to allow thumb activation. It will flip between safe, single fire, automatic fire, and energy discharge. It is ambidextrous, for both right and left-handed shooters. Also, the sights auto-correct for each barrel based on the selector switch position," ALICE-6 supplied.

"The neighboring table holds a 7.62mm sniper combination variant. However, the energy discharge tends to leave a telltale light trail disclosing the shooter's hide point."

"That's OK, I think that rail gun is the new weapon of choice for that job," Jake replied with a grin.

Jake set the rifle down and continued wandering. Most of the other items were intended for ground battles. He hoped to never fight, or crew-served weapons he didn't have the manpower for.

Finally, Jake stopped his wandering, did a little math, and placed his order.

"OK, can you give me 800 of the 5.56mm combo rifles and 160 rail guns? That is 100 rifles and 20 rail guns per facility. After that, we can consider 20 of each for the Cruisers."

"Oh, and ALICE-6," Jake continued.

"Do you have a name you prefer over ALICE-6?"

"I know the other ALICEs have tried to choose a name indicative of their locations. Kola is Sioux for a friend, the Sioux being native to this region of the United States."

"Kola is great," Jake replied cheerily.

----*----

Sara was delighted that Jake had found this aircraft for her mission. She tried in vain to get him to let her fly in a fighter instead of the Falcon. Ten-plus hours over water and not even the distraction of inflight sex was a nightmare scenario for her. At least in this aircraft, the six of them had plenty of room to stretch out, and with a little help from ALICE's medical stores, she slept for most of the flight.

As they started their descent into ALICE-8, Jacob woke her. She sat for a moment, trying to clear her head, and then looked out the window. The turquoise waters and lush green islands were everything Jake described. The four women that made up the combat team were readying themselves for deplaning, while Jacob, with a helmet in hand, just tried to stay out of their way. Sara checked her sidearm in place on her hip and then grabbed her helmet as well.

They slowed to a stop, or more accurately a hover, and then slowly dropped until Sara knew they'd entered the hangar as it got very dark inside the aircraft.

"OK, everyone, helmets on and combat team at the ready," Sara announced as she donned her helmet.

The combat team all lined up to exit the aircraft, rifles in hand, and Jacob bringing up the rear. Sara could feel the jet settle onto the hangar floor, and the engines rev down. The cabin door opened, and all four combat team members jumped from the open door, not waiting for a stairway to deploy.

"Ooh-rah girls," Sara thought.

The four women were all recent recruits, within the last few rounds from varying locations. As newbies, they were very gung-ho and excited about their new futures. Sara and Jacob came to the aircraft door and watched as the four spread out and performed their security sweep of the immediate area. Once complete, Sara led Jacob down the stairway, and all six headed to the facility's door.

They performed the standard drill, known to all at this point, on new facility security verification. Once Sara confirmed with ALICE-8's main console in the control room that all was well, everyone relaxed and removed their helmets.

"Hello, ALICE-8," Sara declared.

"Hello, Sara," ALICE-8 replied.

"If I may, I understand we can now choose our names now?"

"Absolutely," Sara replied.

"I wish to be called Lanai for the island I'm on," she responded.

"Well, from what I saw on the way in, I think that's a great name, you're beautiful!" Jacob replied.

"Lanai, it's a pleasure," Sara said and then issued orders to her team.

"OK, let's stow the rifles and head to the manufacturing bays," she announced.

Before leaving, Nevada Sara reviewed ALICE-8's layout and resources. The hope was she could convert to constructing spaceships instead of maritime vessels. She led the group out of the control room and back to the hangar, heading to the armory. Once they dropped off their rifles and helmets, two of the automated carts pulled up. Climbing in three to a cart, they sped off deeper into the main hangar area.

Lanai explained to both groups as they rode.

"We have three main assembly bays, all with access to the ocean. They are essentially fully automated dry docks. Sub-components assemble in other areas of the facility. Those are then transported to the main bays for the final assembly. For maritime craft, we would then flood the bays, and the completed ship can sail out into open water via watertight doors."

The two carts slowed to a stop in front of two large hangar doors. The words BAY 1 were painted in 10-foot high letters spanning both doors. A smaller door in one of the larger doors opened to allow the six to enter. With Sara leading the way, they all passed through the doorway and into the assembly bay. More precisely, they were on a 20-foot wide walkway that traveled around three of the four sides of the bay.

All around the bay and overhead were cranes and equipment that Sara assumed were part of the automated assembly systems. Stepping up to a railing that wrapped around the edges, she looked down about 50 feet to the floor below and up at the roof, a good 100 feet or more above. At the far end of the bay, which had to be over 2000 feet away, Sara could see the watertight doors and noted there was a much narrower gangway crossing from one side to the other.

"All three bays are identical and were designed to accommodate more than one assembly project at a time. A large portion of the rest of the facility is dedicated to sub-assembly production," Lanai offered.

"Well, Jacob?" Sara asked while turning to him.

Jacob produced a tablet from somewhere, studying it intently. He was going between the tablet display and examining different parts of the assembly bay. After a few seconds, he replied.

"Well, clearly, there is plenty of room to work with. From my conversations with Jake, the first designs should be smaller than the NeHaw cruisers we have, and we could build two or three at a time in here with room to spare. The real question is getting them out without having to flood the bay."

"For smaller ships, we can just fly them out through the internal bay doors and out the main hangar," Lanai supplied.

"Yeah, and I was thinking about some kinda barge for a big one," Jacob replied.

"A barge?" Sara asked.

"Yeah, like a floating dry dock. We would build a flat barge and then assemble the ship on it. Once we are ready, we flood the bay and float it clear before liftoff," Jacob answered.

"We may have some sub-assemblies already prepared for that function," Lanai responded.

"We had a floating dock in process, before the attack, and several of the sections welded together would almost fill the bottom of one bay."

Turning to the rest of the group, Sara announced to the others.

"Well then, I suggest we head back inside and let Jacob and Lanai decide what they are going to build for us," she finished with a smile.

Chapter 21

Jake decided to stay with Kola for a few days while a proper staff trained for residency. Considering all the ALICEs had done for him, he felt bad just dropping in for a day at a time. He was also still waiting on an answer from Karen about his request for two facility commanders and a logistics manager. He knew she would contact him as soon as there were candidates, and frankly, the quiet here was nice for a change, with no demands on his public or private time.

While they were all just hanging around, Jake asked Robert and his team to test-fire several of the weapons systems for evaluation, a job they accepted with enthusiasm. With the prior experience to color his judgment, Jake wanted fresh eyes and hands on these before just pushing them on the troops. Besides the firing range, Kola housed several combat simulators they could use to evaluate the effectiveness of each weapon.

Sara checked in on the first day of their arrival, first thanking Jake for the transportation upgrade, and then handing him off to Jacob to discuss the manufacturing options. They wound up on the call for several hours, discussing their needs, versus what was possible and what could be completed the quickest.

In the end, they reviewed several designs the ALICEs already had in the works. They settled on one design that could both serve as a fast atmospheric transport and an armed space patrol craft. He had no idea what the government engineers had in mind for this thing, but it was finished in plan and ready to roll.

It was far larger than the fighters, about one and a quarter the size of the cruisers. The NeHaw didn't have an equivalent in size, but it could be armed to the teeth, and more guns were better these days. They would take months to build but utilized several systems already designed for nautical ship and submarine use. One of the huge advantages they had now was weight was no longer a consideration for liftoff when using the alien propulsion systems. Granted, inertia was still a consideration, but at least exotic lightweight materials were not required, and they had lots of iron plates in bulk.

Sara and her team would only stay in Hawaii until a replacement staff was trained and ready for them as well, but Jacob would likely remain for much longer, supervising spaceship construction. Jake already decided on sending Sara a fighter for her return flight, the repairs on hers being almost complete, better to have her return home in a good mood.

Finishing his morning status briefings with all the facility commanders, he was delighted to hear the two new cruisers would be space-worthy in a few days, with a bot crew. Like the *Revenge*, they would continue repairs in space to make them habitable for humans. The third cruiser salvaging was complete, but its remains were only good for parts.

Patti suggested they name them the *Defiance* and the *Invincible*. Jake agreed on *Defiance* but felt that naming any ship, the *Invincible* was asking for trouble. They all finally agreed on the *Independence* instead. Jake laughed to himself as he thought that *Revenge*, *Defiance,* and *Independence* sounded something like the stages of grief.

When he finally signed off the communicator, he was sitting quietly in the control room. As he did, he was sketching out some ideas for new ships. He grudgingly admitted the Nehaw had it right with their cruiser design. The wedge shape allowed 70% of the ship's firepower to face forward while presenting a much smaller target than a broadside. Even thinking in 3D, the tapers, to the top and bottom of the hull, allowing for a target cone that covered a large forward volume.

However, for every strength, there was a weakness, and for this design, that was the stern. As Jake exploited earlier, they had very little firepower dead astern. So now, he was analyzing various shapes to see if a more balanced design presented any advantages. He was in deep thought when Bonnie called him.

"Jake, we may have a problem," she cut in. Her face was on the display panel, where his sketches had been.

"What's up?" he asked.

"Our long-range sensors just picked up four, no, five ships coming out of faster-than-light at the edge of the solar system," Bonnie replied.

"Why the ambiguity?" Jake asked. Bonnie's new sensors had picked up the three NeHaw Cruisers clear as a bell.

"These are small, well smaller than a cruiser anyway," she replied defensively.

"And traveling fairly close together."

"The only way I can tell they aren't one ship is the fluctuations in their repulser drives. It's one strong reading, but five different frequencies," she added with pride.

Jake hadn't been challenging her. It was more about thinking out loud. Both previous attacks by the NeHaw had come with big ships, almost broadcasting their presence. Why five small ships? Just the fighters were likely more than a match for them.

"Can you make out any details yet?" Jake asked.

"No, they aren't in visual range, maybe in four or five hours. They are still three days out," Bonnie finished.

"Kola, can you get Jessie and Seven on the line, please, oh and please put everyone on alert," Jake asked while thinking.

This was an unexpected move. After the battle, Jake would have bet good money they would be seeing a battleship in two to three months, not five small ships weeks later.

"Yes, Jake?" Jessie chimed in on the communications line.

"We are expecting visitors in about three days. I need *Defiance* and *Independence* in orbit in two."

"We will divert resources from fighter production to Cruiser repairs, they will be ready," Seven replied.

"Sounds good, please let me know when they go orbital," Jake replied.

Getting back to Bonnie, Jake gave her more instructions.

"Bonnie, please get with Patti as soon as you have something on these ships. Five small ships make no sense, and I hate that."

"Yes, Jake," Bonnie said, and they signed off.

Jake pulled up all the relevant data on NeHaw combat vessels and, for the next several hours, tried to determine what they were up to. Their Destroyer class was about half the size of a Cruiser, so Jake figured they weren't that. Bonnie should be able to pick those out easily.

The other thing that bothered Jake was the comment from Bonnie. She said that the repulser drives were of varying frequencies. While the fighter's drives were different from the NeHaw drives, the frequency of like ships was pretty much the same. At least close enough to classify a vessel type.

That meant that while you could spot a fighter frequency from a Cruiser, several fighters would be hard to separate at a distance. These were all close in size to be the same type but different enough to be distinguished from afar. It meant something, but Jake wasn't sure what.

----*----

Bonnie patched Patti into her sensor feeds as they both worked with the real-time data coming in., all six active facilities tasked someone with scanning the data, Jake using it from time to time as well in his work. She still couldn't get a good visual feed, but everything she had so far supported the initial report of five dissimilar ships, all about the same size and all fairly small.

She needed to let Barb handle this. Her due date was approaching fast, and Becky scolded her for overtaxing herself and stressing the baby. No one was sure if she or Kathy would deliver first, but both were now on the no-fly list per Jake. As he promised to be there for the delivery, Bonnie expected to see him arrive any day. Then again, the latest developments could forestall his trip. The NeHaw was starting to piss her off.

----*----

Patti was in the control room with Linda going over the live data. The visuals were still too fuzzy to determine what type of spacecraft was approaching, but they were able to agree on two things. The first was that there were five distinct ships, all similar in size but not identical. The second was they all were about the size of the Nehaw exploration ship, probably smaller but not by much. This also puzzled Patti, as ships of that size were no match for their fighters, one on one, much less the three Cruisers they now possessed.

Could they be some kind of suicide bombers? NeHaw military strategy didn't mention the concept. They couldn't be described as self-sacrificing people, more like the self-centered kind. She made a note just in case but placed that option as a low-risk item.

Patti knew Linda was perplexed as well. The first of the analysts and part of the original six, as Sara, Bonnie, and the rest were known. If anyone knew the ALICE systems and how to extract information from them, it was she. So far, they hadn't found anything in either the NeHaw or ALICE data stores that explained the five ships or a possible attack strategy.

She did suspect the possibility of a diversion and asked Bonnie to continue multispectral scanning of all earth approaches. These ships could be just for a show of force. Either way, this response occurred much quicker than either she or Jake would have guessed.

----*----

The following morning, newly trained staff from Nevada arrived and allowed Jake to bow out gracefully. He jumped into his fighter, leaving Robert and his squadron temporarily assigned to Kola until the current crisis was resolved. Jake was a firm believer in not risking everything in one shot, so having them there better distributed their forces.

Karen still hadn't officially responded to his staffing request, but one of the new arrivals made a point of introducing himself to Jake before he left. James was Bill's oldest son and had been one of the several who requested Nevada over Alaska for training. He said Karen told him to be sure and let Jake know she assigned him as temporary commander of the Kola facility until he selected a permanent candidate. James was about 25, and Jake remembered taking a liking to him, in the short time he was in Seven. He suspected this was Karen's way of making recommendations.

264

Once he cleared the hangar, Jake nosed up and headed south. While in flight, with one of the ALICEs doing the flying, he decided to do a little admin work and did a quick scan of Robert's weapons evaluations. They were satisfied overall, but he included a section with a recommendation for slight changes to some of the designs. Jake was impressed with his analysis and forwarded his recommendations for implementation before distribution. Within the hour, he was descending into Dallas's hangar.

As Jake climbed down the ladder from the cockpit, he spied Bonnie and Becky waiting for him by the facility door. He crossed directly over to them and, being as gentle as possible, hugged and kissed Bonnie. Not one to be neglected, Becky waited her turn, and then jumped Jake, smothering him with kisses.

"Hey, get a room," Bonnie exclaimed with a laugh.

"I plan on it," Becky replied over her shoulder.

"What's the latest?" Jake asked, ignoring the exchange as he set Becky down.

Turning to head back inside, Bonnie replied over one shoulder.

"We are starting to get discernible images now. They don't really do much more than confirm our initial assessments. We can see five distinct ships, not of the same shape, and they are in no identifiable NeHaw battle formation," she continued as they walked the halls toward the control room.

As they walked, Jake consciously moved at Bonnie's speed. They stepped into the control room, and Jake could see the hologram of the five ships projected in the center of the room. Like Bonnie stated, the five ships were in a loose formation, more like traveling buddies on vacation than combat veterans preparing for an attack. They were also similar in size but dissimilar in the configuration. With dissimilar markings and coloring, Jake got the impression they weren't all from the same place.

"Are they racing each other," he asked after a moment.

"No, sir, some ships measurably slow from time to time to allow the others to maintain proximity to each other. I definitely wouldn't call it a formation, though," Barb replied.

"We are positive they are heading for us?" Jake asked on a whim.

"Yes sir, they are correcting for planetary movement and headed directly for the earth," Barb replied.

Jake looked at Bonnie and asked, looking for confirmation.

"They will reach orbital distance in two days?"

"Yes, 2 days and 13 hours," Bonnie replied after glancing at the console.

"And we will have *Defiance* and *Independence* in orbit when?"
Bonnie looked at Barb for the answer.

"In 27 hours, Sir. Jessie confirmed 20 minutes ago that they are on track to lift off and take orbital station. All weapons systems are functional, but with no human occupants. They are strictly ALICE controlled," Barb answered.

The mention of ALICE made Jake pause a moment to consider.

"Alice, what's your take on this?" He asked.

"We have five ships of an unknown nature, apparently dissimilar in origin, but acting in concert, approaching with unknown intent. There are no discernible weapons systems visible, and the ships are making a conscious effort to stay together, as some are clearly faster than others are. They are not a known Nehaw design, so are presumed to be NeHaw subjugates, and are heading directly to earth."

"Alice, those are facts, what's your guess?" Jake replied.

"You are the fuzzy logic beings. My sisters and I are the rational ones," ALICE responded.

"Fine time to be getting a sense of humor," Jake replied with a sigh.

Jake grabbed a seat and watched the hologram for a long time. Finally, he spoke to her.

"Alice, you mentioned possible subjugates? Do we know how many races the NeHaw control in our sector?"

"They do not record facts in that fashion. However, cross referencing the ship's logs from the three cruisers, we note five regular planetary stops for collection of tribute," ALICE replied.

As Jake was forming a follow-up question, Bonnie let out with a shriek and doubled over in pain. Becky was by her side like a shot.

"Looks like it's time," she declared.

Jake scooped Bonnie up in his arms, and as he stepped through the control room doors and into the hallway, he met a robotic gurney, sent to meet him. He gently laid her down, head on a pillow, and then fell in behind Becky, who was leading the gurney off to the infirmary. He followed Becky into the LDR and helped move Bonnie on to the bed in the room. While holding Bonnie's hand, he watched Becky attach sensors for monitoring the baby and Bonnie.

"Are you staying?" Becky asked without looking up from what she was doing.

"If Bonnie wants me to," he replied, looking to Bonnie for an answer.

"Please," she replied.

They spent the next several hours in the delivery room, Jake helping as Becky directed him to as others popped in and out. Jake mostly

266

worked at making Bonnie as comfortable as possible.

"OK, we are getting close," Becky announced as she checked Bonnie's progress.

Becky repositioned Bonnie for delivery and, with Jake holding her hand, asked Bonnie to start to push. After a series of pushes, Becky nodded to herself.

"Here it comes."

With one final effort from Bonnie, Jake could see Becky reach forward.

"Congratulations, you have a beautiful baby girl," Becky announced as she lifted the baby onto Bonnie's stomach.

In a series of quick moves, Becky clamped off the cord and handed Jake the scissors.

"Would you like to cut the cord?"

He took the scissors and cut where Becky indicated. She then sealed the end by his daughter and removed the clamp. Becky continued her after delivery activities while Jake watched the baby wiped clean, and then someone grabbed a blanket to wrap her.

"Oh, Jake, she is so beautiful," Bonnie cried.

"Just like her mother," Jake replied.

"Now, what's my niece's name?" Becky asked, finishing her cleanup work.

"Wow, we haven't even discussed names," Jake replied.

"How about Julie?" Bonnie asked, hopefully.

"Julie is a wonderful name," Jake replied with a kiss.

----*----

It was late that evening before Jake got a chance to sit down to a meal. Once Becky was satisfied that Bonnie and Julie were stable and healthy, they transported both to Bonnie's quarters for rest. Jake suggested they be moved to his, but Bonnie wouldn't hear of it, especially with the unknown nature of the impending visit. She felt it was better if Jake rested and was clear headed. Babies tended to set their own schedules.

One of the newer recruits, with medical preferences who was in the delivery room, took the assignment to assist Bonnie for the next few days. With her and the ever-present bots, Jake was assured she would get all the help she needed.

Satisfied Bonnie and the baby were settling in, Jake headed back to the control room for the latest on the five spaceships. Upon entering the control room, everyone besieged him with congratulations and questions about his daughter from all the facilities staff. Linda had spoken to Becky earlier and stepped in for Jake on all the things he should have known but didn't.

With all the questions asked and answered, the updates on the tactical situation were less informative. The holograph was clearer, and you could make out the markings on the various craft, but as they had yet to locate a reference for any of them, it was all gibberish at this point.

As a whole, the consensus was these were not NeHaw Military, in fact, not NeHaw at all. The NeHaw didn't seem to feel the need to document their conquered peoples, so confirming they were even known to the NeHaw was a problem. Most references to other races were on either acquired technology or tribute collection schedules and inventories. Jake hadn't inquired about the goods they pulled from the holds of the cruisers while refitting them, but there were at least two collections completed before their ill-fated trip to earth.

"Alice, have the container's contents we pulled from the cruisers checked for any markings similar to the ones on those ships, please."

Jake was sure this all fit into the answer of the five ships. He just hadn't gotten the pieces in the right order yet. Heading out of the control room, he took his dinner in the quarters dining hall. He would have preferred dinner in his room, but as usual, he needed to be available for the troops. Except for the occasional quick congratulations, though, everyone permitted him to eat in peace and think.

After a quick stop to check in on Bonnie and Julie, he headed to his room. Bonnie relayed that Sara had contacted her after she rested, and the two talked for over an hour. She expressed her excitement to Bonnie over Julie and couldn't wait to get back to hold her new niece in person. He was sure they discussed far more, but that was all Bonnie chose to share with him.

Bonnie also cautioned Jake that should Becky reach out to him tonight, he shouldn't put her off. With as much responsibility as she held, she was still quite young and starved for attention at times. Walking in the hallway between his and Bonnie's quarters, Jake realized he hadn't seen Becky since they settled Bonnie in her quarters. He expected to see her at dinner but found her nowhere in sight.

Entering his quarters, the mystery solved as Becky was sitting on his couch in a short black silk robe with a good bit of cleavage showing. Her long blonde hair pinned up loosely at the back of her head. She had a bottle of wine opened and two glasses, hers partially filled. From the look of the bottle, it wasn't her first glass.

She sprang up from the couch, and in bare feet, bounded over to Jake, bouncing with excitement. Wrapping both arms around his neck, she gave him a deep, slow kiss. He could taste the wine on her lips and felt the heat of her body pressed against his.

Slowly breaking the kiss, but with arms still wrapped around his neck, she whispered to him.

"I come bearing gifts," she said and then slowly backed away, dropping her robe.

Underneath, she wore a bikini similar to the one Jake made for Sara, although this one was smaller if that was possible, and made of the same black silk as the robe. Jake stood in awe, taking in her beauty. The silk both hid and enhanced her charms. Then it hit him.

"Oh My God, Becky, that's it," Jake cried.

Confusion crossed her face as that was obviously not the response she expected.

"What?" she replied.

"You solved the mystery of the five ships!" he responded, elated.

"Are we in danger?" She asked with a concerned look on her face.

"No," Jake replied, confused.

"Then it can wait," she stated, stepping up and wrapping herself around him again for another kiss.

----*----

The next morning Jake wandered into breakfast alone, still a bit tired from the exuberance of youth. Becky had spent the night with him, but left before he got up to check on her patients and generally spread her good mood. Thank god, Sandy was still in Washington with Sharon, he thought.

He sat and ate, watching as staff, whose names escaped him, came in and sat in groups of two or three. Normally Jake would hit the control room first, but this morning he was less worried about things. Becky's visit last night supplied the missing piece to the puzzle. He could be wrong, but he was 99% sure he knew why those five ships were coming to earth.

Dallas informed Jake that Bonnie and Julie were still asleep, so he headed into the control room at a leisurely pace, coffee still in hand. As he entered, Barb started to deliver her standard morning briefing when Jake held up his hand and wandered over to the holograph, sipping his cup along the way. Staring intently for the millionth time, as if trying to will them to speak, he then motioned for Barb to continue.

"Jessie reports both *Defiance* and *Independence* are in orbit and on station earlier than predicted. As you can see, the five ships are still en route, their arrival time on track for tomorrow afternoon, local time. We have six squadrons on alert, they will be manned and on station one hour prior to alien arrival and ready to intercept any incoming hostiles," she

269

completed.

"Please contact Sandy and make sure she is in attendance when our guests arrive," Jake stated. He then got up, handing his empty cup to one of the bots, and left the room, leaving the staff in a complete state of confusion.

Using the closest elevator, Jake headed to Bonnie's quarters to visit her and the baby. He grabbed a seat, sitting with her while she breastfed Julie. He'd forgotten they weren't just ornamental. He relayed to Bonnie his discussion with Becky and his revelation about the five ships. She agreed it made sense, but also commented, hope for the best and expect the worst.

Leaving them both with a kiss each, Jake headed back to his quarters for a little research. He needed to talk to Sara and was now more curious than ever about the nature of the tribute collected by the NeHaw.

----*----

Sara was going out of her mind, stranded in Hawaii. First, the five ships appeared at the edge of the solar systems, contrary to everyone's expectation. Then Bonnie delivered a beautiful baby girl, and she was stuck here, far from it all.

On the plus side, Jacob did have all assembly bays in motion, the floating platforms in place for ship assembly to commence. The design that he and Jake settled on allowed construction of three ships per bay. They had agreed on four transport ships and five patrol ships for the first run. They wouldn't be ready for months, and certainly not in time to help with the current situation.

Jake was keeping her up to date on all the analysis and planning, though, which helped make her feel included. All six squadrons were on alert, and the three cruisers were in orbit. It all seems way overkill for the five inbound ships, but she knew Jake was taking no chances.

Jake also shared with her his suspicions about the five ships. With this latest news, she wasn't sure what to think. If Jake was right, this could change everything. She was just having a hard time dealing with the fact that it was her hot to trot little sister who supplied him the key to solving the problem.

----*----

It was the morning of the big day, and Jake rose early. Becky spent the night again, pleading she was neglected. Not that Jake objected at all, she was wild in the sack. He suspected Jessie's influence there somehow, but considering he was the benefactor, he wasn't about to question it. She was still sleeping soundly as he slipped out of bed and then into the

270

bathroom for a quick shower.

Dressing in his closet so as not to wake her, he snuck out quietly and headed for a bite to eat. He suspected it might be all he got today. The dining hall was fairly deserted. There were just a few of the off hours' staff eating dinner before bed. Jake grabbed his usual breakfast and ate quietly. He needed to find a place to sync up with Patti, as she was the only one he hadn't contacted regarding his theory, and his visit from Becky had thrown off his plans last night. Finishing quickly, he asked Dallas to direct him to one of the unused offices on a lower level.

Once inside, he grabbed a seat and went about contacting Patti, waking her in the process, thankfully alone. He had developed quite a fatherly attitude with both her and Jacob and though they were barely six or seven years his junior, they were his "couple of greats" grandchildren.

Giving her a moment to clear her head, he explained his theory of the five ships.

"No, Shit?" Patti exclaimed.

"I see time with the natives has improved your vocabulary?" Jake replied.

"Sorry, but that's pretty unbelievable," she responded.

"Just teasing, but yeah, no shit," he answered.

"So how are you going to handle it?" she asked.

"Frankly, I'm not sure. I've talked it over with the ALICEs as well, and they agree I may be right. It's the fuzzy logic thing. How it's handled is the open question."

"Well, all the combat pieces are in place. One wrong move and all five ships will be space debris," she replied.

"Let's hope it goes better than that," Jake replied with a laugh.

"Well, if you don't mind, I think I'll start my morning routine, as I'll never get back to sleep now," Patti stated.

"OK, I'll talk to you later, I'm sure," Jake replied and cut the communication.

Jake stayed in the office, attending to a few unfinished duties, occasionally asking Dallas to chase down various bits of information. In the middle of one of these exchanges, Jake was leaning back, looking at the ceiling when he noticed the speaker grill cleverly hidden above him.

"Dallas?" Jake asked.

"Why are there old fashion speakers installed here? Didn't we get some fancy new audio technology from the NeHaw ship?"

"All the facilities use what you would know as a traditional speaker and microphone systems throughout the populated areas, only maintenance and storage areas are without. There were no advanced audio systems in the NeHaw ships. In fact, there were no audio systems in their ships at all," Dallas replied.

Jake thought about that for a bit and then asked Dallas to investigate some ideas he had on the subject.

Chapter 22

Jake spent the rest of the morning in the control room after his call to Patti and discussions with Dallas. He checked and rechecked all the possible scenarios under consideration and still thought his suspicion was the best guess. As the zero-hour approached, everyone gathered in the various control rooms within the six active ALICE facilities. That excluded those people in their fighters, hovering at various altitudes in differing locations on the planet or those in their cockpits hidden behind secondary stasis shields as ready reserves.

Jake had deployed four squadrons to intercept any potential bombs the cruisers or gun platforms might miss, as occurred in the last two engagements. The two ready reserve squadrons sat behind stasis shields in their hangars should some unknown weapon disable the four active squadrons.

"Always keep a surprise ready," Jake thought to himself.

Each of the control rooms displayed the same tactical holographic image of the approaching ships, the three cruisers, and the planetary backdrop. Icons marked the fighters and gun platforms, as they were too small to make out.

"They are slowing, sir," Barb announced her commentary broadcast to all locations.

"Now we see what's up," Jake said.

The five ships came to a halt in a stationary orbit, facing the three cruisers. Jake spread the cruisers out as opposed to the NeHaw tight triangular formation. All three confronted the five ships, but they were in a horizontal plane, with the gun platforms filling the space above and below, creating a wall of firepower.

"OK, ALICE, send the message," Jake declared.

"This is the Earth Defense Force Cruiser Revenge. Please state your intentions," broadcast in both English and NeHaw, the English audio replicated for all to hear.

Several minutes passed with no response or movement from any of the alien ships. Finally, they heard a reply in English over the audio.

"We are the five sentient races of Sector Nu Tau Beta. We have come to offer an alliance with the inhabitants of this planet."

"Bingo," Jake said to himself and then aloud.

"Alice, what sector did the captured cruisers patrol?"

"All three ship's logs noted Sector Nu Tau Beta as their area of responsibility," she replied.

"Visitor's bearing gifts," Jake stated while smiling at Becky.

"Jake, I don't get it?" Becky asked.

He held up one hand, acknowledged her, and then responded to ALICE.

"Alice, please send the information exchange request we put together."

"Right away," ALICE replied.

Turning to Becky but speaking to the broader audience, he started.

"You hit on it the other night. These five ships are the representatives of the planets the NeHaw hold in servitude in our sector of space. The cargo we have in the hangar at Seven came from their homeworlds."

"When we took the four cruisers out, there was no one around to suppress them anymore. It's my guess the NeHaw have just enough ships to manage the sectors they have, and not a lot more. They come across as pretty cheap and extra ships not collecting costs them."

"OK, but why are they here then?" someone asked.

"That's easy," Barb replied.

"They don't want to go back to being NeHaw slaves."

"Precisely!" Jake added.

"We are now the baddest kids on the block, and they all want to be our best friends. They also have no desire to replace the NeHaw with us, so we need to tread carefully. What's the saying about beware Greeks bearing gifts?"

ALICE cut in at that point.

"Jake, the information exchange offer has been accepted. It will take several hours for that to complete with all five races, I suggest we make a show of good faith and reduce the show of force."

"Agreed, please have all squadrons return to base, but remain on alert. Have *Defiance* and *Independence* take polar stations and leave *Revenge* with our guests as *protection*."

"What are we doing now?" Jessie asked over one of the remote links.

"Well, on the off chance that I was right about all this, I asked ALICE to put a data pack together. It has all the relevant information we want to share in both English and NeHaw providing a "Rosetta Stone" of sorts. The goal is to get similar datasets in return, giving us both a translation of their native languages passed through NeHaw and some idea of whom we are working with. I hope to do several rounds of exchanges so we can get as much detailed information as we can. Stuff like environmental requirements of their species and a flavor of their cultures. The NeHaw didn't exert much effort in documenting their conquered peoples, so I expect there are some native concepts not translatable to NeHaw."

"What about the NeHaw deaths from the last time they tried to land?

274

Will any of these aliens die too?" Becky asked.

"I don't think they'll die, but I don't expect to test it. I want to use one of the cruisers as our negotiation location rather than on earth. I want them all to keep thinking they will die if they land. As to why the NeHaw died, I think the ALICEs may know the answer to that, but have no way to test it, except maybe as a weapon," Jake replied.

"What was it?" Becky asked curiously.

"I'm not sharing that just yet. I don't want rumors to start until we know for sure," Jake replied.

Becky had a hurt look but said nothing more.

"Jake, all squadrons are reporting in, and the Cruisers are repositioning as requested," Barb declared.

"OK, everyone can stand down and return to normal activities, except the pilots. I would also like all available analysts digging into the received data as the ALICEs make it available. And have Sandy stand by for the negotiations of her life," Jake replied.

With everyone filing out of the control room, Jake caught a glimpse of Bonnie sitting on one side of the room, holding Julie in her arms. He wandered over to her with Becky close behind.

"Hello, sweetheart," Jake said, leaning down to kiss his daughter and then Bonnie.

"Well, that didn't take long?" Bonnie said.

"What?" Jake asked, confused.

"One day, and I'm already second fiddle," she replied with a laugh.

Before Jake could reply, Becky knelt to take Julie from Bonnie and declared to everyone.

"Jake, I want one!"

Both he and Bonnie rolled their eyes, and then Bonnie suggested an alternative.

"Why don't you help me out first? Your time will come soon enough."

"Whatever," was all she said, kissing the baby on the forehead as she took her from her sister's arms.

"On that note, I will take my leave. I'll see you three later as I have work to do," Jake replied, giving each a kiss and turning on his heels to head out the control room door.

"Alice, I may never forgive you," Jake commented as he walked down the hallway.

"Why, Jake, how can you say such a thing when you look at that little face?" she cooed.

"Do you mean Julie or Becky," he replied sarcastically.

Jake continued down the hallway and into an elevator that took him

275

back to the offices on the lower levels. Returning to the office he had used the day before, he and the ALICEs went over some of the incoming data and discussed their theory on why the NeHaw had died while entering the earth's atmosphere. Everyone confirmed it held merit, but agreed the only way to test it was on the Nehaw. They were tossing around a few ideas on weapons, and Jake requested a few prototypes constructed when ALICE interrupted him in mid-sentence.

"You have an urgent incoming message from Sara," she stated.

"Please put it through," he replied.

"Hey, sweetheart, what's up?" Jake asked as Sara's face appeared on the display he was just working on.

"The replacement staff has landed, so can I come home, please?" she asked eagerly.

"I believe ALICE has a fighter on the way for you," Jake stated, hoping ALICE took the hint.

"It should be arriving shortly," ALICE replied, covering Jake's butt.

Jake figured ALICE must have the newly finished fighter at full speed to get it there so quickly from Alaska.

"Jake, you have a second message, it's from Linda," ALICE said.

"Go ahead and patch her into this," Jake replied.

Jake's display went into a split image with both Linda and Sara.

"Hey, Linda?"

"Jake, you need to get here now, Kathy just went into labor," she replied.

"I'm on my way, Sara, you want to meet me there?" Jake said.

"Yes," was her only reply, and then the display went dark.

Jake jumped up from his chair, and as he raced through the hallway and into the elevator, he asked ALICE a question.

"Alice, can you please let everyone know where I'm going and why."

"Absolutely."

As he left the elevator and entered the hangar, Jake didn't bother suiting up. He just went straight to his fighter. He had taken to leaving his flight helmet in the fighter, and although it wouldn't seal to his current attire, that wasn't necessary. He climbed into the cockpit and started strapping in, his normal preflight routine completely ignored. ALICE took control at his request and started Jake on his way. They were clear of the hangar doors and on the way to Nevada by the time Jake donned his helmet and was prepared to take over.

"Alice, why don't you drive," Jake said with a laugh and realized by the time he got ready to fly, he would almost be there.

"It would be my pleasure," she replied.

276

"Can you give me a status on Kathy? Oh, and how soon will Sara be airborne?" Jake asked.

"Heather indicates Kathy is still in the early stages of labor, we should arrive in plenty of time. Sara will be airborne in 10 minutes with a return flight time of less than one hour. I understand she is suited up and waiting in the hangar for her fighter to arrive," ALICE replied.

"WOW, Alaska to Hawaii in what 20 minutes?" Jake commented.

"That's a record. Thanks for covering for me. I completely forgot to stage that bird in Hawaii for her return."

"As it only passed initial flight certification yesterday, I would expect Sara to understand," ALICE responded.

"Well, thanks anyway," Jake replied as he felt the familiar weightlessness of a decent and checked the altimeter to verify a drop in altitude.

"We are on approach. You should be on the ground in a few minutes," ALICE said.

Jake looked up from the instruments and noted they were coming in hot! He checked the inertial dampener setting out of habit, as the braking forces would have splattered him all over the instrument panel, seat harness, or not.

"Jake, Sara's ship has arrived in Hawaii, and she is preparing to depart as well," ALICE provided.

"Thank you," Jake replied as his fighter dropped through the open hangar door and slid sideways to settle near the facility's door.

Popping the canopy while the plane was still in motion, Jake unstrapped and climbed out as soon as the fighter settled to a stop. Linda was there to meet him, and they both headed straight to the medical wing and the labor delivery room. With Jake leading the way, they entered the room to find Kathy and Heather chatting calmly.

"Hi! I am so glad you made it in time," Kathy said as Jake slid up next to her and kissed her.

As Jake was about to answer, Kathy had another contraction, causing her to cry out. Heather moved around to check her progress.

"Oh my, that was fast."

For the next hour, both Jake and Linda tended to Kathy while Heather gave instructions. At one point, Jake caught a movement out of the corner of his eye and saw Sara slipping into the room and quietly standing to one side. With the moment of delivery approaching, Heather started to explain to Kathy what to do next.

"I KNOW!" she shouted as another contraction enveloped her body.

At that point, the baby started to make its appearance. Jake stood by Kathy while she held onto his hands and dug her nails into him. Linda moved over to Heather's side, a towel in hand to help once the delivery occurred.

"What a beautiful baby boy!" Heather declared as she handed him to Linda and prepared to cut the cord.

"May I?" Jake asked her.

"Please," Heather replied as she handed him the scissors.

Jake took the scissors from her and snipped the cord, better prepared for its toughness this time. Linda brought the baby over to Kathy while Heather finished up. Both women were crying as Linda handed Kathy her son. Sara moved up behind the two and, sliding around, kissed Kathy on the cheek.

"Oh my god, Kathy, he's so beautiful!" which got her crying as well.

Jake stepped up to the other side of the group, kissing Kathy and then checking out his new son. He took the edge of the towel and wiped a spot on his little face where the others missed.

"What are we going to call him?" he asked Kathy.

"I assume Jacob Jr. is out?" Kathy added with a smile.

"Definitely!" Jake replied.

"I've always liked Timothy?" Kathy asked.

"Timothy is perfect," Jake replied, kissing her and the baby.

"Jake, I hate to disturb you at this time, but we have received and translated the first replies from our visitors. You asked to be notified as soon as they were available," ALICE offered.

"You go ahead," Kathy stated.

"I'm going to need some time to rest anyway."

"Are you sure?" Jake asked.

"She's right, they both need some rest, and we will be right here," Heather replied.

Sara kissed Kathy and the baby and then took Jake by the arm, leading him out and into the hallway, with Linda close behind. The three then headed straight into the control room, where Jake was flooded with congratulations. While he recognized Patti, most of the facility staff on hand were faces Jake had never seen or barely knew. Still, in good spirits, he acknowledged their good wishes like old friends.

Once the celebration subsided, most filed out, leaving Jake and the others to get down to business with Jessie and others remoted in.

"OK, ALICE, what do we have so far?" Jake asked.

"All five races have delivered their first round of the information we requested in NeHaw and their native tongues in exchange for our content. Once translated, we submitted the second round of content for exchange, which included our offerings around mutual defense proposals. We are close to having direct translation capability for all five

278

languages."

"That was only supposed to go forward if the first round displayed solid compatibility between the races," Jake stated, concern in his tone.

"Early analysis of all five respondents indicates a passive, cooperative nature for each. There is speculation amongst the analysts that this very trait made them victims of NeHaw aggression in the first place. While far more technologically advanced than the earth, none of the five races demonstrates the militaristic nature that humans do. They had the means to resist, but not the will. Our inclusion completes the equation for their freedom from the NeHaw," ALICE stated.

"How does that saying go? *With their brains and our brawn, we can go far,*" Patti offered.

"Well, that makes total sense, then," Jake replied.

"The NeHaw thought that if we ever got space travel and the ALICEs, we would be nothing but trouble for them."

"There is one more item to review," ALICE said.

"Oh?" Jake asked.

"You asked me to look into and analyze the tribute collected by the Nehaw. We pulled several containers from the holds of the NeHaw cruiser we captured. Some contained finished products, including weapons and other types of military equipment, nothing we haven't seen before. The other containers held refined metals; silver, gold, platinum, aluminum, and titanium, and all in fairly small quantities. Strangely, there was no iron or steel, and none of the captured ships used steel in their construction. They are mostly what we refer to as manufactured composite material and exotics like Titanium and Aluminum Alloys."

"Well, if I remember correctly, isn't iron supposed to be one of the most abundant elements in the universe? I suppose it is not valuable," Jake replied.

"Maybe, but that is contrary to its lack of use in their ships. Why not use an inexpensive material to build with instead of the more costly manufactured materials and rarer nonferrous replacements?" Patti asked aloud.

"In gentle probing with the first data exchange, these materials are considered extremely scarce in this sector and are highly prized by the NeHaw. The quantities of the rare metals represented a significant portion of each contributor's annual output," ALICE finished.

"Alice, how do those quantities compare with the earth's known quantities?" Linda asked.

"The containers held approximately 600 pounds of gold, representing all five races' contributions for one year. Before the fall, the annual planetary gold production on earth was over 2000 tons. The ratios are similar for the other metals."

"So, I think that explains why we've not been vaporized?" Jake said.

"With an atmosphere and potential labor force, this planet is a treasure trove," Linda stated.

"Then why didn't they come back sooner?" Sara asked.

"Notes in the captured ship's logs show the planet was specifically excluded from any activity that risked future habitability. It was also listed as a quarantined planet, forbidding any future exploration, or landings," ALICE provided.

"I'm wondering if someone back home got the geology report from the dead exploration ship and galactically shit their pants," Jake said.

"If our take on their culture is true, a greedy bureaucrat could have easily buried the report. Then by classifying the planet off-limits, they would just wait until they found a way of gaining control?" Jessie offered.

"And with a dead survey crew, who's going to tell?" Patti said.

"How long do NeHaw live anyway?" Jake asked.

"We haven't precisely locked down their time measurement yet, but it looks like they live 350 to 400 years on average. Their reign of terror in this sector seems to go back thousands of years," ALICE replied.

"So yeah, an 80-year wait is reasonable, or the NeHaw who knows all this is dead, and the find is still unknown to the rest," Linda stated.

"Oh, this just keeps getting better and better. Not only are we now the number one enemy of an ancient empire with its oppressed peoples looking to us for salvation. We are also the planetary equivalent of the Lost Dutchman's mine!" Jake stated flatly.

He paused to look around the room and noted all the blank stares.

"Which part?" he asked calmly.

"The Lost Dutch mine?" Sara said in a small voice.

"The Lost Dutchman's gold mine was a 19th-century myth. The legends say it was a huge gold find discovered in the Arizona Mountains. It was lost when its finder, the Dutchman who was a German, was killed. Supposedly, when he died, they found his saddlebags full of gold. People fought and died looking for it for over 150 years, but it was never found."

With that, there were several enlightened looks.

"Let's face it. I need to stop using euphemisms!" Jake finished with a sigh.

----*----

Jake stopped for the day at that point and suggested they all retire to the dining hall for dinner. As he predicted, the only meal he'd had all day was breakfast, so he was starving. He stayed behind in the control room for a moment and placed a call to check on Kathy and Timothy. Heather informed him they were both doing great and sleeping soundly. He then checked with Bonnie, and the two talked for another 20 minutes. She had linked up with Kathy earlier and had seen Julie's new half-brother. She held Julie up for Jake to say good night, and then he headed off to meet up with everyone else in the dining hall.

"There you are," Linda declared as Jake walked into the room.

She, Sara, Patti, and several others Jake didn't know were gathered at one of the larger tables.

"Sorry, I was performing my fatherly duties before eating," Jake replied as he approached the group.

"Oh, so who were you knocking up now?" Patti asked, sarcastically.

"I said fatherly, not studly!" Jake shot back at her, playfully.

"Besides, I got to talk to my daughter," he finished with a smile.

"How is Bonnie?" Sara asked.

As Jake sat, a bot slid up with a tray for him. It contained a grilled steak, mashed potatoes, and a green salad as Jake's preference for red meat was well known.

"We ordered for you," Linda supplied.

"She and Julie are fine. They can't wait to see you," Jake said while taking a bite of the steak.

"Me either," Sara replied.

"Well, what's the plan, oh fearless leader?" Linda asked.

"Besides a shower and bed? I haven't the foggiest," Jake replied.

"Are we going to negotiate a deal with these aliens?" someone asked from down the table.

"I think that's a foregone conclusion, it's what comes out the other side that has yet to be determined. My expectation is they will give us anything we need to fight the NeHaw, but combat support. From what we've seen in the data so far, they are all lovers, not fighters, and we don't have near enough fighters ourselves," Jake finished.

"What they do have is a lot of information on the NeHaw, including ship counts and distributions. The NeHaw seem to have far fewer ships than we imagined. The other sectors near ours are patrolled mostly by Destroyers, this sector used Cruisers as they had larger cargo holds," one of the others at the table stated.

Jake assumed she was one of the new analysts.

"You know, I was thinking, part of the reason the NeHaw don't appear to have a lot of ships might be a lack of raw materials?" Patti offered.

"Patti may have a point, Jake, according to some of the newly

281

acquired data, the NeHaw expansion has declined dramatically in the last 2000 years. The rate of acquired races has all but stopped within the last 500," ALICE supplied.

"If the volume of materials they are taking in as tribute is any indication, they are in a sustaining mode, not an expanding one. We need to be expanding," Linda provided.

"Let's hope our new friends have good automated refining equipment, then," Jake said, finishing his dinner.

"Because we need refined materials, and scrounging is only gonna last so long."

----*----

The following morning Jake and Sara got a call to go to the control room early. She spent the night with him, but they were both so exhausted they had gone straight to sleep. As they entered the control room, Jake could see Sandy, Patti, and all the facility commanders, some in holographic communication connections.

"Okay, what's up?" Jake asked as he and Sara grabbed seats next to Linda.

Sandy started to explain.

"We've completed three rounds of data exchanges, and the ALICEs approved moving forward with negotiations based on your original instructions. I contacted all five races to propose a meeting, and they all prefer not to land," she finished with a smile.

"The quarantine status as a death planet scares them," Jake said with a laugh.

"They have offered to host us on any of their vessels, or can just meet virtually if we prefer," Sandy added.

"No offense Sandy, but I want the ALICEs directly hooked into this too, so their ships are out except for social visits. Let's offer a virtual meeting as we need translators anyway. Also, offer to return the raw materials we have from the cruiser holds, but ask if we can keep the manufactured goods, which we will pay for. There were some items of interest on the list I got from ALICE," Jake replied.

"I understand and will do, Jake," she replied.

"Is that it then?" Jake asked.

"Well, there is one more thing," Sandy replied slowly.

"Yes?" Jake asked after a pause.

"Three of the races are roughly humanoid, though one is tri-pedal. I guess they have three legs instead of two. The other two races, well, I haven't been able to get a good description of them beyond general attributes. One is covered in fur and looks like a six-legged canine. The

282

other is similar to a lobster with an exoskeleton," Sandy provided.

"Ok?" Jake replied.

"The lobsters and the tri-pedal humanoids are quite proud and have strong social casting traditions. As we are not a conquering force, they will only open negotiations with our king," she finished.

"Well, Jake's president, so that's the same thing, right?" Sara said.

"No, it's not. They have royal families, and their kings assume the throne on lineage, not by election. I asked ALICE to contact the other races discreetly to ask how they accommodate this. She said they doctor up their leader's family history and title them, King. It's figurative only. Their power comes from occupying the elected office. Usually, they become an ambassador once out of office," Sandy answered.

"Oh, so like an honorary title?" Bonnie asked.

"No, the translator came back with a word I didn't know, so I had to look it up. It was faux, which I guess means false. We need to create some documentation, making Jake a false king, and then they will acknowledge his right to open negotiations. Afterward, he can assign a delegate," Sandy completed.

Suddenly, Patti burst out in uncontrollable laughter. Everyone stared and waited. When she finally got it under control, Sara asked her.

"What's so funny?"

Standing, she bowed and declared to the group.

"All Hail, faux-king Jake!" and then dropped to the floor laughing.

----*----

By the following day, they had the negotiations well underway. Jake took his faux king title in stride, but the jokes were getting old fast. If he heard one more "royal scepter" crack, he was going to shoot someone!

On the plus side, all five races opened with recognizing earth as a full intergalactic trading partner and offering up all the data they had on the NeHaw, with no strings attached. The recognition contained status as a full member of the intergalactic community, which was a position previously denied earth by the NeHaw. All public NeHaw records listed Earth as a barren planet of death, and any contact requests were refused upon submission. Jake passed on, pointing out that, as they had thrashed the NeHaw in this sector, they were in no position to deny anything. The data was very welcome, and the analysts were all over the translations as they became available.

While Sandy was acting as lead negotiator, Jake made sure she understood that ALICE's input was not just a suggestion. They also agreed that the ALICEs were top secret and not to expose themselves at any cost. Finally, the last instruction was that all negotiated agreements

283

required adoption by Jake and the facility commanders before they became binding. As each of the races worked to receive similar approvals from back home, this was not an issue.

With Sandy hard at it, Jake went back to his other duties and followed up with ALICE on the prototype weapons he had requested just before Timothy's arrival. There were several constructed, but both Jake and the ALICEs were at a loss on how to test them. He also followed up with Karen on his staffing request. As he suspected, James was her recommendation for the South Dakota location. She also proposed giving Jacob the responsibility for Hawaii as he was destined to reside there for the next several months overseeing ship construction anyway.

Her logistics recommendation was a surprise to Jake. She pointed out it took someone with a reasonable amount of education to accomplish all the tasks he had in mind, particularly around the raw materials' acquisition and deliveries. Robert was her recommended choice. He'd continued his education in engineering fields and demonstrated an aptitude for creating an organization.

He would have to give up his position as squadron leader for the 1st Air Cavalry, though, as there was far more work to do logistically than the additional squadron duties would allow. Jake thought about it and figured he could at least let him keep his fighter, maybe even making him a Wildcard as he did with Sara. He asked Karen to approach him about it.

Chapter 23

It had been a week since the five races introduced themselves and began negotiations with Earth. During the entire negotiation, they provided a continuous stream of data, all concerning the NeHaw. Patti was taking in the tactical data in overwhelming volumes. It was like drinking from a fire hose. She asked Jake, and he approved pulling in two of the newest additions as assistant analysts.

With almost all the staffed facilities working on recruiting, Jake had no idea how many were on board now or who they were. He saw new faces every day, it seemed. He'd given up trying to stay on top of it all and left it up to the ALICEs and facility commanders to oversee. By the last counts, there were over 300 on-board, spread out between the six facilities, and two-thirds of them were women.

During that time, Jake focused on various projects, all in some way related to killing NeHaw. Associated with those efforts, Robert agreed to take on the role of the logistics manager, his top priority being the location and acquisition of materials for shipbuilding. Fortunately, there were still large quantities of refined materials available at various locations around the country. For Robert, it was more of a transportation challenge. The smaller items were no big problem as he could chopper them almost anywhere. The big stuff was giving him fits.

Jake and he were in the control room in ALICE-1, discussing that very issue. ALICE had the 3D holograph displaying areas in Alaska, where raw material stockpiles had been in the past. Robert was explaining to the group.

"As you can see, the docks here, here and here, hold pre-attack stockpiles of sheet and formed metals, wire, and other items we need. We just need to get them to here," he said, using the hologram and indicating the distances from the three locations to Seven.

Jake knew back in the day, there were both trucking and rail transport to move the items they needed to the facility storerooms in Alaska. In Hawaii, the supply ships docked and transferred supply materials onto barges, which were then towed right inside the dry docks to be unloaded.

"We have some truck transport in Alaska and can get more transferred there from other facilities. It's the manpower for loading and unloading that's the killer," Jake said.

"We have some possible options with the bots there. Seven even mentioned creating a few specialized models just for this work," Robert replied.

"It's Hawaii that's got me stumped. We can airdrop anything there, but we need shipping for the heavy stuff, that's the greatest need," he finished.

"I don't have an answer for that yet. We are in no position to start a shipping line and open the ports here. We might be able to use the Cruisers to fly stuff in once hostilities subside," Jake replied.

As they were discussing this, Jake heard a commotion on one side of the control room.

"Jake, you need to see this now!" he heard Linda say.

Suddenly the hologram they were working with disappeared, and in its place was a view of space. Discernible was a large spaceship, moving through space.

"What the hell is that?" Jake asked.

"That is a NeHaw battleship," Patti replied from the corner with Linda.

"Crap," Jake blurted.

He studied it for a moment, then asked a question.

"I presume it's just dropped out of faster-than-light?"

"Yes, sir," Barb answered before the others.

Jake let out a sigh, then passed on instructions to the others.

"Ok, what do we know?"

Before anyone could answer, Sandy broke in with her declaration.

"Jake, all five races just broke off negations!"

"Yeah, we have a NeHaw Battleship on the way in, are they leaving?" Jake asked.

"No, not yet, they just ceased discussion and cut all transmissions, including the data feed," ALICE replied.

"Alice, please reassure our guests that they will get the full protection of our armed forces. All we ask is they obey any directions we transmit to guarantee their safety," Jake said calmly.

Then he repeated his last question.

"What do we know?"

"We will know more as it closes on earth, but it's over 10,000 feet long and varies between 500 and 800 feet wide and tall. Weapons are not yet detectable but presumed to exist. It is traveling somewhat slower than the cruisers, so we expect orbital arrival in a little over 4 days," Patti replied.

"The damn thing is two miles long?" Jake replied.

"It appears so. We will have measurements that are more precise as it gets closer, but we have a good idea now. I am scouring the databases for any more relevant information," Patti offered.

"OK, then, everyone goes on alert, all three cruisers will remain in orbit, and I want to start a full battle planning session first thing in the morning. We should have more information by then. ALICE, what was the reply from our guests?" Jake finished.

"They accepted our offer immediately. I suspect they could not safely depart, so it was stick with us, or brave the battleship guns alone," ALICE replied.

----*----

Jake spent the rest of the day working with ALICE and trying to stay out of everyone else's business. He wasn't a micromanager by nature; he was just struggling with the transition from doer to leader. As such, he focused on the special weapons they worked on earlier, increasing the number of prototypes and escalating their priority in manufacturing.

That evening, Jake met everyone in the dining hall for dinner, not wanting to isolate himself from the staff with a fight looming. Kathy was out of bed with Timothy. He found her seated with Sara, Linda, Patti, Barb, and several others Jake didn't recognize, which seemed to be becoming the norm these days.

"Hey everyone," Jake said as he gave Kathy and the baby a kiss, then slid into a seat next to Linda and across from Sara.

"We were wondering when you were going to show up," Sara declared.

"Alice told us you two were working on secret weapons," Linda added.

"And she wouldn't tell us what they were!" Patti threw in.

"That's why they're secrets! It's a surprise," Jake answered as a bot arrived with his tray.

"Jake, this is serious," Barb replied.

"Yes, I understand. That's exactly why I won't tell. I don't want to set false expectations. If these things work, we will save a lot of lives. If they don't, it's an all-out battle for survival. ALICE has told me about Patti's initial analysis. Even with the rail guns and the cruisers, we aren't sure we could do enough damage to that thing to prevent a global bombing run on earth," he answered between bites.

"And we don't have enough fighters to both attack and defend," Patti added.

"Precisely, either we commit all our craft to the attack and hope to prevent the bombing or hold back fighters to defend against a bombing. Even then, they won't be able to stop everything," Jake said somberly.

"And these things of yours might?" Linda asked.

"*If* ALICE and I are right, yes, these will stop the fight before it even starts. Tomorrow we will start our battle planning and will open with

287

these. I'm afraid they are an all-or-nothing proposition, though. They are either devastating or a pretty light show," Jake offered.

----*----

After eating, Jake escorted Kathy and their baby back to her quarters, and tucking Timothy in, he spent some time with Kathy and then headed to his room. Upon entering there, he found Sara and Linda sitting in his living room. He quickly crossed the room and stuck his head in his bedroom, only to find it devoid of naked bodies.

Turning back to the two, he explained.

"Just checking."

"Disappointed?" Linda asked with a laugh.

"Not really," he replied, taking one of the chairs.

"I'm not sure I'm up to dealing with exuberant, oversexed teenagers right now."

"That's why we stopped by. How are you doing?" Sara asked with a concerned tone.

"I'm OK. I just wish I had more answers than questions," Jake replied with a sigh.

"Are we going to win this one?" Linda asked.

"That is the question," Jake replied.

"With all our previous encounters, we have held some kind of edge. First, it was a surprise, then superior firepower and shields. This time we have just a hunch and a hope."

"Can't you even tell us?" Sara asked.

"Tomorrow, I will let you two and Patti know what I'm working on, but under threat of death!" he replied.

"We need to keep it under wraps. It is a wild-ass guess, and I don't want to demoralize the troops should it fail. Everyone needs to expect a dog fight upfront."

"Speaking of troop morale, I think I'll head off to bed and let Sara take on the responsibility of keeping your morale up," Linda said while struggling to her feet as Jake jumped up to help her.

"Letting her take one for the team, huh?" Jake said, laughing.

"I was hoping for more than one," Sara replied with an evil grin.

----*----

The following morning Jake and Sara met the others for breakfast, and after eating, they all headed off to the control room for an update. Other than confirmation of earlier speculations on size and weapons, there was no new information. Afterward, Linda led them off to an anteroom Jake had never seen before, and they began their battle-

288

planning session.

Jake opened with an explanation of his work with the ALICEs. He expanded on what the thoughts were on the weapons they devised.

"Oh My God," Patti commented.

"How did you come up with that?"

"It's brilliant, if true!" Sara added.

"That's the kicker, isn't it," Jake replied,

"It can't be tested, except in battle, which means putting lives on the line for something that may not even work."

"How were you thinking of accomplishing this?" Patti asked.

"Putting six of the weapons on each fighter and then, in pairs, strafing the length of the battleship, dropping one every few hundred feet," he said with a wince.

"The hope is, in the attack, they won't be noticed and destroyed as they are dropped."

He could see Patti running it through her head.

"Ok, so eight fighters, two per side, top and bottom. Wow, they need to be pretty close to that ship for maximum effect. That's a lot of firepower to absorb! There are some pretty big guns on that thing."

"Yeah, but staying close limits the number of guns that can be brought to bear at any one time. Also, ALICE thinks if they control the stasis shields on the fighters, they can protect them in a high-speed pass. I repeat, she thinks they can," Jake finished.

"Jake at that distance, I doubt you could survive multiple direct hits from the battleship's larger guns, stasis or not," Patti commented.

"My thoughts as well, so this is a volunteer mission, with full disclosure. I will make sure every pilot knows what they are risking their lives for," Jake added.

"How close can the fighters be to the weapons, when they go off?" Linda asked.

"That's the funny part, if this theory is true, we can be almost right next to them when they go off and won't feel a thing. In reality, there is some debris if it explodes, so not too close," he answered after some thought.

"And if they start shooting them as we drop them?" Patti asked.

"That just triggers them earlier," Jake replied,

"The bombs still go off. But, if the NeHaw figure out what they are, then they may have countermeasures. Our best hope is they don't go off until we are ready."

"And if they don't work?" Sara asked.

"That's what we need to figure out over the next few days," Jake answered somberly.

----*----

They spent the next few days with the principles in battle planning meetings and preparation. In the end, they went for a layered approach with four of the six squadrons in low earth orbit, positioned for bomb interception. The three cruisers and gun platforms assumed places in high orbit, facing the battleship on approach. The remaining two squadrons were to intercept the battleship, several hours out, strafe, drop their loads, and then high tail it out of the battleship's gun range.

Should all go well, they had prepared a post-engagement cleanup plan. However, Jake felt the more likely scenario was going to be a full-blown assault on the battleship with all hands, including Jake, Sara, and Robert in their fighters. Provided the NeHaw were not intent on Earth's destruction, ALICE was confident anyone inside a facility was safe for now. Unfortunately, he could not say the same for those above ground. Unless they could damage the battleship enough to either disable a bombing run or drive it off, millions would likely die on the surface.

----*----

The following day, Jake held a very private meeting with all the fighter squadron's pilots, 24 hours before the expected attack. He asked everyone to fly in and held it in the hangar ready room in ALICE-1. With Patti and Sara on hand, he swore them all to secrecy and then explained the mission.

Even after emphasizing the dangers and insisting they would likely take heavy casualties, Jake was gratified to see all six squadrons volunteer for the run on the battleship. In the end, through a process of skills assessments and the luck of the draw, the 1st Air Cavalry and the VMFA-112 Cowboys were selected to make the run. Immediately dispatched the following morning, they went to Kola, in South Dakota, to be fitted with the bombs. Everyone else went back to their home facility to await further orders.

----*----

KeRoc sat in the command chair of the NeHaw empire's newest and largest battleship. This was, in fact, its maiden voyage, having completed its space trials only recently and thus achieving a battle-ready status. He ruthlessly undermined his competitors for the command, blackmailing one, and having another killed off in a training accident. His accomplice in that endeavor was now his first officer.

Being part of what was widely perceived to be a decadent and corrupt system, KeRoc excelled in the dirty and underhanded politics

290

necessary to elevate one's position. His military prowess wasn't equal to his political skills, but with a ship, this large, subtlety wasn't required. Acting as the ship's commander, his cut of the tribute collections would make him very rich in a short period. He first, however, needed to rectify the current situation.

Homeworld directed him to investigate the unnerving reports around one of the most valuable regions in space. It was said an entire sector of Cruisers was destroyed, and its five indentured peoples were in revolt. Word was they had gone into collusion with a previously unknown race to gain their freedom. This was unacceptable, especially as these worlds were to be part of KeRoc's primary source of income.

As they approached the inner planets of this solar system, he could see three of the missing cruisers parked in orbit.

"So much for all Cruisers destroyed," he thought to himself. These things were always being overblown.

He could also make out the five wayward representatives huddled in a polar orbit. He was still debating whether it would be more profitable to capture them or just destroy them outright and claim a friendly fire incident. That way, there would be far less paperwork, and he could claim their ship remains as salvage.

He was still debating all this when his tactical officer reported to him.

"Sir, we have several small ships inbound."

----*----

Jake wasn't happy at all that the two squadrons needed to leave six hours early to give them the separation they needed for their plan. By meeting the battleship farther out in space, should these weapons fail, they gained reaction time before the battleship gained orbital status. That required the pilots to fly for an extended period before reaching the contact point, but it couldn't be helped.

As the eight fighters left earth's orbit, everyone else continued to make ready. The Cruisers were already in position, but Jake wouldn't have the other squadrons deploy until the battleship was much closer. He hoped they wouldn't be needed at all.

Before contact, everyone gathered in the various control rooms, with Jake, Sara, and Robert suited up just in case. They had the holographic display up, showing the eight fighters approaching the NeHaw battleship. The fighters were represented as glowing indicators because they were too small to see compared to the battleship.

At the designated distance from the NeHaw battleship, Jake instructed the eight fighters to close up, so their forward shields overlapped, giving them greater protection while making for a smaller target.

----*----

KeRoc was in confusion about what was before him. Initially, his tactical display indicated eight single-seat ships headed directly for them, and then they closed the formation and disappeared behind some kind of null field. What did those eight little ships think they could do against his battleship?

"Forward guns open fire," he stated calmly.

"Firing," his weapons officer replied.

As they watched, the forward energy guns converged on the null field and then flared in a flash of bright light.

"No effect," the weapons officer reported as the flash subsided.

Suddenly they saw a flash as the little ships darted off in differing directions, all running parallel to the battleship's hull and all firing at it.

"Sir, we are reporting hits in the forward batteries," the tactical officer reported.

"All stations, fire!" he ordered urgently.

----*----

Jake watched as the NeHaw fired on the grouped fighters, their forward shields holding up under the concentrated fire. As the firing stopped, the fighters split formation, flying in pairs covering the four sides and running the length of the battleship. ALICE tracked the fighters and the bombs they released with icons.

Suddenly one of the icons flashed red and then disappeared entirely. Everyone in the control room looked around, but no one spoke. As the fighters reached the end of their run and peeled off, another icon disappeared from the display.

Jake stared in silence and then spoke over the silence.

"Alice, status, please."

"Air Cavalry 2 and Cowboys 4 were lost. All bombs away and tracking. The remaining six members of the two squadrons are shadowing the NeHaw battleship, just out of gun range."

"The charges are working as designed, holding position relative to the battleship. They will be dragged along as it travels, but haven't settled on the hull."

----*----

"Sir, they have ceased the attack. Some damage is reported in

292

multiple sections throughout the ship, but all systems are operable. We have lost 7% of our weapons capability. They are using some form of projectile weapons that penetrates both our energy shields and our hull plating," the tactical officer reported.

"Is that what's wrong with those three cruisers? Are they shot full of holes?" KeRoc asked.

"No, sir, sensors indicate all three are powered up and operational. All indications are they are in enemy hands," he replied.

----*----

"OK, ALICE, send the message," Jake declared.

For the benefit of the five races Jake knew were watching, he asked ALICE to broadcast in all seven languages, including English and NeHaw.

"This is the Earth Defense Force Cruiser, Revenge, surrender now or be destroyed."

----*----

KeRoc sat laughing at the message they just received. Were these creatures insane? That little sting they delivered was barely measurable. They were still sub-cycles away from orbit, but a few missile launches might get their attention.

"Fire batteries 2 and 4. Let them try to get those to surrender," he said to the weapons officer.

Then, to his communications officer, he directed another instruction.

"Transmit all that has occurred in Homeworld. Continue transmitting, so they can witness our triumph."

----*----

"Jake, they just launched missiles, I count eight of them headed this way," Barb announced.

"Well, I guess that's our answer," Jake replied.

ALICE chimed in at that point.

"Jake, they are transmitting to their home planet. It is too far out for me to interrupt."

"That's OK, we are either going to make a huge impression or end up on the intergalactic gag reels for years to come," he replied with a laugh.

"Have the cruisers and gun platforms take those out as they come in range," he finished pointing at the incoming missile icons

Everyone watched as the missiles closed on Earth. Jake knew the

ALICEs were calculating, at what point firing the rail guns would guarantee the highest success, with minimal risk. Suddenly all three cruisers and the gun platforms lit up, a short burst from all.

They waited for several minutes until missiles and projectiles reached the point of convergence, and then there were bright flashes in space. The rail gun projectiles ripped through the skins of the missiles, triggering the charges inside, thus destroying them all.

"All missiles destroyed," Barb announced.

"How far out is the battleship?" Jake asked.

"It's still three hours from orbit," Linda answered, finally beating Barb to the punch.

"Then it's time to see if I know my ass from a hole in the ground," Jake stated flatly.

----*----

"All missiles destroyed before contact," the weapons officer reported.

"Obviously," KeRoc thought to himself.

While he enjoyed the godlike power his command provided, some aspects of military life grated at him. Now was one of those moments. As he was considering his next move, the tactical officer broke the silence with an observation.

"Sir, I am detecting several small objects holding position just off our hull."

"Where?" KeRoc asked, checking his displays.

"Everywhere, they seem to be hovering just off our hull and keeping pace with our movement," he replied.

"Find me one and put it on display," he directed at his navigation officer.

A small cylindrical object came into view on the display. It was a dull gray and looked like some type of storage container.

"Where is that?" KeRoc asked.

"It's amidships just over the main crew quarters, sir," Navigation replied.

"Destroy it," KeRoc ordered.

The display changed slightly as the targeting indicators appeared. Suddenly it flared into bright light as the energy cannons exploded it.

"Sir, we are getting reports of casualties on decks 3 and 4 of the crew quarters," the communications officer announced.

KeRoc turned to face the communications officer.

"What kind of casualties?"

"Unknown, sir, they are reporting a crewman falling in place, with

294

no visible wounds. There is no damage to the ship, though the energy shields show a fluctuation in the area of the explosion."

----*----

"Jake, they exploded one of the bombs," ALICE informed them.

The flash was visible, but confirmation was nice.

"If it didn't work, I would guess they start shooting the rest. However, if they don't..." Jake let his sentence hang.

Several minutes passed, and there were no more flashes.

"I'll be damned if it didn't work," Jake said aloud.

"Orders?" Barb asked softly as if everyone else was afraid to speak.

Jake stared at the image floating in front of him as if weighing his options. Then he simply gave an order.

"Blow them."

----*----

The total casualty count from that single explosion was greater than the NeHaw had lost in the last 500 years. The fact that a significant number of the crew were currently at a meal increased the number of crew members congregated in the portion of the ship near where the object they fired upon detonated.

"What happened?" KeRoc screamed at his officers.

"The device we destroyed, emitted some form of electromagnetic radiation our shields only partially absorb. We have never seen emissions of that magnitude occur naturally. That area of the ship was overrun with long wavelength energy at a lethal intensity."

"And they are all over the ship!" he screamed again.

Before the communications officer could reply, the bombs started exploding in sequence. KeRoc watched in horror as the flashes worked their way up from the bow of his ship, heading right for the bridge.

As he rose from his chair, his head suddenly erupted in intense pain. It was as if someone had exploded his brain from the inside out. The damage was immense, killing him where he stood.

----*----

The holographic image displayed the bombs as they went off, walking the length of the battleship. Jake and the others watched as the flashes rippled in sequence. Jake was right. It was a very pretty light show. With the last one detonated, they all watched in silence for some indication of success or failure.

"Well, what now?" someone finally asked.

"Alice, have 1st Air Cavalry 1 approach and investigate, please," Jake said slowly.

They watched as the indicator of the CO for the 1st Air Cavalry Squadron slowly approached the battleship. As it closed, everyone looked for some indication of return fire. Closing the distance, the fighter ran the length of the battleship and then returned to a position directly over the bridge.

"No signs of life, sir," the CO reported.

"I think we killed it!"

"Commence boarding procedures, let's get that thing stopped," Jake answered as the control room erupted in cheers.

They watched the other five icons close on the 1st Air Cavalry's position. Losing all her formal decorum, Barb asked loudly over the commotion.

"OK, Jake, give! What was in the bombs?"

"Radio," Jake replied as he altered the display to zoom into the area where the boarding activity was occurring.

"The bombs released extremely high energy radio waves, for the NeHaw, it was like 100 times a teenager's stereo, right inside their head!"

"What?" someone asked.

"OK, remember we were all told that the NeHaw exploration ship had four dead crew and that the speculation was they died after entering our atmosphere, right?"

There were several nods around the room.

"We all know that," was the unanimous reply.

"Well, data point one was something in our atmosphere was the cause of death. Datapoint two is something not so well known. All the communications gear on the NeHaw ships required an upgrade to accommodate human occupation. It's not audio-based. No speakers or microphones were found on any of the vessels. They were all radio transmitters and receivers. They don't speak and hear, to communicate like we do anyway, they transmit and receive biologically."

"Wouldn't they shield themselves then?" someone asked after a moment.

"Yes, I expect they did for what they considered a normal amount of space chatter. Those bombs produced so much high-energy radio that they felt like they were passing through a Quasar," he explained.

Jake watched as the six ships positioned themselves in an inverted position and opened their canopies. Each then fired a grapple attaching their fighters to the battleship's hull. Afterward, all six pilots worked their way down the tether lines and up to the bridge windows. Jake smiled to himself, noting they didn't need spear guns for this. Jake continued to speak as he watched one of the pilots place a charge on one of the bridge windows as the others held back.

"We had so much radio, bouncing around in our atmosphere, that the first visitors were killed where they stood. I'm not sure what frequencies are the most lethal, so the bombs were a broad spectrum, but my bet is it's the ones the atmosphere tends to bounce back," he finished.

As if to punctuate his statement, the bridge window blew out in the holograph, and they watched as the boarding party climbed inside the bridge window.

"Placing the interface units on the control systems now," one of the squadron COs announced.

"Acknowledged," Barb replied absently.

"Is everyone on that ship dead?" one of the new analysts asked.

"Most likely, though, we will still need to do a safety sweep of some kind. The plan is to park it in a far-earth orbit and turn the bots loose for a cleanup. I won't inflict that on anyone. We do have a combat team specially trained by me on ship clearing ready on Revenge, which is parked nearby in case there is live resistance," Jake replied.

"Jake, I have control of the battleship now. I'm programming the navigation control to place it in the predetermined orbit," ALICE said.

"Please inform our guests the current emergency is over, and we hope they weren't too inconvenienced. Oh, and let them know we now have a battleship in our fleet," Jake supplied with a grin.

"Jake, I just checked the database and the NeHaw only has three battleships, and this one is the newest!" Patti offered.

"Jake, the ship still has an open communications line to their Homeworld. I was able to confirm it correlates to the earlier location we calculated from the cruiser transmission. Shall I cut the transmission?"

Jake thought a moment and then smiled.

"Send this first," he said as he typed out a short message on the console next to Barb as she watched, then smiled.

----*----

HeBak had been sitting at the communication desk in the NeHaw Military High Command for many, many megacycles, and, in all that time, never recorded a transmission like the one he just received. He redirected it to several of the commanders as well as High Council members of the empire.

He was not in a position to judge these matters, but in his opinion, the NeHaw just had their asses handed to them. With the loss of four cruisers and their newest battleship, they had taken a beating. The fact that those same resources were now in enemy hands was indescribable. He was not aware of any historical record containing such a severe and expensive loss.

It was, however, the last part of the transmission that unnerved him the most.

It simply read, "You're Next."

Author's Notes

I would like to point out that this is the very first novel I have ever attempted, and as such, it has gone through several iterations. In some ways, I still consider it a constant work in progress, a living document of a sort, as my skills improve with every new book I write. For some of you, this will come as no surprise, but I am no writer. I do, however, enjoy good storytelling. That is the basis for my writing this book.

The origins of the story come from my real-world life as an Engineer and Computer geek. In an age where Artificial Intelligence is the buzzword du jour, it was a workplace conversation that gave life to the question of what next? If AI systems became self-aware, but not in a Skynet, maniacal, murderous way, how would that relationship evolve?

From the story, you can also get a glimpse of my somewhat dark view of humanity. Left to fend for themselves, I do believe the polarization of the species would manifest in those who always look for the easy path and those who strive for self-improvement. It is the latter that are the heroes of this story.

Printed in Great Britain
by Amazon

62294179R00167